I0772616

AWAKENED

The Wevlian Chronicles – Book 3

Aaron N. Hall

Cover design by Shelbi Tietjen

Map illustrations by Joseph Spangler

Beta readers: Russel Haggard, Benjamin Reid, Arianna Vincent, Kaitlyn Smith

ISBN 979-8-9910978-9-5

Dedicated to you.

Thank you for staying with Jason

until the very end.

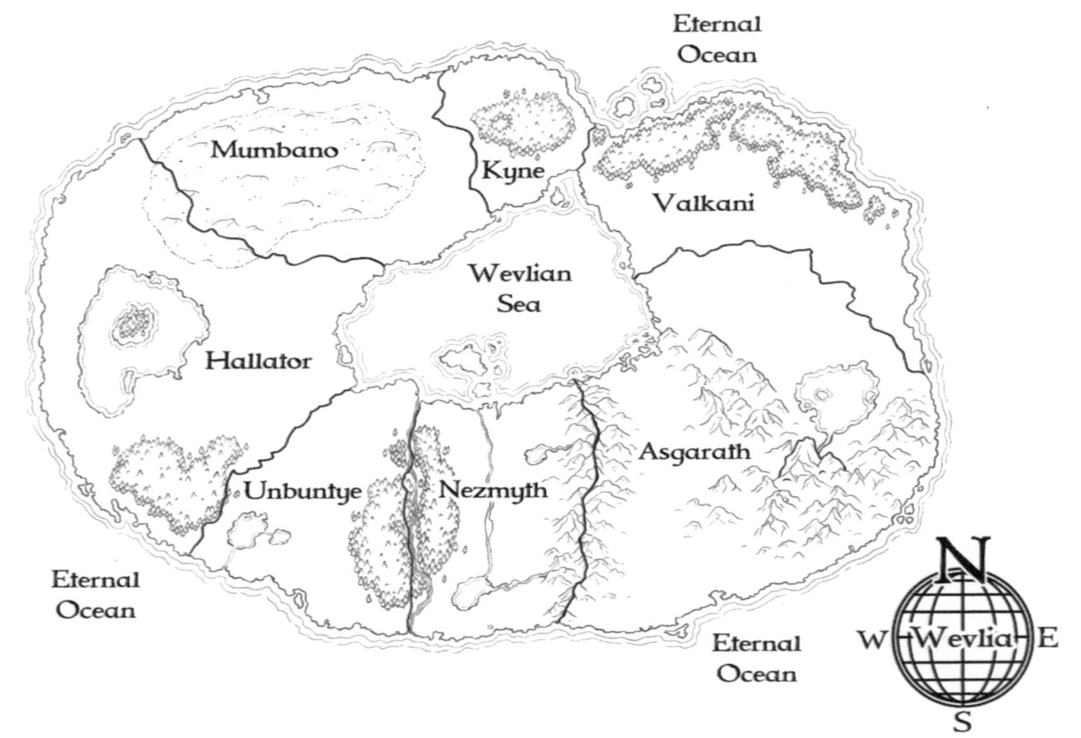

Eternal
Ocean
Mumbano
Kyne
Valkani
Wevlian
Sea
Hallator
Unbuntye
Nezmyth
Asgarath
Eternal
Ocean
Eternal
Ocean
N
W
Wevlia
E
S

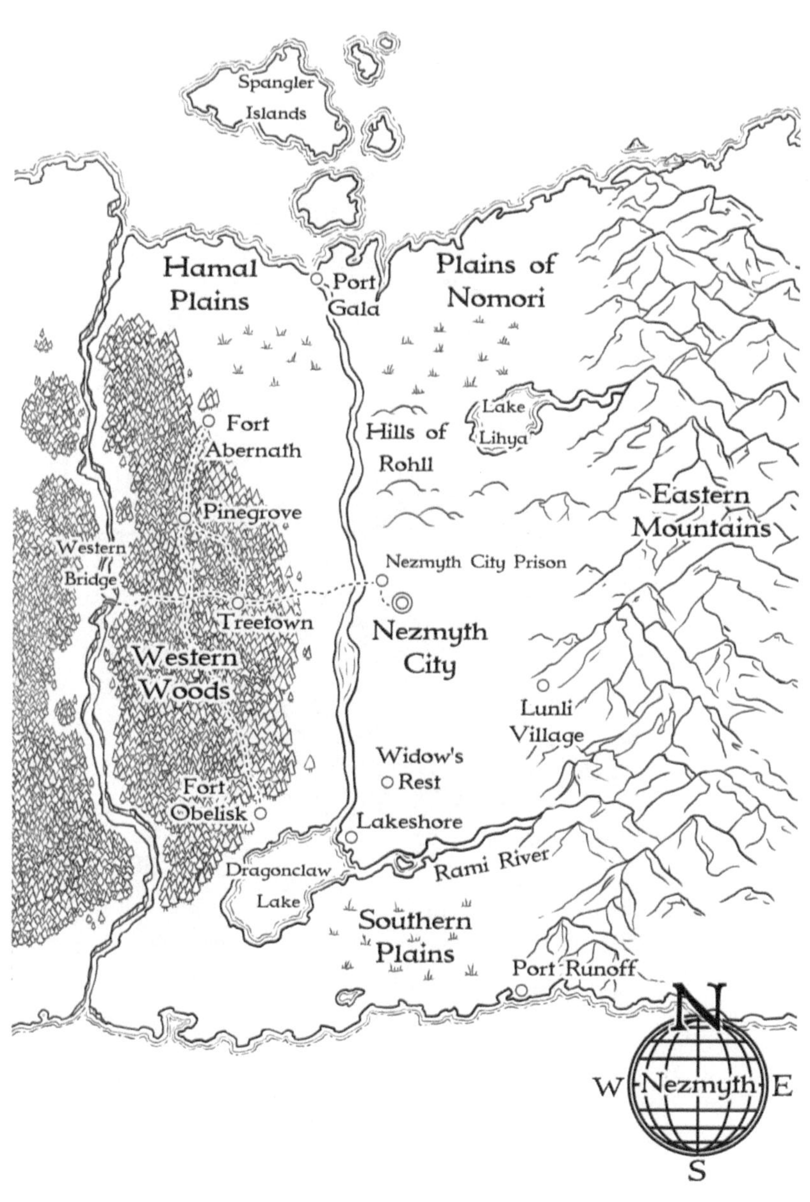

Spangler Islands
Hamal Plains
Plains of Nomori
Port Gala
Fort Abernath
Lake Lihya
Hills of Rohll
Pinegrove
Eastern Mountains
Western Bridge
Nezmyth City Prison
Treetown
Nezmyth City
Western Woods
Lunli Village
Widow's Rest
Fort Obelisk
Lakeshore
Dragonclaw Lake
Rami River
Southern Plains
Port Runoff
N
W Nezmyth E
S

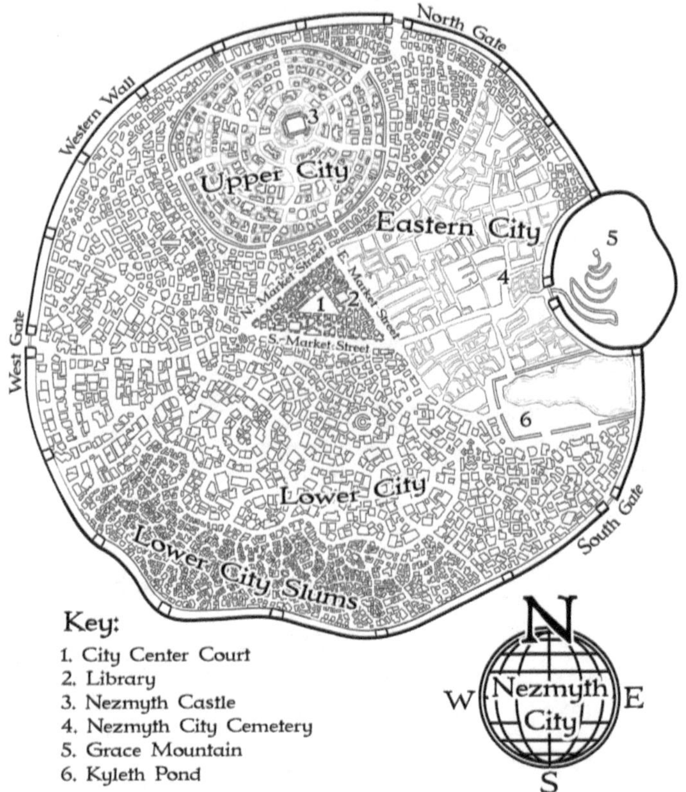

Key:
1. City Center Court
2. Library
3. Nezmyth Castle
4. Nezmyth City Cemetery
5. Grace Mountain
6. Kyleth Pond

I

THE FUNERAL

Long have I waited. Countless suns have set on Wevlia, and through it all, I have been patient. Waiting in the pale dark. Peering from the shadows.

The whispers of my servants have toppled thrones. Decimated kingdoms. But one piece has remained, defying me in the south.

No longer.

The foundation is laid. The pillars of the Old Ways will crack and break. A new era shall begin—an era that I deserved five thousand years ago.

And it begins with her.

* * * * *

Saryan's cries touched every corner of the castle. The soldiers heard them in every hallway and around every corridor. Even the chef down in the kitchen tightened and bristled with every scream. Every time another one rang out, everyone recoiled in their own way. They should be happy on a day like this, but if it turned out like last time… no one would rejoice in Nezmyth tonight.

On the upper floor, outside the royal washroom, Nezmyth's elite were gathered: Advisor Tarren, Captain Barnabas, Master Ferribolt, even the King's parents. Tension pressed all of their faces. The Advisor squatted on his heels with his back against the wall, his thumbs pressed into the inners of his eyes. Captain Barnabas kept his face to the ground while his toes tapped vigorously. Master Ferribolt stood across from him, hands clasped, praying. Tomm and Kara held hands and waited.

More screams reverberated from inside the washroom. Captain Barnabas turned to Tarren.

"Can you feel anything?"

Tarren shook his head. "I'm trying, but I still can't discern feelings like Nadiel could."

The breath that came from Barnabas was shaky and unsettled.

In the washroom, Queen Saryan squeezed King Jason's hand with white knuckles. He had to squeeze her hand back to keep her from crushing his fingers. Behind his lips, his teeth clamped shut. The sweat coating his forehead was glossy in the candlelight.

Saryan's legs were propped up on the tub's edges. Her breaths came in frequent gasps, which caused the water to stir and slosh. Meanwhile, a midwife in a long apron held her stomach and coached her.

"One, two… push!"

Saryan bore her teeth and grunted. She clenched Jason's hand tighter. He tried not to whimper.

The midwife frowned, her face fixed on the birthing canal. She clapped her hands, rubbed them together, then reached in the water to put them on Saryan's bulging belly. Her palms glowed yellow and she moved them around, feeling for something. All the while, Jason watched, his heart pounding.

This time it'll work, he assured himself. *There have been too many prayers.*

Saryan's breaths were becoming shallower. She let her eyelids slide shut and tried to relax. Her grip slackened. In turn, Jason held her tighter.

"Saryan, you're doing great," he said.

"No, I'm not," she half-whispered. "Jason, I can't…"

"Yes, you can!"

More words tried to escape Saryan's lips, but they came out as something unintelligible. The midwife never stopped working. Her glowing hands kept tracing Saryan's large belly. As she did, the worry on her face grew thicker.

Finally, she said, "Your Highness, the baby's heartbeat is fading."

Saryan's head lolled about her shoulders and rested on the edge of the tub. "Jason… Jason, I'm sorry…"

"Don't apologize. We're not done with this yet. There's still a chance."

"Maybe we're just…"

She didn't finish. A long breath trickled from her pink lips. Frowning harder, the midwife's palms left Saryan's stomach and went to her chest. Then her eyes snapped open and she shot a look at the King. All color left Jason's face and he felt his blood go cold. His fingers shot for the spot right below Saryan's jaw, feeling for a pulse.

It was fading.

The midwife slapped one hand against Saryan's heart and one hand on her forehead. Then she started spouting Ancient Nezmythian healing spells at a rate faster than Jason had ever heard. Saryan's pulse lifted barely, like a wave lapping on the shore of a lake, but it wasn't enough.

"Saryan," Jason said, clutching her hand and kissing it. "Hold on! You're going to be fine!" He rubbed her hand and turned to the midwife. "*More!* Give her whatever you know!"

"I'm giving her *everything* I know!"

Saryan's body was still slacking. It was like watching someone drift off to sleep—a terrible, terrible sleep. Jason held her face. She didn't react.

"Saryan?" He pleaded. *"Saryan!"*

* * * * *

A river of white flower petals drifted along the road that stretched between Nezmyth Castle and the Cemetery. Along its edges were every soul in Nezmyth City—the shops, restaurants, and Cathedrals had all closed down for the afternoon. People threw the flower petals onto the cobblestone in handfuls as the procession moved along, creating a rainfall of feathery white silence.

At the front of the procession was Captain Barnabas, leading atop his horse with one hand on his sword. On his shoulder was his hawk, Artemis, with his beak pointed to the ground. The Captain was stiffer than usual, as if his body were under some great weight—suppressing something. Those who stood close enough could see his lips pursed and eyes puffy.

Behind him, the caravan's first wagon held two coffins: one large enough for a grown woman, and one small enough for a baby. The wagon was lined with soldiers on either side, marching in pace.

Following the coffin wagon, a knot of people trudged along, garbed in formal clothing with their faces turned to the ground. There was Advisor Tarren, with his thick blonde beard and eyes like purple gems. Not far from him, Tomm and Kara of Lower City walked side-by-side, holding each other's hands and sniffing. Then there was Master Ferribolt, dressed in his flowing orange robes and devoid of any glimmer.

Lastly, a red carriage crawled along, surrounded by more guards. Inside sat King Jason, garbed in full ceremonial armor. His eyes were glued to the space between his boots and he had to clench his jaw to keep it from shaking. As he did, tears freely dripped from his eyes. In his hands, he clutched a long staff made of Golden Oak.

For the length of the ride, Jason listened to the sniffles and whimpers of the townspeople crowding the streets. The turning wheels of the carriage were quieter with the river of white beneath them. It made the aching in his heart deafening.

How is it possible to feel this empty?

At the Cemetery, two plots were dug next to Captain Garrit and Melody. The public wasn't invited—it was an intimate ceremony for friends and family. The coffins hovered suspended in the air while everyone gave their last words to the deceased. It was all a blur to Jason. Every word was hollow and distant in his ears. But lastly, it was his turn to speak.

He swallowed, wishing the wetness on his face could coat the dryness in his throat. It was only yesterday that she was alive. Smiling. Glowing. How could he speak when his thoughts were still processing her departure?

And what about their unborn son? They managed to get his body out after his mother had grown cold. And it was just as lifeless as hers. The little face never even got the chance to open its eyes.

Jason would never forget looking at both of them—the wave of despair and loneliness it caused. But alas… words needed to be spoken. He tried to swallow again.

"Seven years I had you," Jason muttered. "And every day was better because of you. I don't know what else I could say, my love. You were my everything. And I don't know how I'll get along without you, but I must try. I'll remember you in the little things—your paintings around the castle. The jokes you used to tell. The songs I used to play to help you sleep." He paused. "Maybe if I play one now, it'll feel like you're still here. And you," he turned to the grave of his unborn son. "Please take care of her while I'm gone."

With a clammy, cold hand, Jason extracted his flyra from his pocket and put the instrument to his lips. He played a bending, somber, whistling tune as everyone looked on. Not a single eye was dry. Jason's throat was tight as he played, and he found it hard to breathe at the right times. But he finished the song nonetheless. He always had to finish the song. And when he did, the air was still cold.

It was done. Master Ferribolt lowered the caskets into the earth and pushed the soil on top of them. Tarren stepped forward, put his hand on each mound, and used magic to sprout white flowers across their surfaces. In the background, Barnabas and the guards stood watch, keeping so rigid that they didn't even wipe the tears from their faces. Everyone exchanged hugs and words of comfort as they gathered themselves and left.

In his carriage, Jason looked out the window to the fresh graves of Queen Saryan and Prince Garrit. He wondered if their unborn first child would be with them in Paradise.

And that night, he slept alone.

2

THE POEM

One month went by and the throne gathered dust.

Tarren stood beside it like a watchdog. His eyes were tired and his hands clasped behind his back, much like his old master used to do. Guards stood around the perimeter of the great hall, alert and still. Standing on the red carpet was an Eastern City farmer yammering and griping. His raspy voice was the only sound reverberating off the walls.

"I demand to see the King at once!" he yipped. "You have been most unhelpful!"

Tarren tisked before he replied. "The King is currently indisposed. And I've answered your quarrel with a more than reasonable answer. If he were down here, he would tell you the same thing. Pay the tribute to your neighbor and return what was taken."

"Why—this is outrageous!" The farmer continued, his cheeks burning. "Indisposed? Doing what? What is more important than addressing the grievances of his people? That's his responsibility as King!"

"He's well aware of his responsibilities," Tarren replied. "As am I. You have no more business here. You are free to leave, or I'll have the guards escort you out. The choice is yours."

The farmer grumbled before he flipped around and stormed away. A small battalion of soldiers heaved the double doors open and closed them shut. As the doors boomed and the echo died down, Tarren left out a long sigh and scratched his hair. He took a glance at the throne out of the corner of his eye, then slid his finger along the armrest, rolling the dust with his thumb. He flicked the dust mite away and left the great hall, headed upstairs.

His armor clinked and his blue cape wafted by his ankles as he made his way through a series of corridors. Passing guards stepped aside and nodded dutifully as he passed. Through more hallways, up a few flights of stairs. All the while, a frown pulled at his cheeks. Before long, he was at the doors leading into the King's quarters. Two guards nodded to him and stepped aside. Tarren nodded back, unlatched the handles, and pushed them open.

The musty smell made his nostrils flare. Saryan's side of the room hadn't changed since she passed. Her belongings were still strewn out on a chest of drawers on the right side of the room. The castle's maids had done a good job of tidying the place without disturbing any of her old trinkets. They would have put them away if the King would let them.

Jason's side of the room was a different story. Drawers were left open, clothes hanging out and strewn across the floor. The biggest change was the long couch pushed against the left wall, piled high with blankets and pillows. That's because Jason hadn't slept in his own bed since… that day.

Currently, a blanket covered half of his body as he turned his back to the rest of the room, laying motionless with his eyes still open. Tarren closed the doors behind him and crept inside. Jason didn't acknowledge his visitor. Even after Tarren arrived at the couch and sat at one end, he didn't move.

"How are you?" Tarren asked. "Any better today?"

The King said nothing.

"You would have gotten a laugh out of the last one that came by," Tarren said with a smirk. "The man stole his neighbor's plow because he thought he wasn't using it. The neighbor didn't notice for months, and when the neighbor demanded it to be returned, this man actually thought he had the right to keep it because his neighbor hadn't noticed for so long."

Again, Jason didn't answer.

Tarren sighed. "Jason, I know it's only been a month, but —"

"You don't have to say it."

Finally, King Jason turned over and pushed himself into a sitting position. His eyes were sunken, bloodshot, and his shoulders sagged lower than they used to. "I know I have a responsibility to this kingdom. And I know I should be better at keeping it."

"You're grieving," Tarren said. "We all are. I don't blame you at all. But that also brings up the issue of your new Inheritor. You're way past the customary ten days—"

"I *know*," Jason said. He paused. "Thank you for handling those grievances for me. I know I should do them myself."

Tarren half-smiled. "I have just as much responsibility to these people as you do. I want you to heal from your heartache, but I'm not convinced hiding in your room every day is doing you any favors." He stood. "And I can't do the Succession Ceremony myself. You have to be there."

Oh right. That was today. Jason nodded half-heartedly.

"Now would be a great time to take a bath and get cleaned up," Tarren said. "I hate to tell you this… but you smell. And your beard has gotten scruffy."

Jason tried to smile, but failed. "I'll visit the washroom."

"Good."

Tarren began marching for the door. As he crossed the room, he stopped. He scanned the remains of Saryan's belongings, then he looked at Jason. "I miss her too, Jason. Very much. There's a brightness that left the castle along with her."

Jason's throat lumped up and he pressed his lips together. On that comment, Tarren slipped out the door.

Jason sat there for several minutes more, letting the silence crash down. The Succession Ceremony. Picking a new Inheritor. He looked over his shoulder at the empty bed—the space that was taken by his wife until just weeks ago. Sometimes, he would wake in the middle of the night, turn over, and expect to see her still laying next to him. Then he would snap back to reality.

With effort, he pushed himself off the couch and his feet clapped against the stone floor. All he wore was a pair of cotton pants, cinched up at the waist. The muscles around his stomach weren't tight anymore, but bits of food lingered in the hairs around his belly button. Absently, he staggered across the floor until he went out the door toward the washroom.

A pair of soldiers passed him in the hall and nodded. Something flashed across their eyes that was somewhere between worry and surprise—probably worry for his emotional state, and surprise that he emerged from his room. Naturally. Jason was sure the entire castle was talking about him, if not the entire kingdom. Noting how little he had shows his face anymore. His weight gain. The absence of his commanding presence or confidence.

When Jason reached the washroom, it was prepared for him. Every corner and crevice had been cleaned. The tub was filled with warm water fetched from the boiler. In the middle of the room, a maid was waiting for him next to an empty chair.

"Afternoon, Your Highness," she bowed. "We'll give you a quick trim then you can help yourself to the bath."

Jason dragged his feet to the chair. It creaked as he sat down. The maid expertly snipped without a word, and Jason silently thanked her for not pursuing conversation. He also silently apologized for subjecting her fingers to his greasy hair and beard. When she was done, she slipped her scissors into her apron and put her hand on his shoulder.

"Tub's full of warm water and there's a fresh bar of soap," she said. "Take whatever time you need."

She shut the door and left him alone. Jason stayed in his chair for a while, then with a sigh, stood up, disrobed, and trudged over to the tub. He put his hands on both sides as he sank himself into the water. It was comfortably warm—not too hot, but hot enough to make him feel something. Jason lathered himself up and even put some perfume in his hair to make it smell nicer. Then, he sat and let more silence swallow him.

The soap created a thin film on the water's surface. Bubbles glided along, bouncing off each other, joining, popping. Jason couldn't help but think that this was the same tub Saryan died in. The thought gave him a strange mix of disgust and comfort. Disgust that this was the last place Saryan was alive. And comfort that… this was the place Saryan was alive.

What a dark day. It made him think of when he and Saryan lost their first child in the womb last year—the blood-soaked sheets, the tears, the following void inside them. To expect a first child and miscarry was a pain he thought nothing could surpass.

Clearly, he was wrong.

A knock came to a door, followed by a muffled voice. "All done, Your Highness? It's been nearly an hour."

Had it? Where had the time gone? Jason cleared his throat and said he would be right out. He quickly dried off, covered himself, then changed into some comfortable underclothes to wear under his ceremonial armor. He opened the door to find two maids waiting for him. He sheepishly retreated to his room as they went in to clean up.

When Jason made it to his room, soldiers were waiting to suit him up in his ceremonial armor: a golden set of breastplate, bracers, boots, and a red satin cape. When they were done, they excused themselves while Jason looked at his reflection in the mirror. Had his eyes always been so tired and dull? Or was it just from recent events?

Saryan's old dresser was next to the mirror. She insisted on moving it to the castle after they got married. It was decades old and belonged to her grandmother, then her mother, then her. As he scanned its surface, Jason found himself gravitating toward it.

He pulled open a drawer to find her clothes neatly folded and packed. He dipped his hands in and pulled out an old nightgown. It was silky in his hands, but was made from a fabric that was considered conservative for an Upper City girl. He lifted it to his nose and inhaled. It still smelled like her. He folded it up nicely, put it back in the drawer, then closed it tight. Maybe the smell would last longer that way.

He opened up another drawer and found an assortment of things: a hair brush, ribbons, a music box, scraps of paper with sketches and paintings… and an envelope.

Jason blinked at the envelope as he took it out. As soon as he touched it, he recognized it. It wasn't closed—the seal had been broken years ago. He took the envelope gingerly in his hands and skulked over to the couch. He plopped himself down on the corner, slipped the paper out, and held it with both hands.

To the angel with the golden hair
With eyes that makes pure silver stare
A smile of pearls and a laugh that whirls
The sunshine that floats through the air
To the girl as sharp as a blade

With passion as fierce as the rain
In her is my love and will never be dimmed
Saryan the Queen is her name

When she had read it on her birthday years ago, she smiled and said, "Fierce as the rain? Rain isn't always fierce. Sometimes it's gentle."

Jason blushed and shrugged. "It's the best thing I could think of."

"Well, poetry definitely isn't your strong suit. But I love it anyway." She kissed him on the cheek.

Jason's eyes stung. He folded the poem up and pushed it back in the envelope. His eyes moved to the bed, gazing over the spot where Saryan used to rest.

"You used to lay right there," he said. "Right next to me. Some days I miss you so bad it hurts. But the world keeps moving anyway."

Nothing but the empty room replied. Then a gentle rapping came to the door.

Jason cleared his throat. "Yes?"

A guard's voice came. "It's time to go down to the ceremony, Your Highness."

"Right. Thank you."

Jason cleared his throat again, stuffed the envelope back in Saryan's dresser, and snapped it shut. He squared his shoulders and marched for the door. He was still the King. King Jason. Tonight, he had to show the people that he was strong and collected. Carry himself with dignity.

But the carriage trip down to Center Court still felt as lonely as anywhere else.

3

THE CEREMONY

Center Court buzzed, packed with people standing shoulder to shoulder. Soldiers surveyed in pairs around the perimeter of the plaza, wearing ornate ceremonial armor of bronze and leather. On the north end of the plaza, a stage was erected, sandwiched between two cascading banners of red and blue. In the middle of the stage was an empty chair, almost throne-like in design, facing the crowd but unoccupied. There were more empty chairs on the stage for the Advisor, Chief Patriarch, and Chief Captain.

Facing the stage were two rows of seats—one for each Captain in the Nezmythian Army. They had all traveled to Nezmyth City for the occasion, everywhere from Port Gala to Port Runoff. Now they chatted among themselves, their weapons across their laps as they adjusted and tried to sit comfortably.

Tarren stood on the platform to the right of the empty chair. Not far away, Master Ferribolt and Captain Barnabas sat looking over the crowd. Tarren wished he could sit and relax like they could, but duty dictated that he remain standing until the King arrived. He tried to pass the time by looking for lovely women in the crowd.

Master Ferribolt gazed around delightedly, the golden light reflecting off his smudged glasses and bald head. He brushed the orange robes cascading down his belly as he squirmed in his seat. Barnabas, on the other hand, wasn't nearly as content. He kept his back straight and his hands in his lap, but his jaw was tight as his pale blue eyes took in the crowd. His legs bounced in small, rapid movements.

Master Ferribolt noticed and smirked. "I've never seen you quite this nervous, my friend."

"I don't like crowds," Barnabas muttered.

"It isn't the ceremony's occasion that makes you nervous?"

"Hardly," Barnabas said. "Kierli is a dedicated soldier, a born leader, and the most accomplished Captain in Nezmyth. It's natural that she would replace me."

"And what are your retirement plans?"

"Aid the kingdom from a quieter angle, without the armor or swords. I'll still be in frequent contact with King Jason on matters in which I can assist. But I must admit," he looked around, "I will not miss the ceremonies or celebrations in the slightest."

"So you won't linger for the feast?"

"Absolutely not."

Master Ferribolt chortled. "I will miss working beside you so frequently. I'm grateful you elected to stay in Nezmyth City for your retirement. That means we'll still have tea time."

Barnabas gave a brief smile, then went back to tensing under the eyes of the people.

Near the stage, the King's red carriage pulled up, towed by two white stallions. As it did, the air filled with a steady stream of cheers. Whoops, whistles, and jubilant hollers filled the plaza as the carriage tottered, slowed, then stopped. The driver jumped down from his stoop, swung around the side, and opened the door.

Jason had to shield his eyes from the light. The cheering didn't let up. He waved to his subjects and forced the corners of his mouth into a grin. His gaze drifted to the ground as he climbed the steps to the platform. The claps and whistles continued until he plopped down in his temporary throne. It wasn't as comfortable as the one at the castle, but the one at the castle was never too comfortable to begin with.

The cheering finally settled. Nearly two dozen Nezmythian Captains sat facing Jason with fresh haircuts and polished armor. The emotion on their faces was a sort of pride and admiration—their leader, their King. Jason forced his mouth into a grin again. He shouldn't feel so empty today. After all, his whole people were gathered together. Yet, all he wanted to do was go back to the castle and lay down. Part of him was annoyed with himself, but tried not to show it.

A row of trumpeters blared triumphant notes to the sky. Everything about the song felt grand and majestic. The crowd listened intently, barely breathing, as the notes filled the air then disappeared in a rousing fade. They lowered their horns and Jason pushed himself from the seat. His feet dragged to the edge of the platform and he could feel a soft stir inside his throat. He knew Tarren was using magic to amplify his voice. He cleared his throat and said:

"People of Nezmyth, we welcome you to the Succession Ceremony for the Nezmythian Army's new Chief Captain. Thank you for attending."

Applause.

"As you know, Captain Barnabas has served the kingdom honorably ever since the Ash War. It is under his direction that Nezmyth was able to withstand the forces of the Ash. Without his leadership and experience, Nezmyth would have fallen."

More applause, but not as loud.

"But now, after an honorable tenure, Captain Barnabas has chosen to retire. With careful deliberation, weighing the merits and experience of each Captain, he has chosen a successor.

This person will take on all his rights and responsibilities as Chief Captain. They will coordinate all efforts to keep Nezmyth safe and contend against enemies both internal and external. Captain Barnabas, if you would please introduce the nominee."

Jason sat down and there was more applause. Barnabas got up, gazing over the thousands of people, and swallowed. All the faces looked back at him with either gratitude or impatience. He could still see it in the older ones—they hadn't forgotten what he did or who he was. Their scowls and folded arms were a nagging scratch on the back of his brain. But he tried not to think of them.

"I, first of all, would like to thank you," he croaked, "for accepting my second tenure as Chief Captain. I was once an evil man then, full of darkness and despair. And you suffered because of me. But, through the mercy of King Jason and our Sacred Dragon, I was able to serve you as you deserved. Thank you to those who accepted me and allowed me to reconcile with my crimes to some small degree. I will forever be grateful."

Applause, slightly more spirited.

"Before I announce the newest Chief Captain, I would like to take time to express gratitude to the current Captains that guide and direct our forces across the kingdom. Ladies and gentlemen, please stand up."

All of the Captains stood from their seats and the turned to face the crowd. The audience boomed with clapping and whistles. The Captains, all strong, tall men and women, waved and smiled as their armor glinted in the warm colors of sunset. As the cheers died down, they all took their seats again.

"Thank you. All of you serve in your positions with honor and dignity, and all of you would make fine Chief Captains. But there is one that stands out above the rest."

The crowd held its breath.

"The newest Chief Captain hails from Widow's Rest, just northeast of Dragonclaw Lake. Raised primarily by her mother, she joined the army when she reached the age of womanhood at fifteen. Since then, she has quickly climbed the ranks, building a reputation through her strength, wit, and mastery of magic. She has served as Captain of Widow's Rest, Lower Nezmyth City, and Upper Nezmyth City. She is loved by all, including her equals and subordinates, and is a prime example of dedication, fortitude, wisdom, and charisma."

Excited chatters rippled through the crowd.

"Captain Kierli," Barnabas said, "arise and come forth!"

The crowd burst into cheers. Captain Kierli stood from her seat and marched for the stage—a tall, blonde-haired woman with steely blue eyes and a long scar across her cheek. Somehow, the scar didn't diminish her beauty in the slightest. The other leaders shook her hand as she went by. There was no animosity in their eyes.

Captain Kierli didn't suppress her smile as she climbed the stage. The cheers slowly faded away. The roaring finally ended with a stranger quipping, "Marry me, Kierli!" followed by snickers.

Barnabas stepped aside and Kierli knelt before King Jason. She rested her sword at Jason's feet, then put one elbow on her knee, her face to the ground. Jason stood and unsheathed Nightbane, letting the steel sing in the sunlight. He looked down on his newly nominated Chief Captain, the flat of his blade resting on her shoulder.

"Kierli of Widow's Rest," Jason said. "You have been selected to replace Barnabas of Nezmyth City as the Nezmythian Army's Chief Captain. In this capacity, it will be your life's responsibility to protect Nezmyth from threats both internal and external. You covenant to live a life of integrity, fight for justice, protect all people of the kingdom, serve the Foreordained leaders, and most importantly, the Sacred Dragon. Do you accept?"

Kierli's eyes flashed. "I accept!"

"Take up your sword."

Kierli scooped up her blade and stood on her feet. She was a few inches taller than Jason—almost the same height as Barnabas but slightly shorter than Tarren. She pointed her blade to the sky, and Jason did the same. The tips of their blades touched, creating a pointed arch. Looking into each other's eyes, Jason nodded three times to count them off. On the third time, both he and Kierli shouted, "For Nezmyth!"

"*For Nezmyth!*" the crowd echoed.

Kierli and Jason slipped their swords into their sheaths, shook hands, and Jason said, "Congratulations, Captain."

A swell of more cheers. Kierli shook Tarren's hand and then Barnabas's. When the cheering and hollers and marriage proposals settled down, King Jason addressed the crowd very briefly one last time.

"Thank you for coming, one and all! Let the celebration begin!"

With the efficiency of soldiers, townspeople spilled into Center Court carrying chairs, tables, roasts, stews, vegetables, fruits, and ales. Those who chose not to celebrate in Center Court retreated to their favorite taverns along the Market Street Triangle. Musicians populated the streets, playing tunes that drove people to dance. Through it all, the leaders of Nezmyth stepped down from the stage and a band of soldiers went to work dismantling the structure.

Kierli smiled wide, then bowed. "It will be an honor to serve alongside you, my King."

Jason nodded and grinned, still thinking of his couch back home. Next to him, Master Ferribolt stood with his hands behind his back until he caught Captain Kierli's eye. Then he leaned forward and offered it to her.

"Captain, I regret that I haven't had the pleasure of meeting you yet!" he said. "If you have time before the end of the evening, I would be delighted if you visited my home for tea!

I'm eager to hear your plans for the kingdom and how our Patriarchs can be of assistance."

"Of course, Master," Kierli smiled. "That would be wonderful."

Kierli clasped Master Ferribolt's hand and shook it. When she did, something stirred inside Master Ferribolt—an uncomfortable tensing in the wake of a passing shadow. The feeling surprised him, and he hoped no one noticed. Putting on a smile again, he said, "Thank you. I look forward to seeing you."

Kierli nodded. "Gentlemen, if you don't mind, I'd like to be excused to celebrate with the people."

"Granted," Jason said.

Kierli bowed again and jaunted into the crowd. A crowd of men and women welcomed her with cheers and claps on her back. They lifted their drinks and sang rousing tunes of victory as she disappeared among them. During that time, Master Ferribolt sidled over to Barnabas.

"And there it is," Master Ferribolt said. "You're retired. A free man."

"I was always free," Barnabas replied. "Now it's just easier to rest."

"Tell me… you said Kierli came recommended by the other Captains?"

"It was almost unanimous. When selecting another Chief Captain, it's customary to seek nominations from all the Captains in Nezmyth. Nearly all of them selected Kierli."

"She certainly is popular," Master Ferribolt watched her among the crowd. "And what were your feelings in selecting her? Did you consult the Sacred Dragon?"

Barnabas's response was slow. "I admit I didn't make it a matter of prayer. I just trusted my better judgment. I've worked with Kierli personally for years and always been impressed with her. She's climbed the ranks quickly—much like I did when I was younger."

"Hopefully not in all ways," Master Ferribolt muttered.

Barnabas turned to him. "Sir?"

Master Ferribolt's tone died down even more. "As I shook her hand, I felt a tremor pass through me. It was faint—barely strong enough to notice. I know this might be intrusive, and I don't know what power is still allotted to you, but if there were a way to keep an eye on her, that would bring some peace to my heart."

Barnabas thought about it, then nodded. "I'll see what can be done."

"She's coming to my home after the celebration for tea. Perhaps getting to know her will assuage some of my concerns." Master Ferribolt forced a smile. "You're welcome to join us."

"On any other day, I'd accept, Master," Barnabas said. "But the preparations for this ceremony have taken it out of me. I plan to retire to my new home and read a book. Perhaps with a crackling fire and a goblet of wine. If it's well enough with you, let's reunite for tea another day."

Master Ferribolt's eyes sparkled. "Well enough indeed." He extended his hand. "Thank you for your service, Captain Barnabas. It has been an honor."

Barnabas took Master Ferribolt's hand. He was surprised when Master Ferribolt pulled him in and embraced him. The Captain's eyes popped, but after a second, he held his friend in kind. Finally, they let go, Master Ferribolt wished him a good night, and the Chief Patriarch vanished.

During Barnabas and Master Ferribolt's conversation, Jason and Tarren walked back to Jason's carriage. Their armor clinked, their capes wafted around their ankles, and their Foreordination Rings glinted as the sunset.

Tarren tugged at the shoulder plates and said, "I'll never get used to this ceremonial armor."

"I know. It's so impractical. I hate it as much as you do."

"You don't intend to stay for the festivities?"

"No," Jason sighed. "All I want to do is rest. You know even before Saryan's death I was never one for parties."

"It might be good for you to be among the people for an hour or two," Tarren counseled. "They love you and miss you. Everyone in this kingdom knows what you've been going through and I'm sure they want to be a support."

Jason stole a glance at the crowd behind him. There were laughs and songs and drinks all around, people stuffing their faces with whatever they could find… he smirked. Saryan would have loved something like this—a chance to be among the people. As soon as that thought passed through him, his smile faded.

"No," he said once more. "But thank you. Do you plan on being out late?"

"Not too late," Tarren smiled. "Hopefully just long enough to find a lovely girl. I want to dress in some commoner clothes, though. If I find a woman to marry, I want her to be a hard working Lower City girl. Not some aristocrat."

Jason's eyes got narrow. "You've been acting a little desperate lately. Let love happen naturally. Don't go chasing for it. It'll only get you into trouble."

"That's easy to say when you were married at eighteen," Tarren replied coolly. Then his eyes lingered on the crowd, looking for the new Chief Captain. "Maybe Captain Kierli is available. She's beautiful and strong."

Jason actually smiled. "Now *that* is a bad idea. She's the Chief Captain now, so you don't want anything spoiling that working relationship. Besides, the last girl you courted was a soldier too, and she was awful."

"Hey now, Rosalyn was delightful! Except for her temper. And the occasional lies. And the jealousy."

"Those were two very long months."

"Now that you mention it, they really were."

They both laughed. Then Jason said, "By the way, when is your next trip to Lunli Village?"

"Soon," Tarren said. "Most likely within the next few weeks. The technique I've been practicing uses a mix of healing herbs and Ancient Nezmythian magic. It just might work. And I feel like I'm close to cracking it."

"I've heard you practicing late into the evening," Jason said. "It would do my heart a lot of good to see Niri home with you. Maybe someone else's triumph could heal my heart a little."

This made Tarren's heart pang. He put his hand on Jason's shoulder. "Jason, you're my friend and I love you. You don't have to just lay around in despair each day. Let's go out on the town soon, just the two of us. Like we did when we were teenagers. Before these capes and the responsibilities became who we were."

The memories started to flood into Jason's mind. Playing instruments together behind his parents' old house. Scraping up enough money to buy sweets on the Southern Market Street. The Cranny. Kristof's shop.

"I'd like that very much," Jason said. "Thank you, Tarren."

They hugged, then Jason climbed into the carriage. The driver yaw'ed and took him up to the castle as Tarren stayed behind to mingle with the commoners. Unfortunately, Tarren didn't get to talk to Captain Kierli, and he missed with many other women he tried to approach.

And back at the castle, Jason laid around and despaired until he fell asleep. Just like Tarren told him not to.

4
THE INTERVIEW

Master Ferribolt's writing stick scratched on a roll of parchment with intensity. A lantern burned on his desk just a foot or two away, flickering a soft orange glow. The windows of his study were dark and it was hard to hear the celebrations happening miles away.

The muscles in his hand grew tired and he put the writing stick down. Blinking hard, he held his wrist and flexed his hand as he opened and closed it. It felt like his joints were fighting against him. An evening of prayer compelled him to write the note on his desk.

It was titled, *To my friends.*

A rapping came to the front door. Master Ferribolt covered up the parchment and put his spectacles on, but didn't answer the door. He let Jerem take care of that. Instead, he migrated to an armchair by the fireplace.

He groaned as he let himself down, his muscles thanking him for a chance to relax in a soft chair. He put his hands in his lap and twiddled his thumbs, waiting. He could hear the door opening and some casual chatter between Jerem and the guests.

It sounded like Kierli had brought someone with her—a male voice he didn't recognize.

In the fireplace, the logs were cold and still. Master Ferribolt winked and one of them ignited. As heat began to permeate the room, he found it easier to get comfortable. He sent up a silent prayer for clarity and wisdom.

Jerem brought Kierli through to the threshold of the study. The man accompanying her was clearly a soldier—strong but not brawny, tall but not towering. A well-trimmed blonde beard wrapped around his face, streaked with gray around his chin, which was only slightly shorter than his blonde hair. His gray eyes reflected his age, which had to have been forty or fifty.

"What a beautiful home!" Kierli marveled as she approached Master Ferribolt. "It reminds me of our Cathedral back in Widow's Rest. The mural on the ceiling is magnificent."

Master Ferribolt smiled and stood from his seat. "Thank you! This mansion has been the home of Chief Patriarchs for centuries."

They shook hands. Again, Master Ferribolt felt the tremor —the small shadow pass through him. He composed himself better this time and didn't let his smile falter. He turned to the friend accompanying Kierli. "And you must be...?"

"Captain Yorn, Master," he smiled widely. "Kierli's replacement as Captain over the Upper City garrison. We worked together for the last two years."

"Ah, of course!" Master Ferribolt said. "Tales of your conduct have reached my ears! All wonderful things, a fine man indeed. Please, sit down."

Yorn's chest swelled with pride. Kierli sat across from Master Ferribolt and crossed her legs as if she had been here a dozen times. Yorn sat down next to her, his face as bright as a fan in the presence of his idol.

"Thank you for making the time to visit this evening," Master Ferribolt said. "Now how about that tea? Would you like sugar? Honey?"

The two guests said that would be delightful. Jerem nodded and marched out to prepare the drinks, his footsteps echoing through the main hall. Master Ferribolt went back to entertaining his guests.

"How were the celebrations this evening? I hope you both had your fill of dancing and drinking."

"We both opt not to drink ale," Kierli said. "It dulls the mind. We have to remain vigilant at all times. We did enjoy our share of dancing, though."

"Not me," Yorn smiled crookedly. "I'd rather spar with a bear than dance. Not a gift I was blessed with."

Master Ferribolt chortled. "Well, Captain Kierli, since you'll be working in the capacity of Chief Captain, we'll be seeing more of each other from now on. Tell me more of you. And you as well, Yorn. I'm so grateful you could bring your spirit to my home tonight."

Light could have shot from Yorn's eyes. Beside him, Kierli smirked.

"Certainly, Master," Kierli said. "I was born and raised in Widow's Rest."

"A lovely farming community. I've visited several times."

"Yes, we're very proud of our work. I was raised by my mother. We were poor like the rest of the village, but we managed to get by."

"And your father?"

"Left when I was five."

Master Ferribolt hummed. "I'm very sorry to hear that."

"It's nothing to me anymore," Kierli shook her head. "I hardly think of it."

"Any brothers and sisters?"

"One. My brother, Jax. Died at the Battle of Nezmyth City. He was my best friend and I miss him every day."

Master Ferribolt's heart sank. "Again, I am very sorry. It appears as though you've had no shortage of hardship."

Kierli smiled politely. "Have you ever lost someone you loved, Master?"

Master Ferribolt didn't expect this. But the answer was easy. "Yes. My sweet Rosie. She passed nearly ten years ago."

"Any children?"

"No."

"It seems as though you're no stranger to hardship either."

Master Ferribolt straightened in his chair. "Part of me believes it's a necessary thing. Through my struggles I've learned to lean upon the Sacred Dragon. I suppose it would be easy to lean away and become bitter—it would be less than honest to say I've never experienced such feelings. But death is a part of our eternal sojourn. Mortality is a fleeting thing. I hold to the truth that I'll reunite with my Rosie in Paradise one day. And when that time comes, I'll be grateful."

Kierli smiled. "Of course. Dragon be praised."

There was something about the way she said that. In the underbelly of her tone, it felt hollow and rehearsed. It gave Master Ferribolt pause, but he tried not to look suspicious. At this point, Jerem returned with the tea, so it was easy to deflect his attention to that. The three of them emptied spoonfuls of honey and sugar and sipped quietly. Then he focused on Yorn. The man had been drinking in his words carefully ever since he sat down. Master Ferribolt's eyes sparkled. "Yorn, what of you? Tell me your story."

Yorn leaned forward and rubbed his hands together. "There isn't much to tell, Master. I was born in Port Runoff, joined the Army when I was fifteen like everyone else. I advanced in rank through the years—not nearly as quickly as Kierli." He glowed at his superior. "But I'm happy to be in this new position. I just hope to fill the very large shoes that Kierli has left for me."

"Please make remarks on the size of my feet, Captain," Kierli sneered.

Yorn and Kierli shared a look. Master Ferribolt smiled.

"So," the Chief Patriarch said, "what are your plans for the kingdom, Captain? How do you plan on serving Nezmyth in this new position?"

"Maintenance is key," Kierli said. "Barnabas already did such a masterful job organizing and training our troops across the kingdom. Additionally, I wanted to be of more service to King Jason directly. A more personal level."

Master Ferribolt's ears pricked. "Oh?"

"He's still grieving the death of Queen Saryan," Kierli said. "It's been over a month and I've heard he still hasn't selected an Inheritor. Is that right?"

Master Ferribolt's eyes bent a little. *That kind of information isn't supposed to make it out of the castle.* "I'm sorry, but I'm not at liberty to share the status of that information."

"Even with the Chief Captain?"

Master Ferribolt nodded. "Even with the Chief Captain."

Kierli drummed her fingers on the armrest. "I see." A thoughtful pause. "Well, regardless, I would like to see the King less stricken with grief. If there's anything I can do, I intend to do it."

Master Ferribolt didn't know what to make of this. He took a sip from his tea to mask his pause. This conversation certainly didn't do much to put his mind at ease. He would definitely want to circle back with Barnabas about this later. He set the tea down on his lap.

"King Jason is understandably upset," Master Ferribolt said, "But he has lots of friends and family for support. All of us are doing what we can to help him through this time."

Kierli smiled. "And I intend to do the same."

Master Ferribolt tried to mirror the smile, but some discomfort crept in.

Kierli took a final sip from her tea, draining the cup. "If you don't mind, Master, I'll be going now. I still need to get some things packed up to move from my barrack to the Chief Captain's mansion. I look forward to working with you more."

Master Ferribolt stood and shook her hand one more time. Again, the unsettling tremor. In contrast, he shook Yorn's hand and felt no such thing. Suppressing a frown, he bid his farewells and Jerem escorted the guests out. The main door opened and closed, then Master Ferribolt was left alone with his butler.

He stroked his chin. "Jerem?"

"Yes, Master?"

"What do you make of the new Chief Captain?"

"I've heard she's very cunning and strong, Master. But I don't know her personally."

Master Ferribolt nodded. "Something tells me none of us do."

* * * * *

Two soldiers, one half-drunk and one sober, clomped around Captain Kierli's barrack. According to what they knew, she was still somewhere near Center Court celebrating with the rest of the city. They heard someone saw her walking toward Upper City, but regardless, it meant she was away and her barrack was unguarded. They would only need a few minutes.

"What are we looking for again?" The half-drunk soldier asked.

"Anything unusual," the other soldier answered. "That's what Captain Barnabas requested."

The first soldier shrugged and blew a raspberry. "Looks like a normal barrack to me. A bed, a chest, a water basin… why did Captain Kierli live like someone from Lower City? There's hardly anything here."

"Probably what she's used to. She's from Widow's Rest, remember?"

"And why are we taking requests from Barnabas, anyway? He's not even Chief Captain anymore."

"It's disrespectful to turn down a request from a Chief Captain, former or current."

"I won't miss him," the first soldier said. "I haven't forgotten what he's done. You haven't forgotten, have you? The time before King Jason?"

"Course I remember, my father was taken by the Blacknote. But he's different now. Come on, help me look around."

As the second soldier turned around, his boot bumped into the chest against Kierli's bed. And as it did, something inside rattled and lurched. The two soldiers traded nervous glances. The second soldier kicked his boot against the chest again, and once more, something rattled inside.

"Something is in here," he said.

The first soldier swallowed. "So, you gonna open it, or what?"

"Me? Why don't you open it?"

"I'm inebriated. You're the responsible one."

"Oh, shut up."

"Go on, Captain Barnabas's orders, right? Be a good soldier."

The second soldier rolled his eyes. "Okay, fine. Just a quick look."

Cautiously, the soldier unlatched the lock and lifted the lid. The soft rattling became louder. As he opened it fully, his face became hard and he frowned. "What in the Dragon's name…?"

Pushed in the corner of Captain Kierli's trunk was a cage full of lizards, scampering over each other in a frenzy. They seemed to panic as soon as light touched them, like they expected something horrible. The soldiers exchanged looks again.

5

THE VISION

Lightning cracked the sky. It was close.

Jason jolted up on his couch, gasping. Winds shook his chamber windows, whistling fiercely outside the walls. Another crack of lightning flashed across the stained glass followed by a burst of thunder. It couldn't have been farther than a few miles. Breathing hard, Jason threw the covers off his sweating body and shook his head, trying to get his bearings.

He didn't even bother putting on his armor. He quickly threw on some street clothes, slung Nightbane around his waist, and flew out the door.

No one was guarding his room. And no one roamed the halls as Jason ran the path leading to the castle doors. Through every room and corridor, he found himself totally alone. Jason frowned. Through corridors and staircases he ran until he arrived in the great hall. There, it was no different. Even the soldiers that should have been around the perimeter were nowhere to be seen.

Breaths came heavy and few. All the time he had spent on the couch had taken its toll—he wasn't as resilient as he once was.

There was no one to open the castle doors for him, so he planted his feet, cracked his knuckles and put his hands against them. He focused his magic and uttered Ancient Nezmythian words for strength. With great effort, the doors groaned open just wide enough to let his body through. But that effort made him exhausted—his head swam and his body tingled.

When he stepped outside, his blood ran cold.

The sky was black and rain came down in a violent torrent. Lightning flashed all around, and with each bolt, thunder shook the ground. The wind snapped at his clothes and the biting cold nipped his ears. The most unsettling thing was the ground beneath him. It was… moaning.

He had to move.

Jason picked up his feet and ran for the edge of the castle grounds. The lush green foliage bent and swayed as the downpour assaulted it. As soon as he passed the trees and flowers, they wilted and died—like each step pulled a wide blanket of death that shriveled everything behind him. Jason looked back at a desolate castle ground as he slipped through the courtyard gates.

And the ground kept moaning.

As he sprinted down Upper City hill, he looked over his shoulder. His heart sank and his throat went dry. Not only were the grounds dead, but the castle was no longer a marvelous cathedral of white stone. Instead, it was charcoal black and chilly. Just as it was years ago.

"What…" Jason wondered aloud. "What's going on…?"

He ripped Nightbane from its sheath and kept sprinting down the hill. His heart fought inside his chest. He could feel a dark presence closing in—something that couldn't be seen, only felt.

The rest of the mansions sped by in a blur. As he careened down the street, a myriad of voices echoed through the wind. He couldn't tell who or what they were. There were so many that they drowned out anything coherent—just a garbled mess. Jason's breathing was labored. Nightbane was tight in his hand.

Finally, he passed the Northern Market Street and shot through some buildings until he reached Center Court. What he found only made him colder.

Center Court was completely empty except for one person. The figure stood at the very center of the plaza, their back to Jason, uncaring of the rain that crashed all around them. Whoever it was clutched a sword in their hand with a pure black blade—a blade so dark that it didn't reflect any light.

Jason lifted his hand to block the rain as he edged closer to the figure. As he did, some of the figure's features became clearer. Whoever it was had silky blonde hair, soaked with rain that cascaded down their shoulders. They also had a strong, feminine body.

Jason's eyes grew wide. "Saryan...?"

She turned around and looked at him. At least he thought she looked at him—he couldn't see her eyes from so far away. But he could tell that her face was completely marred with purple scars, cracking and fragmented like a spiderweb. The same pattern was also on its arms and hands.

An explosion rang out.

Jason flipped to see Upper City hill completely blasted into pieces, erupting like a volcano. The castle was no more— reduced to bits of rubble and stone hurtling through the air. But the part that made his teeth chatter were the shadowy figures that climbed into the sky from the remains of the hill. He couldn't make it what they were. All he could tell was that they were large, strong, and fast.

In his awe and terror, Jason let Nightbane clamber to his feet. The steel sang and tinkled on the rain-soaked cobblestone. And as he turned to the figure in Center Court, she was dashing upon him with her dark blade poised for a strike.

Jason cried out. His body popped up on the couch again. There was no wind or rain. No explosion. No attacker. He was alone in his room, a blanket half pushed off him and his entire body coated in sweat.

Footsteps shuffled quickly from outside the chamber doors. Within seconds, a soldier burst through, holding up a lantern.

"Sire! Sire, are you alright?"

Jason's heart thumped in strong punches. With ferocity in his eyes, he said, "I need to talk to Master Ferribolt *now*."

* * * * *

"A vision, you say?"

"It has to be."

"How can you be so certain?"

"I've never felt anything like it. It was so real."

Jason sat in the armchair with his hands laced together. A fire crackled less than a dozen feet away, radiating Master Ferribolt's study with its typical glowing warmth. It was such a comforting contrast to the dream he just had. It wasn't an hour ago that Jason sprang out of sleep in a cold sweat. His coach was assembled, Tarren was awakened, and they both left for Master Ferribolt's mansion immediately. Jason preferred not to discuss the issue until they arrived.

"You've never experienced dreams like this before?" Tarren said.

"No," Jason said. "Not even the dreams Nadiel put in my mind during my Year of Decision. It was so dark and horrifying." He looked up. "Do you think it means anything?"

Master Ferribolt didn't answer immediately. Instead, he sighed and wiped his glasses. "It's not outrageous for kings to be granted special visions in the night. It's happened before. You said the woman in your dream was Saryan? Not anyone else?"

Jason nodded. "I'm sure."

Master Ferribolt scratched his face. "Why do you think Saryan would strike you?"

"I have no idea," Jason shrugged. "The whole dream felt very ominous. Saryan was never one to instigate terror or fear. But that's all I felt."

All the while, Tarren slouched in his seat, tapping his finger on his temple. Master Ferribolt bent his eyebrows. "Mr. Advisor, what do you think?"

"I'm not sure yet," Tarren said. "The thought of Saryan attacking Jason with any *real* intent to harm him is ludicrous. You two used to spar all the time, but this is different. If anything, I think this is just a bad dream."

"No," Jason said. "No, this has to mean something. It felt too real."

Tarren shrugged. "I don't know what to tell you."

"How can you be sure it was Saryan if you didn't quite see her face?" Master Ferribolt asked.

Jason thought about it. "She had her same blonde hair. The same kind of build." He lost his train of thought when he read Master Ferribolt's body language. "Master Ferribolt, what are you thinking about?"

Master Ferribolt leaned forward. "I debated on whether or not to share this with you, Your Highness. It could be nothing, and I didn't want to cause any unnecessary worry. But I had a strange feeling when I shook Captain Kierli's hand this evening after the Succession Ceremony. There's something about her. I can't put my finger on it."

"Like what?" Tarren frowned, suddenly interested.

"She seems perfectly fine on the surface," Master Ferribolt said. "Well loved by the kingdom. Respected. Capable. But when I shook her hand—something just didn't feel quite right."

"Like a premonition?" Jason said.

"Something of the sort. I invited her over for tea after the ceremony, thinking it would give me a chance to question her and get some answers. I didn't notice anything suspicious about her—only that she seemed particularly interested in who your Inheritor would be."

"She and everyone else." Jason rolled his eyes.

"I also asked Barnabas to pull some strings and keep an eye on her if possible," Master Ferribolt said. "I don't know what measures will be taken, but he said he would see what could be done."

Jason nodded. "Well, it sounds like we're taking all the right measures. If you're feeling bad things about her, that's enough reason for the rest of us to be cautious. Let's continue to exercise that caution with her until we've got some definitive answers." He paused. "Also, I'd like to invite you all to make this a matter of prayer. I'll spend some time in the Oracle Stone room this morning supplicating the Sacred Dragon. Maybe it was just a dream. But if not..." Jason didn't finish the thought.

"Agreed," Master Ferribolt said. "Additionally, I'll take some time to research the Ancient Texts a bit in the morning. Perhaps we'll find some things that pertain to your dream. If it truly is a vision, there should be prophecies in the Text that support your experience."

"Then we're adjourned," Tarren groaned. "Let's go home. I'm tired."

They all stood up from their seats, wished each other a good night, and went their separate ways. On the way back to the castle, Jason and Tarren didn't speak much. Tarren did, however, say one thing once they were back in the carriage.

"You know, I stand by what I said. It could just be a bad dream. You're experiencing a lot of grief. Tonight could just be a manifestation of it."

Jason's arms were folded and he was half asleep, but he said, "Or not. We'll see."

6

THE PRAYER

Barnabas scowled. "Lizards?"

"Yes, sir. A cage full of them. There had to be dozens."

Barnabas set his tea down. His little cabin by Kyleth Pond was only one room, furnished with a couch, a fireplace, a bed, and a round table large enough to seat four. The steaming cup of tea rested between his elbows, not far from his half-eaten breakfast.

"Doesn't seem like the proper way to keep them either," the second soldier asked. "Keeping creatures covered and hidden like that. Seems awfully strange to me."

Barnabas put his hands to his lips. "It is. Thank you for your work. Dismissed."

The soldiers marched out of the cabin, leaving Barnabas alone. He sat pondering for a long moment, his hands still pressed to his lips. Kierli keeping lizards reminded him of himself decades ago—a new Chief Captain, secretly keeping small creatures on hand to kill and practice Dark Magic. If Kierli had somehow figured out how to do the same... Barnabas shivered at the thought.

He took another sip, then stood and walked to a nearby window. Through the glass, he could see Kyleth Pond a short walk away. Trees were beginning to turn warm colors, contrasting with the cool gray morning. On the other side of the pond, people walked along the bank or cast their fishing lines into the water.

Barnabas wandered back into the depths of the cabin as he let himself mull over the situation. Memories of his own descent into Dark Magic danced in front of his eyes. If Kierli really was using Dark Magic—of which they still didn't have definitive proof—he potentially put her in a very dangerous position. Someone like that shouldn't be serving in any position of power, let alone a Chief Captain.

He stroked his beard and stood in front of the fire. It crackled brightly as his eyes sunk into it. He sloshed the tea in its cup a little, then threw his head back and drained it before he set it on the mantle.

No use sitting on this information. King Jason had to be told.

Barnabas moved briskly to the window, pushed it open, and gave a little whistle. Within moments, a hawk swooped down, perched on the window sill, then flapped inside until it nestled on a tall wooden perch by the door. In its beak dangled a dead mouse. The bird held it with its talons and used its beak to rip into it.

Barnabas frowned as he watched the fur tufts and bones fall to the floor. "You're making a mess, Artemis."

The bird ignored him.

"I'm going to the castle," Barnabas said as he reached for a coat. "Look after the house while I'm gone. I'll take the horse, so I should be back within the hour." He frowned again. "If you're going to be that messy while you eat, please take it outside."

Artemis lobbed the remains of the mouse into his beak, then stretched out his wings and flew to the window. In a second, he was gone. And a few minutes later, Barnabas was riding for the castle.

* * * * *

Tarren's eyes traveled up and down some parchment clipped to a board in his hand. With his left hand, he made scratches on the sheet as he absently paced in front of the throne dais. The sunrise was fresh outside, but he didn't feel renewed. Thanks to Jason, he hadn't slept much since he returned to the castle hours ago.

More reading. More scratches with the writing stick. Surprisingly, three knocks came to the castle doors. Tarren turned and bent his eyebrows. It was too early for visitors—Jason wasn't even out of bed yet. Nevertheless, he commanded the soldiers to open the doors. Within seconds, a tall figure in Chief Captain armor same sauntering up the red carpet.

Tarren's ears turned pink. He cleared his throat and tried to go back to his clipboard and paper. The woman advanced, moving with purpose until she arrived at the throne dais. Tarren didn't look up at her as she approached.

"Good morning, Captain Kierli."

"Mister Advisor! A pleasure to see you this early."

"I didn't think we were expecting you."

"Is that a problem?"

"No. It's just that the King isn't even out of bed yet."

"That's perfectly fine," Kierli smiled. "I can wait. Besides, that means you and I can get acquainted a little better."

Tarren stole a sideways glance at her. She was nearly as tall as he was, which surprised him. His eyes couldn't help but move up her body to the scar that stretched across her left cheek, but it was her steely blue eyes that caught his attention. She seemed fully aware of Tarren's wandering eyes, but didn't mind. She even smiled at him. Tarren cleared his throat again and went back to his parchment.

"Did you have a lovely time last night, Mister Advisor?" Kierli asked. "Rumor has it you were looking to find a lady."

Tarren smiled. *She's flirting with me. I could definitely do much worse.* He also thought of Jason's admonition about pursuing her... but Jason wasn't here right now. "It's my regret to inform you that my venture was less than successful."

"I find that hard to believe. At least with shoulders like those."

Tarren's ears burned brighter. Kierli tried not to laugh as her eyes sparkled and her lips pulled into a smile. Tarren tried to coolly collect himself and get back to writing, but dropped his writing stick. It clambered by his feet and his cheeks flushed with embarrassment.

"Oh—"

"Here."

Kierli already had it. She stooped down, picked up the writing stick, and extended it to Tarren as she stood back up. But when she stood up, she was closer. Tarren could see more detail in those eyes—the flecks of white that drifted in the deep blue. They were so inviting. And Tarren couldn't help but think that she was everything he wanted: beauty, strength, wit, humble circumstances.

But wait. Master Ferribolt was suspicious of her. That was reason enough to be on guard.

Bring it back, Tarren, he thought. *There are still things we don't know about her.*

Tarren swallowed, smiled, and cleared his throat again before taking back the writing stick. All the while, she smiled with those perfect teeth.

"Thank you," he croaked.

Suddenly, the doors at the end of the hall swung open. King Jason came through, dragging his feet but dressed in his royal armor. The bags under his eyes were visible even from across the room. Kierli bowed to Tarren and abruptly turned her attention to the King, standing with poise and dignity. Jason blinked hard when he saw her.

"Captain Kierli?" he said, half awake. "What are you doing here this early?"

She marched up to him, nodded with a disciplined bow, and locked eyes with him. "Good morning, Your Highness! Oh. Rough night?"

"They usually are."

"Then I won't disturb you further," Captain Kierli said. "I wanted to take the time to thank you personally for the opportunity to serve Nezmyth in a greater capacity. I've admired your work ever since you became King seven years ago —particularly your actions during the Ash War."

"Thank you, Kierli."

"My current plan is to travel to all the villages and cities across Nezmyth to determine their needs. Barnabas already did such a wonderful job. This will give me a chance to determine how we can best maintain the order he established." She paused. "I love this kingdom dearly, Your Highness. I'll do everything in my power to make it even more prosperous and beautiful."

Jason half-smiled. "That's a good attitude. Thank you, Captain."

"Well… thank you, Your Majesty," she said. "As you know, the Chief Captain's mansion isn't far away. I'm already settled, so if you need anything—anything at all—please don't hesitate to call upon me."

"I will. Thank you."

Kierli nodded benevolently, then turned on her heels and marched away. She didn't leave the castle before stealing a look at Tarren—making sure to eye him up and down just as he did to her. Tarren's ears burned again. Then the castle doors opened and shut, reverberating through the great hall.

Tarren turned to Jason. "Seems a little odd for her to wake up early just to come tell you that."

"She's trying to make a good impression," Jason said. "Master Ferribolt said she was interested in who my Inheritor will be. How much would you bet she's interested in the position?" Jason shook his head. "People who aspire to power are rarely worthy of it. Anyway, I need to go pray. I'll share with you whatever the Sacred Dragon tells me."

"Of course. Best of luck."

Jason slouched down to the Oracle Stone chamber. He periodically rubbed his eyes as he went, trying to wipe out the drowsiness. Sleep never came to him even after he came home from Master Ferribolt's mansion. Maybe he was afraid of having that terrible vision again. Or maybe he was just too caught up in his thoughts.

Regardless, there were two answers he needed: who should be his Inheritor, and the meaning of last night's vision.

The final corridor was one of the darkest in the castle—the most secluded and highly guarded. Guards were stationed around every corner. Torches flickered on the wall. Finally, Jason reached the double doors that were completely engraved with Ancient Nezmythian. He pushed them open, and there it was.

The Oracle Stone—sitting on a pedestal in the middle of an empty room. As soon as he entered, a torch on each wall magically ignited, giving the room an orange glow. Jason closed the doors and approached the Stone. It seemed to sense his presence. As he drew closer, the smoke inside its glassy surface swirled a dull yellow. It also seemed agitated. Troubled by something.

A perfect reflection of my soul, Jason thought.

After a deep breath, Jason unsheathed Nightbane. He set it on the ground before him, then knelt in front of the Stone with his hands on his knees. He kept his gaze to the floor. His words came in mumbles.

"Sacred Dragon… my heart is troubled. I'm—"

His feelings surprised him. As soon as he opened his mouth, his throat caught and his voice shook. He tried to keep his eyes from stinging.

"It's been a month without her, Holy Dragon," he fought his whimpers. "I wish this pain would go away. I wish I didn't have so much hurt. But I understand that I still have a duty here." He swallowed hard and took a long breath to regain himself. "I had a dream last night. A vision. The woman in my dream was Saryan, I'm positive. Why was she surrounded by so much destruction? And what about my Inheritor? I know I should have selected someone weeks ago, but I can't think of the right person to take my place. I'm at a loss, Sacred Dragon. Please guide me."

He sat in silence, listening. A few seconds. A few minutes. Nothing. More time dragged on laced with silence. He tried not to grow impatient, but to keep his heart open to direction. After another long pause, he said with more verve and conviction, "Sacred Dragon, answer me!"

There it was. He blinked, and suddenly he was surrounded by endless white. The Oracle Stone floated in the air without a pedestal. And behind the Oracle Stone, King Thomas stood in full royal armor. His dark eyes were fixed on Jason. Upon seeing him, Jason couldn't help but stand. King Thomas didn't say anything. He just stared.

Jason swallowed. "I've only been in this white room once before. At the beginning of the Ash War. It's where you let me know I should set Barnabas free."

"And you've seen the results of that."

"Yes."

King Thomas almost smiled. "You've battled with a great deal of sadness lately, Your Highness. We've seen it."

Jason dipped his head, fighting the tightness in his throat again.

"I wish I had more soothing words for you," King Thomas continued. "I'm very limited on what I can say. You may not like it, but nonetheless, it is the truth, and you are entitled to it as King.

"A pivotal time for the world is approaching. What you must do is follow your intuition—what your heart tells you is right—and endure. Stay strong and true to your calling. Those are the most important things, Your Highness. Trust your heart, and endure. Do you understand?"

Jason mumbled, "That isn't much to go on."

"I know. I'm sorry."

"What about my Inheritor?"

"It is the same," King Thomas said. "If your feelings tell you that you haven't found the right person yet, follow them. When the right person is presented, you'll know."

Jason inhaled a deep breath and let it seep out his nose. "That's it, then?"

King Thomas nodded. "That's it."

"I see," Jason mumbled. He took another deep breath and locked eyes with King Thomas. "Then I'll do my best."

"I know you will," King Thomas said. "But, if the Sacred Dragon doesn't yank me from this vision now, there are a few things I would like to tell you myself."

King Thomas strode around the Oracle Stone and planted himself in front of Jason. He put both hands on Jason's shoulders, but since he was a spirit, Jason couldn't feel them.

"I've experienced this kind of loss, too," King Thomas said. "Your pain doesn't make you weak. It makes you human. You are still the Foreordained King of Nezmyth and you are entitled to that royal strength so long as you live worthy of it. The Dragon will carry you through this time. It doesn't mean that it'll be easy, but the sun always rises when the night is gone. Do you understand?"

Jason's throat was tight again. He coughed to clear it up. "Yes, sir."

"Good. May the Dragon bless you, King Jason. And by the way..." his eyes became soft again. "She sends her love."

Jason clenched his teeth and pressed his lips together to keep his chin from shaking. King Thomas smiled, then the vision disappeared. He was back in the Oracle Stone room, surrounded by flickering torches and staring into the surface of the smoky orb. He couldn't help but deflate. Those answers were hardly answers at all. And a pivotal time was coming? Of what sort?

Jason stewed on the thoughts all the way up to the great hall. By the time he reached it, he could smell his breakfast wafting through the air: eggs, toast, bacon, and sausages. At least that was one thing to look forward to. Tarren was still standing at the throne dais. When he caught Jason's eye, he smirked and strolled over.

"If you were wondering what I was writing earlier," Tarren said while handing Jason the roll. "Here you are, Your Highness."

Jason glowered. "Don't call me that. I've known you since we were five."

"I know, but it's fun to be just a little patronizing with you."

Jason glowered even harder when he read the parchment. It was scribbled with several lines that clearly made up a schedule. There was time blocked out for sparring, magic, meals, and reading among other things. Tarren watched him with folded arms.

Jason looked up. "You're putting me on a wellness regimen? I'm fine."

Tarren shook his head. "No you're not. You've lost more than a step in the last month."

"You can't order me to do this."

"You're right. I can't. But you would be unwise not to take my counsel and you know it."

"I don't know. You're a little too self-assured at times." Jason's eyes narrowed. "And sometimes you're even stricter than Nadiel was."

"I'll consider that a compliment," Tarren smirked. "I've already lined everything up. I'll spar with you, just like the good old days. I've already contacted a local magician that considers it an honor to train you. You're not allowed to leave the dining hall until you've finished each meal. And I've got some *riveting* volumes of literature for you."

Jason looked over the sheet one more time, growled, then folded it and stuffed it in his pocket. "So, when do we start?"

"Right now," Tarren said. "Let's go to the back courtyard. We'll get you started on some stretches."

They didn't get the chance. A soldier came running up to them and said, "Your Highness, Capt—uh, Mister Barnabas is at the castle doors. He says he has something urgent to tell you."

"It must be if he came all the way up here unannounced," Jason said with furrowed eyebrows. "Let him in."

Three knocks on the double doors. They inched open. And in came Barnabas, retired Chief Captain. His pace was rushed and his jaw was locked into his skull. Jason and Tarren traded concerned looks. When he reached the two of them, he looked around and whispered, "Advisor, Your Highness... I suspect that Captain Kierli might be tampering with *Tepnoh Edomah*."

7
THE HEARING

"Based on what?" Jason replied just as lowly.

In a hushed tone, Barnabas explained the lizards found in Kierli's barrack. Jason and Tarren traded looks. They knew what the lizards were for—small animals to be kept in reserve, killed to practice Dark Magic when needed. Barnabas used to do the same thing many years ago.

"Maybe it's a coincidence," Tarren mumbled. "But where there's smoke, there's fire. Jason?"

Jason scratched his beard. Everything lined up, but accusing someone of *Tepnoh Edomah* was too serious a thing to be done on scraps of evidence. He wouldn't make any decision without confronting her directly. A hearing was necessary to examine her and determine their next course of action. He proposed the idea to the others and they all agreed—not only that, but they would send for her immediately. If they could examine her and listen to the Dragon's whispers, maybe they could clearly determine the depths of her practice.

A soldier was sent to fetch Master Ferribolt. He returned within the hour. The four of them moved their discussion to the King's quarters so they wouldn't be overheard. They stood and discussed the implications of another Chief Captain practicing Dark Magic—if that was even the case. The effects of the Ash War were still fresh, but thankfully, the kingdom didn't know the nature in which those creatures were born.

Eyes frequently passed on Barnabas, though. He was the only one to experiment with Dark Magic in the past, so his presence during the hearing would be imperative. He understood Dark Magic better than anyone in the room— probably the kingdom.

"I haven't noticed any outward signs of usage," he admitted, "but the evidence is fairly clear. Among Master Ferribolt's feelings and what we found in her barrack… it's a serious possibility. We must be wary of how she reacts when we confront her."

The others agreed. They concluded their discussion and sent a soldier to Captain Kierli's mansion. In the meantime, the party waited in the great hall. Jason's legs jittered as he sat. Tarren stood silently at his right side, his face to the ground, thinking. Barnabas paced along the side of the throne dais while Master Ferribolt stood with his hands behind his back, meditating.

Finally, three knocks came to the castle doors. They moaned open, letting the cold air seep in. Four guards marched Captain Kierli down the red carpet. As they did, the soldiers lining the walls stared ahead like armored statues, perplexed at the unfolding situation.

Kierli's eyebrows bent, taking in the scene. She was in full Chief Captain armor, freshly-polished bronze plates covering her body, her sword slung around her hip. All throughout her march, she kept her wits about her. It was odd enough that she had to be escorted to the castle by four of her own, but to be met by every Foreordained leader in such a way? She kept one hand on her sword.

No one breathed. They just watched each other. The only sound in the great hall was the clanking of armor and the soft plodding of footsteps. When Kierli finally reached the end of the red carpet, the four soldiers dismissed themselves. There she stood, looking into the eyes of her King and the others—those she had sworn an oath to serve. But the feelings across her eyes were those of a cornered wolf. Cautious. Alert.

"Good afternoon, gentlemen," she tried to lighten the mood. "It's been a while."

Jason smirked. "Captain Kierli. I hope you're getting used to your new living space."

"It's beautiful. Much nicer than anything I've known."

Jason maintained his half-smile, then his gaze washed over every soldier in the great hall. He lifted his voice. "Ladies and gentlemen standing guard, you're dismissed for half an hour. Please don't return to the great hall until then."

The soldiers hiked up their weapons and made for the nearest doors. This gave Kierli even more pause. Her sharp eyes watched every soldier file out of the great hall until it was just her and the four men. Each of them stayed tensely still until they were alone. Not even the dust in the air seemed to move.

The echoes from the closing doors died down. The air was heavy and the silence was suffocating.

"Kierli," Jason laced his hands in front of him. "We have some questions for you. And I trust that you'll answer honestly."

Kierli's eyebrows pointed. "Naturally."

"Some soldiers found a cage full of lizards in your barrack's trunk last night during the celebration," Jason said. "What are they for?"

"I keep them as pets," Kierli said flatly. "May I ask why there were soldiers in my barrack?"

Jason ignored the question. "Dozens of them? In the dark?"

"They seem to like it just fine. Why was my private space invaded?"

Jason exchanged glances with the others. No one was buying it, particularly Barnabas. His arms were folded across his chest and he tapped his fingers against one of his elbows. Jason leaned forward and rubbed his hands against his face. Finally, he said, "Kierli, have you ever heard of something called *Tepnoh Edomah?*"

"That sounds like Ancient Nezmythian, but I never learned the language," she said.

"It is. It stands for Dark Magic."

Something washed across her face, like a child realizing they had been caught eating sweets before dinner. But she reeled back her expression and suppressed it. It didn't matter. It was enough. The dots were connecting behind those eyes, and everyone else saw it.

"Now, what we're about to tell you, you must swear never to repeat," Jason said severely. "Dark Magic is incredibly dangerous—it's the same power that instigated Barnabas's rule and the same power Nartikis wielded during the Ash War. It can only be practiced based upon the death you inflict. It robs you of your ability to feel positive emotion and gives euphoric feelings upon practice." Jason's eyes grew even more serious. "Have you been practicing this magic, Kierli?"

Kierli swallowed and her heartbeat picked up. Her eyes darted to everyone on the throne dais. She had the hard time looking at Master Ferribolt, and an even harder time looking at Barnabas. She straightened her posture and said, "If I had been... what would be the consequence?"

There it is, Jason thought. "That would be decided later. But we need the truth now. It's important to the safety of the kingdom. Are you practicing Dark Magic, Kierli?"

She hesitated... but nodded.

A unified sigh drifted through the four men. The confession. But the examination wasn't over.

"So you've been killing the lizards to fuel your use?" Jason said.

"Yes."

"For how long?"

"Since I was fourteen."

Since she was fourteen? Jason thought. *That means he's been practicing for almost twenty years!*

"Kierli," Jason said. "Tell us the full extent of your practice. Every detail."

Kierli took a deep breath and didn't make eye contact with anyone. "I mostly use it to decompress. It was difficult being raised by my mother—if you knew her, you'd understand. And after some of the things I experienced as a teenager, I discovered it and started using it when I needed a lift. I would only kill small things, like plants or animals. But I've never killed humans for it. The only killing I've done is in my work as a soldier."

There was something in the way she said that last sentence. She continued:

"Once I joined the army, I learned to use it as a source of strength. I would channel it to help me stay up late or wake up early for exercises. I would use it during sparring to make myself faster or stronger. If I'm being honest, it's what's helped me get to where I am now. If I wasn't using this magic, I'd probably still be an average foot soldier in Widow's Rest.

"But with all that being said…" she lifted her eyes. "Could it really be bad if it's helped me so much?"

Jason opened his mouth to speak, but stopped himself. He turned to Barnabas. The man was still standing at the edge of the dais, his eyes intense, bristling like a raw nerve. Jason spoke quietly. "Barnabas, would you like to answer that question?"

"Certainly," he said a little quickly. He stepped forward. "Kierli, if you do not cease practicing this magic, it will destroy you. Just as it did to me and Nartikis."

"With all due respect, sir," Kierli said, calling on her Chief Captain bravado. "I've been using it for nearly twenty years, and all its done is improve me. I've never felt better in my life."

"Kierli," Barnabas squirmed at her contradiction. "Listen to me very closely. That magic is the creation of the Guardian of the Night. It's the magic that's responsible for *my* horrific rule, and for the Ash that Nartikis created—the Ash that killed your brother."

She bristled and courage took her. "No, this magic isn't to blame for my brother's death. Nartikis is. Nartikis could have used this magic to do a great many things, but instead he chose death. I don't blame the magic. I blame that stupid boy for slaughtering our people. I know he's your son, but you should never forget that."

Barnabas's face turned beet red. It took every ounce of his control not to explode. Kierli didn't give him a chance to respond. She turned to the rest of the group.

"Listen to me," Kierli said. "Are you going to punish me for using this magic to serve our kingdom? The magic that's given me strength beyond my normal abilities, that's helped me recuperate when I'm at wit's end? Maybe the problem isn't the magic itself. Maybe it's just overpowering to those who aren't strong enough for it."

With every word, Jason found himself tensing. Conversely, Kierli became bolder.

"Think of it—what could we have done if we used this same magic *against* Nartikis during the Ash War?" Kierli said, her eyes brightening. "We could have ended it so much sooner! Think of the lives that could have been spared!" She brought her excitement back down. "But it seems as though you hold to some ancient tradition that this magic is evil no matter what. I disagree. It's not the magic itself, but the wielder.

"Your Highness, please reconsider. This could be the way of the future. This could be how we usher a new era of peace and power to Nezmyth. I'll help you at every step. I'm strong enough to control this—I'm living proof. Listen to reason."

Jason couldn't believe what he was hearing. He looked to his friends. Master Ferribolt was positively aghast—his eyes wide and his hand holding his chin. Tarren listened with furrowed brows. But Barnabas looked like he could tear the head off a bear. With that, Jason stood from the throne.

"Barnabas is right, Kierli," he said. "You may feel good about this magic now, but over time, it will destroy you. And as Chief Captain, that is a dangerous spot to be in. I don't want to strip you of your new position, but we have been very clear with you. Dark Magic is the work of the *Guardian of the Night*. It is destruction. Dragon's sake, you can only use it after you've *killed* something! Doesn't that speak volumes to you?

"I'm going to give you a choice. You must swear to each of us in this room that you will never use this magic again for any reason. You will retain your position and your status, but you must leave *Tepnoh Edomah* behind. I'm trusting you, Kierli. Do we have your word?"

Kierli was still. Her gaze fell to the red carpet, the gears turning in her mind. She didn't look up to the King. She muttered, "I cannot promise you that, Your Majesty. It's part of who I am. It's what got me here, and it's what gives me strength. If I were to tell you I'd never use it again, I would be lying." She lifted her eyes to him. "I'm asking you to trust me with it. Let me serve Nezmyth with it. It doesn't have to be anyone else—this could be our secret pact. Please... give me your blessing."

What?

Jason was dismayed by the daring Kierli put on display. He couldn't even look at his friends—he knew they were just as bewildered as he was. He clenched his teeth behind his lips and had to take a deep breath before he spoke again. To so pridefully deny the effects of Dark Magic, then to ask the King for a *blessing* to freely wield it? She was either insane or irreparably prideful.

And that was the moment. Something clicked in Jason's mind that shot a bolt of clarity through him. The dream from last night. The girl with the blonde hair and strong build. The darkness all around. The attack on him. It wasn't Saryan. It never was. It was her. It was Kierli all along.

That lit a fire inside Jason. A stone-cold resolution to stop a disaster before it could grow roots.

"Kierli," he said, "it is difficult to articulate my disappointment in you. You have gone against your oath and directly repelled the counsel of Nezmyth's Foreordained leaders. And for what? To clutch onto something that will eventually turn you into a monster. It's reckless, childish, and there is no place for it among Nezmyth's elite. I am stripping you of your position of Chief Captain, and what's more, I'm sentencing you to the Vault of the Damned until you are rehabilitated."

Kierli's mouth went dry. Her eyes showed the reflection of a great tower that had taken decades to build, then came tumbling down in a matter of seconds. Her face burned. Her hands shook and she almost drew her sword, but thought better of it. She spoke through curled lips.

"The *Vault of the Damned?*" She seethed. "*Me?* You want *me,* your new Chief Captain, sentenced *there?*"

"You're insubordinate and disobedient!" Jason commanded. "You are not who we thought you were, Kierli! My decision is clear. You'll be escorted there immediately."

It must have been half an hour, because the soldiers started filing back into the great hall. As soon as a fair number entered, Jason ordered a handful of them to escort Kierli out of the castle and take her to the Vault of the Damned. The initial reaction was shock, but the soldiers followed their duty. They took her and bound her hands with rope.

Before they took her out, Jason looked over his shoulder. "Tarren, if you could go with her. You're a strong magician. If she tries anything, you should be able to handle her."

"Understood."

Tarren joined with the others down the red carpet. Just as they started to leave, Kierli threw her gaze over her shoulder and glared at Jason. She put everything into that look—her disgust, her contempt, her betrayal.

Jason's eyes became hard as he watched that face and thought of his nighttime vision. *Good riddance. Put her in the Vault where she can't do any harm.*

At length, the castle doors boomed shut and the great hall fell to another deathly hush.

Jason slouched in his throne and pinched the bridge of his nose. "Master Ferribolt… you were right. You're always right."

"I wish it weren't the case," the Chief Patriarch muttered.

Jason turned to Barnabas. The man was beginning to settle, but the remnants of Kierli's words still lingered. "I know you had just begun your retirement. But if you would accept your old position until we find another worthy to replace you, that would bring some peace to my heart."

Barnabas pursed his lips. "I accept." Then he shook his head. "I'm sorry, Your Highness. I never should have appointed her. Master Ferribolt asked me if I prayed to the Dragon about her and I didn't. I was a fool."

"We caught it before she could do any harm," Jason said. "Don't trouble yourself on this any further." He paused. "She cut you with the things she said about Nartikis, didn't she?"

Barnabas exhaled like an angry gorilla and nodded stiffly.

Jason tried to smile, but couldn't. "We're going to need some of that famous Barnabas discipline in the coming days. People will have questions. And what's more… she's going to hate being down there with him."

Barnabas thought of his Nartikis alone in the Vault. "May I be excused, Your Highness?"

"Granted. I'll send a decree to the kingdom letting everyone know you've been reinstated. I won't give the specifics of Kierli's imprisonment, just that we discovered things in her conduct that demanded swift retribution." Jason sighed. "Tomorrow is a new day, gentlemen. We move forward."

8

THE CONVICTS

Kierli kept her gaze between her boots as the carriage jostled toward the western edge of the city. There was a soldier on either side of her. And across from her, Tarren didn't blink or avert his stare. His hands laid on his knees, palms up, fingers splayed out, ready to throw magic at a moment's notice. But Kierli showed no sign of resisting. She didn't speak since leaving the castle, and they were nearly at the foot of the Upper City hill.

Finally, she muttered, "This is a mistake."

"His Highness doesn't seem to think so," Tarren replied.

"And you?"

"I trust his judgment."

She smirked cynically. "But you see it, too. My control of this magic. It controlled Barnabas and Nartikis, but not me. I'm different—I know I am."

It was true. Tarren knew one of the telltale signs of Dark Magic use was sapped positive emotions—no joy, no peace, no delight. But it was only yesterday that he watched her celebrate with the townspeople, beaming brightly, dancing and singing.

He wasn't about to admit that, so instead, he just looked out the window.

She scoffed and shook her head. "You're going to have a handful explaining to the kingdom why your Chief Captain was thrown in prison on the first day of her tenure."

Tarren didn't know how to respond to this either, so again, he said nothing. Kierli looked at his open palms—a sign of someone ready to throw magic. She frowned and said, "I have no plan of attacking you. Besides, your friends here tied me up very nicely. So even if I wanted to…" She didn't finish.

Tarren hated seeing someone so beautiful all tied up and defeated. A wave of sympathy washed over him. She was only trying to carry out her duties—he could understand that—but nonetheless, she had stumbled upon something evil and opposed orders to give it up.

But that put another thought in Tarren's mind: *Does Dark Magic affect others differently? Do we just not understand it enough?*

The rest of the trip lasted in tense silence. They both kept their eyes out the windows, watching the houses and shops crawl by as the carriage moved through the city. It passed through the western gates, then tottered along the dirt path for a long while until they reached the Nezmyth City Prison. Guards stood sentinel all around the perimeter of the massive chasm. None of them expected the cargo Tarren carried.

The carriage stopped. The soldiers filed out, followed by Kierli, then Tarren. As the soldiers led her to the edge of the pit, Tarren followed closely behind, still keeping his hands open. He stole glances at the other guards. Their eyes grew wide when they saw their new Chief Captain bound up for incarceration.

As they sunk into the depths of the prison, a dank chill enveloped them. Even the torches on the wall didn't give much warmth. Many prisoners recognized Kierli. For them, she was the cause of their captivity. She became the receiving end of curses, obscenities, and spitting as they descended. She took it all in stride, though. She never fought back or spared so much as a glance. Tarren continued to follow quietly and begrudgingly admire her.

What Tarren didn't notice was Kierli writing words on the palm of her hand. With her wrists bound together, she used her left palm as a surface for her right middle finger to write crude letters. Her fingertip glowed purple as it traced letters, and every letter disappeared as soon as it was written. No one saw it.

Finally, they reached the bottom, where the air was coldest and thickest. There it was. The Vault of the Damned. The soldiers standing guard saw Tarren and opened the door—uttering the incantation and turning the giant crank. As the door swung open, Kierli slid him a look.

"It'll just be me and him down there?"

"Until the King decides otherwise."

"Pity," she said. "Maybe you could come visit me? He's probably not very nice to look at."

She smirked. Tarren tried not to turn pink. The soldiers grabbed her elbows and led her into the depths. Tarren stayed behind. The air grew murky the farther down they went. When they finally reached the bottom, it was too dark to see anything. One soldier walked to the middle of the Vault and lit a tall torch that stood from the floor. It threw dim flickering light through every cell, but only one was occupied.

A young man with pale skin and icy blue eyes watched as another soul finally joined him in a cell opposite of him. The spectacle managed to take him away from the book propped open on his desk. Kierli glowered at him.

Once Kierli was in her cell, the soldiers worked on removing her Chief Captain armor. Wordlessly, they untied straps, unbuckled buckles, and slipped the glorious plating from her body. She resisted the urge to fight or cry as they did. It was like they were peeling away a part of her—stripping away a chunk of her identity. Her body shook with frustration. When it was all taken off, Kierli was left in commoner street clothes.

One soldier looked around the cell. "I… I'm sorry, Captain. Just following orders."

Kierli said nothing. With heads down, the soldiers dragged their feet up the stairs, leaving the convicts alone in the Vault of the Damned. The shuffling of feet on dirty steps became quieter, and finally, the door closed with a metallic slam. Its sound echoed through the Vault.

Kierli took in her new barred home. There was next to nothing—just a pile of hay pushed into a corner. Rats chittered not far away. It was dark. The stones beneath her feet were cold. Just hours ago, she was sitting in the Chief Captain's mansion in Upper City. And now this.

With no eyes on her except that stupid boy's, she roared. She grabbed fistfuls of her hair and pulled. She kicked at the bars. She wished she had a sword to swing or a chair to break, but there was nothing. She even tried to shoot something from her hands, make anything from her hands, but some invisible force stopped it—something damming up the magic inside her.

She tried harder, holding her hands wide open, channeling all her anger into her palms. She could feel the power move through her arms and hands, but that's where it stopped. Nothing. She roared again, grabbing the bars, then slid into a sitting position, staring through stinging eyes.

The boy from the other cell watched the tirade. He closed the book on his desk and set it atop a stack of other ones. He crept to the bars, held them, swallowed, and forced out the words, "Who are you? You're beautiful."

The compliment made Kierli sick. She didn't reply.

After Kierli's silence, the boy piped up again, "Why are you here?"

"You're Nartikis, aren't you?"

The boy hesitated. "Yes."

"My brother was killed in the Ash War."

Nartikis swallowed.

"It's a good thing there are two sets of bars between us," Kierli hissed. She cocked her head back and spat in his direction. Then she turned around and put her back to the bars.

Nartikis swallowed again. "Are you… Captain Kierli? You were wearing Chief Captain armor. My father's talked about y —"

"Speak to me again and I'll kill you."

Nartikis obeyed the command. He felt anger rising inside him. He understood her anger—it was justified—but being a former King, he had never experienced someone snapping at him in such a way. But he had to let it go. Harboring those ill feelings never did any good, especially in a place like this.

Nartikis reached over and took a few books from his stack. Then he reached through the bars and set them on the ground. Concentrating, he held his hand out and the books began to levitate. They hovered inches above the floor and glided along until they bumped into the bars of Kierli's cell. Then they fell to the ground in a pile. Kierli heard the sound and looked behind her.

"If you don't plan on speaking to me," Nartikis said, "you should at least have some books to read."

Kierli didn't stop scowling. "It's too dark to read."

"Your eyes will adjust."

She didn't get up to grab the books. She just sat and scowled. "Why is it that a murderous king gets a desk, a bed, and books to read while I, a faithful soldier, get a pile of straw?"

Gaining courage, Nartikis said, "Oh, you want to speak to me after all? I'll have you know I didn't ask for any of these things. My father had them brought down. None of the soldiers were happy to do it. One of them even tried to kill me."

"They should have."

"You're probably right." Feeling bolder, Nartikis said, "You've been tampering with Dark Magic, haven't you?"

Kierli was silent.

"This place is reserved for Dark Magic users like us," Nartikis said. "We can't use it here. And that's a good thing. Cleansing that darkness from your soul is enlightening." He paused. "How many people have you killed?"

"I'm a soldier, you dunce. I've only killed when necessary. Not like you."

"But you *have* killed. And that's given you fuel."

Kierli didn't reply.

Nartikis shook his head. "Count yourself lucky that you're here. Give it time and you'll see things clearer. You'll be grateful King Jason put you down here."

Kierli scoffed. Unable to think of a response, she put her hand in front of her face. She snapped her fingers, trying again to ignite a little purple flame on her fingertip. Nothing. She snapped again. Still nothing. She glared. It's true. This place was really keeping her from practicing it. She really couldn't do it.

Her frown deepened and her gaze dropped to the books that Nartikis left her. It took great concentration—standard magic was more difficult—but she pointed her finger at them and managed to shoot a little gray flame. The fire took hold of the books and burned them slowly, flicking dull light against her.

* * * * *

Several miles away, afternoon sunlight spilled into Captain Yorn's barrack—just one room built into the army training facility on the lower part of Upper City. Steaming tea sat on the stove, his bed was made, and he sat at a desk with a quill and parchment, scribbling intently. Two soldiers stood guard by his front door. One of them had teased him earlier for using a quill instead of a writing stick. They called it old fashioned. Yorn didn't mind. He liked the feel of it.

His first day as Captain over the Upper City garrison went as expected. He didn't need a lot of pleasantries among the soldiers—he already knew them all. Seeing as he was second in command to Kierli over this garrison for nearly two years, he already knew how everything ran. And everything ran so smoothly under Kierli's direction that he felt no need to make any changes.

The scratching of the quill was soft in his ears. But as the quill traveled down the parchment, something else caught his eye. The corner of the desk—purple lines were starting to form.

Yorn gasped and shot up, toppling his chair and putting his hand on his sword. He watched the purple lines bend and curve on the corner of the table, forming words. After only a brief moment, a message was clearly visible:

YORN, IT'S KIERLI

SENT TO VAULT OF DAMNED. DON'T KNOW WHY. KING WRONG. HELP.

"Sir! What's wrong?"

The two soldiers heard the noise and dashed into Yorn's barrack. Yorn pointed at the desk.

"There," he said. "You see those words?"

One soldier paused and began reading aloud. "To my dearest K—."

"No, not on the parchment. There, on the corner of the table."

"Sir?"

Both of them ogled at him. Yorn frowned. The words were still on the table, but starting to fade. And for some reason, these soldiers couldn't read it. That means that Kierli meant this message for his eyes only.

"Nevermind," he muttered. "I'm fine. Back to your post."

9
THE EPISTLE

Sweat clung to his collar. Breaths came in forced bursts. Jason kept pace with Tarren as they ran laps inside the perimeter of the castle grounds.

The trees and bushes rustled as the autumn breeze meandered through the courtyards. Tarren pumped his fists in front of him, barely breaking a sweat, still breathing through his nose. Jason's heart threw a violent fit inside him and he was quietly thankful that the air was so chilly this morning—it made the sweat feel like a cool, misty coating.

"Keep going," Tarren said. "You're doing great."

Jason wheezed.

They were coming up to the back courtyard. Soldiers patrolling the grounds watched Jason and Tarren as they jogged, and some tried to avert their eyes to avoid embarrassing the King. Jason started lagging behind Tarren as they reached the sparring ring. Tarren strolled to a stop while Jason slumped down with his hands on his knees, breathing in great gulps and letting the sweat pour from his face.

"For someone who's been in bed for the better part of a month," Tarren said, "I'd say you did pretty well with two laps."

Jason didn't reply. He just huffed and puffed.

Tarren paused. "Do you… need a little bit more time?"

Jason nodded tightly.

Tarren smirked. A soldier brought him a canteen, which he drank from a little bit. Then he handed it to Jason, who drank from it deeply. When he was done, he noticed a woman approaching them, escorted by a pair of soldiers. She was fairly young—had to be the same age as them, with short black hair and dark eyes.

"Ah, Alis!" Tarren said. "You're here early! Jason, this is Alis of Pinegrove. She's one of the best magicians in Nezmyth City—probably in the kingdom. She's the magic instructor I mentioned yesterday."

Jason was finally standing straight with his hands on his hips, but still breathing hard. "A master magician? You look… pretty young… to be a master. I mean that… in a nice way."

Dimples poked into her cheeks when she smiled. She stood with her hands clasped in front of her, her feet together, wearing a lavender dress that was modest in both quality and design. Her black hair was cut just below her jaw line, and her eyes were dark as beetles. Everything about her glowed.

"I get that a lot," she smiled. "Comes with being a prodigy, I suppose."

Tarren patted Jason on the shoulder. "I'm going to go back inside and work on some things. You'll work with Alis for the next hour on whatever she has planned. I trust her fully." He winked and smiled. "Don't go blasting holes in any walls."

Jason tried not to laugh through his breaths. As Tarren walked away, Jason took another long drink from the canteen. Alis watched the Advisor depart, then turned to Jason and tilted her head. "Blasting holes?"

"When we were teenagers," Jason explained, "Tarren and I were sparring rivals under the same teacher. Sometimes we would even spar in our free time just to test each other. One time, he beat me so hard that I blasted a hole in his wall with a jeroki." Jason grinned absently. "His father was furious. We worked for the next few days repairing it."

Alis hummed. "Sounds like you used to have a bit of a temper."

"I hadn't come to terms with my Foreordination yet. There were a lot of pent up feelings."

"Clearly," Alis said. "Well, if you have any other unhealthy feelings pent up, they might very well prevent you from practicing magic at its peak."

Do I? The remark made Jason stop and think. But the only pent-up feelings he could think of were his loneliness and stress. Nothing unusual. After a quick pause, he asked, "How old are you?"

"Twenty-four, Your Majesty."

"That's just a year younger than me," Jason said. "How does one become a master magician at such a young age? Nadiel took a lifetime of study to get where he was, Dragon rest his soul."

"He truly was a master," Alis said. "As for myself, I knew how to throw a jeroki before I knew how to read. My father was wise enough to teach me discipline and dedication on top of my natural talent. He's what helped me become what I am now."

"Well then, show me what you can do."

Alis smiled wide. "No."

Jason blinked twice, taken aback. Alis almost laughed.

"Please forgive me, Your Highness," Alis said, "but I will not treat magic like a set of parlor tricks. Some say it's the closest thing we have to practicing the Sacred Dragon's infinite power. Showing off feels inappropriate. You'll find that most of my lessons are more about addressing the things inside you than running laps or doing pushups. Magical strength is found within."

"I'm aware," Jason said, feeling a little irritated.

"Good. Then I'll build on what you already know."

She didn't elaborate, so Jason said. "Well, what's first?"

"I need to get to know you a little better, Your Highness. First off, what are the things that make you truly happy?"

Jason felt lost at this. He wasn't sure how magical strength tied directly to happiness—how forming jerokis or fire whips could relate to laughing or smiling. He had to repeat the question to make sure he understood. "Things that make me happy?"

"Yes. I don't mean things that you do for fun, but things that give you a truly authentic feeling of joy and peace. What are they?"

One thing came to mind. "Saryan made me happy. Even though she annoyed me at times, being with her was the best thing. She made me feel complete."

"What else?"

Jason thought more, but got nothing. "I... I don't know."

"Then you're presented with a great opportunity," Alis said. "It seems as though you felt a major part of yourself was lost when Queen Saryan passed. I understand that you two were only eighteen when you married, and it was on the same day that you became King. That means you two experienced *everything* about royal life together. And *that* means there's a major opportunity to discover yourself as your own person— to readjust your focus as an individual, not as a joined unit."

Jason stared at the ground and soaked in all her words. "That sounds like a lot."

"It will be a journey. But that's life, isn't it?" Alis said. "Besides, I know you two are Melded together forever, so she's probably not far away. Her spirit could be with us right now for all we know. And that means you're not really going through this without her."

That made Jason smile.

But something caught Alis' eye—something that was approaching Jason from behind. He turned around to see. Two more men were approaching the sparring ring. One was a common soldier, the other was Captain Yorn. Jason hadn't many direct dealings with Yorn, but with the few he had, Yorn never looked as distressed as this. His gray eyes were hard and sleepy bags hung beneath them. His rigid posture was clearly forced—Jason surmised he didn't get much sleep last night.

When the soldiers reached the King, they both bowed, and Jason returned the gesture with a nod. He suspected Yorn would come eventually. He was garbed in full Captain armor, complete with his sword slung around his hip.

"Sir," the soldier said, "Captain Yorn said he had some questions for you about the event with Cap—uh, Kierli yesterday."

"I'm not surprised," Jason said. "I'm sorry for the sudden change, Captain. I'm sure you have questions."

"I do, sir," Yorn said.

Jason turned to Alis. "If you could excuse us for a few minutes?"

"Of course, Your Majesty."

Alis and the soldier retreated a respectful distance. Alis busied herself with admiring the ground's flowers while the soldier stood at attention. Jason and Yorn strolled to a bench at the edge of the sparring ring. Any of the patrolling soldiers were dozens of yards away—out of earshot, as far as they could tell.

"You're distraught about Kierli," Jason said. "I heard you two were close."

"Yes, Your Highness."

"What's on your mind? You can speak freely."

"I just don't understand."

"Why she's in prison now?"

"Not just that, but the *Vault of the Damned?*" Yorn said. "The only other person down there is Nartikis! What could she possibly have done to warrant that? That's in complete opposition to her character."

Jason's face darkened. "Yorn, there are some details about her imprisonment that I've sworn a sacred oath to protect. I wish I could tell you, but I'm forbidden."

"Forbidden?" Yorn's eyebrows bent. "But you're the King."

"Even I as King am bound to ancient oaths," Jason said. "You understand. Duty is woven into every fabric of Nezmythian government, and I'm no different. But this is what I can tell you… Kierli was involved in some dark works that we weren't aware of when we called her to be Chief Captain. And they are very serious."

Yorn fell quiet. His hands clasped together and his elbows rested on his knees. He twirled his thumbs together, processing Jason's words. At length, he said, "Kierli and I worked side by side over the Upper City garrison for the greater part of two years. I can't believe that she was involved in anything that would require that kind of discipline."

"It's the truth, Captain," Jason said. "*Dark works.* We gave her a chance to reconcile and turn away from them, but she refused. There is more I could tell you, but it's to your benefit that these things remain hidden. I expect you to trust me on this."

Yorn frowned. He tried not to be too annoyed that a twenty-five-year-old was hiding things about someone he cared for, even if that twenty-five-year-old was the King. He briefly thought about sharing his experience from yesterday about the writing on the table, but didn't.

"Well, sir," he said, "do I have your permission to visit Kierli on occasion down in the Vault? I consider her a close friend."

Jason shook his head. "No, Yorn. I'm sorry."

Yorn's frown deepened. He swallowed and tried to contain a defeated sigh. "Well… thank you for your time, Your Highness."

"I know this is troubling, Yorn," Jason said. "But please believe this is what's best for Nezmyth. I'm sorry."

Yorn stood, gave another bow, and left the castle grounds. All the while, his gray eyes were hard as his mind sorted out the things King Jason said. He wished more than anything that he could just talk to Kierli once—get her side of the story. But no. He was forbidden from visiting her.

But… the King didn't say anything about writing letters, did he? Surely there couldn't be any harm in that. He would stay away from Kierli, but still get the answers from her side.

And there were too many questions. He had to know.

As soon as Yorn got home, he sat at his desk and scribbled out a quick message. When he was done, he folded the paper into thirds, melted some wax, and stamped it shut.

* * * * *

Kierli sat with her arms wrapped around her legs, staring between the bars with her face pressed in a scowl. She stopped counting the rats that scurried by. Across the way, Nartikis busied himself with his books, ignoring her, not speaking. The books he gave her still lay in a pile of ash outside her bars.

She held out her hand, focusing on her palm. Her fingers flexed and the blood veins thickened down her forearm, but nothing came. The anger inside her was still pent up with nowhere to go, stewing inside her like a sludgy black mess. She ground her teeth together, staring across the room at the fallen King. She hated that he was so comfortable here. Not just with his furnishings and books, but with his calmness. His peace. He was responsible for Jax's death—for thousands of deaths—and there he was, laying on a comfortable bed reading a book.

The Vault door unlatched. Kierli's stomach growled. She scooted to the edge of her cell. In a few moments, a soldier came down carrying two trays of food. They weren't lavish meals, but adequate—a cup of water with half a loaf of bread and two modest pieces of cheese. The soldier set down the trays outside both their cages, and the captors reached through the bars to enjoy their bounties as the soldier climbed up the stairs and left.

However, Kierli's tray included something more. A letter, wedged between the cup and the bread. She scrunched her eyebrows and took it. As she pulled it close, she recognized the seal.

Yorn.

Her heart leapt. She hurriedly broke the seal and unfolded the letter. Just as Nartikis said yesterday, her eyes had adjusted to the dark, and she could read the epistle just fine.

Kierli,

I don't know if I'm supposed to be writing you while you're in the vault, but the soldiers standing guard allowed it. King Jason won't let me visit you, so I wasn't sure what else to do.

Why are you in there? I saw magic words appear on the table in my home. Tell me that was from you and that I'm not insane.

I'm including a blank piece of parchment and the stub of a writing stick. One of the soldiers from my garrison will be by tonight to pick up your reply. So many of us are confused. Prison doesn't seem like you, let alone the vault of the Damned.

-Yorn

"A letter?" Nartikis said with wonder.

Kierli ignored him. She found the parchment and the writing stick, then stretched across the floor and flattened the parchment against the stone, completely forgetting about her dinner. The writing stick scooted across the page.

Yorn,

It's such a relief to find your letter. Yes, I made those words yesterday. You're perfectly sane.

I'm not sure what to think anymore. I've never done anything to deserve this treatment. You know my greatest desire has been to make Nezmyth great and to protect its people. I don't belong here. If there's anything you can do to talk some sense into King Jason, please do it.

She folded the parchment into thirds and set the paper back on the tray, then picked up the bread. Carefully, she tore away pieces and stuffed them in her mouth. She stared at the ground as she did, but her mind was elsewhere. From several yards away, Nartikis gambled another conversation.

"A letter two days into your stay here," Nartikis said. "You must be grateful."

"Didn't I say I'd kill you if you spoke to me?" Kierli hissed.

"What, from all the way over there?" Nartikis jumped from his bed, grabbed the bars, and bore his teeth. "I'm trying to be kind to you! Why is there something wrong with that?"

"Because it's *you*," Kierli spat. "I dirtied my hands with the dust and soot of the Ash *you* cast on my kingdom! My brother is buried outside of Widow's Rest because of them. I don't need your kindness. It's poison to me."

Nartikis scrunched his face and kept silent for a second, then said, "I've seen you try to practice that magic down here. Just give up. The sooner you accept it, the better."

"You're the last person I'll take advice from," Kierli hissed again.

"It's the truth." Nartikis's eyes narrowed and he put his face between the bars. "You know, if you think about it, I probably know you better than anyone else. I've used the magic, just like you have. You've kept it secret, haven't you? Because part of you knows it's dirty. You have to kill so you can use it, so even though you justify it and try to make it something small, you know it's wrong. I started it because my mother died and my father abandoned me. So let me ask you…" his voice died down. "Who was the one that hurt *you?*"

In an instant, Kierli cocked her arm back and launched a gray jeroki through the bars. Nartikis tried to dodge, but three years in a cell made him slow. The ball was small enough to slip through the bars and he took the blow in the shoulder. The force threw him backward. He stumbled and tried to catch himself, but his leg caught on the corner of the bed. The back of his head slammed against the wall, then his body slumped to the ground.

Ice shot through Kierli's veins and her eyes grew. Nartikis wasn't moving. He just lay there in a slumped heap on the opposite side of the Vault. He was too far away—she couldn't tell if he was breathing or not. She stared at her hand. If he was dead, she would feel her magic reserve grow. But it didn't.

The Vault door opened up. Kierli could hear it—the metallic clacking and the old hinges squealing. She let herself down into a sitting position and continued in her meal, acting as if nothing happened.

A soldier reached the bottom. "Captain. Nartikis."

Kierli didn't speak. The soldier strode toward Nartikis' cage then bent down to pick up his tray. When she noticed him slumped against the wall, she bristled. "Wow… what happened to him?"

"Fell and hit his head," Kierli said.

The soldier frowned. "Looks like he's knocked out right well."

Kierli chewed her bread and watched. The soldier drew her sword, then a set of keys by her hip. She unlatched Nartikis' door then cautiously walked in. She put her hand on Nartikis's neck, feeling for a pulse. Kierli was quiet, still chewing. Finally, Nartikis groaned. The soldier let out a tense breath.

"Had a nice little fall, didn't you?" The soldier said a little loudly. "Well at least you're not dead. Captain Barnabas would have a fit. Last thing I need is him upset." The soldier marched out of the cage, latched it shut, then went over to Kierli's cage. She stopped when she saw that she had barely broken her bread. "Need a little while to finish your meal, Captain? I can come back down in an hour if you need."

Kierli stared at Nartikis' body, then the soldier. Her eyes couldn't help but slide to the keys jingling around her hip. It got her thinking. Behind her steely blue eyes, gears turned and notches aligned, formulating a plan. Maybe this place wouldn't be her home for long. She had gotten out of tight spots before. If she managed things just right, this place would be no different.

Then she would be free. Free to tell the people her own story. King Jason wouldn't like that. And that made her smile.

"Thank you," she said. "That would be perfect."

The soldier smiled and walked up the stairs, leaving Kierli and Nartikis alone in the dark.

IO
THE FUGITIVE

The air became chillier at the deepest parts of the prison. Barnabas felt it all the way down, sprouting goosebumps on his arms and making his breath smokey. As he descended the curving path around the edge, he carried a small basket with bread, cheese, apples, and milk. As usual, he ignored the typical curses and sputters of the prisoners.

When he reached the bottom, the soldiers outside the Vault bowed to him and unlatched the door. It groaned and cranked before it swung open, letting out a squeal that reverberated through the chasm. Barnabas thanked them, then ducked his head and trudged through.

The Vault felt clammy and pitiful as always. As soon as he reached the cells, Barnabas pointed his finger and ignited the torch in the center of the room. Nartikis stood from his bed, trudged over to the bars, and put both his arms through.

"Hello, father."

Barnabas set the basket down and embraced him through the bars. "Good morning, Nartikis."

He turned around. Just opposite of Nartikis's cell was Kierli's. She stared daggers as she leaned against the wall in a lump, arms folded. And her gaze filled with even more envy as examined the Chief Captain armor that covered his body.

Barnabas frowned. "You have no reason to be angry. We gave you a second chance."

Kierli spat in his direction and made a rude gesture with her hand.

Barnabas pulled a chair next to Nartikis's cell and Nartikis pulled his own chair next to him on the opposite side. The two of them sat within arm's length of each other, and Barnabas handed Nartikis his share of breakfast through the bars. Nartikis picked apart his bread and ate methodically—a little slower than usual. His eyes were unfocused, too.

"Are you well?" Barnabas said. "You seem like something's bothering you. Is it her?"

"No. I'm fine."

Barnabas furrowed his eyebrows, pondering. He tried not to look at Kierli out of the corner of his eye. She hadn't moved at all since he came down. She just stayed against the wall, arms folded, knees up, glaring.

"Is it time for new books?" Barnabas said, nodding to the desk.

"I don't think so. I've actually found this latest volume fascinating. I've read it three times and I intend to read it more."

"Which is it?"

Nartikis took it from his desk and gave it to Barnabas. Barnabas had to hold the cover right to his face to see it in the dark. It wasn't a long volume—one could probably finish it in an hour. The gold leaf letters glinted faintly in the firelight.

"The Legend of the Formation," Barnabas read aloud.

"Mother never told me such stories growing up," Nartikis said, "so this was very new to me. But it's brilliant. I've never read anything like it."

"This isn't just a storybook," Barnabas said, handing it back to him. "It's history. These beliefs have been abandoned by much of Wevlia, but we still hold them to be true. The Sacred Dragon created us as spirits before we were born into this world. It created the world so we could experience mortality. There was a mighty war where the Guardian of the Night was cast out of the Dragon's presence because it wanted Wevlia for its own. And now, the Guardian of the Night and its followers vex us with afflictions and desires for evil as we wander through mortality."

"That wasn't the part that interested me most though."

"What then?"

"The afterlife. The parts about Paradise and Darkness." Nartikis paused, then said, "I wonder where mother is. And where we'll go."

At this, Barnabas stopped chewing. Memories of his life began flooding before his eyes. The treachery of murdering his best friend and usurping the throne. Then all the suffering and despair he caused for twenty years. Sure, he had led Nezmyth to victory during the Ash War, but that was only three short years ago. That couldn't be enough to atone for all the pain he orchestrated. The thought made him lose his appetite.

"I like to think mother is in Paradise," Nartikis muttered. "She was a good woman, even if she didn't know about the Sacred Dragon and these things. I don't know for sure, but I like to think the Dragon would reward her anyway." Nartikis's tone got dark. "But I worry about you and I. I'm the worst person I know. I've done terrible, terrible things. But I feel like I've grown closer to the Sacred Dragon down here. I'm different than what I once was. Can I possibly reconcile for all the death I caused?" He turned to his father. "Do you think I can be forgiven, or am I too far gone?"

Barnabas didn't answer immediately. He looked at the floor. With a deep breath, he said, "I don't know, my son. The Dragon will be our judge."

Nartikis exhaled weakly. As he nodded his head, a sharp pain suddenly shot through him. He winced and held the back of his scalp.

"What's wrong?" Barnabas said.

"It's nothing."

Barnabas didn't listen. He reached through the bars and gripped his son's head. His eyes popped open. On the backside of his head, he could feel the scabbed blood sticking in Nartikis's hair. When he pulled back and looked at his hand, some of the flecks came off and his fingertips were dyed red.

"What happened?" Barnabas commanded.

"I tripped and fell."

"Here? In your cell?" Barnabas's eyes were narrow.

"Yes. It was an accident."

Nartikis tried not to look at Kierli, but failed. As soon as he stole a glance, Barnabas understood. He thought about turning and reaming his most recent prisoner, but thought against it, no matter how badly he wanted to. He would pass this information on to the King. For the next several minutes, Barnabas and Nartikis ate breakfast together in relative silence, then Barnabas said farewell and stomped up the stairs.

As he did, he threw a look at Kierli. She looked back at him just as sourly as she did minutes ago. No remorse. Just like days ago.

Barnabas instructed the carriage driver to forget his house at Kyleth Pond and take him straight to the castle.

When he arrived, he found Jason and Tarren in the back courtyard. A pullup bar had been erected and King Jason was dangling from it. Meanwhile, Tarren stood a few paces away, watching him with his hands in his pockets.

Jason growled and sweat coated his body as his hands clasped the bar above him. Soldiers patrolling the castle grounds marched a little slower as they passed. Some of them stealthily took bets on how many pull-ups the King could do. Jason's palms were sweaty, which made it harder to hang on.

"How many have I done already?" he grunted.

"One," was Tarren's reply.

Jason breathed two quick breaths in and out, then he clenched his teeth. His muscles tightened. His legs flailed. His body inched upward ever so slightly as he tried to pull his chin above the bar. With a few more quick breaths and loud grunting, Jason's chin barely passed it. Then he let out a narrow gasp and he dropped to the ground. Some soldiers nearby clapped, and Jason tried to push down his embarrassment.

"How did I get so out of shape in a single month?" Jason mumbled.

"Poor diet, too much sleep, heartbreak," Tarren counted on his fingers. "But progress is progress. That's one more than yesterday."

At that moment, they noticed Barnabas approaching. He stopped, stood at attention, and gave a dutiful nod. Jason nodded in return. "Captain, good morning."

"Good morning," Barnabas said dutifully. "I just came from the Vault."

"How's Kierli?" Jason said.

Barnabas tried not to scowl. "Just as vengeful as when we saw her last. She doesn't seem repentant in the slightest."

"I'm not surprised. And what about Nartikis?"

At this, the corner of Barnabas's mouth twitched and he flexed his hands. He exhaled loudly. "Nartikis had been injured. He wouldn't tell me much about it, but he tried not to look at Kierli during our conversation. I suspect she had something to do with it."

"How?" Jason said. "She hasn't been able to leave her cell, right?"

"Not that I can tell."

"Does he need a healer?"

"I recommend it."

Jason thought for a moment. "If they're in the cells directly across from each other, move Kierli. Put them in opposite corners—the soldiers should have done that in the first place. We already know how she feels about him. And feel free to send a healer his way."

"Thank you, sir."

Jason was pensive for another second, then said, "Do you think Nartikis could be a positive influence for her down there? I know he hasn't practiced magic for years."

"Yes sir, he's recovered well. But I'm unsure if he'll have any kind of impact on her. I could feel the tension between those two. It was toxic."

Jason nodded and let that thought stew. "Well, separate them. See to it."

* * * * *

Kierli slouched her back against the wall again, staring between the bars. Across the way, Nartikis sat at his desk, reading a book with the cover flipped open. His face was just inches from the page as he drank in every word. The crispy crinkle of a flipping page sounded every minute or so. Kierli grimaced every time.

Nartikis flipped through several more pages and snapped the book shut. He pushed the chair back and stooped down to one knee, as if he were kneeling to someone. Bowing his head, he began whispering to himself. Kierli could only make out bits and pieces from across the room.

"Sacred Dragon, ... misdoings ... I ... forgive ... truth ... thank you ... unworthy ..."

Kierli tore her eyes away. Nartikis whispered for a few more minutes before laying on his bed and curling up with his back toward her. Kierli thought about the bed that was hers for only one night at the Chief Captain's mansion. She had never felt anything so soft. Now she had trouble picking the straw out of her hair every time she woke up.

The door swung open at the top of the Vault. Nartikis perked up. Kierli's heart began thumping. It was hard to discern the passing of time here, but it still felt too early for their next meal. Why were they coming down then?

Two soldiers came to the bottom. They lit the torch. Kierli blinked hard to adjust to the light. Wow, had her eyes really adjusted to the darkness that well? The soldiers were unlocking Kierli's cage.

"Captain," one of them said. "We've been instructed to take you to one of the other cages. Please follow us."

Kierli's heart thumped faster, but she remained calm. The plan she had been forming in her mind was coming to the surface. But this soon? That wasn't part of the plan. Plans change, though. You have to be precise, but flexible. The pieces in her imagination shifted and came together. It could work. But there wasn't much room for error.

She nodded and pushed herself up, fighting the aching in her knees. The soldiers didn't bind her or restrain her. They just stood by her sides and cautiously marched her down the room.

As Kierli's feet dragged across the stone floor, they stopped in front of the cell farthest from Nartikis. He wouldn't be able to speak to her from here. They would be at opposite corners of the room.

Kierli flexed her hands. Her eyes jumped all over: the keys on the guard's waist, the bars, their weapons, their helms, shoulder plates, breast plates. All her muscles tightened.

"Thank you for your honorable work, both of you," she said.

The soldiers didn't have much time to think of the remark. She was too quick.

Her hand shot out and grabbed the first soldier's head, smashing it against the iron bar. The soldier slumped down, out cold. The second soldier grabbed for the sword by her waist, but Kierli toppled her and wrapped around her body, clamping her neck. The soldier squirmed and struggled until her body went limp.

Nartikis dashed to the bars and pressed his face up to them, trying to see what happened. It was a stretch, but managed to see the unconscious bodies laying outside Kierli's newly-assigned cell. A sliver of dread trickled down his spine. Kierli rummaged through their bodies and managed to procure the cell keys, some money, and a dagger.

She quickly lashed the dagger around her waist and slipped the money into her pocket. The cell keys dangled from her fingers. With them in her hand, she looked over her shoulder at Nartikis. Nartikis shot back from the bars. But even when he couldn't see her, he could hear her footsteps approaching.

With menacing slowness, he reached his cage, took out the keys, inserted one in the lock. It got stuck—wrong one. But she had four more to go. As she went through the ring, trying every key, she spoke to Nartikis in a low tone.

"This should have been done years ago," she droned.

Another wrong key. Nartikis trembled.

"Do you know what it's like to hold a dying person in your arms?" Kierli mumbled. "To watch the life leave their eyes as their blood stains your hands?"

Key number three. Wrong again.

"That's what happened at the Battle of Nezmyth City three years ago. It was my brother. His name was Jax. Not that you care."

Key four. Stuck again. There was only one left. Nartikis was sweating, trying to scream for help, but his dry mouth didn't let him.

"Let me do you a favor," Kierli's tongue slithered. "I'll help you answer your questions about the afterlife."

Key five clicked the lock. The door swung open on squeaky hinges. Nartikis tried to backpedal into the wall, but there was nowhere to go. He swallowed hard, trying to wet his throat enough to let out a cry. But nothing but a wheeze left his lips. Kierli stalked up and flashed the dagger.

A thrust. Nartikis felt the steel pierce his lung, then she twisted the blade as hard as she could. A sickly gasp leapt from his mouth, and immediately his surroundings started to fade.

"It's ironic," Kierli whispered. "You stopped using the magic. But now, killing you is going to give me enough magic to escape."

She yanked the dagger back, letting the steel shimmer with red. Nartikis exhaled, and with it, his body slumped onto his bed, a pool of blood soaking onto the mattress. The life in his icy blues faded, and within seconds, Nartikis, fallen King of Unbuntye, was no more.

And with his death, something big grew inside Kierli. She could feel it. It was inside her, waiting to be let loose.

But first, she had to get out.

The bodies on the other side of the Vault began to stir. Kierli sheathed her dagger and darted out the cell, bounding up the stairs. She skipped steps as she leapt upward, heading for the entrance.

When she reached the door, she knocked casually. After a brief moment, the door rippled, clacked, then swung open. She staggered back as the light crashed into her face. It was blinding —her eyes had adjusted to the Vault too well. But she only recoiled for a second. There was no time to lose.

She held her breath, and as she leapt into the light, she pushed magic through her entire body. Her limbs disappeared as soon as they passed the threshold, completely invisible. The guards at the door squared up and drew their weapons. They *knew* they saw Kierli at the top of the stairs before she jumped out the door and disappeared. And that meant she could be anywhere.

"Did you—"

"Yes, I saw her too!"

"*Show yourself!*" one barked as he turned all around. Then he turned to the other guard. "Go down and check on the others! I'll try to find her!"

Kierli was already running for the path leading to the surface. Dark Magic was pumping through her body again, filling her with sweet tingles. As she looked back at the Vault, she almost laughed. She was free. Even the deepest, most heavily guarded cell in Nezmyth couldn't hold her.

But wait. How long could her powers last? If she was going to make it back to Nezmyth City, she might need more fuel. She turned her attention away from the path—instead, she ran to a cell on the opposite wall. This was the lower level—the worst villains in Nezmyth were down here.

One of the cells had a criminal she recognized: a stringy middle-aged man that had been imprisoned for abusing and murdering young girls for years. Kierli's jaw clenched.

The man had run to the bars after he heard shouting. That made it all the easier for Kierli. Through her invisibility, she pushed more magic into her feet to make them soundless as she ran up on his cell. With his face already pressed against the bars, she unsheathed her dagger and jammed it into his neck.

The man gurgled and collapsed, blood pouring out his slit throat. Kierli felt more of the power course through her. It doubled what she got from Nartikis, and it would definitely be enough for her to get home.

With that, she thought of a location just outside the Southern Market Street. As she closed her eyes and focused, a purple cloud enveloped her body. At the prison, she disappeared. Her body tensed and floated through space for just a moment, then another wall of purple smoke appeared at that place just outside the Southern Market Street, miles and miles away from the prison.

An alleyway. Separated from the noise and commotion of eager shoppers. Kierli looked up. The sky was turning orange —sunset. And at her feet, a cellar door. She looked around, finding herself alone. Then she threw open the door and slipped inside.

As soon as the cellar door was shut, she gasped for breath. She had never attempted transportation and invisibility at the same time, and it took a larger toll on her than she thought it would. She wiped the sweat from her forehead and stumbled down the stairs into the cellar, cradling her dizzied head.

The cellar still had some barrels, a bookcase, and a single chair, but it was clear that this place had been abandoned for months. Cautiously, Kierli wandered around the large room. Some rats scurried about the corners and she shot them all with jerokis, killing them. Lastly, she noticed a bedroll pushed into a corner. Looks like someone had decided to squat here. Perfect. If they attacked her (and they probably would), she could defend herself and get more fuel. Then she would have a roll to sleep in.

In the meantime, she had something else to do. She didn't have much left, but she had enough. On the wall, she lifted her finger and pressed it against the stone. It glowed purple as it formed words in the dark.

YORN, I'M FREE. MEET TOMORROW OUTSIDE OUR SHOP, SUNRISE. BRING FOOD. I HAVE MANY IMPORTANT THINGS TO TELL YOU.

II

THE OMEN

Kara wrapped her arms around Jason and held him gently. "It's so good to see you, my son."

"You too, mother."

"Don't forget me!" Tomm came up and held them both, smiling widely. "I look forward to these weekly dinners."

The table had been set for the four of them in Jason's old Lower City home—a dinner of cooked beef, carrots, green beans, and pudding. The curtains had been pulled back from the window, letting the orange sunset seep through the glass and shine on the table settings. Tomm led Kara to the table and seated her while Jason sat opposite of them.

"A lot of our neighbors have talked about Captain Kierli getting locked up," Tomm said as he began carving into his meat and vegetables. "Have to admit, it was a little surprising to all of us, especially since she was just made Chief Captain the day before."

Jason stabbed a carrot. "Surprising is right. We discovered some things about her that were pretty serious. It was the right thing to do."

"Are you allowed to share?"

"No. Sorry."

Tomm was content with that answer.

"So, Barnabas is reinstated as Chief Captain for now?" Kara said.

"Yes. Back to his old duties until we can find his replacement."

"I must admit he grew on me," Kara said. "When you first released him to fight in the Ash War, I felt as confused as anyone. But you were clearly inspired. He served well."

"I'll tell him you said that."

There was a bit of quiet, then Kara let out a hefty sigh. Her body sagged and she gazed deeply into the eyes of her son. Their browns were nearly identical. She tilted her head.

"Jason, how are you? In here?" She pointed at her heart.

Jason slowly stopped carving his food. As he collected his thoughts, he said, "It happens the most at night. During the day I see little reminders of her everywhere, but it's when I get ready for bed that it's the hardest. I go upstairs… take off my armor… hang it up… and she's not there." His voice died down. "It's really hard sometimes."

Kara reached over the table and took Jason's hand. Her eyes were glistening.

"She's never too far away," she said. "Don't forget that."

Jason smiled and squeezed her hand back.

They ate the rest of their meal with minimal chatter, only occasionally talking about the neighbors, Jason's duties, or things Kara had seen at the market. As the sun began to fall over the horizon and stars dotted the sky, Jason wished them goodnight and started back for the castle. They exchanged hugs and I-love-yous as Jason stepped outside. Two guards were waiting to escort him into his carriage.

The reins snapped and the carriage lurched to a crawl. Jason sat by the window, staring into space as the wheels ground against the cobblestone. The faint sound of horses' trotting was faint in his ears and far from his focus. Meanwhile, he drank in the autumn air. The leaves were turning golden colors. Winter would arrive in just a couple months.

They had barely made it to the Southern Market Street when Jason heard shouting from outside the carriage. Suddenly, it slammed to a stop that nearly threw him to the floor. He staggered to his feet, clutching Nightbane at his side.

Before he could throw open the door, a soldier did. Her eyes were wild, hair matted, and face glistened with sweat.

"Your Highness," she said. "Kierli has escaped and two prisoners are dead. One of them was Nartikis."

* * * * *

Barnabas's jaw clenched and eyes widened when the soldier broke the news. One hand was on the doorknob, the other hand was trembling at his side. He remained in the doorway of his new home, in his night clothes, looking for words but finding none.

"Barnabas," Jason said softly, "I understand what you're—"

"You know what to do," Barnabas fired at the soldier. "Find her. Send hawks to every garrison across Nezmyth. Let them know she's loose. Then search every home, alleyway, and shop in Nezmyth City. Every corner of every room. Gather our local magicians to see if there is anything they can do to help find her." He paused. "Where is Nartikis's body?"

"They're still moving it from the prison, sir. We're bringing it to you… you were his only family, after all."

This made Barnabas's lips push together. But he managed to say, "Go."

The soldier mounted a horse and rode into the night. Jason's carriage and two guards were behind him, but he wasn't thinking about them at all. Instead, he was still focused on Barnabas, who was standing numbly in the door frame.

"Barnabas," he said, "I can stay with you until the body arrives. Is that okay?"

Barnabas was numb, still processing, his eyes glassy and vacant. He did manage to come to himself just enough to nod and step aside.

A fire crackled in the fireplace, radiating the home with warmth. Barnabas led Jason to a table in the middle of the cabin, then kept walking to a stove. His tone was distant when he spoke. "Would you like some tea, Your Highness?"

"I'm alright, thank you."

Barnabas left the stove and sat across from Jason. Both of them rested their elbows on the table. Jason felt his heart ache for Barnabas, looking for the right words to say. But he knew all too well there's nothing you can say in a moment like this. Meanwhile, Barnabas's face was paler than usual and his thoughts were clearly far away from here.

Finally, after needing to say *something*, Jason said. "I know exactly what you're feeling."

"I know."

Silence. Jason didn't want to speak if Barnabas didn't feel like talking. But then Barnabas said, "The last time someone I loved died, I was the murderer. This is different."

His lips trembled, then he pushed himself up and marched over to the stove. Dishes clinked as if he were preparing tea, but Jason suspected Barnabas was just making himself busy so Jason couldn't see his face. He knew he and Nartikis had breakfast together just this morning. Barnabas was probably thinking about what he could have said if he knew that would be the last time he saw him. Things he could have done to ensure his safety.

And that made him think of Kierli. Escaped the Vault of the Damned—no one had ever done that before according to his memory.

"We'll find her, Barnabas," Jason said. "Then I'll punish her to the full extent of her crimes. Count on it."

Barnabas nodded and tried to withhold a sniffle, but Jason heard it. He coughed and rubbed his face, then went back to the table. Those icy blue eyes were getting puffy and swollen.

"If I wouldn't have called her to Chief Captain," Barnabas muttered. "This wouldn't have happened tonight."

"Barnabas, don't," Jason said forcefully. "You made the sensible decision. She was recommended by every other Captain in Nezmyth. You made the natural choice."

Barnabas wanted to argue, but knew that Jason would try to beat down any assertion he made. In his mind, he knew what he did, and nothing Jason said could change it.

A knock came. Barnabas squared his shoulders and made for the door. Jason stood and followed him. When they opened, they were greeted by another soldier looking grim and nervous.

"I, uh… heard you were expecting us."

The soldier stepped aside. Behind him, a cart was pulled by two horses. In the cart, he was there, wrapped in cloth from head to toe and tied together with rope.

Barnabas swallowed. He forced his feet forward. Jason didn't follow. When he reached the cart, he reached inside and lifted a flap on the wrapping. Jason couldn't see what he uncovered, but he knew. When Barnabas lifted the flap and saw his face, it nearly took him to the edge. It took every ounce of his discipline not to crumble. He forced himself to be collected and thanked the soldiers for delivering the body.

"What should we do with him, Captain?"

Just to the side of his house, a tall oak tree was splashed with orange and red leaves. Barnabas looked at it. "Come with me."

For the better part of an hour, Jason and the soldiers helped Barnabas dig a long hole under the tree. The soldiers brought shovels and Barnabas had one in his cabin. Jason tried to improvise some magic to help move the earth. Occasionally, he would catch Barnabas sniffling or pressing his lips together as he shoved his spade harder into the dirt. When the hole was done, they used some rope to lower Nartikis's body into the grave, then they covered it with the overturned earth.

They all stepped back from the mound. The silence danced with the night air nipping that at their arms and necks. Jason turned to Barnabas. "Would you like me to offer some words, Captain?"

"No, I will." Barnabas moved forward and knelt next to the mound. He held out his hand, resting it on the mound's crest. "Nartikis, I pray that your soul finds rest in the Third Life. I pray that you find peace in the bosom of the Sacred Dragon. It was a brief time… but I'm grateful for the chance I had to finally be your father."

That broke him. With a cough and a sputter, Barnabas wept. He buried his face into his hand as the tears fought their way out. Jason met him where he was, kneeling down and wrapping his arm around his shoulders. The soldiers stood in the background, their faces down.

* * * * *

In his study, Master Ferribolt sat in an armchair by the fire. A mound of scrolls gathered at the side of his chair, stacked in a neat pyramid.

He had a hard time sleeping. Soldiers had just arrived at his doorstep hours ago to inform him that Kierli had escaped. He thanked them then went into his study to pray for the safety of the kingdom, and for the well-being of her soul.

A cup of tea sat on a nightstand by his chair. Steam still wafted from its surface as Master Ferribolt blindly gripped the handle and pressed it to his lips. His eyes never left the page.

Exasperated, he set down the tea and looked to the ceiling. "Sacred Dragon… I'm concerned for our kingdom. I fear dark things are coming. How can we prepare? What is to be done?"

Nothing. No feelings in his heart or mind. His body deflated. The Ancient Nezmythian on the scroll before him was dimly visible in the firelight, but nonetheless, Master Ferribolt's eyes traveled down the page.

Then he caught something. And another thing. Fragments. They triggered a stirring inside him—something that told him that these were significant now, even though he had read those words before. They didn't seem to be directly connected with Jason's dream or Kierli, but nonetheless, something about them made him sharpen and tense.

"*The tall sunflower shall make the moons bright,*" Master Ferribolt translated aloud. "*The great tree shall rend asunder as the stars reach up from the ground. Bones and wings of old shall vex the tormentor. If the last stone remains, all that lives shall depart and be free.*"

Master Ferribolt stared at the words, reading them over and over again.

12

THE HUNTED

Yorn anxiously tapped his fingers on a table outside Sue's restaurant. There were three tables just like it outside this Northern Market Street establishment—each of them wide enough to seat two people. As he sat, he looked around and waited. So far, the tables were vacant except for the one farthest from him. A woman with dark hair sat there.

There was a modest sack of food by his feet, filled with apples, carrots, guabos, bread, and some dried meat. He even bought a few sweets that he put in the bottom as a surprise. Not knowing how much food she might need, he stuffed the sack to the brim.

He adjusted in his chair and folded his arms. Letters had reappeared on his desk late last night—he saw them glowing across the room as he laid in bed. Kierli had escaped. By this morning, he got the official order from the King: find her immediately. She had killed two people, including Nartikis. Yorn spent the morning making a plan for his unit to search every house in Upper City, every Market Street, and every building in between. It could potentially take weeks.

Silently, he wondered why Kierli would want to meet him in broad daylight like this. She knows everyone would be looking for her, including him. Yorn himself was obligated to take her into custody if found. But first, he wanted answers.

He cleared his throat and set his hands on his lap. Unwittingly, he caught the eyes of the dark-haired woman sitting at the far table. He pressed his lips into a polite smile. The woman smiled back, then stood and sauntered over to him. She was tall, with a strong shapely figure. Strangely, the clothes she wore were very plain—trousers, boots, and a white cotton top. Definitely unusual for a woman on the Northern Market Street.

"Waiting for someone?" She asked.

"I am."

"Why do you seem so nervous? Is it a woman you fancy?"

Yorn half-smiled. "We've known each other a while."

"I see. Well, perhaps you can make due with me for now." She leaned forward. "You seem good at following instructions."

That's when Yorn noticed the eyes. Steely blue—unmistakably steely blue. He had seen them a thousand times. His jaw unhinged and his face went pink.

"*Kierli?*" he breathed.

She winked. When Yorn saw her last, her hair was long and blonde. Now, it was short and black. Her face was different, too—somehow structured differently, but still attractive. And no scar. She took the sack of food by his feet, pulled it onto her lap, and began rummaging through the contents. She held up the various fruits to inspect them, looking for bruises or blemishes.

"Call me Evelyn," she said without looking at him. "You never saw Kierli. She's still on the run as far as you know."

"Kie—Evelyn, what's going on? How did you change your appearance?"

Evelyn sneered. "You know Kierli is a powerful magician. If she could change her appearance, it would be temporary, which means she wouldn't have long to talk."

"I understand. I have lots of questions."

"That's why we're here, isn't it?"

"What's going on? And why the *Vault of the Damned?* Nartikis is down there! Or at least he was."

"He should have been in a grave instead. Kierli did the right thing."

"I'm sure Barnabas took it hard."

Evelyn rolled her eyes. "That's his own fault. He shouldn't have gotten emotionally attached. Nartikis was a killer, even if he was kin."

Silently, Yorn thought it ironic that she would call Nartikis a killer after what she had just done. But he wasn't about to point it out.

"So, what did King Jason tell you about Kierli?" Evelyn cinched the sack up and put it at her feet.

"Good morning! What can I get you two?"

It was a waitress from the restaurant. Her sweet young face was completely oblivious, like she hadn't heard a single word of the conversation. Yorn's words got caught, so Evelyn took over. Smiling brightly, she said. "Two cups of booshum berry juice, please? It's our anniversary."

She reached out and held Yorn's hand. Inside his chest, his heart thumped harder. The waitress beamed. "Of course! Congratulations! These rounds are on the house."

"Why, thank you so much!"

The waitress scurried away. Evelyn pulled her hand away, and out of sight, she rubbed it on her trousers. Yorn cleared his throat.

"He didn't say much," he said. "Just that y—she was involved in dark things that he was under oath not to discuss."

Evelyn scoffed and shook her head. "Under oath… he's *King*. There's no oath."

She stayed quiet, staring into the distance. Dozens and dozens of Nezmyth City's upper class walked around the Northern Market Street. Their footsteps clacked and clopped against the cobblestone as they carried bags of fruit and fine garments. Yorn looked out of the corner of his eyes. Kierli seemed so relaxed—fully confident in her disguise. No one seemed to notice or care about either of them.

"It boils down to two things," Evelyn held up fingers as she counted. "One, when he realized how powerful a magician Kierli is without Ancient Nezmythian, he saw it as a threat. And two, he found out Kierli saw things he didn't want people to know."

"Like what?"

"Like all the money he kept after Barnabas's rule."

Yorn's eyebrows bent and he leaned forward, unsure if he had heard correctly. At that moment, the waitress brought their drinks out and set them down. When she noticed the intense look on Yorn's face, she opened her mouth and closed it, then retreated into the restaurant. Yorn didn't speak until she was gone.

"You're joking," he breathed. "After people in the slums have struggled for so long? How did you find out?"

Evelyn took a long drink from her juice, then wiped her lips. "Kierli went over to visit him the morning after her Succession Ceremony. He was taking a long time to get out of bed, so she went exploring the castle. It was in a secluded room deep underground—boxes upon boxes of Bars and Blocks. When King Jason finally got out of bed and she confronted him about it, he denied everything—said she was talking nonsense. But Kierli knows what she saw. He was already intimidated by her magic, but when she found out his secret, that's when she became too much of a problem." She shrugged and took another long drink.

"I don't understand," Yorn muttered and shook his head. "If he has all that money, why does he tithe farmers, butchers, and seamstresses for their needs at the castle? If he were so greedy, couldn't he just tax people like other kings have done before? King Jason grew up poor, too, so he knows what it's like—"

"Yorn," Evelyn interjected. "I'm telling you what I saw. King Jason is a liar. Do you believe me, or not?"

Yorn never had any reason to distrust Kierli in the years that he knew her. And Jason locking her up so suddenly was incredibly suspicious. Faintly, he nodded. "I trust you."

"As you should. Now, I need your help." Evelyn leaned in. "Where did you have the soldiers take Kierli's things? She had just taken them to the mansion in Upper City when she got summoned and thrown in prison. Where are they know?"

"They're at the barrack. There wasn't much to bring back, and the King has us busy looking for y—her. So we haven't had time to go through the belongings and determine what to do with them."

"Perfect. Tell the soldiers you'll inspect them yourself and leave them in your room. I'll take care of them."

Yorn frowned. "You don't have a key to the barrack anymore."

"Doesn't matter. I'll manage."

She scooped up the bag of food and threw it over her shoulder. Then she stood and looked down on Yorn. His eyes didn't leave the surface of his booshum berry juice as he processed everything she had said. She smiled like a big sister watching her little brother, then lifted her own drink and drained it.

"Kierli is innocent, Yorn. You'll see. King Jason will come to his senses. Then you won't have to wrestle with your conscience about this." She smiled. "I'll see you again soon."

She put her empty cup on the table before she turned on her heels and marched away, swaying her hips as she went. Yorn folded his arms again. He didn't even take a sip of his juice. He reached into his pocket, dumped some change on the table, and left.

* * * * *

"Breathe in."

Jason breathed in.

"Breathe out."

Jason breathed out.

Alis sat across from him, cross-legged, her hands on her knees in the middle of the sparring area. A sweet smile stretched across her face, seemingly content and comfortable. Conversely, Jason struggled to relax as he sat across from her, mimicking her position. His mind was too much on Kierli's escape. He had just helped bury Nartikis last night, and he couldn't help but wonder if she had it in her to murder again.

"Trouble concentrating?" Alis said.

"That's putting it lightly," Jason grumbled. "It's difficult to concentrate on anything when a disgraced Chief Captain has escaped prison."

"You've sent the order to track her down?"

"Yes. Every village and city should have received a hawk this morning."

"So you're doing all you can?"

"Of course."

"And there is nothing else you can do?"

Jason tried not to feel annoyed. "No."

"Then, for now, there is only you and me and your breathing," Alis said. "Breath in and out again, Your Highness."

Jason closed his eyes and tried to lock everything out. But the image of her scowling face in the great hall kept coming back. Vault of the Damned. Escape. Murder. Searching. Nothing. Finally, after another huff, he slouched and opened his eyes.

"Alis, I'm sorry," he said. "We need to continue this another time. I just don't know if I'll be able to concentrate until we've found Kierli. I want to give your lessons my full attention, and right now, I can't."

Jason got up and dusted off his pants, but Alis didn't budge. She looked up at him, studying. Before Jason could get too far, she said, "The situation of her imprisonment is very curious, I must admit. I heard people in the market discussing it this morning."

Jason stopped. "I know. And I knew people would talk about it. But believe me, it was for the best. We saw her true colors that day."

"I believe you, Your Highness," Alis said. "I have the utmost trust in your judgment as our Foreordained King. You made some perplexing decisions in the past, but it has always been for the best of the kingdom. Like freeing Captain Barnabas. That was a very brave move that looked absurd. But you did it nonetheless. And I admire that."

With a shrug, Jason muttered, "Thank you."

"From what you have told me, you *are* doing all that you can to find her. There is much out of your control at this moment, so let the Sacred Dragon handle that. You've seen the results of that in the past, haven't you? You have no reason to doubt things now."

Jason put his hands on his hips. "You're right."

"Now, do you remember what we discussed yesterday?"

"About my grief being an opportunity to rediscover myself?"

"Yes. I asked you to think about things you love doing— things that give you peace. Did you do that?"

"No," Jason scoffed. "I used to play the flyra, but that was when Saryan was alive. She asked me to play her songs to help her sleep, so playing it now feels... incomplete. Besides, I think it's fair to say I've been a little distracted."

"That's alright," Alis said. "So I'm renewing the assignment for you. Think about the things that make you truly happy. Bring you peace. Alright?"

Jason nodded.

Alis smiled. Then her eyes shot open as if a light turned on behind them. "Oh! I just had a thought! When was the last time you read your Blessing of Fate?"

My Blessing of Fate? Jason couldn't even remember where he put it. "Oh my… it's been years."

"I think you should revisit it. Remember, a Blessing of Fate isn't just to determine if you've been Foreordained to something. It's also a chance for the Sacred Dragon to give you direct instruction. Please find it and read it before we visit again. Okay?"

Jason nodded again. "Yes, teacher."

"Good," Alis said. "Now come sit back down, please. Thank you. Breathe in… breathe out…"

* * * * *

Stars came out as a sheet of black spread over the sky. Along the Southern Market Street, candlelight flickered in windows, but for the most part, everything was still. Shops were dark and doors were locked. Aside from the plodding footsteps of patrolling soldiers, only the taverns and inns made any sound. And those muffled sounds were usually raucous singing, clinking of dishes, and overblown laughter.

Tarren took his carriage down to the area but had it parked a short walk away from his favorite tavern. He also opted not to wear his Advisor armor, but donned average street clothes like he did before his ordination. Not that it would do much to make him less conspicuous.

The name of the place was the Wilted Rose—a tavern directly in the center of the Southern Market Street. It wasn't far from The Cranny, the music shop that he used to run.

When the Harvest Tax ended and he had more money to spend, he began frequenting the Wilted Rose for a pint of something sweet on a regular basis. The barkeep even grew to know him by name.

The tavern was marked by a dangling wooden sign reflecting its name. Glowing lanterns dangled on the exterior of the building. Tarren almost made it to the door when a man and woman drunkenly stumbled out, clinging onto each other. They giggled and mumbled sweet nothings as they staggered down the street.

Tarren watched them for a while, his heart heavy with envy, wondering what it must be like. Then he thought of Kierli and her compliments on his physique. Her eyes. Her body. Then he tried to cast out those thoughts. She was a fugitive now. He shook his head and pushed open the door.

Muffled sound turned into a dull roar as he crossed the threshold. The bitter scents of alcohol and body odor battled with incense burning on a mantle. All around him, the people of Nezmyth City happily shared drinks and swapped stories as they gathered around tables and crowded the bar. Tarren tried to slip in quietly, but as people recognized him, it became impossible to remain covert.

"Aye, the Advisor! All hail!" "*Hail!*" "First round's on me, friend!"

Tarren sheepishly waved and pushed his way through the crowd. As he went, he surveyed the tavern for pretty girls, but most of the girls were already accompanied, and the ones that weren't accompanied were hardly pretty at all. When he reached the bar, one person volunteered to give up their seat to him, which Tarren declined. He finally found an empty seat near the end, a few spots away from anyone else. As he sat in his chair, he let out a heavy sigh.

The barkeep made his way over to him—a short man with a thick mustache and porky, hairy arms. His cheeks were rosy as he smiled. "Evening, Master Tarren. The usual?"

"Yes, Gus, thank you."

Gus pulled a stein from under the bar and a bottle of something murky yellow. He drained nearly half of it into the stein before setting it down in front of Tarren. Tarren kept his back to the rest of the room as he took his first sip.

"You must be pretty popular around here."

Tarren turned and his eyes popped. The speaker was a delightfully beautiful brunette sitting not far from him. In his head, he wondered how he possibly missed her during his walk in. Her smile was sugary as she looked him up and down. Tarren didn't mind at all.

"I used to live in this area," Tarren said. "I actually used to run a shop not far from here."

"Oh? Where do you live now?"

Tarren took a sip from his drink. "Upper City."

The woman's eyes flashed. "You must have been very successful! Clearly a man of dedication and vision."

Tarren remembered the nights of studying with Nadiel. The Ash War. The Purge Ordinance. The smile slowly slid from his face and he took another drink. "Sometimes it's vision, sometimes it's fate."

The woman's eyes narrowed. "What are you drinking?"

Smirking, Tarren held the stein out to her. She took it and held it beneath her nose. Then, her face brightened. "It's just guabo juice!"

Tarren took it back and had another sip. "I don't drink wine or mead. I already make poor enough decisions as it is. I don't need alcohol to help me with that."

The woman laughed. "I'm the same way. What is your name?"

"I'm surprised you don't know," he held out his hand. "Tarren. And yours?"

The woman took his hand and shook it. "Evelyn. It's a pleasure."

13
THE BLESSING

Jason chewed on the end of a writing stick as he stared at the parchment in front of him. At the top, he had written "Things that make me happy." So far, he had written "Saryan." The rest of the parchment was empty.

A lantern glowed at the edge of the desk, trickling feeble warmth on his arms and face, but the rest of his body remained cold. A faint drizzle of rain pattered the windows. Maybe Kierli was caught in it somewhere. Who knows? There was still no sign of her.

After a bit more gnawing on the writing stick, Jason put the tip on the parchment, withdrew it, then put it back again. With a few more scribbles, he wrote, "Serving Nezmyth."

He dropped the writing stick and rubbed his eyes. Then he folded his arms and set his head down, looking out the rain-streaked windows. How long had he been sitting here, racking his brains? Too long. This wasn't his only assignment, either. He still had to find his Blessing of Fate. Knowing he needed to cool his tired mind, he pushed out his chair and went for the dresser.

Jason was embarrassed to realize his Blessing of Fate was so difficult to find. He rummaged through drawer after drawer before he found it tucked away behind some musty old street clothes. It was still rolled up and tied together with that same orange ribbon, but it was slightly bent and creased along the edges.

Carefully, he peeled off the ribbon and unraveled the Blessing. The smell of the parchment and ink brought up a burst of unpleasant memories—mostly angry teenage years. The weight on his shoulders. The fear. Most of that was gone… most of it.

The Blessing was just one page of hastily-written text. The last paragraph was the one burned into his brain since he was twelve, but the Blessing had a lot more written before it. Maybe he ignored much of it because the last paragraph drew so much weight.

Jason's eyes panned from side to side with every line. There was more content than he initially remembered, but as he read, the memories of his twelfth birthday came flooding back in detail. Going to the Cathedral with Kara and Tomm. Patriarch Willows putting his fingers in a triangle above his head. The wonder and horror that ran across their faces when they heard he was Foreordained to be King.

But what of the Dragon's instructions before then?

Jason, son of Tomm, the printer.

You have been born into a family of modest means. The Dragon does this for your benefit. It is not meet that a special soul like yours should know the taste of luxury. Privilege could impede your judgment and impair your ability to relate to the common man. This will be of great worth to you.

Your greatest strength lies not in your body nor your intelligence, but in your heart. The Sacred Dragon has blessed you with a sound conscience. Follow it and heed its council. The decisions you make when you are at peace are those that are the best for you and for those that follow you.

Struggle and pain are the refinery of life. Know that all trials ebb and flow like the waves of the ocean. You will have times of great prosperity, and times of great sadness. When the times of adversity come, rely upon the Sacred Dragon for comfort and direction, and you will come off conqueror. This is one of the great truths of your life.

One day you will find a woman that will love you and you will love her. She will be yours, Melded for eternity, along with beautiful children, if you live up to your responsibilities. But this blessing is only assured based on your dedication and loyalty. Do not falter. Do not fail.

You will be a magnificent light that shines upon the world of Wevlia. You will imprison the vulture. You will restore the Kingdom of Nezmyth to harmony and peace. Your blood is the blood of the next King of Nezmyth.

Jason's hands shook and his jaw tightened. Some of the promises came true—like being Melded to Saryan for eternity. But being blessed with beautiful children? *Twice* Saryan became pregnant, and both of those times, children never came. Had he not lived up to the responsibilities? Had he not followed the Dragon's promptings and done as he had been commanded? Why was he alone?

Jason threw the Blessing aside and buried his face in his hands, trying to gulp down the lump in his throat.

What did I do wrong?

He sat still, thinking quietly until he couldn't take it any longer. He tied up his Blessing, grabbed some street clothes, quickly changed, and the carriage was prepared. It crawled through Upper City until it arrived at Master Ferribolt's mansion. The gatekeeper was almost getting used to midnight visits from the King. He obediently opened the gates and Jason didn't stop until he was knocking at the door.

Jerem answered within seconds. "Good evening, Your Highness."

"Is Master Ferribolt awake?"

"As a matter of fact, he is. Come in."

Jerem took his coat and Jason went right to the study. He found Master Ferribolt sitting at his desk scribbling intently on a long piece of parchment. Master Ferribolt never looked up as Jason crossed the floor and sat across his desk. The two sat in silence for a long moment as Master Ferribolt continued pushing the writing stick along the paper.

"Please do not think I'm ignoring you, My Liege," he said. "I'm just finishing up a few things."

"That's alright." Jason tilted his head to read it. "'For My Friends.' You're not writing your will, are you?"

"Please, as if I would leave one Shard of anything I own to the likes of you," he looked up and winked. "Besides, you know I haven't much in terms of material possessions—this home and all things in it will be passed to the next Chief Patriarch. But I am growing old, Your Highness, so it may come sooner rather than later. No, this is just the last message to my loved ones when the time comes." He set down the writing stick and looked up. "What's wrong this time?"

"I'm confused."

"About?"

Jason pulled out his Blessing of Fate and handed it to Master Ferribolt. "This. You remember my Blessing of Fate?"

"How could I forget?" Master Ferribolt undid the string and unraveled it.

"It says that I'll be Melded to a wonderful woman and have children if I lived up to my responsibilities," Jason said. He tried to keep his voice from shaking. "Master, my wife is dead and I have no children. What did I do wrong?"

Master Ferribolt's eyes were darting across the page, but when Jason asked that question, he stopped. Everything inside him lurched, like Jason's pain was transferred to him. He wanted to help. He wanted to soothe it. He got up from his desk, came around the side, and knelt by the King. His thick, wrinkled hands held Jason's. Meanwhile, Jason tried to compose himself.

"My King," Master Ferribolt said with passion. "You have done *nothing* wrong and you have lived up to your responsibilities admirably. I've watched you struggle and fight for the good of Nezmyth year after year. Nothing is more honorable than that."

"Then why am I alone, Master?" Jason sniffed.

"I don't know. But I do know that often the Sacred Dragon fulfills Its promises in ways we don't expect." He thought for a moment. "What of your kingdom? Do you not hold stewardship over your people like a father to his children?"

Jason wiped his eyes. "It's not the same."

Master Ferribolt sighed. "I know... but if it lifts your spirit any, I understand exactly how you feel. Rosie and I tried for years to have children. When we finally knew it wouldn't happen, I felt sad and angry at the Sacred Dragon. It took me a long while to let it go."

"Sometimes I feel bitter, too," Jason said with a cough. "Sometimes I get angry that It took my wife away so early. Then I feel guilty that I blame the Dragon for something that just *happened*. But I wish so badly that I could have been a father. When will these feelings go away, Master?"

Master Ferribolt shrugged and shook his head. "They don't. You just learn to live with them. It takes time, too. That's the worst part. But I want to be clear on one thing, Your Highness: the Sacred Dragon fulfills Its promises. Always. We don't know how or when, but It always does. So you'll get to be a father somehow, someway."

Jason let out a shaky breath. "That would be nice."

* * * * *

It took a while for Kierli to shake him. Thankfully, he was pleasant enough with conversation. They had sat and talked at that tavern for the better part of two hours before Kierli insisted she should go home. He offered to walk her, but she politely declined. Hopefully that wasn't too suspicious.

She moved through the alleyways, hugging the shadows as she made her way to the cellar. As luck would have it, she passed a stray dog foraging for scraps in the cobblestone. It turned and growled at her as she got close. She didn't have to think about it—she slipped the dagger from her side and hurled it at the animal, lodging in its neck. The dog whimpered and fell over, and as Kierli passed by, she extracted the dagger and flicked the blood off.

She felt her inner reservoir fill a little. Using the magic for her disguise already created a small blanket of pleasure through her whole body, but with the dog's death, she pushed a little more to ease her nerves. She turned a corner and spotted the cellar door. She almost started for it, but that's when two soldiers walked through an intersecting alley. She stopped dead and ducked behind a wall.

One of the soldiers noticed the movement. "Did you see that?"

"No. What was it?"

"I don't know. But it was coming from over there. Come on."

Footsteps grew louder. Kierli held her breath. As the soldiers came to the corner where she stood, she held her breath and pushed more magic through her body. She vanished. The soldiers were upon her, standing in the intersecting alleys, only a few feet away. Kierli pressed against the wall, invisible, keeping perfectly still.

One soldier frowned. "I swear I saw something."

"Did it look like her?"

"It could have been. I'm not sure."

The other soldier meandered around the intersection, looking around. "I heard she can turn invisible."

"What? Is that even possible?"

"I don't know. One of the women in my last regiment transferred to the prison—she was one of the soldiers guarding the Vault when she escaped."

"You're kidding. What happened to her?"

"She escaped."

"Not Kierli, you idiot! Your friend!"

Kierli remained a transparent statue, watching and listening.

"She was transferred to another garrison," the second soldier shrugged. "Doesn't look good when you can't guard someone stuck in the darkest cell in the kingdom."

"It *is* Kierli, though," the first soldier muttered. "She's incredible—especially her magic. I've seen her spar. She had four soldiers on her. *Four.* And that's normal for her. No wonder she became Chief Captain."

"Maybe," the second soldier said. He sniffed, then a smirk spread across his face. "She's beautiful, too, even with that scar." He turned to the first soldier. "You know what I would do if I were left to guard her?"

Something flared inside Kierli—a rage buried deep down, but granted a small hole to burst forth. The soldiers had no time to react. She dropped her invisibility, planted her feet, and launched a jeroki at the first soldier. The soldier took it in the face, unconscious, and toppled to the ground. The second soldier gasped and tried to flip about, but Kierli was too quick. She was on him with her hand over his mouth and her dagger at his throat.

Kierli put her lips right next to his ear. "Tell me. What *would* you do?"

The soldier let out a stifled whimper. Kierli's grip got tighter on his mouth.

She pressed her lips closer to his ear. "Want to know what *I* would do to *you*?"

A pull. A flash of steel and a spill of red. The soldier's body fell to the ground, limp. Kierli flicked the blood off and belted through the alleyway. When she reached the cellar doors and closed them behind her, she didn't reflect on the events of the evening. She didn't rejoice that she had put more power into her body. Instead, she went straight to her bed roll and wrapped herself tightly, trying not to think of the soldier's words. She ground her teeth and her eyes stung. Then she heard a voice.

"My child…"

Kierli sat up. There was no one in the cellar but her. But she heard something—a creeping whisper in her ear that made her stir. And with that voice, something flashed across her eyes. A dark vision of a place familiar—the Vault of the Damned. The last place she wanted to go.

But somehow… it was pulling her there.

She blinked. Just as quickly as the whisper came, it disappeared. She was left alone in the cellar with nothing but the darkness for company. She pulled the bedroll tightly again and tried to sleep.

* * * * *

The sun was bright and warm as it hit Jason's face, but it still made him think of the impending winter. Autumn was a beautiful time of year, but its beauty always surrendered to a biting chill. He didn't look forward to trudging around in the snow, and he knew he irritated the soldiers around the castle with all the firewood he demanded during those months. He couldn't stand cold feet on a stone floor.

Alis clasped her hands behind her back and walked in circles around him. The King was on his back in the middle of the sparring arena, his hands laced over his chest and his legs stretched out.

"You're not keeping your mind blank," she admonished.

Jason frowned, opened his eyes, and looked at her. "How can you tell I'm—"

"Eyes closed!"

Jason snapped them shut.

"Good. So you completed the assignment I gave you yesterday?"

"I did. I could only think of two things that make me happy: Saryan, and serving Nezmyth."

"That's a start. We'll work on building that list a bit more. I think you need more granular ideas on how you could spend your time in a meaningful, uplifting way. And what about your Blessing of Fate?"

Jason didn't answer immediately. "That one was a little more difficult. The Blessing mentioned promises that the Sacred Dragon hasn't fulfilled yet—things about me being a father. I went over to Master Ferribolt's house late last night to talk about it."

Alis nodded thoughtfully and let silence hang. "I'm sure that must be difficult for you. But you and I know the Sacred Dragon never breaks Its promises. That must mean you'll have some opportunity to be a father someday."

"That's what Master Ferribolt said."

"Then you know it's true. Sit up."

Jason sat up, still keeping his eyes closed, crossed his legs, and put his hands on his knees. Alis made her way around him and sat across from him, mirroring his pose. She took a deep breath and let the air seep out her nose. Jason opened one eye to look at her, waiting for her to speak. But then he closed his eye again, fearing her reproof.

"I find it profound that you listed serving Nezmyth as a thing that makes you happy," Alis said. "But there might be more immediate opportunities for you to serve others on a more personal level." She opened her eyes. "That is my next assignment for you. Every day, look for three opportunities to serve others in a meaningful way. And as you do it, explore yourself. Look for other activities that make you feel fulfilled. Will you do that?"

Jason nodded.

"Good. Now, I want to ask you another question."

Jason opened one eye, waiting.

Alis said, "When was the last time you felt genuine peace?"

Jason's mind went blank. Peace? He was born into a kingdom ruled by a tyrant. When he was twelve, he learned that he was Foreordained to lead that kingdom. When he was seventeen, he was tested for the throne and nearly died. Since then, it's been the well-being of a kingdom resting squarely on his shoulders, including a war.

Peace?

Jason blinked. "I don't think I've ever felt real peace. There's always something."

"Something what?"

"Something blocking it."

"There's never anything blocking peace."

Jason frowned. He opened his eyes and stared intensely at Alis. Still, her face was just as soft as ever—almost expectant. Through his scowl, Jason said, "Of course things block peace. Suffering. Pain. Death. Haven't you experienced that?"

Alis's eyebrows furrowed. "I'm from Pinegrove, Your Majesty."

Jason's heart sank. During the Ash War, that village was decimated. Half of the town was slain while the other half fled for their lives. Jason remembered the battle—he was there. The flood of Ash that spilled into town from the south, the massacre that ensued. The air filled with soot, the smell of death, and the clashing of steel. It was awful.

Jason's gaze fell. "I'm sorry. Forgive me."

"Forgiven," Alis said. "But please don't assume I am the way I am because I've never known suffering. It's quite the opposite." She paused. "Your Highness, would you like to know the keys to obtaining peace?"

"Of course."

"Acceptance and gratitude."

Jason didn't respond. Alis almost smiled.

"I lost a lot of loved ones in the Battle of Pinegrove," she mumbled. "Many of my friends fought against the Ash on the south side of town. I used to think that focusing on healing magic instead of combat magic was morally superior but… that night changed my mind. To watch your people slaughtered like animals and feeling so helpless to stop it all…" She took a breath. "I've come to terms with what happened. I know I did my best to help in that moment. But to recompense, I've learned volumes of combat magic so the next time someone threatens people I love, I can be ready." She smiled.

Jason listened quietly, then he half-smiled. "You're an exceptional woman, Alis."

"I know," she smirked. "Try to add that acceptance and gratitude in your life, Your Highness. There is always something to be grateful for."

14
THE CAMPAIGN

Kierli emerged from the cellar before sunrise. Sleep came in scraps after she killed that soldier last night. It wasn't the guilt that haunted her—hardly. It was the memories that his words brought back. She tried for hours to push them down as she curled in her bedroll, but relived them every time she closed her eyes.

When she fully awoke, she rummaged through the abandoned cellar for any traces of metal. To her delight, she found several: the bindings of some old barrels, a rusty dagger, and an iron club by the door. She put all of them in a pile and held her hands over them, focusing. She felt the metallic fibers twist and warp, reshaping, recoloring. With a bit of strain, they glowed purple and deteriorated. In their place was an eye-popping pile of Pieces, Bars, and Blocks—almost identical to real ones. She scooped them into a sack. It nearly reached the brim. After some brief debate, he took a handful and stuffed it into her pockets.

Taking account of her internal reservoir, she surmised that she'd have just enough power for the day, but she'd have to be conservative. No transforming into Evelyn. She had to be stealthy—not that stealth was a problem. After her breakfast with Yorn yesterday, she managed to swipe a cloak and a sack from a nearby shop without notice.

She threw the cloak around her shoulders and made for the cellar door. The hinges whined quietly as she poked her eyes out. Seeing no one around, she crept out and darted through the alleys like a cat, moving southward. When she emerged onto busier streets, she blended in with the rest of the people and acted natural, avoiding the potential gazes of passing soldiers.

Further south she went—past the Southern Market Street and through neighborhoods. She hardly drew any attention. Eventually, the cobblestone turned to dirt roads. The cabins turned to tents and huts. Hardly any of the soldiers made their way down here. After all, what was there to see? It's the slums of Lower City. There's nothing there.

In the slums, people walked slower. Coughs and mumbles were everywhere, made by the tired and ragged people. A man passed her that had to walk with crutches—his left leg ended just below the knee. Hard to get work with a condition like that. Another man leaned his back against a hut, chomping on an apple. His right arm was shriveled and ended in a hand that resembled more of a claw. Kierli frowned. It was like a shadow of Widow's Rest. Like most southern villages, honestly.

There was a gathering place in the slums known simply as the Crossing. As the name implied, it was an intersection of several streets that converged into something like a town square, but lacked the energy of Center Court. The edges were lined with merchants selling scrap wood, flimsy crafts, and half-rotten produce. A couple of street performers danced and crooned in the center of the Crossing, their overturned and expectant hats home to just a few Pieces and Shards.

Kierli scrunched her nose at it all. It was pathetic. But more importantly, it was ripe. The emotions here were thick, and they were just the audience she needed. As she looked around, she found an unattended box and snatched it up. She planted it firmly, stood on it, and lifted her voice. But not before she pulled the hood off her head.

"My friends!"

The people stopped and looked. It took them a second to realize who she was, but when it dawned on them, it led to shouting and pointing. "It's Kierli!" "The Captain that escaped!" "Find a guard!"

"Please, *please!*" Kierli held her hands in the air. "I mean none of you harm! I'm here to bring you the *truth!*"

That got their attention even more. Kierli felt the weight of one hundred eyes fixed on her. But something about the pressure was exciting. It always was. It pulled her lips into a smile.

"There's a reason King Jason won't talk about my imprisonment," Kierli said. "Seven years ago he distributed the wealth that Barnabas collected from the Harvest Tax. Every last Shard was sent out to neighborhoods like yours. Or so he said." She held up the sack of money. "I'm here to tell you that King Jason is a *liar!* Boxes upon boxes full of gold are kept within the castle walls! In my hand is all I could take from the King's secret treasury! And I'm sharing my spoils with you!"

Kierli hurled the sack into the middle of the Crossing. When it hit the ground, a jingling cascade of Pieces, Bars, and Blocks spilled to the dirt. The people gasped, stared, then dove for the bounty like a pack of wolves. Through the ruckus, cries leapt out like "Down with King Jason!" and "Kierli for Queen!"

"My heart hurts for you, my friends," Kierli continued. "I know what it's like to survive on the scraps of those above you. So long as I'm a free woman, I'll do all I can to help you. Bring me your sick and your maimed! I will heal them with my magic!"

Raucous cheers. Any thought of finding a guard was abandoned. In a matter of seconds, slum people lined up at

Kierli's feet. She went one by one, using her magic to mend altered bones, diminish lingering coughs, and replace missing appendages. She only got through six people before her head started feeling light. When she finished mending a broken leg, she staggered and clutched her head.

A woman nearby noticed this. "Cap'n Kierli, you alright?"

Kierli nodded, but felt dizzy and nauseous. The magic was euphoric during use, but when fully expended, it left a slogging weight that made her entire body feel like tar. She pinched her eyes shut and tried to keep her balance. A small crowd was still gathered around her. Finally, she sighed and forced a smile.

"Please forgive me, but my magic is nearly diminished. Don't worry, I'll be back again soon. I won't leave you to suffer. Not like the King has done so many times before. Farewell, my good people! The truth shall be known!"

They cheered. They clapped and whistled between their fingers. They shouted things like "Dragon bless Captain Kierli!" and "Kierli for Queen!"

The cheers died out as she threw her hood back on and snaked her way to the east. Her head swam and she felt weak.

I need to find something, she thought. *Anything... it can be small...*

As if on cue, a stray cat slid into view, tucking itself to the side of a hut, sniffing for prey. Kierli felt the dagger by her side. Through aching eyes, she focused on the cat and hurled the blade. She barely missed, lacerating the cat but not killing it. It hissed and whined a high-pitch moan, laying in the dirt, bleeding out. Kierli moved swiftly, scooping up the dagger and ramming it through the cat's brain.

A trickle of power seeped into her. Kierli let out a relieved sigh as she pushed magic, activating a soft drip of pleasure. No more aching limbs. No more swimming head. Back to normal.

That's when she was able to revel in her small victory. Looking back at the Crossing, she smirked. The seed was planted. Soon, the news of her visitation would spread across the city—the news that she had healed people in Lower City and given money that King Jason had selfishly kept. And how would that look for him? She smiled wider and continued east.

The journey was more shanty homes as she moved among the slums, but as she got closer to the southern gates, the crowds grew thicker. When the roads got more congested, she slowed her pace and tried to blend in. Her eyes darted in their sockets. Whenever she spotted a pair of soldiers, she sidestepped to hide from their view.

Eventually, she reached the southern gate. As she gazed upon its short size, memories of the Ash War came flooding back. At this part of the wall, there was little to no protection—the builders had focused so much attention on the western wall. Through Kierli's leadership, many lives were protected, but even more were slain. A chill slid down her spine as she remembered the Ash climbing this ten-foot wall and leaping onto the people below. They fought back for hours, but it wasn't enough. Even with Kierli's magic.

And in her walking, she could make out the spot where Jax bled out. Right there, outside that house that got rebuilt. His horrible, gurgling coughs. His warm, sticky blood on her arms and hands. The light leaving his eyes.

She put her head down and kept walking until she reached some of the stables inside the gates. There, multiple carts were being loaded with supplies, waiting to depart for various villages across the south. Among them, a few of them were being loaded with people. Drivers held signs indicating their destinations. There was one for Fort Obelisk and another for Port Runoff. But she couldn't sit in a carriage full of other people. That was out of the question.

Instead, she moved for some carriages filled with livestock and farming supplies. Painfully, she pushed whatever magic she had left through her ears to pick up on conversations. She saw carriages of pigs, sheep, chickens... finally, she heard one conversation that stuck out.

"...not the finest, but it'll do."

"That's the army way, isn't it?"

"The folks down in Widow's Rest won't be picky, either."

Perfect. The drivers were carrying a carriage piled with hay, nothing more. Kierli's feet hardly made a sound as she darted over and hoisted herself inside. Quickly, she covered herself in the hay, giving herself just a small pocket to see through.

The drivers took their time. Several minutes went by before the carriage began to jostle, but finally, they snapped the reins and the horses pulled forward.

"Hold it!"

The wagon stopped after only ten feet. Kierli nearly inhaled a mouthful of hay. She could see through her peephole that it was a couple of guards.

"Sorry, new orders from the King," one of them said. "Gotta check every carriage going in and out of the city. This won't take long. It's just hay, right?"

The drivers mumbled in the affirmative. Kierli held her breath and watched. The guards didn't spot her in the pile. One went around the other side of the wagon, and together, they jammed their swords into the hay, searching. All the while, Kierli didn't breathe. She felt the stabs getting dangerously close—one even cut her pants, but the soldier didn't notice. What could she do if she got caught? A headache was coming on again because her reservoir was so low. She wasn't in any condition to battle.

One last stab. The sword's tip stopped just an inch away from Kierli's eye. She didn't move. The guard pulled it out, sheathed it, and said, "You're good. Travel safe."

The wagon tottered out the gates and Kierli could breathe again.

∗ ∗ ∗ ∗ ∗

The sky was red, but it fractured into more colors as it streamed through the windows into the dining hall. Tarren and Jason sat at one end of the table, waiting to be served. Tarren buried himself in a book on healing magic, written completely in Ancient Nezmythian. Meanwhile, Jason forced himself to read from a storybook that Tarren recommended as part of his wellness regimen. It was about a sparrow that befriends a dying lamb. Jason found it unbearable, but Tarren assured him it was a classic that deserved reading.

Finally, the royal chef brought out plates and set them down in front of the King and Advisor. Jason closed his book, set it aside, then stared at the meal in front of him. There was hardly any meat or potatoes on his plate—just various vegetables.

"There's asparagus here," he said sourly.

"Very astute, Your Highness," Tarren said.

"You know I'll eat *any* vegetable besides asparagus."

"It's good for you. Just eat it."

Jason stole a glance to the royal chef, who was standing not far away with his hands behind his back. He gave a very nervous glance to the King. "It... was on the Advisor's recommended menu, Your Majesty."

"My friend, I want this removed immediately."

The chef started forward.

"*Don't,*" Tarren said severely.

The chef stopped.

Jason threw a look at Tarren. "You can't overrule my orders."

"Of course I can."

"You're making that up. Chef, please come remove this."

He cautiously moved forward.

"I said *stop.*"

The chef stopped and swallowed, his eyes shifting between the two.

Jason glared at Tarren. "Why are you undermining my authority?"

"I'm not undermining you. I'm trying to—"

"Yes you are! Just look at what you're—"

"Your Highness? Mister Advisor?"

A soldier entered the dining hall, standing at attention and wearing a perturbed expression. When he got the two's attention, he marched forward and gave a respectful nod.

"Sire," he said, "there's a large gathering of people outside the courtyard gates. They look like slummies and they're demanding entrance to the castle. They're… very angry." The soldier saw the plate and licked his lips when he noticed the asparagus.

Jason's face became hard. "Demanding entrance to the castle? Why? They know if any one of them has a grievance they can visit me during the day."

"They're saying that Kierli visited them this morning at the Crossing. She healed their infirm and told them you're hiding boxes of gold in the castle. That you've got rooms full of it."

Jason's face twisted like something smelled bad. "That's absurd."

"A total lie," Tarren muttered.

Jason put down his fork and stood from the table. "I'll go speak to them."

"I'll go with you," Tarren said. "Then you can come back and finish your asparagus."

Jason ignored that.

As the three of them crossed into the great hall, Jason spoke to the soldier. "You said Kierli healed the people down in the slums?"

"Yes, with her magic, sir. She must be a powerful healer, because from what the people said, she was helping people with missing legs, gouged eyes… I didn't know that sort of thing was possible. I've been to an infirmary before, but that kind of healing takes weeks, not a single morning."

Jason sent Tarren a look. The Advisor didn't return it—he was too busy processing the idea. *Healing through Dark Magic? Is that even possible?*

They made it through the southern courtyard and arrived at the gate, where a crowd of nearly thirty gathered outside. All of them were shabbily dressed and armed with cheap weapons— clearly the people of the slums. Jason marched up to the gates, where a row of bars separated the people from him.

"Kierli told you I'm hoarding gold?" He frowned. "Is that right?"

"She sure did!" a gray-haired man in the front piped up. "She took a sack full o' your money and brought it to us! Now I can finally afford to get my family new clothes, no thanks to you!"

"I don't know *where* she got that money," Jason said, "but I can assure you it wasn't here. Every Shard and Piece left in this castle was distributed to you seven years ago when I took the throne. Nothing was kept for myself."

"That's what you *would* say!" someone shouted from the back. "Cease the lies! Show us where it's hidden!"

"There's nothing hidden!" Jason barked. "Kierli is playing you! Don't you think I'd put her away for good reason? She's trying to put you against me out of spite. Be smarter!"

"Show us then, if you have nothing to hide!"

Jason rolled his eyes. "I have nothing to prove to you. I've given you the truth. You can shout and holler at these gates all night if you want. The choice is yours."

As Jason turned and stalked away, his back was met with boos and hisses. The soldiers stood by the gates and kept an eye on them as Jason and Tarren made their way back to the castle doors. Tarren's eyes were hard as they followed his feet.

"Do you really think Dark Magic has those kinds of healing properties?" he muttered.

"I didn't think it was possible," Jason said. "I always thought Dark Magic was for destruction and bondage, not restoration."

Tarren was quiet, thinking. "Maybe there's properties to it that we're not aware of."

"Perhaps. If Kierli is going around the city healing people and spreading lies, this could become dangerous for us. All the more reason to find her."

"That might turn her into a martyr for these people."

Jason didn't reply.

* * * * *

Sweat coated Barnabas's entire body and breathing came in gasps. His shirt was off, revealing the stretch marks that covered most of his body. The brightly colored trees around him rustled in the breeze. He kicked, spun, punched, jumped in place. Not far away, Master Ferribolt sat with his legs crossed, reading a book while a cup of tea steamed on a table next to him. In the not-so-far distance, the surface of Kyleth Pond shimmered with golden light.

With a final spin, Barnabas shot three yellow jerokis in different directions. Each of them hit their marks, knocking off small branches that dangled nearby. The branches fell, along with handfuls of crinkly brown leaves. Master Ferribolt looked up and applauded.

"Well done!" he said. "I remember when you had first gotten out of the Vault and you struggled to throw a straight jeroki."

Barnabas trudged over to him and took a seat on the opposite side of the table. "It's only taken three years. Standard magic is difficult to relearn after using *that* magic for so long." He grimaced and stretched his arm. "And getting old doesn't help."

"Well, for what it's worth, you don't look a day over fifty."

Barnabas grinned, then spotted the oak tree out of the corner of his eye. The fresh mound of dirt right below it. His grin dropped. "Thank you for blessing Nartikis's grave today, Master."

"Thank you for asking me."

"Jason told me not to blame myself. But I know if I wouldn't have appointed her, Nartikis would still be alive right now."

"Jason is wise. We would have discovered Kierli's methods eventually, then we'd be in the same predicament we're in now."

"I should have prayed to the Dragon about it."

To this, Master Ferribolt didn't reply right away. Instead, he chose to say, "Let it go, my friend. Let it go."

Barnabas cracked his knuckles. "I'll let it go when we find her."

15
THE DISCIPLE

"Hey! *Hey!*"

Kierli's head hurt and her eyes fluttered open. When she did, she gasped and shot up. Two men were glaring at her through the hay—one short and stocky, the other tall and lanky. The tall one held a short sword, so Kierli slipped the dagger from her side, ready for a fight. But that wasn't the thing that disturbed her most.

Her face was uncovered. Exposed. That was enough to take her mind off her aching head.

"What are you doing in there?" Shorty shot. "This ain't a passage carriage!"

Kierli swallowed. "Sorry. Didn't have any money for the passage carriage."

"Hard to believe a lady lookin' like you would need any money," Lanky sounded more bitter than flirtatious. "Alright, get up. Out you go."

Shorty tried to take one of her arms, but Kierli slapped it away and rolled out of the carriage herself. Frowning, she ignored the hay clinging to her body and squared up, flashing the dagger. In the movement, Shorty and Lanky heard the money jingling in her pocket. They both bristled and matched her fighting stance.

"What was that?" Shorty pointed. "You've got money on your pocket, don't you?"

Kierli's glared. "Come look, if you're feeling bold."

Lanky's eyes grew wide, like a spark suddenly lit behind them. "Wait just a minute… I know who you are! Captain Kierli! The wanted fugitive! They were looking all over the city for you!"

Shorty's jaw fell and Lanky's face turned pale, but he still kept his short sword pointed at her. Finally, Shorty slapped Lanky's hand.

"Put it away, idiot!" He said. "You expect to fight a Captain?"

"That's right," Kierli said. "I could kill both of you without a problem. And that's why you're going to give me passage to Widow's Rest, no questions asked."

Lanky glared. "I have a sword and all you've got is that little dagger! Besides, I bet you'd fetch a handsome reward."

"*Shut up!*" Shorty slapped his hand again. "Haven't you heard about her magic, too? Just do what she says!"

"Sounds like your friend is the sensible one," Kierli flicked her head at Shorty.

The two were silent. Clenching his jaw, Lanky finally slipped his sword back in its scabbard. Standing up straight, he held up his hands and said, "Just to Widow's Rest?"

Kierli nodded.

"Fine."

Without taking their eyes off her, Lanky and Shorty climbed back into the driver's perch. Kierli hoisted herself into the pile of hay and hunkered down, covering herself so passersby wouldn't see her in the pile. But she kept a hole where she could clearly see the two drivers.

"Don't try anything funny," Kierli said. "I'm not taking my eyes off either of you. I can do this for hours."

The two didn't reply. They just yawed the horses and they got off to a steady trot. Several minutes went by and Kierli barely blinked. The carriage wheels ground softly on the dirt road. Neither Shorty nor Lanky spoke. They just stayed rigid and stoic, facing forward.

Good, Kierli thought. *Keep it that way.*

Several minutes more went by before Lanky nudged Shorty. "Might want to pick up a little speed at this part."

"Reckon you're right. It's pretty clear."

Shorty snapped the reins and the horses picked up the pace. Kierli stayed poised in the back. She never once let go of her dagger. The carriage shook and rattled as it moved faster. Then, suddenly, the wheels hit a rock in the road, throwing the carriage's load in the air.

The drivers saw it coming, but Kierli couldn't. That fraction of a moment was all Lanky needed. He flipped around, threw out his arm, and locked Kierli into a Paralyzing Curse. Kierli gasped as she felt her entire body constrict and become rigid.

He knows intermediate magic! She thought. *Looks like I underestimated this one.*

What's more, Lanky dove into the pile of hay. A length of rope was in his hands.

"Yeah, you got 'er!" Shorty yipped from the front.

Lanky only had seconds, but it was enough. He expertly kicked away her dagger, lashed together her ankles and wrists, then used another length of rope to gag her. He stayed hidden in the hay, holding her close, pressing his short sword to her throat.

Kierli started to regain control of her limbs. She growled through her gag and struggled against the bonds, but Lanky grabbed her hair and held his sword tighter against her throat.

"I can stay like this for hours, too," he said, "especially considering the reward *you'll* fetch us. So stop moving, or I'll cut your throat."

Kierli's eyes could have set him on fire. Rage boiled inside her. Gears turned in her throbbing head. It's not like she hadn't been in similar situations, but to escape, someone always wound up dead.

Her mind kept drawing and scrapping various plans. She kept looking for alternate solutions, something where she wouldn't have to draw blood, but pulled a blank. Lanky had her in his clutches, steel to her throat. Trapped. Restrained. That feeling made everything inside her scream.

Do it, an inclination whispered to her. *You're justified. End him.*

That thought came with a feeling that almost frightened her. It was a pull—a pull to the violence. The clash of steel, the hot sticky red, and the surge of power that always came with it. It could soothe this aching head. It made excitement and anticipation swirl deep inside her. Yesterday she did it. She escaped the Vault with it. Today, it would be the same. Two victims. Enough power to transport to Widow's Rest, and then some.

He threatened your life, the itch came again. *Do it. He deserves it.*

She hesitated, but only for a moment.

With what little magic she had left, she made the ropes catch fire. Lanky gasped and tried to squirm away, but the surrounding hay was rapidly burning. Lanky scrambled toward the driver's perch but Kierli caught his ankle and pulled him back. She disarmed him and rammed the short sword through his chest, making him gurgle and sputter.

There it was. Replenished. The headache went away.

Gasping like a frightened child, Shorty leaped out of the drivers perch and rolled into the grass, struggling to get to his feet. Kierli snatched Lanky's short sword and scrambled through the burning hay. She jumped out of the jostling carriage and was on Shorty within a manner of seconds. The man lay on his back, eyes welling with tears, squirming along the grass as Kierli approached. Meanwhile, the need pounded in her head.

Kill.

"Please, I won't tell anyone!" Shorty begged. "Please! Have m—"

Kierli didn't look him in the eye as she gutted him. Shorty was dead, blood pooling. The reservoir inside her doubled. Kierli looked over her shoulder. Plains stretched for miles, but she couldn't see anyone down either end of the path. Meanwhile, the carriage was hundreds of yards away, engulfed in flames and pulled by two panicked horses.

She quickly ransacked Shorty's body for goods. If he didn't have any valuables, this would look like a bandit attack. She found another dagger and some pocket change. Nothing else. Not surprising for someone making a delivery to Widow's Rest.

The horses were getting away. Maybe she could transport to the carriage, free them, then ride one of the horses to town. Or better yet, she could kill the horses and get that much more energy. Yes, that's it. She transported in front of them, launched two large jerokis at their heads and shattered their skulls. The horses crumbled and slid across the ground, no longer alive to fear the growing flames behind them. And with their deaths, Kierli felt the power inside her double again. Her body shivered at the feeling—the pleasure almost made her laugh. She pushed a deal of it through her, letting it swirl and drift inside her, sparkling and sweet.

But what of the aftermath? Two dead men. Two dead horses. And a ten-foot-tall fire of wood and hay.

She stood with her hands on her hips and watched. "What a mess."

"My child…"

The voice again. The otherworldly whisper that slipped in her ears and fluttered in her mind—the same one that happened after she killed yesterday. And with it, the same vision of the Vault. The same pull to return. She turned all about, looking for a source, but there was no one around but her. In every direction, it was just green hills.

Kierli focused on Widow's Rest, pushed magic through her body, and in the crest of euphoria, she vanished.

She reappeared at a familiar place. A broken bridge reached over her head and a stream babbled at her feet. Her secret spot. The moment would have felt comforting if it were complete, but it wasn't. Jax wasn't here. So it could only be half of whatever it used to be.

The place was over a mile outside of Widow's Rest, so she took it as a chance to rest. She knew word was now spreading in Nezmyth City about her visit to the slums. If she reappeared in Widow's Rest less than a day later, people would know she was using her magic to travel. That wouldn't be prudent. She caught some fish from the stream and cooked them over a small fire for dinner. Then she slept.

The next morning, when the sun peeked over the Eastern Mountains, Kierli crept around the edge of the bridge. Just as she thought, there was no one around. But it wouldn't be wise to walk to Widow's Rest from here. She held her breath, turned invisible, and transported to the edge of town. When she reappeared, she was slammed with the smells of livestock and manure and her boots sank into the mud. She moved silently across multiple slabs of property, each a tiny house with its own patch for pumpkins or squash.

As she went, she passed the dirty-faced farmers who lived here. When she could, she snatched farm tools that were left leaning against houses. She found an old shovel, a spade, a hoe, and a metal pail. They all turned invisible and soundless with her as soon as she held them. Satisfied, she kept moving. She didn't stop until she reached a single-room cabin with a door dangling on its hinges. She didn't feel the need to knock—she just grabbed the jittery handle and pushed the door open.

Inside the cabin, there was hardly a thing. Every corner gathered dust and dirt. There was an outline of where a stove used to be. No table. The only furniture was a rickety chair and a single straw mattress pushed into the corner.

On the mattress was a woman with blonde hair, sickly and frail, sprawled out. Her eyes had been vacant and fixed on the ceiling until the door slammed shut, then she mumbled and tried to sit up. A small bowl rested by her bed, half filled with the ground-up remains of a Mulak Flower. Kierli glared at it and released the invisibility from her body.

"Looks like you've hardly changed, mother," she said. "Even after Jax and I begged you for years. At least you don't feel like you have to hide it anymore now that you're home alone."

"Hnnng?" her mother mumbled as she sat up and tried to focus. "Wha? Kierli?"

Kierli ignored her. She took the gardening tools to an empty corner and dropped them on the floor, letting them clang loudly. Then she knelt down and held her hands over them, pushing magic. With some strain and a purple glow, they all transformed into more Bars and Blocks. Kierli scooped them all up and pushed them into a sack, cinching it shut.

Meanwhile, her mother stared, blinking hard, struggling to stay balanced. "Kierli... it's so... give me some of that, will you...?"

"So you can what?" Kierli spat. "Go get spun on Mulak Flowers again? As if you don't have a perfectly good patch of soil to grow and harvest like everyone else?" She looked around. "Looks like you sold all the furniture. You don't even have a blanket for that mattress."

"I'm so tired all the time..." her mother mumbled. "I need this for strength..."

"You'd have more strength if you *stopped*. That's what's sapping your strength all the time. Here... so you don't have to whore yourself out for a meal again."

She reached in the bag and pulled out a few Bars, then dropped them at her mother's feet. Her mother's hands shot for them and scooped them up, holding them close to her heart. She nodded tearfully and sniffled.

"My kind daughter," she said. "My wonderful, beautiful daughter… thank you…"

"Your wonderful, beautiful daughter that you love so much," Kierli echoed mockingly. "The one that you loved enough to come support at her Succession Ceremony. I know you got the letter weeks ago, mother. I made sure someone from the garrison delivered it in person."

"Oh, I… it must have slipped my mind."

"That happens when you're always spun. Jax never would have done that." She threw the sack of money over her shoulder and rolled her eyes. "Goodbye, mother."

As she crossed the room, she looked over her shoulder. Her mother was laying back down on the mattress, reaching for the bowl of ground-up Flower. Briefly, Kierli considered it. No one would miss her. No one would find her for days. And that would give her more power. After teasing these thoughts for a moment, she felt disgusted with herself, then left.

She walked in silence, hood covering her face, until she emerged onto the square. It looked more similar to the Crossing than it did to Center Court, with just a few soldiers standing guard around the edges. She marched near the entrance of the village chief's mansion, still glaring at every board in its walls until she turned to face the crowd. Then she pulled off her hood and raised her hand, revealing her face.

"My friends!"

People stopped to look, and it was a repeat of the Crossing from yesterday. The collective gasps and pointing fingers. Two guards rushed forward while a third dashed away from the square, looking for a superior. Meanwhile, the crowd stopped and stared.

"It's wonderful to be home!" Kierli said brightly.

The voices started popping up from the crowd. "Why were you imprisoned?" "How did you escape?" "What's going on?"

"I will answer any questions that you have," Kierli said. "But first, allow me to plead my case. I was wrongfully imprisoned!"

"Stop right there, Kierli!"

The two guards were upon her, pointing their spears at her. Nervousness was scrawled across their faces, but they tried to project confidence. Kierli glowered at them.

"Not another word," one of them said. "We have direct orders to take you in, Captain."

Kierli cocked her head to the side. "I understand. But how will you do that without any weapons?"

She blinked and their spears snapped into purple dust, trickling to the soil. The crowd gasped and murmured, becoming a blanket of hisses and whispers. Kierli raised an eyebrow and smirked. Meanwhile, the soldiers gulped, traded looks, and backed into the crowd.

"Good," Kierli smiled. "As I was saying, I was imprisoned because I wanted to bring you the *truth!* The truth that King Jason has hidden for so long! He didn't distribute all of Barnabas's wealth when he became King. There are still boxes filled with riches at the castle! Here in my hand is what I was able to retrieve for you good people!"

She raised the sack in the air, then threw it into the crowd. Someone caught it, pulled it open, and their eyes filled with wonder as they saw the money filled to the brim. People shouted with awe as they passed it around and everyone took a handful. Residents at the edge of the crowd ran to the nearby houses to pull people into the square. As they money got distributed, questions popped up.

"Why would King Jason do this?" "He's been greedy all along!" "Down with King Jason!"

"With my power and the knowledge of the truth," Kierli continued, "King Jason knew I would be dangerous! But I escaped because the people of Nezmyth deserve to know! Let King Jason know that you won't stand for this! Nezmyth deserves the *truth!*"

The crowd cheered. When the applause died down, Kierli said, "Bring me your sick and your maimed! I will heal them!"

There should have been more cheers, but instead, the noise died down to a hush. One person moved through the crowd— a man in armor more ornamented than the other soldiers. His face was young and hard, with stiff cheekbones, yellow hair, and an eyepatch.

As he approached Kierli, he didn't advance on her, but kept a modest distance and put his hand on the hilt of his sword. Kierli put her hand on her short sword as well.

He nodded. "Kierli."

"Captain Felix," she said. "You're looking well."

"Can't say the same for you. You look a little more pale since your Succession Ceremony."

"Life on the run does that, I suppose."

Captain Felix smiled. "Surrender yourself. You know we have orders to take you in. Dead or alive, actually."

"Dead or alive? Now, that sounds a bit extreme."

"*Down with King Jason!*" Someone from the crowd cheered, then the crowd applauded before Felix got to speak again.

"We took an oath," Felix said. "*You* took an oath. Extreme or not, they are orders, and we are bound to them."

Kierli scanned Felix and the crowd, calculating. She could challenge him to a duel and she would definitely win—although he was an excellent warrior, his eyepatch put him at a disadvantage. And his magical ability was nowhere near Kierli's. But that wouldn't be the smart move. Felix was popular. If Kierli killed him in a battle, that would repel more followers than attract. That's the last thing she needed. This had to be handled with precision.

After a while, Kierli nodded and said, "I see. Well, then I won't resist. But I have one request, since I *was* your Chief Captain, if only for a day." She smiled. "Let me heal your eye. You can keep a dozen soldiers trained on me. You know I won't make any sudden moves. You have my honor as a soldier. No tricks."

Felix's eye narrowed. The crowd held their breath, waiting. They had the money in their hands—the money from King Jason's secret treasury. And Kierli was such a powerful magician, who was to say that she couldn't heal an eye? Felix stared hard at her for a long moment.

"Fine," he said. "But we're taking you straight to the prison afterward. You understand."

"I do."

One by one, the guards surrounded Kierli, putting their swords and spears inches from her. They made it so she could barely move. But Felix cautiously removed his eyepatch, revealing the empty, fleshy socket. Kierli put her whole hand over it, inhaled a large breath, then pushed magic from her body to Felix's.

Felix took a sharp breath as the sensation hit him. The soldiers around Kierli tensed, but she didn't move. She kept her hand on his socket, and under her palm, she could feel the soft, squishy eye materializing. All the while, the people of Widow's Rest watched with thick silence. Then, at last, Kierli removed her hand.

Felix blinked with two eyes. He looked around, enjoying the morning sky and the autumn colors with his whole field of vision. He forced himself not to smile—not to let a happy tear fall—but turned and looked at the crowd. When they saw his eye fully restored, they erupted into celebration.

It was hard to hear over the roaring of Widow's Rest, but Felix ordered, "Take her away. Thank you, Kierli. I'm sorry."

She held her wrists out. Soldiers bound them. She stayed penitent as a group of soldiers escorted her through the square. Meanwhile, half the village chanted her name.

"*Kier-li! Kier-li!*"

The prison was on the southern edge of town—a large brick building with a basement and ground floor, all separated into single cells. Rats were aplenty. Dirt and straw scattered everywhere. Somewhere out of view, a prisoner sang a tune that sounded more like a mumble and another prisoner used profane language to try to shut them up.

Kierli was escorted to a cell and the door was locked behind her. Through the rest of the day, many people tried to visit her—people with missing fingers or sick family members. The soldiers denied them entrance, citing their instructions from King Jason.

"Those orders don't seem to be in the people's interest, do they?" Kierli jeered.

The soldiers didn't reply, but their faces said enough.

It didn't matter. Nightfall would come eventually, then Kierli would move.

As the hours passed, a soldier brought her dinner: a fistful of bread, a cup of water, and a half-bruised apple. Kierli ate it all. The sun set to the west and the sky turned to black. She snapped her fingers and a purple flame danced in her palm. She drank in the feeling, letting it settle and curl inside her. The sounds of the guard's footsteps grew and faded with each patrol that passed her cell.

The vision of Nezmyth City was vivid in her mind—particularly the cellar. She knew she could transport there just like she did when she escaped the prison. All she had to do was focus and disappear.

But footsteps were becoming loud again. She breathed an annoyed sigh and slumped against the wall, waiting for them to pass.

They didn't pass, but stopped at her cell. It was Captain Felix. He squatted down so their eyes were level. Kierli couldn't help but think about how lovely his eyes were—a vivid brown that reflected brightly in the moonlight. They were almost as nice as the Advisor's, but Felix had a stronger jaw.

"You probably could have killed me today if you wanted to," he said.

"I thought about it. You embarrassed me." Kierli smirked.

Felix half-smiled. "With that kind of magic, you would probably have no problem breaking out of a place like this."

Kierli shrugged.

"I've been thinking," Felix said. "And I want to follow you. You showed your true colors today, and if you're saying that King Jason is hiding something, I believe you. I've already left a note at my barrack, so the soldiers will know by tomorrow morning that I've left. Will you take me as your follower? I can get you out of here tonight."

Kierli's face softened. "I could never say no to you. But you don't need to spring me out of here. Come closer."

Perplexed but curious, Felix unlatched the door and slipped inside. Still sitting, Kierli extended her hand. Felix took it. She imagined the cellar and pushed magic through their bodies with a strong snap. Purple smoke overtook them both. In a matter of seconds, they were both in Nezmyth City.

16

THE RECURRENCE

No. Not again.

That's what Jason thought as his eyes filled with another vision of destruction. He could have sworn he was laying on the couch just moments ago—he knew because it took him hours to fall asleep. But now, he was floating in the air with a perfect panoramic view of Nezmyth.

To the south, he could see all the way to the Eternal Ocean, including Dragonclaw Lake and Port Runoff. To the north, the shining waters of the Wevlian Sea were clear on the edge of Port Gala. But once again, black clouds gathered in the sky and rumbling tremors moved through the ground.

His eyes fell to Nezmyth City. A shadowy mist was gathering, blooming out from Nezmyth City and spreading until it touched every corner of the kingdom.

The ground shuddered, a quick calm, then Upper City hill exploded. The castle was rent asunder, chunks of stone and debris hurling through the air. In its place, a gaping hole opened its mouth to the sky. It was deep and dark, but Jason could hear something monstrous stirring from within its depths.

Then a great rush. Just like the black mist, it touched every corner of the kingdom. All the greenery disappeared—the trees, bushes, grass, everything. As far as Jason could see, the kingdom was completely devoid of life.

He watched in horror, powerless. Then he realized someone was standing beside him—a beautiful blonde woman in a white dress. It wasn't Kierli. Instead, this woman was just a little shorter than him, with silver eyes and a splash of freckles around her nose.

"It'll be okay," she said.

She reached out her hand, inviting Jason to hold it.

Saryan? Jason wondered.

He reached out to take her hand, but before he did, he blinked and the vision ended. He was back on his couch, staring at the ceiling with his hand outstretched to someone who wasn't there.

Jason clenched his teeth and threw off his blankets before he shoved his feet into some boots.

* * * * *

Tarren rubbed his eyes and slouched against a pillar, but Jason stood at full alert. The door to Master Ferribolt's mansion had already been knocked. After a moment, Jerem answered it and led them to the study. It took a few minutes for the Chief Patriarch to arrive. His slippers dragged across the ground and he straightened a powder blue nightgown.

He yawned and rubbed his eyes as he sat down. "Good evening."

"If it were a good evening, I'd still be in bed," Tarren mumbled.

"I had another vision, Master Ferribolt," Jason said. "Another dream about Nezmyth's destruction."

Master Ferribolt snapped his fingers and the fireplace ignited. As the warmth grew, Tarren burrowed in his seat more.

Master Ferribolt leaned forward and laced his hands over his mouth. "Go on."

Jason explained it in detail—Upper City exploding, the vegetation disappearing, Saryan. Meanwhile, Master Ferribolt listened and Tarren struggled to stay awake. When Jason finished, Master Ferribolt scratched his head. "What do you suppose it means?"

"The dark mist started in Nezmyth City and grew outward," Jason explained. "Maybe it represents Kierli's influence."

"We've already alerted every village and across Nezmyth," Tarren groaned. "They'll be on the lookout for her. What more can we actually do?"

Jason's face pressed. "There's just got to be something."

"Your Highness, Mister Advisor, I have found a prophecy recently."

At this, even Tarren perked up. Master Ferribolt went to the wall of scrolls and pulled one off the shelf. He unraveled it on his lap, making the ancient parchment crinkle softly. His eyes traveled its length while he cradled it.

"*The tall sunflower shall make the moons bright,*" Master Ferribolt said. "*The great tree shall rend asunder as the stars reach up from the ground. Bones and wings of old shall vex the tormentor. If the last stone remains, all that lives shall depart and be free.*"

The words sent a chill down Jason's spine. Tarren frowned. Master Ferribolt rolled the scroll back up and placed it back on the shelf. As he went, Jason said, "If there's anything that sounds like a prophecy of destruction… it's that."

"These words and your dreams sound like they could be connected," Master Ferribolt said. "But it's very cryptic."

"Or Jason could just be having bad dreams," Tarren said.

Both Master Ferribolt and Jason gave him looks.

"Listen," Tarren raised his hands. "I love Jason and I know he's in tune with the Sacred Dragon. But we also need to remember he's been under a *lot* of emotional stress lately. Have we counted out the possibility that these *visions* are just a reaction to his grief? Both dreams had a person who resembled Saryan. I'm not trying to minimize your pain, Jason, I'm just trying to think objectively."

This gave Jason pause. *Could these really just be a manifestation of my grief? Is it nothing more than a nightmare and I'm overreacting?*

Master Ferribolt, however, felt differently.

"I believe you need to take this more seriously," Master Ferribolt said sternly. "You as Advisor should know that nighttime visions have been given to Kings of the past, often as a form of warning. The fact that they're happening repeatedly should raise flags to you. Nadiel wouldn't have brushed away something like this."

A prickly silence fell over them. At the mention of his old master, Tarren's swallowed and dried up in his seat. He slouched, folded his arms, and looked away. Almost imperceptibly, he muttered, "I'm sorry, Jason."

"Don't become too confident in your position, young one," Master Ferribolt continued. "Being Advisor doesn't make you naturally more intelligent than anyone in this room."

"Did I not just apologize?" Tarren snapped.

As the tension swelled, Jason cleared his throat.

"Listen, Tarren," he said, "I appreciate your feedback. You make a good point. And thank you for validating my feelings, Master Ferribolt. These could be real, or they could just be bad dreams. But I do know that in my last prayer, I was told to trust my instincts. And my instincts tell me these visions should be taken seriously. So we move forward as such. Agreed?"

Both his friends nodded quietly. Tarren, still folding his arms and slouching, asked, "So what do we do then?"

Jason deflated. "I don't know."

✳ ✳ ✳ ✳ ✳

"My child... I await you... Come... and feel... true... power!"

Kierli moved with lightning speed through the streets of Nezmyth City. Out the western gates. Toward the Prison. Down to the bottom. Then she was at the Vault of the Damned, but she didn't go down. Instead, the stones beneath her cracked and a fissure opened up, seeping out purple and green smoke. Something was pulling her down, but she didn't feel frightened.

She felt ecstatic.

Suddenly, she jolted awake. She sat up and splayed her hands out, making sure she was back in the cellar. Only the darkness responded. Next to her, Felix stirred as the bedroll was lifted off his naked body. His eyes painfully slid open. "What's wrong?"

Kierli let out a thick sigh. "Nothing. Nothing at all."

"Then come here."

Felix tugged her arm and pulled her against him. Laying her head on his shoulder gave her some comfort, but the vision she received was still fizzing behind her eyes. There was something beneath the prison. Something that was calling to her. And it was getting stronger.

It took a while for her to fall back asleep. When morning arrived, they both crawled out of the bedroll and put their clothes back on. It only took a moment before Felix started asking about Kierli's magic.

"You know me," Kierli sneered. "I'm gifted. Always have been."

"Among other things," Felix purred as he looked her up and down. "But your mastery is something else. Not even specialized healers can heal ailments that fast. What are you doing differently?"

Kierli winked. "I'm just special. Come here. If we're going to go out in public, I need to change your face."

Felix smiled and obeyed. She put her hands on his face, and within moments, his look was transformed. His jaw was narrower, his eyes blue instead of brown, and his ears smaller.

A completely different man. When she was done, she transformed her own face and turned into Evelyn.

"You still look beautiful," he smirked.

Kierli ignored him. "Come on."

They made sure the coast was clear when they emerged from the cellar. From there, it didn't take long to reach Center Court. Even in the morning, it was a bustling hive. The shops and eateries around the edges were populated with hungry people. Merchants slung out rugs and carts burdened with wares. Residents walked about with sacks full of goods, their pockets jingling with money. There were a couple of street performers, but what was most curious was a man standing on a box near the south end of the plaza. Kierli recognized him.

"...no leg for thirteen years! And look at me! Good as new!"

Kierli's ears perked and her feet took her toward the man. Felix followed, keeping close. A small crowd had gathered to listen. The man's clothes were fine and rich with color, his face shaven and washed. He stood atop an apple box, making himself a head above the crowd.

"Kierli deserves to be *free!*" He preached. "She came to the slums, healed us and gave us money, while *that* bastard—" he pointed at the castle "—has done nothin' for seven years! Set Kierli free! Or I say… Kierli for *Queen!*"

Half of the crowd clapped in agreement. One person piped up, "You don't know what she was locked up for! Maybe she —"

"No one knows!" Someone else shouted. "The King's not saying a word! Don't we deserve the truth?"

More claps among the crowd. The man standing on the apple box held out his hands for silence. "Here's somethin' I know: I've been missing a leg for thirteen years since a horse stomped it, but Captain Kierli used her magic to fix me up good as new. *And* she tossed me enough money to feed my family for weeks! Now if that isn't someone who lives to serve the people, I don't know what is! Kierli for Queen!"

"Kierli for Queen!" The crowd responded, following rousing applause.

"Brothers and sisters, please consider what you're saying!"

The voice was accompanied by flowing orange robes— Patriarch Willows, the Patriarch of the Lower City Cathedral. As he walked by, many people nodded respectfully, but he was also met with scowls and scoffs.

Patriarch Willows raised his hands and tried to muster the strongest voice he could. "The Sacred Dragon instituted the system of Foreordination over two thousand years ago, and since then, it's protected us from corrupt people that aspire for power!"

"What about Barnabas?" someone shouted. Many in the crowd applauded in agreement.

"Yes, at times corruption has slipped through the cracks," Patriarch Willows continued. "It is not a perfect system, but it is nonetheless what the Dragon has given us. Do you consider yourself wiser than the Sacred Dragon? Do not be so easily deceived! The Sacred Dragon knows the purity of each spirit. If Captain Kierli was put away, King Jason surely had a reason for it!"

His remarks were met with boos and hisses from many, while others applauded him and patted him on the back. The man up on the apple box shook his head and started a chant while Patriarch Willows shuffled away.

"Kierli for Queen! Kierli for Queen!"

At the edge of the crowd, Kierli watched Patriarch Willows shuffle along with disdain. Felix leaned toward her and said, "Look at that. Not only are they demanding a pardon, they're demanding that you're instated as *Queen*. Imagine that."

Kierli's eyes flashed. "Yes. Imagine that."

17

THE EPIPHANY

"How are you feeling about last night?"

"Fine."

"Master Ferribolt was pretty blunt. Are you sure you're okay?"

"I said I'm fine."

Tarren stood a little more rigid today. Jason sat in his throne with his head propped on his fist, looking up at his friend. Meanwhile, Tarren kept his face forward, avoiding eye contact.

"He had a similar conversation with me during the Ash War," Jason said. "I hated it at the time, but it turned out to be good advice. He's just trying to help."

Tarren still didn't look at him. "The jeweler should be here by now. What's taking him so long?"

Jason exhaled and shook his head.

Minutes later, three knocks came to the castle doors. The soldiers pulled them open and in came a wispy old man with a button-up vest and a large gray mustache. His feet moved like long, spindly scissors as he made his way to the throne platform. Then he put his hands to his hips and gave a generous bow.

"Your Highness. Mister Advisor. Please forgive my tardiness."

"Mister Jahki, thank you for lending your expertise this morning."

"Certainly. I take it, you have the specimens?"

From his pocket, Tarren procured two Bars—one officially minted, and the other reportedly from Kierli's stash. He handed them to Jahki, and he held each one in a different hand, his face twisting thoughtfully.

"Right away, I can tell there's a weight difference," the jeweler said. "This one is lighter."

"That's the Kierli sample," Tarren said.

Jahki held both of them up. "They look remarkably similar. I can see how the common eye would pass it for the real thing."

He extracted a magnifying lens from his pocket. The glass against his eye made it comically large. After scanning its surface for a thoughtful moment, he hummed. "Yes. This is made of iron, not gold. There are small pocks across its surface —too fine to tell with the naked eye. But this is clearly a counterfeit."

"There we have it," Jason said. "What do we do about it? How can we get these off the streets?"

"If I may be so bold, Your Highness," Jahki handed the pieces to Tarren. "I do not believe you can. It's clear this is iron instead of gold, but it's been magically altered somehow. The similarities are very close. You would have to track down every piece in the kingdom and have experts such as myself analyze each one. It's too great a task."

Jason deflated and stole a glance at Tarren. The Advisor nodded in agreement.

"Very well then," Jason resigned. "Thank you, Mister Jahki. You may go."

Jahki bowed and exited the great hall. After the doors opened and shut, Jason rubbed his face in his hands. "She's good. Really good." He turned to his friend. "Are you ready for our exercises this morning?"

"I'll give you a day off," Tarren said. "I'm sure you're tired from last night."

"No, I'll be okay."

Tarren smirked. "Alright then. If you insist on some punishment."

He took Jason to the back courtyard and put him through several rounds of sparring. Tarren, of course, beat him every time. As the hour progressed, Jason became more and more sweaty, panting like a dog on a hot summer day. Tarren, however, was infuriatingly comfortable as always. After their last session, Jason found himself once again on his back, bleary eyed, blinking up at the sky. Tarren sighed and holstered his wooden daggers. "Alis should be here soon. I'll give you a little bit of a break before she shows up."

Jason painfully pushed himself into a sitting position. "Thanks, I guess."

"Besides," Tarren said. "I have a technique I want to keep meditating on before I go to Lunli Village. I know I was planning on going in a couple weeks, but I decided to go tomorrow. I think I'm nearly ready."

"That's alright. I really hope this is the one. I'd love to see her come home with you. Be safe on your trip, okay?"

Tarren smiled and gave a little bow, then strode toward the castle and disappeared through a door.

Back in the sparring area, Jason caught his breath and got on his feet, pacing absentmindedly. His thoughts drifted to Kierli and his visions. Destruction. Finding her. As his stare floated along the courtyard, he spotted the rack of practice weapons that hung at the circle's edge. There was still a staff hanging on it—the staff that Saryan used to practice with before she got pregnant.

Jason eyed it for a good while before he approached it. He picked it off the rack, holding it firmly in his hands. He spaced his grip apart, trying to remember where she would have put her hands. Then maybe it would be like his hand touching hers. Just a little.

A sigh. His shoulders sagged and he placed the staff back on the rack.

"I thought you used a sword?"

Alis's voice was so close it made Jason yelp. There weren't any footsteps that crept up. She was just instantly upon him, right over his shoulder.

"You and Master Ferribolt!" Jason gasped.

Alis blinked curiously.

"He likes to startle people like that, too. It's his idea of fun."

"It *is* fun." Her eyes sparkled.

"Maybe to you," Jason said as his heart rate started to settle. "Good morning, Alis."

"Good morning, Your Majesty! How have you been doing with my most recent assignment?"

"Fine. I've been looking for chances to serve just like you asked. I helped Tarren organize some of the books in the library yesterday. And I helped the royal chef prepare one of our meals—he seemed pretty surprised when I offered. As for hobbies, my mother suggested knitting, but that doesn't sound interesting to me. Some guards recommended hunting, but I don't like killing things." He stopped. "If you don't mind, I have other things I'd like to ask you. I feel like the Sacred Dragon has been keeping instruction from me."

"Oh?"

Jason went on to explain his recent visions and his answers after he prayed to the Sacred Dragon. All the while, Alis listened carefully.

"So what's bothering you," Alis clarified, "is that you've had so much weighing on your heart lately, and the Sacred Dragon hasn't been giving you direct orders."

"Exactly. I've just been told to trust my instincts."

"My, that's a great honor."

Jason scrunched his eyebrows. "An honor?"

"Yes, why wouldn't it be? To know the Sacred Dragon trusts your judgment enough to leave you to your own devices! What a blessing! Besides, did you expect to be commanded in all things all the time?"

Jason didn't answer right away, but put his hands in his pockets. "When you say it like that, it does sound a little silly."

Alis grinned. "I'm not Foreordained to this position. You have a special link to the Holy Dragon that I could never have. But from my limited perspective, it seems like it would be a great gift for the Sacred Dragon to tell you to trust your instincts." She paused. "What do your instincts tell you?"

Jason was quiet. "...that Kierli could destroy Nezmyth."

"And what do your instincts say about stopping her?"

Jason was quiet again, let the moment hang, but at length shook his head. "I'm still not sure."

"Then I believe the natural path is to keep going until you do," Alis said. "You don't need me to remind you of this, but our path isn't often clear. Sometimes you must walk through the fog before you can see the sun." She smiled. "Let's meditate for a bit, then we'll begin."

* * * * *

Tarren's eyes scanned every corner of the Wilted Rose as he passed through the door. The chatter and noise were all the same—people from every corner of Nezmyth weaving tales and bragging about recent exploits over pints of mead. He kept gazing through the crowd, searching for the dark hair and blue eyes. No luck. His head swiveled all around even as he made it up to the bar.

"Evening, Advisor," Gus said. "Sorry, haven't seen her at all since the other day."

"That's okay."

"The usual?"

"Please."

The barkeep poured him a tall pint of guabo juice and set the tankard down in front of him. Tarren pulled it to his lips and drank from it conservatively. He stole a few more glances over his shoulder. No sign of her. Occasionally he would make eye contact with a commoner and they would raise their drink to him. He would raise his drink back politely.

Until there was one man not far away from the bar. As soon as Tarren looked at him, he bristled—a wide man with hairy arms and a big, round nose. Tarren tried to smile, but the man frowned deeper. He pushed his seat out from under him and lumbered over to the Advisor. Half of the tavern stopped and watched.

The citizen's eyes became slits as he got closer. Tarren's face grew hard and he put his hand on his dagger.

"I got sumfin' to ask you," the citizen said.

"You have my attention."

"Why you after her?"

Who, Kierli? Tarren paused, not sure what to say. He was about to respond when the man tugged at his sleeves. "Ya see this?"

"Your clothing?"

"Yeh," he said. "Bran' new. Haven't had a new shirt in years n' years." He scowled harder. "I'm from the slums. Down near the southern gate. Couldn'a got this if Cap'n Kierli didn' come down and give money t' people who need it."

Tarren nodded. "It looks good on you. I'm happy for you."

"She's doin' good things," the citizen said. "Helpin' people who need it. Healin' people. Why you got a problem with that?"

Truthfully, Tarren didn't have a problem with that. All he said was, "It's complicated."

The citizen blew a raspberry and shook his head in disappointment. "No s'not. Free the Captain. Free her." Then he lumbered away, disappearing into the crowd.

The tavern's buzz picked up again and Tarren sat still, recovering from the situation. His hand moved off his dagger. All the questions he had been suppressing were brought to the surface by a drunken slummie. Kierli really did seem like she was bent on helping people, even as a Dark Magic user. So was it truly possible to become the master of Dark Magic? That goes against everything he was taught. What if those things were just… wrong?

A feminine voice came to his left. "Wow. That was a little tense."

There she was, with her jet black hair and striking blue eyes, sitting just two seats away, cradling an identical tankard of guabo juice. Tarren couldn't help but smile.

"It's you!" he said. "I've been coming here every night looking for you!"

Evelyn's eyes sparkled. "Really? Why?"

"Just to talk to you again," he shrugged and went a little pink. "I really liked our conversation."

She smiled. "I liked it, too. How goes the hunt for the wanted fugitive?"

"Not great," Tarren said. "We have no idea where she is. And all the reports we've had of her are that she's healing people and giving away money the King *definitely* doesn't have. There have been some reported murders inside and outside the city, and I know some people suspect it's her, but we have no proof. It could just be coincidence."

"Doesn't make sense for someone to go around healing people and killing people at the same time."

"You're right. It doesn't." Tarren mused. "On another note, I'm getting ready to leave for Lunli Village tomorrow. I should be gone for several days."

"The crazy village? Why?"

Tarren prickled when she called it that, but he tried to act cordial anyway. "My mother lives there. She went insane in prison during Barnabas's reign. I've tried for years to cure her madness, but nothing's worked. I think I might have found something, though. A new spell. If I can do it right, I might just bring her back."

Evelyn's eyes grew soft. As Tarren talked more about his mother, she leaned in and put her hand on his forearm, stroking it with her thumb. Tarren sprouted into goosebumps.

"I'm so sorry. I shouldn't have said that," she said. "After all that, Barnabas became Chief Captain… that must have been difficult for you."

"It was for a time. But he helped us during the Ash War, and I'm grateful."

"Are you going to the village by yourself?"

"Just me and a small detail of guards."

"I envy you. I've never left the city. I've always wondered what it's like in the towns outside."

An idea struck Tarren. He smiled wide. "Well, perhaps this is a little forward, but… maybe you'd like to come with me? I don't know what you're doing for the next several days, but it would be nice to have some company not in uniform."

Evelyn's eyes brightened. "You mean it?"

"Of course."

"Then yes!"

* * * * *

The night was waning and the two moons hung heavy over Nezmyth. Jason's bedroom was empty.

In the north courtyard, the King ran barefoot under the moonlight, his feet clapping against the stone. Nightbane was slung over his back and sweat dripped down his whole body. The patrolling guards nodded at him as he went by, huffing and puffing and swinging his arms.

Things that make me happy… become my own person… trust my instincts…

Finally, he slowed to a stop and put his hands on his knees, gasping for air. But he didn't allow himself to rest for too long. He jogged over to the sparring area and slipped Nightbane out of its sheath. As he swung it around, he muttered Ancient Nezmythian. Words of fire. Words of ice. Words of speed, light, and strength.

Nightbane caught fire as he swung it around. Snowflakes sparkled between his fingers and he built towers of ice, only to cut them down with his burning steel. He somersaulted through the air, occasionally two or three times as the magic moved through his body, making him more agile and precise. At length, the magic and the physical exertion wore him down, and he sat cross-legged in the middle of the combat arena, drenched in sweat.

All around, he was surrounded by segmented sections of foliage—fruit trees, shrubberies, flowers, all dancing and losing their resilience in the autumn chill. Jason drank in their colors with his eyes.

They're growing, just like we do, he thought. *Funny how life takes different forms.*

He pushed himself to his feet and forced himself to walk over to the nearest garden box. He cradled some of the flowers in his fingers, gently stroking the petals and leaves. So delicate. If he wanted to, he could squeeze the stem and pluck it right now. Cut it down. But why would he do that? Why end something so lovely?

Why is it so easy to take life, he thought. *But so difficult to nurture it?*

Then a thought struck him. A spark that shot between his ears and ignited his mind.

Dark Magic. It's fueled by death. That's the Guardian of the Night's power. And what of standard magic? That's reinforced by study, practice, and a spiritual connection. But what if there was more to it? If Dark Magic is powered by sowing death, is not standard magic powered by sowing life? By nurturing? By growing?

Jason stared at the flower, bending and swaying in the night air. The spark in his mind would not be denied. There had to be truth in it. He could ask Alis during his next lesson, but until then, his deepest feelings told him this was true.

A couple of guards were patrolling nearby. Both of them snapped to attention as Jason called to them.

"Guards! When the morning comes, give a message to the courtyard gardener. Tell him I want a dozen plants taken up to my quarters as soon as possible, and send him up so he can teach me how to take care of them. Do you understand?"

The guards looked at each other, then the King. "Uh—yes, Your Majesty!"

"Good. I'm going to bed. Carry on."

18

THE CHASM

Kierli let her face revert back to normal as soon as she returned to the cellar. Felix was reading a book by lamplight, waiting for her. He licked his thumb before turning another page. "How did your date go?"

"He wishes it was a date," she rolled her eyes. "But very well. I'm going with him to Lunli Village tomorrow."

Felix looked up. "Excuse me?"

"I have plans. Plans that will change the course of our mission. But if I'm going to be in a carriage with him for a couple days, I need to fully replenish my magic."

"How?"

Kierli folded her arms and stared at her feet as she paced. "I've felt something beckoning me back to the prison—a voice. It's happened several times. The Vault of the Damned... I think there's something there. Something waiting for me. We have to go there."

Felix snapped his book shut. "Go back to the place you were thrown into? That's madness. They'll arrest you as soon as they spot you."

"Which is why having you is so helpful."

"I suppose I'll have to finish this later. It was just getting to a good part." He patted the book. "And how do we plan on getting in and out of the Vault without winding up captured or killed? You're the most wanted person in Nezmyth."

"Leave it to me."

"I'm trusting you."

"As you should. Put your cloak on."

Felix followed orders. They both donned on their cloaks and put the hoods over their faces. Kierli checked the alley outside the cellar. All clear. Then they moved like darts through the night, dashing between buildings and slipping through the shadows. Throughout the entire city, more soldiers were out on patrol than usual. It didn't matter. Kierli and Felix evaded all of them without a problem. They made it all the way to the western gates without turning any heads. Kierli's magic muffling their footsteps definitely helped.

When they arrived at the gates, there were more guards than a dozen guards. They checked every carriage that tottered into the city, holding torches to their faces and inspecting every inch of cargo. Kierli frowned at the sight and turned to Felix. After some brief deliberation, they both agreed that they should transport to the prison. Kierli hated using that much magic at a time like this, but the option was clear. The western gates were too secure to sneak over. They held hands, she focused on the bottom of the prison, and they both disappeared in a flash of purple smoke.

The darkness carried them, then they materialized at the bottom of the pit. Part of them hoped it wouldn't be so guarded, but it was even worse than expected. Eight fully-armed guards were waiting in the pit—strong, tall, armed, and alert.

One of them shouted, "*It's them!*"

Kierli and Felix both tore their weapons from their sheaths. Kierli brandished a dagger and shortsword. Felix held a longsword with both hands. In seconds, they were completely surrounded. These weren't average soldiers, either—the decorations on their uniforms showed that these were upper ranked. The kind of soldiers that were on their way to becoming Captains. They wouldn't be easy.

"Put the weapons down, you two!" One shouted.

"No," Kierli sneered.

"You're wanted dead or alive! Don't force our hand!"

Kierli's eyes became slits. Eight people… it would take plenty of magic to bring them down, but conversely, eight people is a lot of fuel. Perfect for the upcoming journey. Just the thought of that much in her reservoir made her teeth chatter.

Yes, she thought. *Attack. I dare you.*

"Put the weapons down!" Another soldier shouted.

"Make me," Kierli said.

The soldiers converged.

The prison's depths filled with the singing of swords. Kierli swiped, dodged, and deflected as five soldiers descended on her. Likewise, Felix swerved around all the blows that were dealt. Two Captains, fighting a small horde of rising underlings.

Kierli slashed her dagger and got one soldier in the neck, spraying blood onto her hand. With the move, she exposed herself. Another soldier swiped at her leg, cutting her deep. Kierli cried out as she clutched her leg, but let go long enough to get a swing in. She caught the soldier in the throat.

Felix managed to kill two soldiers. His move on the first one was agile and swift, but the second one came after he pierced the soldier in the arm. She dropped her spear and clutched her wound, baring her teeth and groaning. That's when Felix swung and bashed her head with his sword's pommel.

One of the soldiers yelled to another. "Go! Alert the others!"

Another soldier turned tail and ran, sprinting up the curving slope that led to the surface. Kierli killed a soldier with a stab in the back, letting their body topple to the ground. Then she set her eyes on the escaping one. She spoke lowly to Felix. "I don't have any long range weapons."

"Nor do I."

Kierli thought about it, watching the soldier run. Throughout the fight, she felt her power multiply with every death. There was definitely enough within her. She reached out her hand. Her fingers glowed purple. The veins in her forearm popped. Then, she quickly clenched her hand in a fist. Nearly one hundred yards away, the soldier's neck cricked sideways, and she fell in a heap on the ascending path.

Felix watched the soldier collapse, feeling sick. As he looked around, eight dead soldiers were littered around their feet. His face wrinkled. "This isn't going to help you."

"They attacked first," Kierli replied. "We only killed in self defense."

"That doesn't matter. We killed *eight* soldiers," He put his hand on the forehead of another soldier, feeling for warmth. "Eight Nezmythian families will mourn tonight."

Kierli ignored him. All those deaths had filled that reservoir even more than she was used to and it made everything inside her swell. And like always, she heard the voice.

"*My child...*"

There it was—the pull toward the Vault. But there was something new here. A low pulsing... oscillating beats that rose up from the ground and filled her chest. Vibrating. Lurching. Calling.

She turned to Felix. "Do you feel that?"

"Feel what?" Felix frowned.

Her feet carried her toward the Vault, almost without command. As she moved closer, it became stronger. When she was nearly to the door, she found that the pull wasn't coming from the Vault itself, but from somewhere else.

She bent down and put her hand on the ground. Yes. She could feel it. It wasn't coming from the Vault... it was coming from underneath.

Kierli knelt down and put both hands on the stone. Using her magic, she could feel an emptiness beneath it. Something hollow. She closed her eyes tightly and focused energy into her hands, pushing. Magic seeped out of her fingertips and into the stone. The stones began to rumble. The mortar between them cracked. She sank deeper into the ground as Felix watched with terrible apprehension. Lower and lower she went until finally, the ground around her collapsed.

In a shower of dirt and stone, Kierli landed in the mouth of a long tunnel just large enough to stand in. She could touch the wall on either side of her—it was so narrow. But all around her feet, gems of green and purple glowed a ghoulish hue, casting dim light on the path before her.

"Kierli!" Felix shouted from above. "Kierli, what is this?"

The pounding in her chest was getting harder—the exciting, frightening force inside growing more intense. She shook her head. "I don't know... but I will soon."

She started on the path. It sloped downward, going deeper into the earth. The gems lit the way, and after a while, the opening to the tunnel disappeared behind her. The force in her chest became stronger. It surged through her heart, turning it into a war drum. It was like the very air down here sparkled with something otherworldly. It made it easy to ignore how damp and muggy each breath was.

The path came to an end, opening into something large. She lifted her weapons that were still stained with blood. Her feet moved slower. She almost came to a complete stop, but when she entered the room, she gasped.

It was a cavern filled with sparkling minerals like the ones that illuminated her path. But these were massive—gems as large as bodies, glowing their pale purples and greens and dancing in their own light. They dangled from the ceiling like great fangs, and paved the ground before her like multicolored cobblestone. Eerie, but magnificent. Nothing man could ever conceive.

In the middle of the cavern, a large pool of stagnant, black water reflected the colors of the gems. Kierli started toward it, keeping her wits about her. But the feeling in her chest had spread to her entire body. The very air was sweet. She drank it in, but remained tense.

Now, the voice was no longer a whisper in her ear, but echoed all around. "*Welcome, my daughter.*"

Kierli tightened. She waited, then said. "Who are you?"

"*I am the master of this world,*" the voice said. "*Its true guardian and keeper.*"

Kierli hesitated to say it, but she chanced it.

"The Guardian of the Night," she scowled. "That's who you are, aren't you? The one who the Sacred Dragon cast away from Paradise when the world was created."

"*There is no Guardian of the Night,*" the voice replied coolly. "*It is a farce. A lie told for centuries. My power far exceeds that of the Dragon's.*"

Kierli stayed quiet, processing. Could that be true? She said, "So why are you in this place?"

"*It is my refuge. A place of rest. For thousands of years, I have waited for one such as you. You were destined to come, and I am grateful.*"

"Is that why you gave me these visions? To bring me here?"

"*Yes, my child. Step closer.*"

The water. Cautiously, Kierli trudged forward, still holding her weapons high. As she arrived at the pool, she gazed down at the water's surface, still and shiny as glass.

"*Come. Dip your feet. Feel what lies in store for you.*"

Kierli squinted. "Why should I trust you?"

A sudden breeze rushed from the pool. And on it, a sparkling sensation that danced all over Kierli's face and arms. She took a deep breath, soaking it in. It felt a lot like the pleasure she experienced when she practiced magic. She let out a shaky, sugary breath.

"*Because you and I are one,*" the voice said. "*Come. Step into the pool. You shall not be harmed.*"

She hesitated. Even debated. But not for long. She inched forward, stepping in the water just enough for the liquid to lap up on the edges of her boots. But it was enough. The effect was immediate. The power shot up from the soles of her feet to the tip of her head, crashing through her. The hairs on her neck stood up and she felt like she could shoot lightning from her fingers. It even made her smile. Finally, she stepped out, grinning wide.

"*I know your heart,*" the voice said. "*I have seen your suffering—those who have sought to suppress you. They are fearful. They are small. They do not deserve to rule. We can bring justice upon them.*"

Kierli trudged through the dirt, her face down, thinking. She said, "Why are you helping me? What do you get from all this?"

"*My child, remember, I am the true master of this world. After the Dragon stole this world from me so long ago, the time has come to reclaim my rightful stewardship. And I select you as my denizen.*" It paused, and you could hear a smile on it. "*Return when you desire. I will give you further knowledge and power. Until then, I shall watch you and guard you.*"

Kierli rubbed her arm, still feeling the sparkles. And the way it filled her body with energy! She had never felt her reservoir so full. She would be able to hide her identity for days. Even if she didn't fully trust this voice yet, she couldn't deny the awesome force it put inside her.

She grinned and said, "I will."

"*Good,*" the voice said. "*You may conceal the entrance to this place. Your eyes have beheld it. Call for me when you wish to return.*"

Kierli didn't say anything else. She turned and marched back up the tunnel, letting the twinkling gems guide her. At length, she arrived at the hole she created in the prison floor. She bent her legs and sprang through the opening. When she emerged, she found that Felix had lined up the bodies, placed their hands on their hearts, and closed their eyes. Prepared for a soldier's burial. Kierli turned to the hole, holding her hands over them.

With loud crackles and snaps, the stones and mortar leapt into place as if nothing happened.

Looking on, Felix frowned. "What was that? Where did you go?"

Kierli marched up to him and smirked. "I'll tell you later. We're done here."

"Kierli," Felix bristled and stepped forward. "I just killed three soldiers for you tonight. This is not what I had in mind when I chose to follow you. And *that*." He pointed to the hole. "I felt something when you opened up that hole. I didn't like it. What was down there?"

Kierli rolled her eyes. "You're being a child. I said I'd tell you later. Are you ready to go or not?"

Felix thought about it and said, "I don't think I am."

"Felix," Kierli's face grew hot. "I don't need this right now. They attacked *us*, remember? If you're with me, you're with me. If you're not, you're against me. You were ready to follow me anywhere just yesterday. If you're having second thoughts, you better say something."

Felix looked over his shoulder. Eight bodies. And for what? He didn't even know. A sight trickled from his lips.

"Patriarch Willows did say that good people can be fooled by those aspiring for power. Maybe that's exactly what you're doing. Or maybe I'm wrong. Who's to know? Just you, I suppose."

Tense, deafening silence. Then Felix lunged, throwing a barrage of jerokis. Kierli dodged all of them, bending and spinning. She was upon Felix before he could react—one hand was on his throat, the other hand around a dagger.

Felix gasped horribly as Kierli slammed the dagger into his chest. His eyelids slackened and his last breath spilled from his lips. Kierli withdrew her dagger as his bloody body slumped to the ground.

She flicked blood off the blade and thought, *I can't leave his body. People will know I killed him.*

She held out her hand. Her fingers glowed purple. Then Felix's body disintegrated in a hiss of black and purple flakes. His blood, his flesh, his clothes all evaporated into the air. Nothing of his body remained. And with that, Kierli disappeared in a puff of purple smoke.

What she didn't know was that one of the soldiers was alive. Her hand was pressed to her wound, stealthily trickling healing magic into her side to be sure she didn't bleed out. While laying down, she kept her eyes nearly closed, but managed to see the whole thing. After Felix was killed Kierli disappeared, she forced herself to stand.

* * * * *

A chilling bolt snatched Master Ferribolt from his sleep. Rarely had he felt a premonition this aggressively dire. His spirit told him exactly what and where, but there was no time to lose.

His hand slammed on the nightstand, feeling around for his glasses. He shoved them on his face, smudged and dusty. The last thing was his slippers. He threw them on, then he vanished from his bedroom.

The chill of the prison was brisk on his ill-prepared body. His slippers shuffled against the stone not far from the Vault of the Damned. As he rubbed his eyes and looked all around, his mouth went dry and his chest tightened.

Seven soldiers, lying dead in neat rows. The ground stained with blood. But there was one who was alive, struggling to stand, pushing healing magic to her side. Master Ferribolt scurried over and put his hand against the wound. He muttered some Ancient Nezmythian, focused his energy, and the wound mended. The soldier coughed and sputtered as she took her first steady breath. Master Ferribolt's eyes were wild.

"What happened?" he asked. "Was it Kierli?"

"Yes, Master," the soldier said. "Her and Felix. They killed all of these, then Kierli went underground over there. When she came up, she killed Felix, burned up his body, and disappeared."

Master Ferribolt turned white. *Went underground? Here?* "You're sure it was Kierli who did it? You're certain it was her?"

"Yes, Master. No mistake."

Master Ferribolt waddled to the mouth of the Vault, his heart racing. He slapped his hands on the door, frantically spoke more Ancient Nezmythian, and the door flew open on screeching hinges. He flew down the stairs as quickly as his portly body would take him. When he reached the empty ground level, he threw fire into the room's torch, then he knelt down, his hands on the floor, feeling.

He prayed it wasn't true. Prayed it was false. But the magic inside the Vault enhanced his senses. He could feel the power that was sealed underneath this place—the power that had slept for thousands of years.

It was stirring. Growing.

Master Ferribolt shot to his feet, his hands shaking. "Dragon help us."

19
THE EXCURSION

Captain Barnabas sat on a chair by a mound of dirt under the oak tree. The chair creaked a little bit as he shifted, holding a plate in one hand and a fork in the other. His breakfast consisted of eggs, some bread, and a few strips of bacon. It wasn't long ago that he could have enjoyed this meal with Nartikis, talking with him in the depths of the prison. But now he laid beside him, still as the earth. And that would have to be sufficient.

The leaves around Kyleth Pond were getting brighter and warmer. The colors didn't do anything to arouse his senses after the night he had. Hours ago, two soldiers came pounding on his door, alerting him of what happened at the prison. Eight soldiers dead, including Captain Felix of Widow's Rest, but his body was nowhere to be found. One surviving soldier claimed she saw it burning up, citing Kierli as the assailant.

He was also told there were other matters that needed to be discussed at the castle first thing in the morning. For that reason, Barnabas got up earlier than usual to make breakfast.

When his plate was clean, he took it into the house. He didn't bother to take the chair with him—he knew he would just bring it back out the next morning. For the next few minutes, he got his armor strapped on. Meanwhile, Artemis slept on his perch not far away, his chest rising and falling as his head rested down his front. As soon as Barnabas was fully dressed and marching for the door, Artemis awoke. The hawk shook his feathered body and flapped his wings a little. Without a single command, Artemis hopped onto Barnabas's shoulder as he strode through the door and locked it shut.

By the next hour, Barnabas was at the castle gates. Artemis swooped into the air and perched somewhere on the castle's roof. The doors opened and down the red carpet he went. He didn't stop at the throne dais—no one was there. He went through a door at the end of the great hall, down a corridor, down some stairs, and arrived at the Oracle Stone room.

The others were already waiting for him—Master Ferribolt, King Jason, and Tarren, all displaying varying levels of seriousness. Barnabas closed the door behind him.

Master Ferribolt was the first to speak.

"Gentlemen," he said, "the seriousness of what I'm about to tell you cannot be overstated. The hunt for Kierli has just taken a drastic turn."

"I'll say," Jason said darkly. "I heard of the murdered soldiers at the prison."

"It goes deeper than that," Master Ferribolt said. "She's awakened a power that's remained dormant for thousands of years. A power that lies directly below the prison."

"Below the prison?" Tarren frowned.

Master Ferribolt nodded. "You understand that Grace Mountain is one of the most sacred places in the kingdom? A place touched by holiness and light so we can gain a better understanding of the Dragon's wishes?"

"Of course."

"As you know, everything the Guardian of the Night does mirrors the Sacred Dragon in an evil way." Master Ferribolt began pacing the room. "Since there is a place where we can communicate with the Sacred Dragon, there is also a place where we can communicate with the Guardian of the Night. It's called the Chasm, and it's directly below Nezmyth City Prison."

The air suddenly felt heavier. Master Ferribolt continued:

"The area below the Vault of the Damned was made as a plug to the Chasm's influence at the end of the Dark Era two thousand years ago. It took Nezmyth's mightiest magicians to construct and enchant it. When the prison was built not long after, they built the Vault of the Damned on top of that plug due to the fierce magical energy it exuded—they knew it would be a place where no one could practice *Tepnoh Edomah* even if they tried. However, it looks as though Kierli found an alternate entrance to the Chasm. One of the soldiers saw her leaving it just last night."

Silence. Jason drummed his fingers on his arms. "So what does this mean?"

"It means Kierli could be drastically more dangerous than originally anticipated," Master Ferribolt. "If she's had this chance to commune with the Guardian of the Night... who knows what kind of power she's capable of?"

Jason began pacing up and down the room. *Instincts, instincts, instincts...* he turned to Barnabas. "Have the soldiers found any leads on where she might be hiding?"

Barnabas clenched his teeth and shook his head.

"Then it seems like there's only once sensible thing to do," Jason stood up straight. "I'm going to Grace Mountain. If Kierli has communed with the Guardian of the Night, I'm going to commune with the Sacred Dragon. If I learned anything from the Ash War, it's that our good needs to be stronger than her evil. And I intend to become such. Anyone who wishes to come with me is welcome to join."

Master Ferribolt and Barnabas both volunteered.

Tarren said, "I'd love to, my friend, but the caravan for Lunli Village is leaving this morning. I'll have to postpone my visit until I return."

Jason nodded. "I understand. Let's go, everyone. No time to lose."

They all left the room and made their way back to the great hall. As they went, Jason and Tarren walked side by side. Something stirred inside Jason as they went—a foreboding feeling in the pit of his stomach that churned just faintly enough to notice. His face pressed into a frown. Next to him, Tarren walked with purpose, his long strides faster than Jason's. They were barely out of earshot from Master Ferribolt and Barnabas, so Jason turned to his friend.

"Tarren…" he said. "I have a feeling about your trip to Lunli Village. Something about it doesn't sit well with me."

Tarren pointed his eyebrows and looked at him. "What do you mean?"

"I don't know. Just an uneasy feeling. In light of what's happened, maybe it would be prudent for you to postpone your trip. Come with us to Grace Mountain instead."

Tarren was quiet for a moment. By now, they were entering the great hall. Barnabas ordered some soldiers to prepare a coach for the three of them. As they reached the throne dais, Tarren turned and folded his arms, thinking. He was eager to heal his mother, but he was also eager to spend some alone time with Evelyn. It would be rude to cancel the trip when Evelyn was so excited to go.

"Jason," he said. "I don't think my being here will affect what answers you'll receive on Grace Mountain. This may be the time that I *actually* bring my mother home. Besides, you know I'll only be gone a few days."

The uneasy feeling inside Jason didn't subside. "Tarren, I love you. You're like my brother. And I won't force you… but it would do my heart good if you stayed."

Tarren's face softened and he placed a strong hand on Jason's shoulder. "You've been under so much pressure for weeks. And now all of this with Captain Kierli. We live in a wild and dangerous time. But I don't have any of the same foreboding feelings as you do. Things will be okay, you'll see. I'll be back before you know it."

Jason took a deep breath and tried to smile. "Alright then. Well, send a hawk when you arrive. Be safe and stay on your guard."

Tarren winked and ruffled Jason's hair. Jason smiled and tried to smooth it back out.

Finally, the coach was ready and the three filed inside. On the south castle grounds, Tarren's carriage was waiting for him, along with some other supplies for the trip. The coach for Grace Mountain wasted no time. The rider snapped the reins and made its way eastward through the city.

It wasn't long after that Tarren's caravan left. It snaked its way through town, heading for the south gate. But as it passed through the Southern Market Street, the coach stopped so it could pick up a passenger—a pretty dark haired woman with steely blue eyes.

Tarren threw open the door and Evelyn climbed in. Beaming, he said, "Are you ready?"

"Am I ever!" She said brightly. "Wow… this carriage is so fancy!"

"Make yourself comfortable."

She could have sat across from him—the bench seat was padded and certainly gave her more space. But instead, she sat right next to Tarren, nuzzling into his side and holding his arm. It made his cheeks burn pink.

Miles away, the others arrived at the foot of Grace Mountain. Directly to their left, the Nezmyth City Cemetery sprawled with lush green grass dotted with gravestones. As they climbed out, Jason couldn't help but stare. The others noticed and kept their silence. Then Jason looked over his shoulder and said, "Would you two mind if I paid a visit before we ascend? I won't be long."

Barnabas and Master Ferribolt nodded. As Jason entered the gates to the cemetery, he listened to his feet clomp along the stone pathway. It wasn't far inside the gates. Just a brief walk.

Jason arrived at the headstone and put his hand on Nightbane. There it was, freshly engraved. A large stone ornamented with flowers, mountains, and streams. And her name:

SARYAN, QUEEN OF NEZMYTH
WIFE TO JASON, KING OF NEZMYTH
DAUGHTER TO GARRIT, CHIEF CAPTAIN
DAUGHTER TO MELODY

The other grave was right next to her, small enough to carry in Jason's arms. Besides the name, this headstone had a single flower engraved on it—a budding one, very small and delicate.

PRINCE GARRIT
SON OF KING JASON AND QUEEN SARYAN

Jason let out a deep sigh. Had it really been a month since they left this world? It felt like a lifetime. And all the while, he stayed here, simply existing. He stooped down and put his hands on the headstone. Its surface was cold.

"So much has happened since you left," he whispered. "I really wish you were here to help me through it. Having our friends for support is good, but it's not the same. I miss your strength. Your warmth." He paused. "Rest well and wait for me."

He kissed the surface of the headstone, imagining her forehead. But it wasn't the same—too cold and rough. Then he knelt down and stroked Prince Garrit's grave. His little boy. He swallowed and let out a huff before he put his hands in his pockets and retreated down the path.

When Jason reunited with Barnabas and Master Ferribolt, they walked up the face of Grace Mountain. There wasn't much to say. Master Ferribolt put his hand on Jason's shoulder and gave it a fatherly squeeze, which the King appreciated. But the climb up Grace Mountain was arduous. Jason didn't remember it being so exhausting. Inwardly, he was grateful that Tarren had forced him to exercise so much lately.

The sun had fully risen over the Eastern Mountains and was bathing the valley in warm light. As Jason gazed to the west, he breathed deep. Home. Then the memories of his recent visions intruded his thoughts. Destruction. Black clouds. Tremors. The castle reduced to rubble. All of it made him shudder.

The three tread across the clean, chiseled stone and made their way to the Dragon statue. A few other people were here paying their respects to the Sacred Dragon, but when they noticed the three approaching, they bowed respectfully and walked away. They knew that whatever the King had to ask had to be more important.

Jason and Barnabas unsheathed their swords, laying them on the ground. Master Ferribolt knelt with both knees, chin down, breathing deep. Jason and Barnabas fell to one knee, facing the Dragon statue. Jason offered the prayer:

"Sacred Dragon, a dire threat is rising among us. We've learned terrible, horrifying news of Kierli's exploits. What is to be done? If she's awakened this force of evil... how do we combat it? How do we prepare?" Jason paused. "I fear for Nezmyth, O Sacred One. How can our good become stronger than the evil we face?"

The others were quiet as Jason prayed aloud. When Jason was done, he stayed still for a long time, listening. He expected King Thomas to suddenly appear and impart wisdom—grant him an extra nugget of truth since they sojourned to Grace Mountain. But what he got was much different.

A voice. Tender and delicate, yet infinite. Like the rushing of great waters or the rumbling of armies. It filled Jason's mind and heart and echoed through his bones. It said:

"You have been told before. Seek light and trust your heart."

Jason gasped and stood up. He had never felt anything like that. He flipped around to face the others. They were both still kneeling.

"What? What is it?" Barnabas said.

Jason blinked. "I heard a voice."

Master Ferribolt advanced on Jason. He put his hands firmly on Jason's shoulders, his eyes intense. "What was it like? Describe the feeling."

"It was small," Jason said, "yet colossal. Like standing under a waterfall but floating through the air. I don't know how else to describe it."

Master Ferribolt nodded, his gray eyes flashing and a smile spreading across his face. "You've been touched, my young friend. It's not often that anyone can hear the voice of the Dragon itself. That happens maybe once or twice in a lifetime."

Jason's eyes grew. "That was the Sacred Dragon itself speaking to me?"

Now Barnabas was on his feet. "What did It say?"

Jason shrugged. "Seek light and trust my heart. The same thing I've been told."

"Then our course of action remains the same," Master Ferribolt said. "We follow your lead. It appears as though the Sacred Dragon has put Its complete trust in you, Your Highness. I can't think of a higher honor."

Maybe he should have felt better about it, but it gave Jason no comfort. He kept thinking about the times during the Ash War where his own judgment led to the deaths of others. He swallowed. "What if I do something wrong?"

"The Sacred Dragon gave you its blessing, Your Highness," Barnabas said. "How can we fail?"

Jason couldn't smile.

20
THE VILLAGE

It was the same news as usual. No sign of her. Soldiers were still patrolling the city up and down. Yorn knew she was out there somewhere—or at least, that Evelyn was out there somewhere. He had thought about asking soldiers to keep a lookout for a woman with jet black hair and blue eyes, but how much less specific could you get when describing a woman in Nezmyth City?

Besides, Kierli could be innocent. He heard of her exploits in the slums and the rumors that trickled up from Widow's Rest. She hadn't hurt anyone. As a matter of fact, she healed people and gave money to the poor. What was wrong with that? He could sympathize with the "Kierli for Queen" chants he heard in Center Court every day.

But some things still didn't make sense. Like her accusations of King Jason hoarding money. Jason was the *King*. If he wanted money, he could get it. He could instate a tax and no one would bat an eye. So why would he need to hoard?

Then there was the prison attack.

Yorn listened to the soldier's account from that evening and helped coordinate the burials for the murdered soldiers. The survivor swore it was Kierli who did it. But why? Why would Kierli murder her own people? Especially fellow soldiers?

Now, Yorn sat at the desk of his barrack, pinching a quill in his hand, ready to write letters to the soldiers' families and share his condolences. But he couldn't get his hand to move. The quill just hovered above the parchment, dripping ink.

Finally, he threw the quill back into its ink bottle and pushed the parchment aside. At the corner of his desk, there was another roll. Frowning, he snatched and unraveled it. The writing on the parchment was inconsistent—evidence of a constant starting and stopping over a long period of time.

To my dearest Kierli,

Words can't express how proud I am of what you've become. You've experienced more hardship than anyone I know. And through it all, you've used it to become one of Nezmyth's finest. For that, my admiration runs deep.

But I must finally speak my mind. I can keep it concealed no longer. My feelings for you extend beyond those of a friend or colleague. As I've served beside you these years, my heart has grown fond of you. I find that

He glared at the words. Were they too much? Were they enough? Or necessary? They were written to a woman that he didn't seem to understand anymore. A specter of who he used to know. It made him wonder if he ever really understood her at all.

She was healing people and giving money to the poor. She was also stripped of her position and accused of slaughtering soldiers.

So which Kierli was the real one?

He rolled the letter back up, tied it, and stood from his desk. Quickly, he strapped on his boots and stormed out of the barrack, headed for the foot of Upper City.

His armor clinked as he marched across the Northern Market Street. As he went, people hailed him and clapped for him from the storefronts and restaurants. They gave him cheers like "We know you'll find her!" and "Bring her justice!". But they didn't know what was stewing in his mind—the conflict, the confusion. That's one thing he never liked about serving in Upper City. These people were so disconnected. Their biggest concern was probably that Kierli would make the slummies their equals.

His feet took him to the grounds of a towering Cathedral close to the Northern Market Street, sandwiched between some magnificent brick buildings decorated with ivy and shrubbery. He found some solace that this one didn't look any different from the Cathedrals across Nezmyth—including the one in Port Gala where he grew up.

The grounds weren't crowded—just a few people walking through the gardens here and there. Yorn ignored most of them and went straight for the doors, which were opened wide. As soon as he stepped through, his footsteps reverberated off the stone walls and multicolored windows. Creaky, worn pews lined in two rows facing the back of the building. And in the back there was a podium, a wide pedestal with a triangle on the base, and a magnificent statue of the Sacred Dragon. Yorn fixed his gaze on that Dragon and took a deep breath.

There was only one other person in the entire Cathedral—a man in orange robes, kneeling in the middle of the pedestal, head bowed, muttering. Yorn opted not to disturb him. He slipped up to the front pew and sat at the end, lacing his hands together and staring between his knees.

Sacred Dragon, he prayed silently. *What is this business with Kierli? I don't know what to believe. She was always such a fine soldier and now I've been hearing things that… well, are they true? What can I believe?*

He looked back into the statue's eyes and they returned an inanimate stare. No feelings inside him. No sparks. Just silence.

He picked at a loose pant thread as he stewed over the issue. After a short wait, shuffling footsteps came up and a man sat next to him. It was the man in the orange robes that was praying earlier—a fellow with deep wrinkles and a hunched back, weighed down with age. His eyes were bright, though, which was amazing considering the pupils were nearly black.

"Captain," the man said.

"Patriarch Juun," Yorn replied.

"I imagined I would see you here before long," the Patriarch said. "It seems like we keep learning new things about the former Chief Captain. Much of it unsavory, if the rumors hold any weight."

"Yes."

"Tell me what's in your heart."

Yorn leaned back and folded his arms. "None of this sounds like her. I don't know if you've heard, but eight soldiers were killed at the prison. The survivor swears it was Kierli, but I can't imagine her ever killing anyone maliciously, especially *soldiers*." He paused. "It confuses me, Patriarch."

After a silent moment, Patriarch Junn said, "Sometimes people take us by surprise. And sometimes rumors are just that: rumors."

"But how can I know what's true?"

Patriarch Juun looked at him. "I saw you praying. Did your heart say anything afterward?"

Yorn shook his head.

"Then the answer is still preparing itself," Patriarch Junn said. "Your spirit is good, Yorn. The Dragon gives answers to those like you. It will come."

* * * * *

Halfway to Lunli Village, Evelyn fell asleep on Tarren's shoulder. The corners of his smile could have tickled his earlobes. He tried to be still as he propped a book in his lap and read from its contents. The smell of the tall field grass drifted into the carriage, making the moment even more pleasant.

The sun set almost an hour before they pulled into Lunli Village. Evelyn stirred awake and Tarren stretched his arms. Two crackling torches on the edge of town greeted them as the carriage pulled in. Evelyn's eyes peered out the windows as they moved along. The village didn't look entirely made of the insane. In fact, it had everything else a normal village had: farmers, blacksmiths, merchants. For the most part, everything about it seemed like an average poor village settled on the foot of a mountain. So what made this the destination for maddened people of Nezmyth?

She sat upright and rubbed her eyes. Tarren watched the townsmen through the windows as the carriage pulled through.

"So this is it?" Evelyn asked blearily. "Lunli Village?"

Tarren nodded absently.

The carriage continued to totter through town. A few pairs of soldiers stopped to shout "Hail!" at the Advisor's carriage, aside from "Dragon bless Advisor Tarren!" and "Hope it works this time!" he got from passing villagers.

Eventually, the carriage slowed to a stop. Tarren stood and stretched the best he could, then addressed Evelyn. "Time to get out. They don't allow carriages this far."

The carriage driver opened the door. As they filed out, Evelyn noticed the area ahead of them and her eyes grew wide. *This* is why the insane were kept here. Before them, an entire district of town was blocked by a tall wooden fence and sealed off with an iron gate. Four soldiers guarded that gate. There was one person by the gate, however, that clearly wasn't a soldier—a stout man with bags under his eyes and trousers that had trouble staying up. Tarren approached him, then nodded politely.

"Chief Marlo."

"Advisor Tarren. Good to see you." Chief Marlo raised a handkerchief to his mouth and coughed into it, then wiped his nose and cleared his throat. "We've been taking good care of her—or at least the best we can. Crops haven't been great this season."

"I'll see if we can reroute some of the donated crops in Nezmyth City here."

"That would be magnificent," Chief Marlo hiked up his pants under his round belly. "She's in the same place as always: the group house at the end of the street. Would you like some guards to escort you? Some of the more spirited residents are likely asleep by now, so they shouldn't give you trouble."

"No need. I think we'll be alright."

"Alright, then. I wish you the best of luck."

Chief Marlo motioned his hand and one of the soldiers unlocked the gate. Then as Tarren and Evelyn walked by, he tried to smile optimistically. Evelyn smiled in return. Something about her smile made him do a double take at her. Something about her felt… it was probably nothing. Evelyn returned to Tarren's side and they both trudged up the eastern street together. Behind them, the soldiers locked the gate shut again.

As their steps crunched on the dirt path, Evelyn surveyed the eastern neighborhood. It wasn't large—maybe a dozen small cabins not much different than the ones in Lower City. Tarren noticed her curiosity. "There's usually three or four people in every house," he said. "My mother lives in that one just over there."

"Do you ever get nervous before you see her again?"

"Every time," Tarren sighed. "I never know how she'll react. Sometimes she remembers me. Usually she doesn't."

Evelyn didn't know how to respond to this, so she stayed quiet. Tarren led her to a cabin with foggy windows and splintering panels. The steps leading up to the door were creaky and old. He unlatched the door gingerly. As he edged it open, they were greeted by a single flickering candle on the far side of the cabin. The other tenant, a stringy haired woman with a thin body, sat in a chair and stared at it, not even acknowledging their visitors. There was no one else in the cabin except for one shape curled up on a straw mattress in the corner.

Evelyn looked at Tarren. Tarren took a deep breath, then entered. Their footsteps made the aged hardwood whine, but neither of the tenants seemed to notice or care. When they arrived at the bedside, the curled up person didn't move. They stayed facing away, curled up, silent.

It was a woman, maybe in her late forties. There was a blanket bunched up at the end of the mattress, barely covering her feet. Her long blonde hair was nearly identical to Tarren's, spilling out in greasy strands over the bed. He knelt down and began reaching for her shoulder, but caught himself. He took another deep breath.

"Please stand back," he whispered.

Evelyn shuffled backward. The woman on the mattress still didn't acknowledge either of them.

Tarren inhaled three times, his hands on his knees. He retrieved a pouch from his side that contained some ground up herbs, then dusted his fingers with it. With his index finger, he wrote Ancient Nezmythian characters on the floor. The characters glowed orange as he went, radiating a feeble light. He muttered under his breath more Ancient words. At last, he extended his hand, the palm facing his mother's head. The whole hand glowed while the veins in his arms popped.

He strained, keeping his arm extended. He could feel something moving inside him, an energy that wanted to perform, but something was damming it up. He tried to will it toward his mother, but something about it felt under-prepared. Nothing. He tried it for a moment longer while sweat beaded on his forehead. Still nothing.

His palm stopped glowing and he dropped his arm. The words on the hardwood disappeared. Still, his mother slept soundly just a few feet away.

Evelyn's words were barely a whisper. "Did it work?"

Tarren didn't answer. *Maybe? I'm not sure.* He swallowed, leaned forward, and gently placed his hand on his mother's side. "Mother?"

As soon as he touched her, she gasped like a thunderbolt crashed through her. She flipped about and slammed her back against the wall, her hands splayed and her eyes wild. She kept trying to push herself away like a rabid animal. Breaths were shallow and frequent.

Tarren let his arm droop to his side. "No. I suppose not." He sat there, staring into her wild eyes for a long moment. "I'm sorry, mother. I'll study harder and try again soon. I promise."

Tarren carefully pushed himself to his knees and turned to leave the house. He didn't make eye contact with Evelyn and tried to push the lump in his throat down. "I'm sorry Evelyn, I —"

She was already moving. Her steps were swift and decisive. Tarren didn't even have enough time to ask her what she was doing.

Evelyn slammed her hand over his mother's eyes, locking her thumb and forefinger on her temples. Tarren's mother cried out a blood-curdling wail, scratching and clawing blindly at Evelyn, but Evelyn held true. Her hand glowed purple as she pushed magic through her. Tarren ripped the daggers from out of his side, ready to move, but his mother's thrashing started to slacken. The wails died down. Her breathing became deeper and more even. Until finally, Evelyn removed her hand, letting herself back quietly.

Through the entire ordeal, the flatmate kept her eyes fixed on the candle, completely oblivious to everything that had happened. Meanwhile, Tarren stood with eyes like saucers, his hands still tight on his daggers.

Tarren's mother blinked, coughed, and lifted her head. When her gaze fell upon her son, her face softened. "Tarren? It's you... isn't it?"

Tarren's jaw fell. He looked at Evelyn, then his mother, then he clenched his teeth to keep his lips from shaking. He dropped his daggers, then fell onto the mattress and threw his arms around her, pulling her close. His body shook and he tried desperately not to weep, but the tears leaked out all the same. As he nestled against her, he felt one with her again. After so long. After so many prayers and tears.

Meanwhile, his mother stroked his back and held him tightly. "Ssshh it's okay… I'm here… you're okay."

"Evelyn, how did you…?" Tarren started to say.

But that's when Tarren's mother's eyes grew wide. She noticed the blue cape spilling from his shoulders.

"You're—you're Advisor now!" she gasped. "The blue cape and the armor and all! For how long? How long has it been?"

"Three years!" he gasped through tears. "And Jason is King!"

"Your *friend* Jason?"

"Yes!"

They both gasped and cried and laughed and hugged. Meanwhile, Evelyn stood off to the side, smiling and clasping her hands in front of her. Coming to himself, Tarren stole a look at her.

"I'm so sorry," he said. "I'm not trying to ignore you."

"No, please don't apologize!" she said. "This is wonderful to see. Hello! I'm Evelyn. So nice to meet you."

"I'm Niri," Tarren's mother said with a smile. "So you're the one who healed me? Are you two…?" Her eyes glowed as she pointed between the two of them.

Tarren flushed pink. "Mother…"

"I'm his company for the trip down here," Evelyn smiled. "We've only met recently. But I think very highly of your son. He's wonderful."

Tarren's ears burned.

"I can't wait to hear more about everything," Niri said. "I remember… pieces of things after the prison, but… oh

Dragon, it must have been years and years ago. Tarren, could you help me? I feel so weak."

Tarren helped lift Niri by her shoulders. "Don't worry. We'll take you to the inn and get you a nice meal and a softer bed. Tomorrow morning, we'll take you home to Nezmyth City."

The three of them left the cabin and walked toward the main part of town. In the meantime, Niri asked Tarren dozens of questions about everything that had happened in the last ten years. He jabbered on about Jason's Foreordination, the Ash War, and Barnabas's reinstatement as Chief Captain. He didn't see it, but Evelyn scowled when they got to that part.

When they made it to the gates, the guards lit up with glee and frantically unlocked them. One guard punched another's arm and commanded them to go share the news. The guard scurried away, shouting to the night that the Advisor's mother was well again. Gradually, people started coming out of their homes to see if the news were true. When they saw Niri walking down the street with the Advisor and his friend, cheers couldn't be suppressed.

"She's healed!" "The mother of the Advisor is healed!" "Dragon be praised!"

People began crowding them to clap Tarren's back and shake Niri's hand. The crowd continued to congeal all around them, loudly making impromptu plans for drinking and dancing to celebrate. Everyone followed the three of them to the town inn where they placed special requests to the bards and ordered barrels worth of drinks.

The next hour went by quickly. Niri gobbled up hot soup while she, Tarren, and Evelyn talked at a table in the corner. They traded jokes and told stories, basking in each other's company. Interruptions from celebrating townspeople were often—a relentless shower of praise and well-wishes.

It was what Tarren always wanted. She was back. Fully restored. Ready to come home. Not only that, but he had a beautiful girl by his side. But curiously, she was the one to heal her, not him.

How did she do it? He wondered.

They could have talked for hours, but it was all beginning to be overwhelming for Niri. Evelyn offered to pay for a room, but the barkeep offered one for free as a gift. Evelyn opted to wait down in the tavern while Tarren took Niri upstairs and got her settled down.

The room was comfortable enough with all the basics. As Niri removed her shoes and climbed under the covers, she said, "I cannot tell you how happy I am."

"I feel the same," Tarren said with a big smile.

"Thank you," she said as she held his face. "Thank you for never giving up on me. Thank you for always trying."

Tarren's throat got tight. "I'm glad you're back."

Her brown eyes glistened. She held her boy's cheeks, pulled his face in, and gently kissed him on the head. "I love you and I'm proud of you. I'll see you in the morning."

"I love you, too."

With a wide smile, Tarren walked out of the room and closed the door behind him, drinking in a deep, cleansing sigh.

"What a touching reunion. I'm so glad I got to be part of it."

It was Evelyn's voice, but when Tarren turned to look, his blood turned cold.

Captain Kierli was standing right beside the door. The blonde hair. The blue eyes. The scar across her cheek. She was leaning against the wall with her arms folded and looking very pleased with herself. It took Tarren a second to collect himself, but once he did, his hands shot for his daggers. It didn't matter. As soon as his hands grabbed the handles, his whole body froze. He couldn't even move his lips.

"Come now," Kierli smirked. "That's not a very graceful way to say 'thank you.'"

Tarren wanted to retort. He wanted to yank the daggers from his side and attack, but was completely immobile. It made Kierli's sultry confidence all the more aggravating.

"Let me tell you how this is going to work," Kierli said. "You're in my debt now. I've given you the very thing you want the most. You're welcome. Now, if you spoil this gift by telling anyone how it really happened, I can send sweet Niri back to the way she was like *that*." She snapped her fingers.

All Tarren could do was breathe.

"So watch your step, Mister Advisor," she said. "Run those sweet lips of yours and I'll know. Until then, I think we'll work very nicely together." She stepped uncomfortably close to him, eyeing him up and down. "You know… knowing I have this kind of power over you gives me all sorts of ideas."

She ran her finger down his jaw and neck. Tarren shivered.

"Good night, Mister Advisor," she sneered. "Try to sleep well. I'll see you again very soon."

A wall of purple smoke enveloped her, and in a second, she was gone.

Tarren snapped back into control. His heart thumped inside him. A thin sweat coated him. And icy cold dread touched every corner.

21

THE EXPANDING

When Jason, Barnabas, and Master Ferribolt came back from Grace Mountain, they went up to Jason's quarters to formulate a plan.

Barnabas and Master Ferribolt were surprised to see the vast collection of foliage Jason had amassed. There were small plants perched on shelves and bookcases, in the window sills, and some large plants pushed against the walls. All of them seemed healthy and vibrant, with thick leaves and cascading vines. Last of all, there were two large watering cans tucked against the door. Jason took one of them (clearly empty) and left it outside the door. The other one, he picked up and began to water each plant.

"This… is quite a collection, Your Highness," Master Ferribolt said.

"I had a realization the other night," Jason said as he watered along. "Dark Magic is fueled by wreaking death. So standard magic must operate in an opposing way—becoming stronger when you sow life. Hence the plants."

Barnabas had meandered to one of the taller plants and tenderly stroked the leaves. "Perhaps I'd like a few as well."

"I'll talk to the courtyard gardener for you," Jason said. "So gentlemen, what are your impressions after today?"

The two of them sat at a small table on the right side of the room. Master Ferribolt laced his hands together and peered down the grains in the wood. "The tactics she's been using are giving money and healing the afflicted. However, news is slowly spreading of the instance down in the prison."

"Many of her supporters don't believe that's actually her, though," Barnabas said. "They refuse to believe the same Kierli that killed those guards is the same Kierli that's been healing them. They've even said"—Barnabas tried to keep his temper down—"the killer at the prison is probably someone you've sent to frame Kierli."

Jason stopped watering and shot a look. "They think I would slaughter my *own people* to cover up riches that I *don't have?*"

"I know. It's madness." Barnabas pursed his lips. "But Kierli has built herself as their savior. After she gave them what they want, they won't believe she can do any wrong."

Jason set down the watering can and plopped down in a chair, thinking. After a moment, he said, "What if we invite a representative from the slums inside the castle? Let them wander around. Go into any room they want, go through cupboards, bookshelves, everything. Let them see for themselves that I'm not hiding anything. What do you think?"

Master Ferribolt dipped his head and shrugged. Barnabas wasn't sold.

"That *could* work," the Captain said. "But the villagers could assume that you just moved the gold out of the building before they came over. Or they might think you bought off the representative to keep them quiet. I'm not convinced this effort will be strong enough."

"Well, it's the best thing I can think of," Jason said. "So unless either of you have any other ideas?"

Barnabas and Master Ferribolt thought about it, then Master Ferribolt said. "It's worth a try. If that's what your instincts are telling you, it must be correct."

"My instincts are telling me," Jason said, "that we have to at least try something."

* * * * *

"Aaahh, you have returned."

The gemstones greeted Kierli with sparkles and gleams as her boots met the glistening tiles. By her feet, the pool of water stayed glassy and smooth just as it had before. She folded her arms and paced the floor.

"Yes, I have," Kierli said. "I healed the Advisor's mother of her madness and now he's indebted to me. He's going to be a valuable tool."

"Very clever. Well done."

"Now it's time for you to give me the power you mentioned before."

"Oh child, you thought I would give it to you so easily?"

Kierli frowned and advanced on the pool's edge. "You didn't say anything about a price."

"You know of the King's power," the voice said. *"The power that surpasses the limits of his mortal body? The power both ancient and mighty?"*

"I've heard stories. Haven't seen it myself."

"I, too, possess a similar power. It can be yours."

Kierli's eyes narrowed. "How?"

"It shall be given when you are ready."

"I'm ready now."

"You are not."

Kierli yanked her sword from its sheath and stabbed it into the pool, making the water ripple. "And what do you really know about me? What are you, really?"

"I know the fear and anger that live in your heart. The torture that you harbor behind that smile. Your beauty that masks the pain. It has given you strength. Your broken parents. Your dead brother. Your village chief that—"

"That's enough," Kierli threatened.

"This power will be yours in time," the voice said. *"But I am still benevolent. I will not send you away with nothing. Come forth."*

Silently, Kierli waded into the pool, a little deeper than last time. She felt the power surge from the soles of her feet up to the top of her head. Pulsing, vibrating the bones and joints inside her. She breathed deeply, letting the cool rush soak over her. After a long moment, the euphoria subsided, and she stepped out of the pool. No water dripped off of her— somehow, she was completely dry.

"I have doubled the reservoir inside of you." The voice said. *"Return again in six days, and the power you seek shall be ready. I will be waiting."*

"What do I do until then?"

"Whatever you wish," the voice said. *"Farewell."*

Kierli didn't control it, but somehow she was transported back to the cellar off the Southern Market Street. Everything was as she left it. As she looked around, she noticed the bedroll where she and Felix had slept together. She frowned. It looked a little narrower than she remembered.

Suddenly exhausted, she slipped into the fur skin and exhaled. Tomorrow would be a new day. And in six more, she'd have all the power she could ever need.

* * * * *

Yorn drummed his fingers on the table as he looked around. The Northern Market Street was just as busy as usual. People were starting to wear thicker clothing as autumn grew deeper. He drew a sip from a tankard of booshum berry juice. The sweet, tangy flavor wasn't enough to distract him from the unsettling feeling in his stomach. He frowned as he stared at the nectar's filmy surface.

It wasn't long before a pair of footsteps came jaunting up to him. A woman sat across from him at the same table and tapped the space next to his glass. "Hello! It's been a while, hasn't it?"

"It has. You've been busy, it seems."

Evelyn propped her head on her hand and tilted it as she gazed at Yorn. It almost felt flirtatious. Yorn actually felt himself turn pink—partially from embarrassment and partially from anger. Did she really think she could act so sparkly at a time like this?

"You're right," she said. "I have a lot to tell you."

"I heard about Felix. The news is spreading across the kingdom."

"That he joined Kierli's cause then left?"

"That's not what I heard."

"What did you hear?"

"That he was murdered."

Evelyn sneered. "If he was killed, where's his body?"

Yorn didn't say anything.

Evelyn smiled and shook her head. "Felix realized how hard it was going to be for Kierli to clear her name, so he gave up and left." She shrugged. "Guess he couldn't take it. Kierli doesn't know where he is now—she didn't bother to ask where he was going. Maybe he was embarrassed to return to Widow's Rest, and that's why no one can find him."

"That doesn't explain the others."

"What others?"

"Seven other soldiers were killed at the prison the same night."

Evelyn frowned. *There should have been eight.* "You're joking. You think *Kierli* would do that?"

"There was one survivor, and she swore it was y—her. Blonde hair, blue eyes, scar on her cheek. Fought with a shortsword and dagger. That sounds like Kierli."

Evelyn's face got dark. "Perhaps it's someone who looks like Kierli, but it couldn't be her. She's been traveling the kingdom giving out the King's filthy money and healing people. That's not a murderer."

Yorn tapped his foot, wrapped his arms tight in front of his chest, and stared at the juice in front of him. After a long pause, Evelyn leaned forward, placing her hand on his knee. His heartbeat picked up.

"Has Kierli ever lied to you?" Evelyn asked. "You've known her for years."

"As far as I know, she never has," Yorn conceded. "But you know what all of this looks like, right? Everything points to—"

"I *know*," Evelyn said. "But Kierli could really use someone right now. She needs to know that someone is on her side."

Yorn was quiet again. He kept his arms folded, looking away. He thought about what Patriarch Juun told him just yesterday. He didn't look Evelyn in the eye, but he said, "I'm always on her side."

Evelyn squeezed his knee. "Good. Now tell me, do you know of any plans that the King has made to push back on Kierli's followers?"

"Nothing yet. He doesn't want to restrict the people's right to protest in Center Court. But that's it."

"Are you sure?"

"Yes."

Kierli smiled. "Thank you, Yorn. You're so cute when you're helpful. I'll visit you again soon, alright?"

Yorn gave her a half-smile. Evelyn stood from her chair, pushed it in, waved, and pranced away. In her wake, Yorn stayed leaning against the back of his chair, deep in thought. He lifted his glass and drank up the last of the juice, then dropped a few Pieces on the table, stood up, and marched away.

The plan was to head back to the barrack. He even thought about the letter he was writing for Kierli. But then he saw the castle looming in the distance—a great white beacon of holiness.

He stopped. He could feel it pulling him, beckoning him. And with that pull, a frightening level of dread. The King had to know. He had to know about his visits with Kierli. It was his duty not just as a soldier but as a *Captain* to make the King aware of these things, and he had failed. His actions were borderline treason. He knew there would be consequences. He would have to resign as Captain of Upper City. But… if Kierli really was a monster, keeping quiet about these visits meant more people could die. The King *must* know.

He cast up a little prayer. Deep down, he knew the Dragon was smiling upon his decision. Even though he hated it.

Curse you, Yorn, he thought. *It has to be done.*

He closed his eyes, growled inside himself, and started for the castle.

When he arrived at the gates, the guards let him in without question. He moved through the grounds, passing the knight fountain that stood in the middle of the front courtyard. As he looked up, he noticed a stained glass window on the castle that was nearly identical—the only difference was that the sword it held was bright orange.

Three knocks, and the doors creaked open. He exited the cold and entered the castle, where it felt comfortably warm. Surprisingly, King Jason was sitting at his throne, but the Advisor wasn't anywhere to be found. Yorn approached the dais and gave a dutiful nod. "Good morning, Your Highness."

"Good morning, Yorn," King Jason said. "What's the problem?"

"Erm… if I might ask, where is the Advisor?"

"Lunli Village," King Jason said. "He left just yesterday to visit his mother. He should be back either tonight or tomorrow. Is something troubling you?"

Yorn swallowed hard and his shoulders sagged. "Kierli has visited me twice."

A variety of emotions flew across Jason's face—shock, bewilderment, anger. He shook his head and muttered "What?"

"She never tells me where she is or what her plans are," Yorn explained. "She keeps me completely in the dark, only popping up when she needs something. And she always appears to me in the form of someone else as to remain conspicuous—each time, it's been a dark haired woman named Evelyn."

A thousand thoughts started firing through Jason's mind, but the last thing caught his attention. Evelyn. The name sounded familiar—the name of the woman that Tarren was enamored with. *Could they be the same? I hope to the Dragon they're not.*

"She has the ability to change her appearance?" he repeated with horror.

"Yes, sir."

Jason stepped off the throne dais, his face growing hot. He tried to stop himself from raising his voice, but failed. "Why did you wait until *now* to tell me this?"

"Because I didn't know what was true, sir. I was torn between your account and her account of recent events. But the incident at the prison shook me." Yorn swallowed again. "And if I'm being honest, my feelings are strong for her, sir."

Jason's face burned and he started pacing the floor in mincing steps.

Bowing heavily, Yorn said, "Sir, I understand the gravity of my transgression. This is my formal resignation from—"

"Oh, shut it, Yorn!" Jason retorted. "We need your experience now more than ever. I'm not letting you go. As a matter of fact..." Jason's eyes widened. "This presents a monumental opportunity. She trusts you, doesn't she?"

"Yes, sir," Yorn stammered.

"And she'll likely visit you again?"

"I'm expecting it."

"Good." Jason paced and stroked his chin. He wanted to get to the point, but Yorn was clearly distressed. He had to make him feel at ease. The King said, "You have no idea where she is or what her plans are? She tells you nothing?"

"Nothing, sir," Yorn said. "She swears she hasn't done any wrong. She even denied killing the guards at the prison."

"That's a lie, as far as we know. And she still claims she stole money from some kind of secret treasury?"

"Yes, sir."

"Another lie. You can search this castle high and low, Yorn, but you won't find any money. There's no need for it here." Jason paused, then said, "That was brave of you to come here and confess this. I'm still very upset with you, and I believe you should be punished for your obstruction, but we'll save that for another day." He paused. "You care about her. That must have been very frustrating when you came here for answers and I didn't give you much."

Yorn didn't nod. He didn't have to.

"I'm sorry, Yorn," Jason said. "But as I told you before, we as Foreordained servants have taken oaths much like you have. I'd tell you more if I could."

"I understand, sir," Yorn said. "But I'm so confused. This is unlike her. I served with her for years and the thought of her killing soldiers is ludicrous."

"We all thought Kierli was someone else," Jason said. "She fooled all of us. But I swear to you, on the Foreordained power within me, that I am being truthful with you. I will never lie to you or the kingdom. I may keep things secret to protect you, but I will never lie to you."

Something tapped Yorn's heart as Jason spoke. A reassurance. With it, Yorn swallowed and said, "Thank you, Your Highness. I believe you."

Good, Jason thought. *Back to the point.*

"The next time she visits you, I want you to try to get as much information as you can—what she's planning, where, and when. Then come straight here. Do you understand?"

Dutifully, Yorn said, "Yes, Your Highness."

Jason reached out and took Yorn's shoulder. "You're a strong man, Yorn. I wish I could ease your mind more. But my mind is troubled as well. Let's get through this together, shall we? I'm counting on you."

Yorn bowed. "Of course, Your Highness. Good day."

With that, the Captain turned on his heels and marched down the red carpet. As he went, Jason watched him and scratched his chin. *Yorn is the kind of man that Nezmyth needs. Imperfect, but he clearly has a strong desire to do good. Even when it goes against what he wants. That's what makes him mighty, I think.*

22
THE EXPERIMENT

Niri's eyes were wide as she soaked in the sights and sounds of Nezmyth City. The clomping of horse's hooves on clean cobblestone. The laughter of children. The people that no longer carried a fear of abusive soldiers or listening spies—a vastly different world than the one she left. Even in the southernmost parts of the city, people waved at the carriage with a brightness that she could scarcely remember. A smile absently stretched across her face.

"All of it is so clean now, even Lower City!" She said with childlike wonder. "This is what it's like now that Barnabas is gone?"

"Well, he's not *gone*," Tarren said. "He's just not King anymore."

Niri was barely listening. Her eyes were wide as they pressed her nose up against the carriage window. Tarren wanted to smile, but found it difficult. His back protested against the lack of sleep he got last night. He tried to get some shut-eye, but a singular thought kept haunting him:

Dark Magic healed her. I couldn't, but Dark Magic could.

He tried not to let himself think of it too much because it always created a curl in his stomach. But it moved through his brain like a slithering snake, whispering the truth whenever he tried to push it away.

Dark Magic healed her. I couldn't.

The blue carriage crawled through the lively streets until it passed through Center Court. Niri noticed the statue of Barnabas was gone, and Tarren told her it was demolished on the day of Jason's Ordination Ceremony. Niri's gaze also drifted to a crowd gathered on the east side of the Court. There, a person with fine clothing was perched on a large crate, preaching about Kierli. Among the crowd gathered were those who had erected signs saying "FREE KIERLI" or "QUEEN KIERLI". Soldiers stood off to the side of the gathering, weapons in hand, ready to quell things if they got too rowdy.

Tarren had already told Niri about the situation, so she frowned at the sight.

"Do these people have no sense?" She asked.

"She's healed a lot of them," Tarren said. "Given them money, too."

"It's never occurred to them that they're being used?" Niri said. "That they're just tools to her?"

That made Tarren think of his debt to Kierli. He tried to squelch the thought. "They've spent their entire lives scraping to get by. You remember how it was during Barnabas's reign. It's still like that in the slums. These people are the filth of Nezmyth City and they know it. Now they've found someone that's validated their suffering and offered them a new path—a path to become equals with everyone else. Can you blame them? She's giving them exactly what they want."

"But it's all a lie," Niri muttered.

Tarren deflated and looked out the window. "Yes. It is."

The sun was beginning to set as the carriage climbed the hill of Upper City. Niri's face darkened as her eyes fell upon the manicured gardens and beautiful brick homes of the wealthier district. This area looked exactly as it always did: perfect. It made her tone icy.

"Many of these people were rich during Barnabas's reign, too," she said. "Not much has changed here."

Tarren nodded. "You're right. Merchants, noblemen… they've mostly remained the same. But it didn't take many of them long to see that Jason had no interest fraternizing with them. They even tried their hand at me for a while. But we're both two boys from Lower City that know what they are. Everything to them is connection and power. Building their own little empires."

Niri kept thinking. "If you as King and Advisor don't tax the people to support yourselves, how do you get things like food and clothing?"

"Folks like these," Tarren nodded to the mansions. "We require donations from them. It's what the Patriarchs have done for centuries, and after Jason looked at it, he thought it made sense that the King and Advisor do the same. We don't take advantage, we just require enough to cover our needs. Nothing more."

"Why doesn't Jason require them to give to the poor?"

"He does that too," Tarren said. "But they donate their lowest quality goods. Food that's nearly rotten. Clothing with holes or missing stitches. For a while, Jason punished them for giving poor goods to those in need, but after a while it became too hard to track. The rich paid off soldiers to give false reports. And we couldn't imprison them—many of them employ hundreds of people on the Market Streets that rely on them. Eventually, Jason figured it was better that they donate something than nothing at all."

Niri hummed. It was a sobering thought, but looking at her son in his royal regalia made it hard to think negatively. He was so strong and intelligent now—a fully grown man. So courageous. So good. Her dark eyes glinted in the fading sun.

"I'm so happy to be here with you," she said.

Tarren smiled. "Me too."

But the thought never left: *Dark Magic healed her. I couldn't.*

They were quiet for a long while, then the castle came into view, bold and large against the sky. Niri gasped. "Dear Dragon… it's *beautiful!* It looks just like it did when King Thomas was alive!"

Indeed, its white stone surface was brilliant against the sunset, with bushy, healthy foliage blooming around its feet. Currently, pairs of soldiers patrolled around the guardian boxes and between the trees. One of the castle gardeners was out picking fruit. The last time Niri saw the castle, it was a looming black fortress surrounded by nothing but parched soil. She got a better look as the carriage approached the gates.

"Good evening, Mister Advisor!"

"Good evening, gentlemen," Tarren said. "This is my mother, Niri."

The soldiers gasped and their faces brightened as they bunched against the window to see her.

"She's cured!"

"Dragon be praised!"

Niri blushed and waved. The gates opened and the carriage jittered through, moving on the path sandwiched by rows of trees. Niri inhaled the smells of ripe fruit and dancing flowers. Nothing like this grew anywhere near Lunli Village, and even if there did, it's not as though she'd remember it. She admired the knight statue as they curved around it. Before long, the carriage came to a halt in front of the massive doors and they both filed out.

The soldiers guarding the doors let out holy praise when they saw Niri, then one of them picked up the hammer and gave three knocks. They shook her hand and congratulated the Advisor on a successful trip. Tarren thanked them graciously and tried desperately not to think of Kierli. The double doors crept open, Niri's eyes grew to the size of saucers, and Tarren led her inside.

The excited whispers started up as soon as they entered. Even the soldiers posted in the perimeter of the great hall couldn't help themselves. Niri moved down the red carpet as if she were in a dream, drinking in everything her eyes could behold—the statues, the chandeliers, the mural on the ceiling. At the throne dais, Jason sat up in his seat. When he saw Tarren marching down the red carpet with a woman beside him, his heart leapt and he jumped to his feet. He stood tense and silent for a long moment, stretching his neck, trying to see if it was really her. At last, he saw her face. His heart leapt and he ran the length of the red carpet, his face beaming and his arms outstretched.

"*Niri!*" He shouted. "Niri, you're home!"

He threw his arms around the woman, lifting her off the ground. Niri laughed like a child as her arms clung around Jason's neck. He swung her around and finally let her down on her feet. She looked up red-faced with wonder.

"Jason, you're so *big* now!" She said. "King of Nezmyth—so strong and tall! The last time I saw you, you were still only this high!" She held out her hand.

"Not as tall as I'd like to be," Jason patted his own head. "But so much has changed. I'm sure Tarren has told you all about it. I'm so thrilled that you're home! What are your plans? Where are you going to stay?"

"I'm taking her home to father tonight," Tarren said. "He doesn't know that she's well again. We didn't stop on the way."

Jason tried to imagine Gulaf's reaction at his wife's return. Secretly, he was glad he wouldn't be there for that reunion. He could only imagine the tension there would be at the house. But he tried to think of something else. "You need to visit my parents before you do. They'll be so happy to see you."

As Jason spoke, Niri felt his cape and brushed some dust from his armor, admiring every inch of it. "Who would have thought that my Tarren would serve side by side with his best friend!"

Jason slid Tarren a look as if to say, *Mothers will always be mothers, won't they?* Tarren just smiled sheepishly. Jason's attention focused back on Niri when she put both of her hands on his shoulder plates. Those dark brown eyes were serious, but full of empathy and love. Her voice was soft as she spoke.

"Tarren told me about your wife. I am so, so sorry. You are Melded to her?"

Jason's heart dropped a little, but he said, "Yes."

"Then she's still yours," she beamed. "And she's never far. Don't forget that."

He forced a smile.

"This one, however!" Niri pushed Tarren's shoulder. "Tells me that he hasn't had much luck with women! Imagine that, my Tarren, as strong and tall and handsome as he is. I think he's being too picky. He came down with a lovely young woman yesterday but she left before sunrise. You didn't chase her away, did you?"

That's when the lightning bolt went through Jason's head. Evelyn. Kierli. He tried to mask his emotions, but the look on his face must have been evident, because Tarren swallowed and bristled slightly.

"Um, Tarren," Jason said, "could I speak with you privately for a moment?"

Tarren nodded stiffly and walked away with him. Meanwhile, Niri meandered through the great hall, filling her eyes with the décor again. When they were out of earshot, Jason leaned in closely. "Captain Yorn was here just this morning. Said he had been visited by Kierli twice since her imprisonment."

Tarren's eyebrows bent. "Twice?"

"Yes. She's been moving under the disguise of a dark-haired woman named Evelyn," Jason said. "Isn't that the woman you've been seeing at the tavern?"

Immediately, Tarren felt himself start to sweat. But he straightened his posture and tried to look self-assured. "No.

You're thinking Jesslin. The names sound similar, but it's a different woman."

"You're sure?"

"Of course I am. Why wouldn't I be?"

Jason let out a deep breath. "That gives me some relief. I would hate to hear that she was targeting you somehow." His face brightened. "But you've given us cause to celebrate. Niri is finally home. I'm sure you're anxious to show her the rest of the city, too. I'm going to my parent's home for dinner tonight. Would you two like to join?"

Tarren did his best to smile. "We'd be delighted."

Jason and Tarren rejoined Niri and told her of the dinner invitation. Niri's face lit up with glee. And so they went. They loaded into Jason's carriage and traveled to Kara and Tomm's home in Lower City. Kara burst into tears when she saw Niri then hurried everyone inside for dinner. As the crickets chirped happily in the evening air, the five of them enjoyed piping hot cups of tea, fresh bread, cheese, and lean steaks. They talked about old times, scraping by during the Harvest Tax, Jason and Tarren's experiences as children... anything under the sun. Laughs were shared. And though the chill was getting stronger with the onset of winter, the company felt very warm indeed.

But ratting in the recesses of Tarren's brain was that thought, continuing to haunt him: *Dark Magic healed her. I couldn't.* It took a murderous traitor to bring his mother back to health. His hundreds of hours of study weren't enough. It was her that broke the curse—*her.* The thought was poison that contaminated what should have been a joyous reunion. Spoiled. Ruined.

The reminder bombarded every corner of the evening. It made the laughs and hugs hollow. They shouldn't even be happening. Not like this.

Finally, he couldn't take it anymore. He stood from the table and excused himself for some fresh air. Everyone dismissed him absently as they went on jabbering with Niri.

Tarren's boots crunched in the dirt as he slid his way around the house. He brushed a cockroach off a small wooden box and sat down, his face in his hands. He half-expected Kierli's voice to come slipping into his ear like some dark whisper reminding him of his debt. But it didn't come. Instead, he stayed glaring at the grass in the moonlight, thinking about recent events.

Tarren pushed his fingers through his hair and rested his elbows on his knees, trying to get the thoughts to fit together. He was in Kierli's debt now. She would come asking for things. But what? Maybe there was a way to outwit her. But was it worth the risk? No matter what he did, she could send his mother back into madness. He was under her thumb. The thought made his blood boil.

And then he thought of Dark Magic. Was there more to the magic that they didn't understand? Can some handle it better than others—actually use it for good and not become consumed by it? If there was, they had missed out on thousands of years of potential power.

After all, how could something so evil bring about something so good?

In frustration, Tarren stamped his foot. A soft crunch sounded beneath his boot. He lifted his foot to check and found the gooey remnants of the cockroach he brushed off earlier. Then an awful thought crept through his mind.

Try it.

Maybe he was strong enough to handle it. He was Foreordained to be Advisor, after all. Not like Barnabas, Nartikis, or Kierli. His spirit was special. Chosen.

But he had also sworn an oath on the day of his Ordination that he would fight against it. He fought against it during the Ash War. Was he really in a position to experiment? There would be dire consequences if anyone discovered him.

He looked around. There was no one else but him. The others were happily laughing inside, their voices muffled by the wall, completely unsuspecting and oblivious.

Do it. Just do it quickly and get it over with. No one will know.

Without letting himself overthink it, Tarren imagined himself pushing the life of that cockroach into his hand. He could feel it move, along with his feelings of confusion and anger. And then, with a soft spark, a purple ember danced in his palm.

He nearly gasped from the feeling. Waves of pleasure flowed through his body, pushing out the confusion and despair. The purple flame seemed to recognize this. Its pale flickering light held him gently, nudging him to put aside the pain for a while and simply be.

And then, it snuffed out. When Tarren was left alone, he took a deep breath and clenched his fist. Part of him felt dirty —ashamed. He had touched its surface, dipped his finger into its pool. It felt incredible. But what was he left with when it was over? Nothing.

But the *feeling* of it…

"Only once," he reassured himself. "Never again. Not again."

He stood up, brushed off his armor, and went back inside.

23

THE PLEDGE

The next morning, a crowd was gathered outside of the castle gates, protesting King Jason and his stocked up treasures again. Following orders, one of the soldiers selected one of the townspeople to come in and investigate the castle according to their wishes. Leave no stone unturned. The townspeople were cautious and puzzled at first, but eventually elected a leader and sent him off.

The man was escorted through every room in the castle— even the Oracle Stone room, which was considered sacred and inaccessible to people outside the King's circle. But the man spent most of the morning searching every corner he could. King Jason himself stayed in his bedroom and watched like a hawk as the man went through Saryan's old things. When he was gone, the King immediately folded everything neatly and put them back where they belonged.

When the man returned to the crowd, he revealed that he found no riches. But that didn't quell the suspicions of the townspeople. They accused Jason of moving the riches to another location before inviting the man in. They even accused the man of being bought off or threatened, which he denied.

One thing remained: they were still certain that King Jason was hiding something. When the soldiers reported that to him, he wasn't surprised.

Miles away, Evelyn walked briskly with a cloak over her face to hide it from view. Not that she needed it. In her pocket was a small handful of money—freshly minted from some rusty nails just this morning. She decided to treat herself to some goods on the Northern Market Street today. The fruits and vegetables were always freshest here, and that made them more expensive.

She pushed through the crowd, trying to be conspicuous. It wasn't too congested today, but enough to be uncomfortable. Perhaps that was a good thing. Easier to blend in.

A cart of booshum berries caught her eye. Her mouth started to water. When she got closer to the cart, she bent over slightly to smell them.

"Don't you love the smell? We talk about the sweet flavor all the time, but not enough about the smell."

Evelyn turned to see a cute, petite black-haired woman standing next to her, looking over the cart with a wide grin. Her hair only went down to her shoulders and her cheeks pressed into dimples with her smile.

Evelyn smiled in kind. "Yes, it's lovely."

"Between you and me, booshum berries from the Western Woods are even better," the girl said. "The ones that grow on wild bushes are more tart than sweet."

"You don't say."

The dark-haired girl handed some Pieces to the man at the cart and filled a small satchel. Happily, she cinched it shut and dropped it into a larger tote she carried over her shoulder. Then she touched the stranger on the shoulder, flashed a smile, and said "Have a lovely day!" before she disappeared into the crowd.

Evelyn returned an insincere smile for just a second before dropping some money into the man's hand and gathering some booshum berries for herself. Then she ventured the opposite direction, frowning and peering around.

Even as Evelyn ventured away, she could feel herself being followed—her slow burn of magic made her more spatially aware. She began ignoring some of the fruit carts and slinking through the crowd with her wares closely in tow. Everyone ignored her. None of the faces she passed seemed to recognize who she was. What's more, the soldiers passed her by as well. So why this sense of dread? And it wasn't fleeting, either. If anything, the feeling was getting stronger. Her pursuer was getting closer.

She ducked into an alleyway. Then crossed into another. Then another. She was alone, but could feel the presence of another. As she darted about, she threw glances over her shoulder. But her eyes convinced her she was alone. All that was left was a feeling.

The patter of footsteps sounded ahead. She flipped about. No one was there. Then she heard rustling behind her. Again, she spun around. No one. Sweat thickened on her brow. She dropped her satchel and ripped the sword and dagger from her cloak. Then she bent her knees.

"It's you, isn't it?"

Evelyn flipped around with a swipe of her sword. *Clang!* The blow was blocked.

It was her. The girl from the market. Somehow, she had enchanted her forearm and blocked the blow with it as if her skin was steel. Evelyn jumped back and brandished her weapons again.

"What do you mean *is it me?*" Evelyn hissed.

"Kierli," the girl said. "I can feel the darkness emanating from you. The only thing I can compare it to is the Ash when they came to Treetown years ago. Strange." She tipped her head sideways. "I heard your brother was killed in the Ash War. So why is your aura the same?"

Evelyn lunged. The girl blocked. Then parried. Then ducked. Then Evelyn tried to jump back again, but was seized. The girl's hand shot forward and grabbed Evelyn's face. Her fingers were like a branding iron that immobilized all of Kierli. It burned fiercely. Her muscles refused to move. After a few agonizing seconds, the girl released her and Kierli staggered backward. She didn't realize that the spell had turned her face back to normal—with the steely blue eyes, golden hair, and long scar.

"Just as I thought," the girl said. "You *are* Kierli. My name is Alis, by the way. I'll be capturing you now. It's in your best interest not to—"

She didn't get to finish. Kierli flipped her cloak and disappeared in a wall of purple smoke. In her wake, Alis hummed and frowned.

Kierli reappeared in her cellar, huffing and frowning. She threw off her cloak and stormed around the cellar, angry that she left her goods behind. As she paced, she heard a voice.

"You didn't let me finish."

Kierli yelped and flashed her weapons again, which Alis dodged and parried, then dashed a safe distance away.

"Anyway," Alis said. "It's in your best interest not to resist. Just come along and make this easier."

"How did you follow me here?"

Alis put her hands on her hips. "Listen, I don't mean to brag, but I'm a much more powerful magician than you."

Kierli smirked. "I doubt it."

"Okay, let me show you."

Kierli didn't see it coming. Alis didn't even have to move. Kierli's body lifted off the ground as if clutched by an invisible hand, then was launched against a wall. Then the floor. Then the opposite wall. Each hit made a sickening thud that reverberated dully through the cellar. When Alis released her magical grip, Kierli staggered to her feet, clutching her side.

"Stop resisting," Alis insisted.

At least one or two ribs were broken. No matter. Kierli pushed the magic through her body to numb the pain and disappeared in another puff of smoke. Alis sighed.

Kierli reappeared in the middle of a grassy field a mile south of the city. There, she waited, knowing that Alis would appear soon. She tightened the grip on her weapons and the blades ignited with purple fire.

Alis didn't announce herself when she reappeared. Kierli felt the Paralyzing Curse fall on her and her limbs start to tighten. She pushed it back with the magic inside her and freed herself. Then she could feel Alis nearby. She flipped around, slashing her sword and sending a wave of purple fire through the air. It singed the grass beneath her, creating a crackling wave of black.

Alis raised her hands and sliced through the embers. She leaned forward as she darted toward Kierli. Kierli's eyes sharpened. This girl was fast, but not that fast. She raised her weapons, ready for the strike.

Suddenly, an arm wrapped around the back of her neck and yanked her to the ground.

Kierli landed on her back with a thud that knocked the wind out of her. The Alis that was running in front of her disappeared, instead replaced by the one who snuck up behind her. *Casting an illusion. She's clever.* As Kierli lay on the ground, the grass beneath her trembled. Before she could act, thick mounds of earth sprouted up and bound her arms and legs. No matter how she struggled and grunted, she couldn't break free.

Alis half-smiled as she looked down at her. "Don't worry, I don't want to hurt you. I want to understand you."

Kierli struggled, but to no avail. Alis knelt beside her, pointed her finger, and pressed it against Kierli's forehead. After she muttered an Ancient phrase, her fingertip glowed and images began to flash across her mind.

A father walking away. Kierli chased after him, but he ignored her. Then she was an older child, pushed in the mud by other children. Kierli wiped tears away as she shakily pushed herself up. The next image was the worst—Kierli in her early teens, on her back, crying and struggling as a man in fine clothing groaned on top of her. The last image was of Kierli standing by a stream, the man's body at her feet. She was clutching a bloody dagger.

Kierli bellowed a shriek that could have split the heavens—it pulled Alis out of the vision. In a feat of strength and passion, the mounds of earth encasing her hands exploded and her hand shot for Alis's throat. The veins in Kierli's arms glowed bright purple. Her hand clenched around Alis's jugular, tightening, staring into Alis's reddening face like a wild animal.

The mounds over Kierli's body dissolved and something ethereal lifted her onto her feet. Meanwhile, she held Alis aloft, her feet dangling as she struggled to break free of Kierli's suffocating grasp. Alis was about to cast another spell to break free, but with the magic coursing through Kierli's body, she cocked her arm back and threw.

Alis tumbled across the grass, bumping and bruising her body as she toppled backward. When her body came to a halt, she forced herself onto her hands and knees, coughing horribly. Her eyes were misty as she lifted her gaze to Kierli.

"I'm so sorry," she said. "You poor thing."

"*I don't want your pity!*" Kierli shrieked. "He's dead! I killed him! I'm *free!*"

Kierli was upon her in an instant. Alis cast a barrier to block her slashing blows. The blades connected with the barrier, and the sadness in Alis's eyes didn't dissipate. "I'm not unfamiliar with that pain, Kierli. I understand perfectly. No wonder you carry such anger."

Kierli leapt back and brandished her blades, breathing heavily. Something about Alis's words stirred something inside and caused her lips to tremble. But she couldn't entertain those feelings. This girl was an enemy, not a friend.

Alis dropped the barrier. "I'm sorry for everything you've endured. But nonetheless, you are a threat to Nezmyth. For that reason, I'm taking you now. Please forgive me."

Bonds like glowing white vines suddenly sprouted around Kierli's wrists and ankles. They were warm, but felt stronger than a Paralyzing Curse. They forced Kierli to drop her weapons. As the bonds started to grow and encase her arms and legs, Kierli pushed magic into her extremities to break them.

Several yards away, Alis held out her hands, controlling them. "Don't resist them! It'll only hurt you!"

Kierli didn't listen. She moaned and grunted and forced more magic through her body. The veins in her arms and legs thickened like purple roots. The bonds were coming loose… but it was putting even more strain on her limbs. Finally, she pushed too hard. At the same moment she broke the bonds, the force of her magic snapped her wrists and ankles. Kierli let out a cry of agony as she crumbled to the ground.

But she was free. And with that fraction of a second, she got control of herself. She called to a voice she had heard before. The voice answered. A wall of purple smoke took her and she disappeared.

Alis humphed and shook her head. As she thought of the vision she had just been granted, she breathed deep and tried to soothe the stinging in her eyes. That poor child. It's no wonder.

She was about to transport to wherever she was… but stopped. She could feel it heavily—that magic that Kierli was using. Wherever she transported to, that place was rife with the same energy. No. She wouldn't follow. Instead, she transported back to the castle and told King Jason exactly what happened.

In the cavernous depths of the Chasm, Kierli suddenly appeared on the edge of the dark pool. Her cries slammed against the gleaming walls, echoing back at her like a chorus of agony. Her hands lay useless at her side along with her broken legs. She tried to push her magic into them, mending them, but it wasn't enough. The bones only twitched—they wouldn't push back into place.

"You! Spirit!" She barked through the pain. "Heal me!"

"That will come at a price, my child."

"Whatever it is, I'll pay it. I have nothing else."

"That is correct. I am your truest friend. Do you pledge your loyalty to me?"

Kierli tried to stop and think—to be strategic about this. But the pain was too great. And what else could she do? Who else could she go to? She nodded. "I swear it."

"Good," the voice purred. *"Now, prepare to be baptized and become anew in my depths. Through my grace and benevolence, I will bestow my greatest gift upon you. Receive me, and free your spirit."*

The murky black water inched up the soil until it trickled all around Kierli. Then somehow, it cradled her body and pulled her into the depths of the pool. Kierli's heart pounded with fear. The water reached up her arms, legs, touching every part of her until eventually she was submerged. She held her breath and tried to stay in control, but the pain was too great. Under the water, she gasped.

But she didn't drown. She blinked with wide eyes as she realized… but she could breathe it. With it filling the pores of her lungs, the tingling of the cavern's magic touched her deeper, encasing her with pleasure and power. Her bones moved into place, becoming whole. The pain dissolved.

And as she turned and looked, she noticed something at the bottom of the pool.

A blade. A sword jutting out from the center. It called to her —inviting her sweetly in her ears and chest. A euphoric ripple lapped through her entire body. Her feet grazed the bottom of the pool as she glided toward it. When she was upon it, she wrapped her hand around the handle and pulled it free. Then she swam back to the surface.

When she stepped out of the pool, no water dripped from her body—perfectly dry, just like before. But in her hand was one of the most mysterious swords she had ever seen. The blade was pure black, reflecting no light. It was almost like looking into a shape cut out of the air where nothing could return. The handle was intricate, beautiful, and fine—silver and gold with shining green and purple emeralds.

"This is Starshadow," the voice said. *"A weapon forged and preserved for thousands of years. A weapon that signifies my chosen denizen. It is yours whenever you call for it."*

Kierli opened her hand as if to drop it, but the sword disappeared in the familiar purple smoke. Then when she clenched her fist, it reappeared in her hand. It was so light she could barely feel it.

"It's magnificent," she breathed. "This is part of the power you promised before?"

"Yes," the voice said. *"A power greater than anything in this world. But it comes at a price. Those that wield Starshadow cannot achieve its full power easily."*

Kierli turned to look at the pool. "What must I do?"

The voice paused. *"Bands must be broken. Thousands of oppressive years must be amended."*

"How?"

"You must destroy every Foreordained person in Nezmyth."

Kierli fell silent. The pool didn't elaborate any further. What it spoke was madness… Foreordination had been in place for nearly two thousand years. Kierli considered the implications. "All of them? Every Patriarch, Blessing Bearer… even the Chief Patriarch, King, and Advisor? You realize what you're asking, don't you?"

"I know it all too well, my child. But it is necessary. The Old Ways are folly, used by the Dragon to control others. Corruption has seeped through. To deny it is madness. It is I who was destined to protect this

world from the beginning. I would bring peace, harmony, and security to all. No more suffering. No more strife. If you complete this task and restore me to what I once was, the world shall know beauty as it never knew before. And I shall reward you beyond anything you can imagine. That, I promise you with surety."

Kierli's imagination reeled on the possibility. Yes, the Old Ways have been oppressive—King Jason is proof of that. And this spirit could promise her rewards beyond her reckoning… did that mean justice for her imprisonment? A role as Queen? She thought of the people chanting her name in Center Court every day. Her monarchical rule becoming real possibility excited her… the ultimate revenge on King Jason. She tried not to smile.

"I know you're right," she said. "But this will be no small feat. Many of these Patriarchs are good people—it'll be a shame to shed their blood. The people must not know it's me."

"You are cunning. You will find a way. It is a worthy sacrifice. The people will see their deaths as an act of providence. I know, for I have foreseen it."

Kierli was silent. Putting her hand in a fist once again, Starshadow appeared in her hand. As she gazed into the endless black of the blade, she muttered, "Then I suppose I have work to do."

24

THE MARTYR

The evening was late and Tarren felt somewhat lifted as he left his mother's room at the Wilted Rose. Earlier in the evening, they got dinner together and bought her some new clothes, then they came back to the tavern to simply sit and talk. The room would be her home for the next while, since there was an altercation with Gulaf back at their house. Niri said she didn't want to talk about it, but Tarren surmised that she had a hard time living with a husband that gave up on her. He wasn't terribly surprised, but hated seeing her upset about it.

Gus the barkeep said she could stay in one of the rooms for as long as she needed if she agreed to help in the tavern occasionally. Niri jumped at the opportunity, seeing it as a chance to make new friends for the first time in years. From what Gus said, Niri did a wonderful job for her first shift.

When Tarren was ready to leave, he came down the stairs and passed through the tavern, weaving through the huzzahs of Jason loyalists and dirty looks of Kierli supporters. The blue carriage was waiting for him outside. He didn't wait for the driver to hop down and open the door for him. He took care of it himself.

But when he climbed inside, he wasn't alone.

"Look, darling. It's where we first met."

Kierli, taking the appearance of Evelyn. She sat back on the bench, her legs crossed, her blue eyes shimmering in the moonlight.

Tarren slammed the door and sat across from her, arms folded. "What do you want? You've sure spoiled my evening."

"I think I've made your evening," Kierli purred as her face reverted back to normal. "Weren't you just visiting with your mother? You should be more grateful."

"I said *what do you want?*"

"Names."

"Of who?"

"Of every Foreordained person in the kingdom, including where they are."

Tarren's eyes narrowed. "I hate the sound of that."

"Almost as much as your mother's maddened screams? Her wild eyes oblivious to who you are?"

Those words sent a chill through his body. He clenched his teeth behind his lips and flexed his hands, wanting desperately to lash out, but knowing better. "I can have it by tomorrow night."

"Wonderful," Kierli said. "I'll meet you just outside the castle after sundown. Don't be late."

Poof. Gone. Tarren scowled for the rest of the trip.

* * * * *

Master Ferribolt's writing stick scratched on the parchment as it went, his gray eyes hard and focused. It was nearing the bottom of the parchment and his hand was growing tired. He would stop, then write some more, then stop and sigh, then keep writing. At last, he ran out of room and dropped the writing stick, stretching his hand once more. He grinned absently and felt a swell in his heart as he reviewed the contents of the page.

Yes. This is enough.

From out of a drawer, he pulled two other blank sheets of parchment and set them down. Raising his hand over the written document, he mumbled some Ancient Nezmythian and swept his hand over the empty pages. Magically, words appeared on them, perfectly copied from the written one.

He took some thread and bound up each parchment as its own roll. The first one, the second one... as he rolled up the third one, he looked at the page header one more time. He smiled, then cinched it up.

Holding all three rolls in his hands, he uttered another Ancient phrase. The pages glowed white for a short moment, then faded back to normalcy. Then he opened a drawer in his desk, carefully set the rolls inside, and slid the drawer shut. For the last touch, he took a key from his robes and locked the drawer shut, then patted it like an obedient dog.

He grunted and his knees protested as he stood up. He scooped a saucer and cup of tea that was sitting on the corner of the desk and took it over to the fire, soaking up the heat. Gazing into the flames, he brought the cup to his lips. The fire crackled so brilliantly. So bright. They nearly matched the colors of his robes like a mirror. He looked up to the ceiling as if to stare into the night sky. As he did, he let out a sigh.

"The time is getting closer, isn't it?" he said. "I can feel it." Looking back at the fire, he took another sip of his tea, then remembered some words he read not so long ago. "*The tall sunflower shall make the moons bright. The great tree shall rend asunder as the stars reach up from the ground. Bones and wings of old shall vex the tormentor. If the last stone remains, all that lives shall depart and be free.*" He sipped again. "I suppose I was never meant to understand all things."

He drained the cup, then set it down on one of the end tables. He marched through the main hall, up the stairs, until he arrived at the door of his butler, Jerem.

He gave the door three gentle knocks. After a minute, Jerem sleepily answered the door. "Yes, sir?"

"Good evening, Jerem. Please come chat with me in the study."

"Could it wait until morning?"

"I'm afraid not."

Jerem half-staggered through the house as he followed Master Ferribolt. When they finally arrived in the study, Jerem sat across from Master Ferribolt in one of the armchairs. Jerem tried to remain attentive with lackluster results. Meanwhile, Master Ferribolt leaned forward in his seat, his hands laced together and his eyes serious.

"Jerem, how long have you served in this house?"

Jerem tried not to yawn. "Something like fifteen years, Master."

"And you've served honorably. I've admired your service and dedication. Tonight, I'm dismissing you from that service."

Suddenly, Jerem was very awake. "Pardon?"

"Don't think of this as an expulsion," Master Ferribolt said. "This isn't a question of your quality or dependability. You've always been wonderful. This is a matter of your safety."

Jerem swallowed. Master Ferribolt continued:

"The Sacred Dragon has been impressing feelings upon my mind for some time now. And they've been getting stronger. With Kierli still on the loose and with the murders at the prison days ago... there's no telling what she's capable of or who she will target next. I can take care of things here from now on. I'm asking you to take your things and leave as quickly as possible."

Jerem's throat was dry and he tried to swallow again. "I see. Well... I suppose I can stay with my mother until I find my next opportunity." He sat up straight. "I will always consider my time here an honor, Master."

Master Ferribolt smiled and thanked him.

"But, Master, if I may…" Jerem asked. "Would you bestow a blessing upon me before I go?"

"Yes, a brief one."

He stood from his chair and walked over to his young friend. He held his forefingers and thumbs in a triangle over Jerem's scalp, and the servant bowed his head. Commanding the heavens within his breast, Master Ferribolt said, "Jerem, the Sacred Dragon will reward you handsomely in the next life for your service in this house. You have shown dedication, dependability, grace, cleanliness, and honor. With this blessing, I assure you that you shall never taste the sting of death, but shall be taken up by the Sacred Dragon in due time."

With that, Master Ferribolt took back his hands, and Jerem stared with glistening eyes. The butler embraced the Chief Patriarch like a father, and Master Ferribolt returned it. When they let go, Master Ferribolt held the man in the Nezmythian Grasp of Brotherhood. "Go, my friend. Be safe."

Jerem was out of the house within a matter of minutes. Master Ferribolt admonished Jerem to warn the gatekeeper and the carriage driver as well, which he did. They took Master Ferribolt's carriage to the southern end of Upper City where his mother lived. His mother was perplexed at their midnight arrival, but alarmed when Jerem told her of the circumstances. They all prayed together for Master Ferribolt's safety.

Meanwhile, Master Ferribolt meandered the halls of the mansion, taking it in. His bedroom. The study. At length, he found himself in the main hall, admiring the polished tile and the Dragon statue standing triumphantly in the middle of the floor. He took a mental note that he hadn't stopped and admired that statue as often as he should have. The craftsmanship was obviously by blessed hands—so smooth and detailed. Majestic. Absently, he reached out and set his hand on its stony claw.

"It's been an honor," he breathed.

He wandered to the middle of the room and waved his hand. One of the chairs from the study magically appeared behind him. He sat down, crossed his legs, and put his hands in his lap as he faced the door.

It only took a few minutes.

The door crashed open, and there she was. Her blonde hair flicking in the breeze and her face pale with violence. The two moons hung in the sky just over her shoulder. And she clutched a weapon in her hand that was otherworldly—a sword with an ornate handle and a blade that reflected no light.

Master Ferribolt sat unphased. "That's an interesting weapon."

Kierli sneered and ignored the comment. She dug her heels in and tried to charge, but as she clutched her weapon, it refused to enter the Chief Patriarch's mansion. It even seemed to pull her back—stopping at the threshold. No matter how Kierli tugged at it, it wouldn't budge.

"That must be a weapon of dark nature," Master Ferribolt said. "Those have no power here. They know this place is blessed by the Sacred Dragon, just like the Cathedrals. If you wish to kill me, it'll have to be with something else."

Kierli exhaled irritably and Starshadow disappeared. She kicked the door closed behind her and cocked her hand back.

"Fine then," she sneered.

She threw her hand forward, expecting to launch some sort of dark blast of magic. But nothing—like throwing a ball that wasn't there.

"*Tepnoh Edomah* won't work here either," Master Ferribolt said. "That's the ancient name of the magic you've been using, if you've forgotten. Please have a seat."

Master Ferribolt waved his hand and a chair appeared next to Kierli. Again, she ignored it. Instead, she ripped a dagger from her belt and dashed toward him. Master Ferribolt hardly flinched. He lifted his hand and suddenly Kierli was thrown against the door. She slammed against it and the dagger clambered by her side. She sat up painfully rubbing her neck. Meanwhile, Master Ferribolt adjusted comfortably.

"We can do this all night if you'd like," Master Ferribolt said. "But I won't let you kill me until I have some answers."

Kierli harrumphed and pushed herself up. "Fine then. It's been a while since I've had a relaxing chat with anyone. All this running has been exhausting." She holstered her dagger and sat down. "Ah, it hasn't been too long since I sat in this chair."

"Indeed. You and Yorn. I hope he's doing well."

"I haven't seen him, if that's what you're wondering."

"I wasn't going to ask."

Kierli smirked. "So what did you want to know? Are you going to try to save my soul? Rescue me from the abyss?"

"I thought about that. But I also think anyone with the darkness in their heart sufficient to open up the Chasm might not be interested in the musings of an old man."

"Well spoken."

"If I were a betting man, and I'm not," Master Ferribolt said, "I would wager that your plan is to usurp the throne from King Jason and take it for your own. I would also wager that you have been planning this for quite some time. Years, even."

"Not quite."

"You can be truthful with me; it's not as though I'll survive the night."

Kierli looked around. "There's no one else here?"

"No. Just me. And you know I'm a truthful man."

She folded her arms. "I never truly considered being Queen until the lot of you threw me in prison for learning some magic tricks. All I did was serve Nezmyth with that power, and I was punished for it. What kind of King does something so hasty and reckless? Someone who doesn't deserve to rule.

"That whole situation woke me up to how oppressive the Old Ways really are. No wonder so many kingdoms have abandoned it. It's foolish, misguided, and doesn't block corruption as it should. When I met the god that lives under the prison, it told me the truth—told me that the Dragon has been controlling people for years through the Old Ways, and it's time to make a change. When the Old Ways are overthrown and we've joined the rest of Wevlia, I'll rule as Queen."

"The 'true' god," Master Ferribolt echoed while shaking his head. "So how will you dismantle a system that's stood for thousands of years?"

"Destroy every Foreordained person in Nezmyth," Kierli said flatly. "Spare no one. I don't find joy in that, but it's necessary. When they're all gone, the people will naturally call me to be Queen. They already want it."

"So you're starting with me. The first to die under your conquest."

Kierli nodded.

"I see," Master Ferribolt nodded thoughtfully. "Well, I hate to be the bearer of bad news, but your venture is folly. You will never rule Nezmyth."

Kierli frowned. "Oh?"

"There are two things standing in your way," Master Ferribolt held up two fingers. "One, King Jason and the Sacred Dragon. This is the last kingdom in Wevlia that clings to the Old Ways, so you best believe the Sacred Dragon will defend it, even as It did during the Ash War. Two, which may surprise you, is whatever you awakened down in the Chasm days ago."

Kierli didn't respond, but just listened.

"Let me be absolutely clear to you, Kierli," Master Ferribolt continued. "The forces of good and evil in this world are alive and very real. There is the Sacred Dragon, who gives light, truth and peace, and there is the Guardian of the Night, who sows destruction, lies, and bondage. That entity that you awakened down in the Chasm represents the latter. Whatever power it has given you will be fleeting. It will use you to get what it wants, then abandon you like trash. That, I can guarantee."

Kierli shook her head and smiled. "No, you can't. You can't guarantee that in the slightest. You talk of how the Sacred Dragon defends Nezmyth... where was it twenty-seven years ago when Barnabas came to power? Where was it when women like me were being abused by our village chief? Where was it when thousands were being slaughtered by the Ash? The Sacred Dragon picks who it protects and abandons who it wants. My power comes from a higher force."

Master Ferribolt took a deep breath and deflated. "I'm so sorry you see things that way."

"I've just been blessed with clarity."

Master Ferribolt half-smiled. "So is this when you kill me?"

"Only if you don't plan on throwing me against a wall."

"I won't."

Kierli stood from the armchair and dusted off her knees. "It's a shame, really. You've always been a pleasant man. But you understand where I'm coming from. It must be done."

"I'm sure you will do what you think is best. But understand with the murder of a Chief Patriarch, your place in Darkness will be forever secured. You remember the old stories—the place of misery and endless torment."

"Stories are just that—stories," Kierli said. "Don't worry. I'll make it quick. Oh, and say hello to Rosie for me. I'm sure she'll be delighted to see you."

"I won't," Master Ferribolt sneered. "She wouldn't like you at all."

Kierli flipped the dagger in her hand and darted for the Chief Patriarch. All the while, he stayed calm and collected in his seat. There was nothing inside him commanding him to retaliate. Nothing inside him screaming for survival. In his heart and his soul, his duty in mortality was complete. He had done what was required. He had loved greatly and deeply. And he had issued a warning to his assailant. At this point, he commemorated all that he was to the Sacred Dragon.

The dagger plunged through his ribs and he coughed. He felt himself thrown into a dark tunnel. The senses fled from his eyes and his body lost its strength as blood seeped from the wound. He did not fear and did not grow cold. Because just as the darkness enveloped him, so did a light. A warmth—familiar and sweet.

Conversely, a fiery bolt shot through his body and into Kierli's hand. She cried out, dropping the dagger and falling to her knees. She held her hand to her face as shallow fissures of purple cracked across her fingers and palm. Breathing came in unnatural bursts until her body finally jerked back to normal. It left her breathing in shallow gasps. She turned the hand in front of her eyes as she inspected every crack and pore. It wasn't disappearing. Was this permanent? Purple, web-like fractures etched into her skin?

By now, Master Ferribolt's body was slumped at her feet, lifeless. She thought of saying some words, but didn't. He was a pillar of oppression, even if he didn't know it. So good-natured and kind. It was a shame, really.

She got to her feet, stormed out of the main hall, and slammed the door behind her. Starshadow appeared in her hand. As she gripped the dark blade, the purple cracks in her hand glowed brighter. She ogled it, stiffening her lower lip.

Kierli almost disappeared into the night—almost transported herself away. But she knew she had to dress the scene. Make it look divinely orchestrated. It didn't take her long to think of it.

She lifted her hand and shot a plume of purple fire at the door. The flames danced in her eyes, then the door toppled backward and the embers crawled through the mansion. The last thing she did was point her fingers at the porch and carve large green words at the threshold:

THE TRUE GOD HAS SPOKEN
KIERLI FOR QUEEN

Kierli didn't stand to watch, no matter how much she wanted to. She disappeared in that curtain of smoke, and within minutes, the entire mansion was engulfed in flames.

As the fire devoured the building, the chandeliers fell in the main hall. The books in the library were reduced to ash. The Ancient Texts were no more—their history and lore gone from Nezmyth. But mysteriously, three letters in Master Ferribolt's desk drawer disappeared. They had vanished as soon as his spirit left his body. And instead, they reappeared on King Jason's dresser, Captain Barnabas's dining table, and Advisor Tarren's pillow.

25

THE TRUTH

Barnabas had a hard time keeping his emotions in check. The coals were still hot beneath his boots. The sun was rising in the east but he would not feel its warmth. Last night he lost a friend and he never had the chance to say goodbye. Just like last time.

In the middle of the night, two soldiers arrived at his door and beat it until he got out of bed. When they told him the situation, he frantically put his armor on and mounted his horse. By the time he arrived at the mansion, it was too late. It was completely swallowed in flames.

Did he make it out? Where was he?

He prayed to the Dragon that Master Ferribolt made it out alive during his ride home. The soldiers told him that the fire wouldn't spread to the other homes nearby, but they wouldn't have a chance to look through the wreckage until it died down. When Barnabas came home and began taking his armor off, he noticed the note on the table.

He frowned at it, then reached out and picked it up. It was in Master Ferribolt's handwriting.

To my friends,

My time has finally come. The Sacred Dragon is taking me into Its peaceful rest. My mortal sojourn has concluded, and I'm returning to my sweet Rosie. Thank you for providing some of the sweetest experiences I enjoyed in mortality.

The Sacred Dragon has permitted me to see my fate, and has informed me that my life will be taken at the hand of Kierli. I'm not clear on her motive, but I do not intend to fight back or struggle. I am ready, and the hand of death brings me no fear.

Jason, you have been a valiant and wonderful King. It has been an honor to serve beside you. I have watched you grow from a fearful boy into a mighty warrior, scholar, and magistrate. Rosie and I never had the pleasure of raising a child, but you have been the closest thing to a son I have had.

Tarren, your wisdom and determination to heal your mother are inspiring. I'm so glad I was alive to see the restoration of Niri and the joy it brought to your heart. I hope the Sacred Dragon continues to bless you in your role as Advisor, and that you and Jason continue to lead the kingdom with inspiration and honor.

Barnabas, my dear friend. You are special. Your heart was once filled with darkness and anger, but you have become a mighty saint, leader, and father. The Kingdom of Nezmyth owes you a great debt. I look forward to embracing you when your time arrives to join me in Paradise. Your story is my favorite of all.

Farewell, my dear friends. Do not weep for me and do not linger in grief. The bridge to eternity is a small one to cross, and when your time arrives, I will welcome you with open arms.

With love, Ferribolt

Do not weep, Barnabas repeated the words in his mind. *How?*

He busied himself right away. *Have to do something. Have to take my mind off.* His feet took him to the stove where he put on a kettle. With shaking hands, he struck some stones and lit a fire. Then he stood and numbly watched the kettle as the water started to boil. His lips pushed shut and his chin shuddered as he shakily poured hot water into a cup.

He sat alone at the table, hands trembling, trying to drink the tea. The silence built, echoing violently off the walls until his emotions bubbled over. He hurled the cup across the room, shattering the ceramic, then slammed his fists on the table. Artemis cawed angrily from his perch.

That was two that she had taken now. Two.

He didn't get any more sleep for the rest of the night. Now, he stood in the middle of what was once the main hall. Everything around him was scorched and broken—that is, everything except the Sacred Dragon statue. Its stone was still creamy and pristine. The only things that looked out of place in the main hall were two smokey gray chairs facing each other. But no sign of a body. As a matter of fact, neither he nor the other soldiers could find any bodies anywhere.

Did he actually die? Barnabas thought. *Or did he get away? No. Otherwise I wouldn't have gotten the letter.*

A crowd had gathered around the property and the soldiers worked to keep them away from the wreckage. Many townspeople held each other close, whimpering, trying to comfort each other. Even some of the soldiers suppressed tears under their helmets.

In due time, the red carriage pulled up and the people parted. Both Jason and Tarren jumped out, running for what used to be the door. When they approached it, they saw the letters on the porch. *The true god has spoken. Kierli for Queen.* Jason bore his teeth and stepped on them as he crossed the threshold.

And when he did, all the air left his lungs. His chest tightened and his eyes stung. The charred smell. The black, desecrated remnants of what used to be a place of refuge. Tarren frowned as he looked around, but Jason had a harder time keeping it together. His bottom lip quivered and his teeth clenched together. Barnabas marched toward him to give him a report.

"There's no body," Barnabas said. "Not him, not even Jerem or the others."

"Maybe they got out," Jason's voice shook. "Maybe he and the others are still alive somewhere."

"But that wouldn't explain the letters," Barnabas said. "I'm assuming you both got one."

Jason nodded tightly. He had read the letter just minutes ago. It was a truth that he didn't want to acknowledge. Aimlessly, like wandering through a nightmare, he found himself moving toward the ruins of the study. He knew he probably shouldn't—it would only make things harder. But still, he had to. He crossed the remains of the open arch and arrived in the room. The floor was completely covered in ashes and torched debris.

The fireplace was nearly intact—a blackened pillar of stone. He stopped. How many times had he sat by that fireplace during times of despair and trouble? How many times had Master Ferribolt gazed into his eyes and told him things that he needed to hear? And where would that be now? Jason took a deep breath and wiped his eyes, then his nose, fully aware of the townspeople watching from several yards away.

I'm the King. I have to show strength at a time like this. But how? Jason looked at the faces gathered on the street and watched their tears. Grownups and children alike, crying and comforting each other. How many lives had this man touched? Could anyone begin to count? He was a pinnacle of righteousness and love. A hero if there ever was one. But now he was gone.

That thought pushed him over. Jason turned his back on the crowd so they wouldn't see the tears slide down his face.

Tarren lingered near the entrance of the building, shuffling his feet and kicking over burnt boards. Barnabas ventured into other rooms to search for anything useful, but what was there to be found? They already knew who the killer was. Maybe it was just a feeble hope that he would be alive, buried somewhere. But no. The mansion's remains were completely vacant.

Barnabas and Jason both returned to the main entrance several minutes later. Jason's eyes were visibly puffy and swollen, but he cleared his throat and said, "Why do you think she targeted Master Ferribolt? What does she have to gain from killing him?"

"I don't know, Your Highness," Barnabas muttered.

Listening to both of them, Tarren swallowed. He had just seen Kierli last night. She had demanded a list of every Foreordained person in the kingdom. As the thought gripped him, a cold rush slid through his body. *Dear Dragon... does she intend to kill all of them?*

Jason turned to a nearby soldier. "Check on the other Patriarchs in town. Being the longest practicing Patriarch, Ragy is now the official Chief Patriarch. Tell them of the news and make sure they're safe. Then come back to the castle and report to us."

The soldier nodded and strode away. Jason and the others didn't linger. What else was there to see? They started for the carriage that would take them to the castle, but it was at that moment that Yorn arrived.

Two guards accompanied him. He marched up the soot-laden garden that led to the mansion's front porch and stopped. The color left his face as he surveyed the burned, imploded wreckage of the mansion.

"I came as quickly as I could," Yorn said as he nodded to King Jason. "Is everyone okay? Did the Chief Patriarch get out?"

Jason took Yorn by the shoulder and led him away from the crowd. When they were a reasonable distance away, Jason's face got dark and his voice was low. "There weren't any bodies here, but the three of us each received letters last night from Master Ferribolt. He's dead, Yorn. Before he died, he received a vision of who his killer would be. It was Kierli."

Yorn's mouth went dry. He looked around as if an explanation would be floating in the air somewhere. He swallowed, his lips forming words, but nothing came. Jason squeezed his shoulder again and said more seriously, "Yorn, if you get *any* kind of information from her, tell me. I don't know why she would target Master Ferribolt, but if this is the start of something else, your help will be imperative. That's my order to you as King. Do you understand?"

Yorn clenched his jaw and nodded.

"You have no other reason to be here," Jason said. "There's nothing left. No books, nothing. I recommend you go about the rest of your day as usual."

Jason patted his shoulder and followed the others to the carriage. Yorn watched them as they moved through the crowd, climbed inside, and trotted back toward the castle. All the while, Yorn wrestled with the truth the King just gave.

Kierli did this?

It was bad enough that she was accused of killing those guards and Captain Felix, but now *Master Ferribolt?* If it were true...

He swallowed and clenched his teeth again, then he marched back through the crowd—a singular destination in mind.

The two soldiers that accompanied him looked expectantly for an order. "Uh, sir?"

"I have no orders for you here, gentlemen," Yorn said firmly. "I have an errand to run. Keep patrolling the streets as you usually do. I'll see you back at the barrack tonight."

Through the crowd he went. Then down to the edge of Upper City. Northern Market Street was busy this morning—people were buzzing in tight knots, chattering about the destruction of the Chief Patriarch's mansion. Was he dead? If so, who could have done it? Silently, Yorn marveled at how quickly news traveled. Some hypothesized that it was Kierli's doing. Others whispered a theory that King Jason set it on fire to better frame Kierli. Yorn scowled at these.

When he reached Sue's, there was an available table outside. He sat down, and within minutes a sweet young waitress came out with a tankard of booshum berry juice. Yorn didn't even drink from it. He just waited.

It was a stretch and he had doubts it would even happen, but incredibly, she arrived. Evelyn. Looking a little sleepy, but otherwise as chipper and bright as usual. She slipped into the seat opposite from Yorn, propped her head on her hand, and batted her eyes at him.

"Fancy meeting you here," she said lightly. "Busy morning?"

"You could say that. I saw it."

"Saw what?"

"Don't be dumb," Yorn said. "Master Ferribolt. He's gone and the mansion is destroyed. They're saying he's dead."

Instantly, Evelyn's expression dropped. "He's *dead?*"

"They say Kierli did it."

"Who's they?" Evelyn frowned.

"King Jason. Said Master Ferribolt was granted a vision of who his killer would be, and said it was her."

Evelyn rolled her eyes. "Of course King Jason would say that."

"Was it or wasn't it?"

"Of course not!"

Yorn's gaze was intense—he kept his arms folded, not blinking or tearing his eyes off her. Evelyn's feet shifted and she swallowed a little bit. Stirring up confidence, she said, "Is this all you were hoping for? If that's it, don't waste my time. Kierli isn't a criminal. I'm sorry, but I have to go."

She got up to leave, but Yorn hadn't forgotten Jason's admonition. He had instructions to get any kind of information from her. There was definitely an opportunity here, and if he sold it just right, Kierli wouldn't suspect anything. Then maybe he'd find some relief for that feeling in his stomach.

"You know," he said, "I served with Kierli for nearly two years. I'm sure if she really did these things, she'd have a good reason. If I knew exactly what she was doing, I might be more useful."

Evelyn stopped. Cautiously, she turned and crept back to the table. The flirtatious facade was gone. Her face was cold and serious.

"I'm sure," she said. "You've always been a good soldier. She probably doesn't have anyone else to trust, and that help would be a great relief to her. But that would bring you into a whole new world. You'd have to forsake the things of the past, including your oaths as a soldier."

Yorn shrugged. "Perhaps some oaths are meant to be broken."

Evelyn's eyes flashed. "Are you sure that's what you want?"

This is it. Yorn nodded.

Smiling and giggling, Evelyn grabbed Yorn's hand and pulled him up from his seat. He managed to drop some Pieces on the table before she led him away. With her hand laced in his, Evelyn projected the image of an affectionate couple enjoying an autumn morning. Yorn did his best to mirror it, smiling and clutching her hand as they strolled.

Evelyn took him into an alley, out of sight. That's when they both disappeared—enveloped in a curtain of smoke. Yorn couldn't breathe, but only for a second. Suddenly, he and Evelyn had been transported to a mysterious cellar he had never seen before. It was dank and dirty, but a recently-used bedroll was pushed into the corner.

Evelyn was gone—instead, Kierli took her place. The blonde hair, the long scar. It was her. She let go of Yorn's hand, folded her arms, and leaned against a wall. There was nothing bright or fun about her appearance anymore.

"Fine," Kierli said. "Here's the truth: I killed Master Ferribolt. And Captain Felix. And those soldiers. But for good reason."

Yorn's face went pale. *The truth.* "Why?"

"Because great change is coming, Yorn," she said, pushing herself off the wall. "The Old Ways are dying. It's time Nezmyth moves on to a new era—an era of freedom and prosperity. I worked tirelessly for the benefit of Nezmyth and I was rewarded with a cell. There is more, but I'll keep it brief: I'm growing in power in ways that you couldn't imagine. Before long, I'll rule as Queen. And if you help me get there, you'll be rewarded."

The truth, Yorn thought. *She finally gave me the truth. And it's this.*

"Wait until I give you further orders," she said. "Glorious change, Yorn. Glorious. Thank you for being someone I can trust. But if you betray me." She advanced on him. "I *will* kill you. You understand that."

He swallowed, smirked, and nodded. "I could never."

"I know you wouldn't. Enjoy the rest of your day."

In another curtain of smoke, Yorn was back at his barrack, just as he had left it earlier. His bed was still made, his water basin full… and a paper titled "To my darling Kierli" was still on his desk.

She lied to me, he thought. *She actually lied to me. After everything.*

With stinging eyes, he crossed the floor, snatched up the parchment, and tore it to pieces. Then he started for the castle.

26

THE INHERITOR

"Your Highness," Yorn said, "I have a report."

King Jason had been sitting on the throne with puffy and swollen eyes when Yorn entered the castle. He wiped his face and sat up straight as Yorn approached the throne platform. To the King's side, Barnabas and Tarren discussed plans for Master Ferribolt's funeral. But when Yorn entered the great hall, their discussion died down.

Jason coughed and said, "Already?"

"It was a long shot, sir, but I chanced it," he said. "She arrived at the shop we used to frequent and appeared with her usual disguise."

Jason stood. "What did she say?"

"She said glorious change was coming, Nezmyth is entering into a new era, and that she intends to rule as Queen," Yorn said. "She admitted to killing Master Ferribolt, along with Captain Felix and those at the prison days ago. And she told me she'd reward me for serving her."

Barnabas flexed his jaw and glanced at Jason out of the corner of his eye. Jason felt a shiver of anger move through him. Next to him, Tarren had to clamp his jaw to keep it from chattering.

"Dragon curse me," Barnabas muttered. "I can't believe I called her to be Chief Captain."

"Shut up, Barnabas!" Jason spat.

Unsatisfied, Barnabas still kept his eyes to the ground, brooding. Then he turned to Jason. "Your Highness, I recommend we guard Master Ragy day and night. If he's the new Chief Patriarch, she might make him the next target. I'll personally front the battalion protecting him."

"Granted," Jason agreed. "Guards, see to it!"

Some soldiers nodded and ran out of the room.

Jason stepped down from the platform and approached Yorn before putting his hand on his shoulder. He used a tone that only they could hear. "I haven't forgotten what you told me. This must be very difficult—working against her instead of for her."

Yorn's voice was shallow. "Not as difficult as you may think, sir."

"But you are serving your kingdom, and for that, I am grateful. It does put you in a volatile position, however—you'll have to be especially careful. Please keep your wits about you and report any other information she gives you. She's opened the gate to something terrible, but having you does give us some leverage. I'm counting on you."

"I understand, sir."

"Thank you. You're dismissed."

Yorn snapped his feet together, nodded, and turned on his heels. As he marched toward the double doors, Jason couldn't help but notice how he carried himself. A man of goodness and truth. A man who cut through distractions and trusted his instincts. Perhaps he was lonely and torn, but despite his hardship, there was something dignified about him.

Even royal.

That's when the spark erupted in Jason's mind—like a flame igniting in a dark room. The question he had been pondering for weeks had been answered, clear as day. And there was no hesitation.

"Yorn, stop. Come back."

Perplexed, Yorn returned to the throne dais. Jason put his hand on his shoulder again, then turned to Tarren and Barnabas. For once, a smile graced his lips. And it didn't feel out of place.

"Gentleman," he said, "I've made my decision. After weeks, it's finally become clear to me. Yorn will be my Inheritor. You are both witnesses to my decision."

Surprise jumped across every face, especially Yorn's. His jaw dangled and his knees nearly gave out. He coughed as his heart skipped and his mouth tried to form words.

"I, uh—Your—Your Highness!" He said. "This is, uh, so unexpected. Are you sure about—"

"Captain, this is a question that has plagued me ever since Queen Saryan passed," Jason said. "The Sacred Dragon has impressed upon me that you are worthy to take up my mantle if death takes me. You still have a choice, but I am officially extending you this offer. Captain Yorn, do you accept?"

How could I say no? Yorn picked up all the dignity he could muster, then straightened his posture and croaked the words. "I accept."

"Good."

Jason pulled Nightbane from its sheath. He held out his arm and gripped the handle so the blade pointed toward the ground. Yorn squared his shoulders, then reached out and held the blade's pommel so his hand was on top of Jason's. They locked eyes, and Jason recited the oath:

"With Tarren and Barnabas and these soldiers as our witnesses, I hereby instate Yorn, Captain in the Nezmythian Army, as my primary Inheritor. As such, Yorn will be entitled to every right, privilege, and responsibility I hold if death take me before succession by Foreordination. This includes full command of the Nezmythian Army, the throne, the castle, and stewardship over the Kingdom of Nezmyth. Yorn, do you accept this sacred charge?"

Yorn's throat was dry, but he nodded and said, "Yes."

"For Nezmyth!" Jason shouted.

"For Nezmyth!" Yorn echoed.

Jason put Nightbane back in its sheath. "Thank you, Yorn. You've brought some peace to my mind. Now go and serve Nezmyth as you were. I await your next report."

Forcing a smile, Yorn bowed and marched away. His heart raced and his knees felt like water as he went down the red carpet and passed through the doors. Inheritor—something he never aspired to, given to him so freely. He felt honored and grateful, but also fearful.

If Kierli were to find out, what would she do?

The doors closed with a boom, then the great hall fell to a thoughtful hush. That was until Barnabas broke the silence.

"So," he said, "there it is, then. Your new Inheritor."

Jason nodded. "The impression was unmistakable. He's the one."

Tarren's mind had been far from the present ever since this morning. All that had just taken place felt like a blur to him—a stage play that he was barely watching. His stomach felt sick ever since he saw the ruins of Master Ferribolt's home and connected it with Kierli's request.

She's going to kill all of them. She's going to murder every last one of them and she's making me help her. She's making me a piece in her conquest.

"Barnabas, Your Highness," he said. "I'm not feeling particularly well. I'd like to be excused to my quarters."

Jason blinked at him, concerned. "Of course, Tarren. You're excused."

Tarren stiffly bowed and walked away. His feet took up through some corridors, up some stairs, and into his room.

There, he reflected on the events of the last day—Kierli's demand, Master Ferribolt's death, Yorn as Inheritor… and among it all, the ghastly task of the list.

He unrolled a sheet of parchment and picked up a writing stick. He knew each of their names—he had a directory tacked on the edge of his desk. Names, what position they had been Foreordained to, which village they lived in, the date in which they received their Blessing of Fate… everything. Some of them had just received their Blessing this year, meaning they weren't even in their teens yet.

Dear Dragon, he thought. *Is she going to kill even these?*

The writing stick shivered in his hand. He pictured Kierli barging into the homes of innocent children to slaughter them for what they would become. Their parents screaming. Their blood smeared across the floor. And it would start with this writing stick in his hand.

He felt the bile creeping up and he couldn't stop it. He dove to a large plant nearby and put his face in the vase, then the vomit came. His forehead glistened with sweat and his hands shook. He couldn't write the words. But he had to. If he didn't, Niri would go back to her maddened state. Then Kierli would just find another way to find these people and kill them. Why did she have to rope him into this?

And on top of it all, a searing iron of guilt against his conscience. The loving words from Master Ferribolt's letter—so supportive and overjoyed of his mother's wellness, unaware of the awful circumstances.

Tarren sniffled and pushed his fingers through his hair, grabbing great tufts. And yet, the empty page remained. If he filled it out, his mother would remain fine and healthy. If he didn't…

The agony and stress were too much. He needed release. Something to numb and distract him. Only one thing came to mind, but it was awful. Could he do it? Here? He looked at his open hand and remembered the dancing purple flame.

He could do it again. Just once more. Then that's it. Not again. But what could he use? He hadn't killed anything lately.

He looked at the plant that he had just vomited into. It was the only other living thing in his room. He swallowed, his eyes darting to the door. It was closed. Quietly, he slipped from his seat, crossed the room and locked it shut. Then he went back to the plant. He coughed loudly and pushed it over, throwing soil onto the floor. The smell of vomit became more pungent as it seeped onto the stone. The plant definitely wasn't going to grow after that, but he ground out the roots for good measure.

Would that be enough? He held out his hand and pushed his feelings into his palm. Then it appeared. The purple flame, dancing and waving in his hand. His eyes stopped stinging and his body stopped trembling. He let himself down into his chair and leaned back, taking a deep breath as the flame flickered and swayed. The euphoria dipped and moved inside him, making itself at home, filling every digit and joint with pleasure. Then, after a moment, it disappeared.

And with it, the same dilemma arrived. The empty paper. Kierli's demand for every Foreordained servant in the kingdom. Tarren sat staring at the empty paper for a long while, a part of him missing the soft feelings that Dark Magic gave him. Finally, he picked up a writing stick.

She'll find these people even if I don't do anything, he justified. *I have no choice.*

And with that, he wrote.

* * * * *

At the end of the day, Jason dragged his feet to his bedroom and peeled off his armor. After hanging it up, he forced himself to the couch and got on one knee. When he closed his eyes, he pictured the wreckage of Master Ferribolt's home. The creaking floorboards laden with soot. The torched remains of books and furniture. Normally, they would prepare a Patriarch's body for burial, but there was no body to prepare. Maybe the Sacred Dragon really did take his body, like the stories of ancient Patriarchs before the Dark Era.

It all made his soul heavy. Every ounce of him weighed down with the numbness of grief. He rubbed his face and let out a long breath.

"Sacred Dragon," he whispered. "I don't know if I'm strong enough for this. With Saryan gone, and now Master Ferribolt… We're looking for Kierli, but even Yorn doesn't have any clues. I worry for Nezmyth. I know I've been told to trust my instincts, but it's hard to trust myself when I feel so burdened."

Jason listened for an answer, but there was none. Just a long, consuming silence. His heart ached with frustration, longing for a sign, inwardly begging for some kind of confirmation. But again, the silence was the only thing that held him close.

Defeated, he crawled onto the couch and pulled the blanket over his body, trying not to think of the gaping hole inside him. He didn't notice it, but he began to drift to sleep.

Then there was a voice.

"It's okay to be weak sometimes. The Dragon fills the difference."

He was on top of the castle. The air was stale and the sky was black—coated with the familiar swirling clouds. Tremors crept up and down the landscape, shaking the trees in the Western Woods and making the Eastern Mountains shudder. Under Upper City hill, something was churning. And Jason was right on top of it.

But for some reason, the impending doom didn't frighten him. That's because Saryan stood across from him, smiling. The silver eyes. The freckles splashed around her nose. She was also garbed in white, looking as beautiful and pure as ever. Her appearance was like a diamond against a black sheet.

"But I can't be weak," Jason said. "I'm King. There's too much on my shoulders."

Saryan grinned. "You're so dumb sometimes. Through everything, you still need to be reminded that the Dragon is the one who leads this kingdom. Not you."

Jason smirked. "Is this really you? Or just a dream?"

Saryan didn't answer the question, but kept smiling. "How have your lessons been with Alis? Do you feel like your own person yet?"

"No. Everything is different without you. You were everything to me—you still are."

Saryan's feet didn't make a sound as she strode toward her husband—a brilliant white specter moving through darkness. She put her hand on his cheek and held it gently, but Jason couldn't feel it. All the same, those silver eyes were close. He wanted to kiss her. To hold her. But he knew that was impossible.

"There is so much you've forgotten," she said tenderly. "Just because I left doesn't mean I'm lost. I've never been far. And as for yourself..." she smiled wide and shook her head. "You've always been Jason, King of Nezmyth. With or without me. I'll be fine, and I'll be waiting for you. But for now, you still have a responsibility. Nezmyth needs you."

The ground trembled more. Upper City hill was edging near explosion. Jason could feel it coming.

"You're complete, Jason," she said. "You are. You always were."

The ground gave one last shudder. Saryan leaned in to kiss him. Just before their lips could touch and the Upper City hill could burst, Jason awoke.

Jason blinked, and suddenly, he was back on his couch, facing up. Moisture gathered in his eye sockets, and as he sat up, they dribbled out the sides of his face. He sniffed and swallowed.

You're complete.

A tremor of strength shook through him. He threw the blanket off his body and trudged over to the window, putting his fist on the glass. In the moonlight, he overlooked Nezmyth City. The candles dancing in the windows. The smoke rising up from chimneys. Fragments of thought aligned. Clarity brewed and became brighter. What was lost was revealing itself.

And for some reason, he knew she was here in the room with him. He could feel it. Something inside him said so.

"I'm complete as I am," he whispered half to himself. "I am Jason, Foreordained King of Nezmyth. And this is the last night I linger in fear."

He didn't go back to the couch. Instead, he went to the bed. He nestled under the covers and pulled the blanket up to his shoulders, just like he used to do. Within moments, he was asleep.

And on the opposite side of the bed, the sheets were warm as if she were laying beside him.

* * * * *

Tarren's feet were heavy as he trudged out of the castle, eyes to the floor. A list of names was clutched in his hand. The guards didn't question where he was going as he slunk through the castle—they just kept to their duty, silently following orders as Tarren commanded the double doors to open. With creaking hinges, they opened and closed and he entered the evening chill. The two moons hung in the sky like two great eyes watching him.

He swallowed and his heart pounded. The trees, bushes, and shrubs swayed and his eyes kept darting about. She said she would meet outside the castle walls, but where exactly? For that reason, he stayed close to the building, skulking in the shadows where he could. Guards were out patrolling the grounds as usual, and he wanted to draw as little attention as possible.

Suddenly, he felt a strange force fall on him. It didn't make him feel sleepy or energized, but instead made it feel like he was walking through water. And it was like a pair of hands had sandwiched his head together, muffling all sound. He turned all about, trying to discover the source, but it didn't take long. Kierli was standing right behind him, leering at him.

"Hello, handsome," she said. "Got a present for me?"

"Take it," Tarren stuck out his arm.

Kierli brushed his fingers as he took the list, which made his ears pink. He stole a glance at her body before he looked all around, frowning. "What did you do to us? The soldiers are just walking by."

"Encased us in a stealth dome," she said, unraveling the list and reading its contents. "It should last several minutes. Everyone walking by us won't see or hear us. It's just you and me."

Tarren swallowed at the sound of that. Satisfied, Kierli rolled the parchment back up and put it in her pocket. Then she eyed Tarren up and down. "There's something different about you. What is it?"

"I don't know what you're talking about."

She took a step closer. Tarren leaned back. She smiled. "You've let the magic touch you, haven't you?"

Tarren's blood turned to ice. "You can tell?"

"I suppose I can." She stepped forward again. "It's amazing, isn't it? What it makes you feel. The power that it gives you. There's nothing else quite like it."

"I've only used it a couple of times," Tarren said. "I don't use it like you do."

Kierli rolled her eyes. "So traditional. When will you wake up and realize how much more you could be with it? How much more powerful and cunning it makes you? After all, this magic healed your mother, remember?"

"And it's the same magic that killed your brother."

Instantly, he regretted saying that. She was too quick. Her fist was around his collar, yanking him close at unnatural speed. Her eyes were fiery and she bore her teeth like an animal.

"*Nartikis* killed my brother," she hissed. "I'm using this magic to build Nezmyth, not destroy it! I suggest you hold your tongue. Don't forget I control your mother's destiny."

Tarren clenched his jaw. "You're cruel."

"I'm a visionary."

She released his collar and the hunger returned to her eyes. Her hand traveled down his chest and stomach. Tarren tried not to quiver. To deflect the attention, he said, "You're going to kill all of them, aren't you?"

Kierli blinked innocently. "Yes. But you won't say a word of that. No hints, no ideas, nothing. Because I'll find out, and then you'll have your mother's body to deal with. Do you understand?"

Tarren didn't know why he said it, but he did. "Why are you pulling me into this? You could have found these people without me."

Kierli smiled and shook her head like a patient teacher with a slow student.

"I'm doing you a favor," she said. "You think these people love and appreciate you the way I would? Here you are, working as the Advisor, and has it ever brought you the things you truly wanted? Your mother's health? A beautiful woman beside you? With me, you'll have both of those things and more. This Sacred Dragon has done a shoddy job of rewarding you for all your sacrifice."

Tarren had no response for this. As he looked upon the last three years, he hated that she was right. He hated that he had worked so hard and been so obedient and had been rewarded with none of the things his heart longed for. And here she was. With all of those things on a silver platter.

Kierli smiled, then said, "It's time for an age of freedom, Mister Advisor. We'll finally join the rest of Wevlia in moving forward. And I've discovered means to bring about beautiful, glorious change. It will be magnificent. You can stand with me as I usher Nezmyth into an inspired new beginning. That's where I want you to be."

Kierli leaned in and planted a kiss on Tarren's lips, pulling his head against hers. Tarren was ashamed that he sunk into it, closing his eyes and letting her lead. After a long moment, she pulled back her perfect, soft lips and locked with his gaze, holding his cheek. Then she gave a playful wink.

"I'll see you again soon," she said.

She vanished. Tarren felt his ears and body go back to normal—no longer encased in the stealth bubble. He stormed back into the castle, feeling filthy as Kierli's words bounced inside his head.

That night, he had a hard time falling back asleep, so he killed a spider and used the Dark Magic to calm his nerves.

27

THE CAPTAINS

An entire week came and went. No sign of Kierli.

The protests in Center Court grew more intense. The soldiers had to stop frequent fistfights between Kierli supporters and Jason loyalists. On one occasion, townspeople even drew their weapons. Vandalism was beginning to blossom with words like "Queen Kierli" and "Share the spoil" smeared on the walls of public buildings, especially if they were frequented by loyalists. Soldiers were ordered to clean these up, but Jason didn't press them on finding the perpetrators.

Through it all, Jason carried himself with a new air of confidence. Everyone at the castle noticed it. He didn't drag his feet or stare at the ground like he used to, but instead, he squared his shoulders and walked with purpose. The couch in his room was removed and his houseplants thrived. He even meditated, read books, and exercised according to Tarren's regimen without grumbling or complaint.

Tarren, however, was a different story. He spent most of each day locked in his room, studying. He would emerge when duty called, but was usually irritable and short. He only fully emerged in the evenings when he went down to visit his mother at the Wilted Rose.

Lastly, Barnabas guarded Master Ragy every day without fail. The Eastern City Cathedral became more or less a second home. He was always accompanied by a dozen soldiers keeping watch inside and outside the building. Every evening, they would load Master Ragy into a carriage and escort him home. There, soldiers guarded his house until the sun came up and he was brought back to the Cathedral.

Tonight, Barnabas stood at the back of the Cathedral with his hand on his sword. The sun was just about to set—he could see the light growing dark through the windows. He kept his gaze fixed on the new Chief Patriarch, thinking of Master Ferribolt's death and his last talk with Nartikis. Both within days of each other.

Where's Kierli? He thought. *What has she been doing?*

Magically, torches ignited along the walls as the sun disappeared. Master Ragy stood from the prayer platform and made his way to the Cathedral's entrance, shuffling his feet as he went. Eventually, he reached Barnabas and the other soldiers. They all stood at attention.

He was a tall man with thick, short black hair and dark eyes. He knew the circumstances in which the soldiers were here, but showed no sign of discomfort or fear. He just bowed a little, shared a smile and said, "Ladies and gentlemen, I'm ready to depart."

They all formed a circle around him with Barnabas in the rear. When they reached the doors, Master Ragy turned around and looked Barnabas directly in the eye.

Barnabas nodded respectfully. "Master Ragy."

"Captain," Master Ragy said. "I'm sure recent days have been very difficult for you. I heard you and Master Ferribolt became good friends after the Ash War."

A blossom of hurt swelled in Barnabas's heart. "Yes, Master. He was the first person to accept me after prison."

"I don't doubt it," he smiled. "I have the pleasure of knowing all Patriarchs across Nezmyth, but if I'm being truly honest, Master Ferribolt was my favorite. He was special."

Yes. He was.

The doors swung open and the battalion advanced, keeping Master Ragy in the middle. They kept their weapons drawn and their eyes about them, ready for anything. All the while, Master Ragy didn't seem the least bit worried.

"Is there anything more troubling your mind, Captain?" he asked.

Barnabas had to think about it. Was there? He had been so consumed with Kierli and the deaths of his loved ones that he rarely had time to worry about himself. But as the Chief Patriarch asked that question, he remembered. There *was* something nagging at the back of his mind, like a dog scratching on a door in the middle of the night. He had just tried not to entertain the thought.

Nervously, Barnabas said, "Sometimes… I worry about the destination of my soul, sir."

"That's an old man's worry," Master Ragy laughed a little. "When you look at yourself honestly, where do you feel you belong?"

"I'm not sure."

Master Ragy gave a thoughtful pause. "You'll discover it when the time is right. If it eases your mind, you're likely doing better than you think you are. Remember, the Sacred Dragon takes pleasure in being merciful."

On top of the carriage, Artemis's face moved in staccatos as he looked all around. The soldiers checked the interior to make sure it was empty. When it was, Master Ragy loaded himself inside. They slammed the door shut and the carriage moved forward. Meanwhile, a few soldiers followed on either side of the carriage, and Barnabas mounted his horse and followed from behind. Artemis didn't move from his perch as the carriage crawled up the street.

Master Ragy's home wasn't far from the Cathedral—less than a mile. And thankfully, there weren't many buildings nearby. The Eastern City Cathedral was on the edge of three intersecting farms, so there weren't many places to hide. If anyone were to stage an attack, they would likely be spotted sprinting through cabbage fields or carrot patches.

Nevertheless, Barnabas kept his grip tight on his sword. His icy eyes surveyed every inch of the landscape, looking for any strange movement.

They trotted through town for several minutes, undisturbed. The dirt roads of Eastern City crackled under the carriage wheels. Crickets chirped not far away. It should have been a peaceful, crisp evening. But every soldier was on edge. They clutched their spears and swords, waiting.

They didn't see what happened next.

Master Ragy sat twiddling his thumbs in the carriage, looking through the windows. A curtain of purple smoke suddenly appeared across from him, revealing Kierli. Her eyes flashed as they locked on him. The color drained from Patriarch Ragy's face and he tried to cry out, but something caught his throat. Across from him, Kierli held her hand like a claw, using magic to clamp his neck. With her other hand, she pressed her index finger to her lips and winked.

Gurgling, Master Ragy started pushing his own magic through his body to free himself. It nearly worked, but Kierli felt what was happening and quickly summoned Starshadow. Gripping the blade tight, she reached across the carriage and rammed it through his chest. Master Ragy let out a sharp gasp, then slumped down in his seat.

Then the pain hit Kierli, just like it did with Master Ferribolt. It took every ounce of her control to stay quiet as it ripped through her. The purple cracks formed on her opposite hand, creeping from her fingertips to her wrist. Her insides burned and froze and scraped and tore, but when it was done, she breathed in a new breath. With the pain, her power had grown. Another one down.

Briefly, she inspected Master Ragy's body. Amazingly, there was no blood on it. The only sign of a puncture was a slight tear in his robes.

Kierli smiled and examined Starshadow. "Interesting."

She put her hand on the space next to his body. Under her palm, green words formed: *The true god has spoken. Kierli for Queen.*

Then she vanished.

Throughout the whole ordeal, Artemis flapped his wings and cawed loudly while keeping his talons latched to the carriage. As he did, everyone swiveled about looking for a potential threat, but there was nothing in sight. Several yards behind him, Barnabas frowned.

What's the matter with that bird? He thought.

In the ruckus, one of the guards trudged a little closer to the carriage. Leaning her head over, she asked, "How are you in there, Master Ragy?"

No answer.

"Master Ragy?" she called again.

Again, no answer.

"Stop the carriage!" she ordered.

The carriage jammed to a halt and the other soldiers squared up, facing outward. The first soldier climbed up and threw open the door. There, Master Ragy lay across the seat, his arms splayed out and his eyes fixed open, unblinking. She slapped her hand against his neck, feeling for a pulse. There was none.

"*He's dead!*" She called out. "I don't know how, but he's dead!"

Every soldier tensed and kept looking around for a potential threat. Barnabas leapt off his horse and drew his sword. His furious eyes studied every carrot patch and field surrounding them. Nothing could have gotten in. They checked the carriage before they left, and nothing had entered since.

"Are you sure he's dead?" Another soldier asked.

The first soldier put her hand on Patriarch Ragy's chest. "No heartbeat. But no signs of struggle, either—his robe is just torn a little. And there are words next to him... *the true god has spoken, Kierli for Queen.*"

Soldiers traded looks with each other.

Barnabas was barely listening. He already knew. He lifted his voice as loud as his lungs would carry.

"*Kierli!*" he bellowed. "*You coward!* Show yourself!"

No answer. The soldiers surrounding him stared.

"Only killing in the shadows?" Barnabas continued shouting. "Afraid to show everyone what you really are? I'm sure that would make your brother proud. Face me like a true warrior! *Show yourself!*"

Nothing. Unbeknownst to the battalion, Kierli sat on a fence just a ways off, cloaked with invisibility and witnessing the whole scene. She watched it all with satisfaction until Barnabas mentioned her brother. Then her smirk slid away, leaving an empty scowl.

After the silence hung, one of the soldiers said, "Captain... there's nothing we can do. Should we prepare his body for burial?"

Barnabas ground his teeth. "Yes. We'll need another Patriarch for that. Send for Patriarch Willows and make sure there's a battalion of soldiers keeping their eyes on him *at all times.*" He glared. "I'm going to the castle to inform King Jason on the news. Until then, you're in charge. Report to me when everything is done."

"Yes, sir."

Barnabas jumped onto his horse and snapped the reins, turning tail and heading for the castle. Artemis leapt off his perch and followed his master, flying just a short distance above. The horse kicked up dust as it galloped along the dirt path. Through the night they rode. The wind nipped at his face and arms.

Why am I so powerless to protect anyone?

There was a sick sound of metal through flesh and the horse recoiled, crumbling to the ground mid-gallop. Barnabas flew off the saddle and tumbled down the road as the horse crumpled under the weight of a slit throat. His ears rang and his body screamed in pain as his body tumbled through the dirt. When he finally slid to a stop, he scrambled to his feet and ripped his sword from its sheath, looking all around with blurry eyes. Half of his body ached with pain—he was sure at least one of his ribs was broken.

It was her. Standing right by the remains of his horse, carrying a black blade doused with blood.

Artemis cawed and dove at Kierli. In the dark, she saw it coming. She pointed a finger at the bird, and in a flash of green, the bird's spirit left its body. Artemis plummeted to the ground, hitting the dirt with a gross thud. He didn't move or shudder. Just as dead as the horse beside it.

Through it all, Kierli stood in the middle of the road, her eyes radiant and sharp. Barnabas ground his teeth. Nartikis, Master Ferribolt, now even Artemis and his horse... does she know when to stop?

"I feel like you're going to be a nuisance as time goes on," Kierli seethed. "Well, here I am! Just as you wish! Might as well see my face before I end you."

"Did you give my son the same honor?"

Kierli took two menacing steps forward, thinking of the time just weeks ago. She smiled.

"Yes," Kierli said. "He gasped for air as I pushed a dagger between his ribs. I wish you could have watched."

A surge of fury shot through Barnabas. "You're turning into what he was, you know. That magic you're using? It's the same magic Nartikis used it to create the Ash. And now it's your turn. How did it fare for him, Kierli? You think you'll be any different?"

"I know I will," Kierli breathed. "The true god has spoken. But you won't be around to see it."

She threw out her hand and instantly Barnabas was immobilized. He became a human star—his arms and legs outstretched as his body hovered just inches above the ground. His sword was still clutched in his hand. He tried desperately to resist, but no. Kierli's magic held him tightly.

Sacred Dragon, Barnabas prayed. *Please help.*

She kept advancing. With another wave of her hand, Barnabas's armor started unraveling, leaving him unguarded in his street clothes. But even though Barnabas was bound tightly, he could still speak.

"I know exactly how you feel," he grimaced. "Brimming with pain and anger. Becoming more willing to sell your soul to a force that you can't begin to fathom. Just because you want to *feel* something. Anything at all. But it's still eating at you. I can see it. What frightens me the most about you, though, is that you don't seem to care."

She was upon him. Without a word, she pulled back and stabbed his shoulder. The blade ripped through his muscles as blood seeped onto his chest. Barnabas groaned through clenched teeth.

Interesting, she thought. *So this does create a wound. Maybe it's because I want to watch him bleed.*

"We better even it out just to make it neater," Kierli mused.

Then she stabbed his other shoulder. Again, blood poured out as the dark blade ripped him. Barnabas felt himself get lightheaded. He coughed.

Kierli tipped her head sideways. "Hm... I know a way to finish this out. A nice even cut right there."

She pointed across his throat. Then she lifted her sword. Barnabas closed his eyes. But when he did, he saw something. It was only for a fraction of a second, but it was unmistakable.

Master Ferribolt's face—the rosy cheeks, the gray eyes. He turned and looked at him, then gave him a sly grin and a wink. He vanished as quickly as he appeared.

The blade hit Barnabas's throat, but made no wound. It rebounded off his skin like steel. And what's more, Barnabas felt himself unbound and dropped to his feet. The wounds in his shoulders closed up like they were never there. He scooped up his sword, brandishing it.

What was this? He felt more energized than he had in years. It was like light was surging through him, making his head clear and his body vibrant.

Thank you, my friend, he thought.

From Kierli's perspective, Starshadow rebounded off Barnabas's throat then he scooped up his sword and sprang to his feet. That was frightening enough, but there was something else that had changed. Something about his aura. His eyes shone brighter—the blue in his eyes were more electric than icy. This was the energy of a young warrior, not a withering old soldier. And as she watched this happen, something inside her shrunk.

She swallowed and clenched her jaw, focusing her magic again on restraining him. No good. Escape was the only other option. She thought of another location in Nezmyth City and tried to transport there, but as the purple smoke started to envelop her body, an aching pang sprouted across her mind and stopped her. It was so strong it almost dropped her to her knees. She shook her head to cast out the dizziness.

"You're not much without that magic, are you?"

Barnabas swung and swiped with the strength and precision of a dancer. Every move was calculated and swift, and Kierli struggled to keep up. She breathed hard and tried to push the magic through her body to help her fight, but it was blocked. She was left to herself.

Swing. Block. Parry. Swipe. Then Barnabas got her—her leg, then her arm, then her face.

"*Augh!*" Kierli cried. She jumped back and clutched her face —the side opposite to her pre-existing scar. Kierli could feel the slice from her eye down to her lip. Blood dripped onto her hand. Meanwhile, more blood dribbled from the wounds in her arm and leg.

"Now you have a matching one," Barnabas snarled. "You like to make things neat, after all."

Kierli spat at Barnabas's feet. He ignored it.

"You have no strength to run," he said. "I know how much you love revenge. Tonight, the Dragon has granted me mine— for Nartikis and Ferribolt. The best thing you can do now is pray to It for mercy."

Kierli clutched her face and raced for a solution. The light aura around Barnabas still hadn't subdued, and it was clearly affecting her magic. She had to break whatever was radiating from him. Maybe all she had to do was put a little of that anger in him. Remind him of what he used to harbor. It had to still be inside him—it never leaves completely. It just had to be tapped into. And with Nartikis and Master Ferribolt, some of that could still be fresh.

"I suppose you'll do what you must," she said. "But before you do, would you like to know what your son's final moments were like?"

Barnabas's eyes grew and his jaw flexed.

"His screams were incredible," Kierli said. "I took my time cutting him up so I could enjoy them. Then to watch the life leave those eyes that looked so much like yours… and how he begged for you. *Father! Father!*"

Barnabas trembled. He could have ground his teeth to powder. The glowing aura was leaving him. In his head, a soft voice told him to put it aside, to remember the moment. But he didn't listen.

Incrementally, Kierli could feel the light starting to loosen its grip on her.

"Oh, and you're probably curious about Master Ferribolt," she said. "He was a little trickier, but eventually he folded to my blade, among other things." She laughed. "Men are so predictable and weak. It's the ones like him that have the dirtiest secrets. I bet you never knew."

"*Liar!*" Barnabas cried.

By now, the Chief Captain's face was scarlet and his hands shook. He entertained thoughts of ripping her to shreds. Dancing on her grave. And those thoughts were the ones she wanted. Kierli felt the conduits of darkness free sufficiently. Barnabas raised his weapon, but before he could strike, she disappeared in purple smoke.

It was just him now—alone on a quiet Eastern City road with a dead horse and hawk. He threw his sword on the ground, letting it clang in the dirt. Then he dropped to his knees, clutched his hair, and roared.

28

THE COIN

"You're lighter."

"I know. I feel it."

Alis sat across from Jason in the middle of the sparring circle. Both of them were meditating with their hands on their knees, cross-legged. Deep, even breaths seeped from both of their lips. All of Jason's muscles were relaxed, and he felt a calm inside him like a spring breeze passing through a wheat field. Alis kept her eyes open, observing her student.

"What changed?" Alis said.

"I remembered who I am."

Alis wanted more explanation, but Jason never gave it. That was okay. As long as he was doing better, that was enough.

"So you've found yourself as your own person?"

"I learned that I was always complete," Jason said. "I just needed to be reminded."

"That's good. So does that mean you no longer require my visits?"

Jason opened his eyes. "I'd like them. I feel like there's still so much more you can teach me. But I suppose that's up to Tarren—he's the one that planned my entire regimen." He frowned and looked down. "But… he's been a little distant lately."

Alis blinked. "Is that unusual?"

"Yes, very. I thought he'd feel much happier once his mother was well again. But instead, he's been more isolated. He's even developed a little bit of a temper."

"Have you talked to him about it?"

Jason shook his head. "I haven't wanted to pry."

"He's your best friend," Alis said. "Ask him how he's doing. I'm sure he'd appreciate it." She paused. "Now, keep taking some deep breaths, then we'll move on."

Jason kept breathing deep, inviting the calm into every pore. Things inside him felt aligned for the first time in ages. Even though Nezmyth was in turmoil and Kierli was still on the loose, there was a stillness that rose up from his innermost depths—depths that were unattainable until just days ago. The grief was still there. He missed Saryan and Master Ferribolt, but among it, there was an assurance. Peace. The quiet knowledge that all things came together for a purpose and there were no stray pieces.

"Very good," Alis said. "Now hold your hands out and charge a jeroki, but don't throw it."

Jason did so. He kept his eyes closed and charged a jeroki between his palms the size of an apple. As he did, Alis tilted her head sideways and ogled at it. "Interesting. Your jeroki grew much faster than I've seen before. And it's a brighter shade of yellow. That means your spirit has strengthened. Like you've awakened to something."

Jason didn't reply, but let himself soak in the calm.

"Stand up," Alis said.

Jason kept his eyes closed and arose to his feet in a smooth motion.

"This is how you open the door to some of the mightiest magic," Alis began pacing circles around him. "You've acknowledged your suffering. But you've learned to *accept* it and let it have its place. You are not a fleshy mortal instrument to be acted upon, but a unique spirit with the power to act, to create, to *be*." She stopped in front of him. "Expend all your magic. Summon your greatest energies and show me what you can do."

Jason smirked. "I'm sorry... but I was taught magic shouldn't be treated like a set of parlor tricks."

She punched his shoulder. Hard. Something about it almost reminded him of Saryan, and he couldn't help but smile. He heard the smile on her voice as she replied.

"I'm your teacher, so this is different," Alis said. "Now do it."

Jason took another breath, settling in. Then his eyes snapped open and released.

He bent his knees and leapt into the air, soaring the entire height of the castle. On the ground, soldiers looked in awe at their King, shooting into the air like a geyser. When Jason reached the crest of his leap, he focused on disappearing. His body became encased in something—something between darkness and light, and after a short second of constriction, his feet touched the ground again. For the first time, he had transported.

He ripped Nightbane from its sheath and instantly the blade ignited with fire. With his other hand, a sparking ball of blue electricity hissed. He held it to the sky, and great bolts of blue shot into the air. He swung his sword around him, and he was encased in a crackling dome of fire. The heat made sweat form on his brow.

Feeling himself expended, Jason sheathed Nightbane, clasped his hands together, and the fire dome extinguished. His head felt light and breathing was labored. Soldiers all around the grounds applauded, but Alis merely folded her arms.

"Very theatrical," she said, "but a bit messy. The execution could use a lot of work, but that would have been very impressive to someone who knows the craft less than I do." She grinned.

Jason scoffed. Alis laughed and took out a vial of magic elixir from her belt. Jason uncorked it and threw the liquid down his throat. It burned and tingled on its way down, but within seconds he was back to normal, excluding the sweat and heavy breathing.

"I think we've done enough for today, Your Highness," Alis said. "I'm very happy to see you healing. Thank you for letting me be a part of your journey."

It wasn't sudden, but she walked up to Jason and gave him a hug. Her petite frame put her head just under his chin. Jason didn't expect this, especially since he was so hot and sweaty, but there was a purity in her expression like a sister clutching a brother. That wasn't the only thing he noticed. He could feel her spirit, and it was *strong*. No wonder she was able to go magically toe to toe with Kierli.

When she unwrapped herself from his arms, she looked up at him. "Sorry if that was a bit sudden. It just felt appropriate."

Jason smiled. "You know… I think it was. Thank you."

She bowed and disappeared with a pop, then Jason trudged into the castle. He made his way through the stairs and corridors, nodding to soldiers along the way as he eventually made it to his room. He closed the door behind him and sighed, taking it all in. The plants around the room grew beautifully—he hadn't missed a single day of watering. He stroked some of the leaves on a taller plant standing next to the door.

He took off his sweaty sparring clothes and began rummaging in his dresser for something clean. There were plenty of street clothes to choose from, but nothing quite fit his fancy. As he reached into the back of a drawer, looking for something appealing, his hand found something small and round.

He blinked. *What's this doing in here?* His hand wrapped around the parcel and he pulled it out.

A coin. But not just any coin—the coin Master Ferribolt gave him the night before his Ordination. He had entirely forgotten about it. It had a little orange ruby encrusted on the center and some strange designs around the edges. Frankly, the gem reminded him of the same one in his Foreordination Ring. But Master Ferribolt had told him years ago this was just a useless trinket, nothing more.

Now it's priceless, Jason said. *Because it was once yours.*

He rolled the coin between his fingers and plopped himself down at the edge of his bed. Rubbing the orange stone with his thumb, he said, "I'm sorry we couldn't even make time to have a burial. Barnabas thinks it would be smarter to wait until after the turmoil is over—until after we've caught Kierli and dealt with her properly."

Guard all the Foreordained in Nezmyth.

Jason perked up. It was more of a feeling than anything, but he could have sworn it came from Master Ferribolt. There was a brightness and seriousness to it that felt like his voice. His eyes focused hard on the little orange gem.

"That was you, wasn't it?" he said. "I know it was. But… what about the young ones that haven't begun their Year of Decisions? If we're guarding them, their identities will be known."

He didn't hear words again, but the feeling was the same. And he knew what to do. Somehow, Master Ferribolt was telling him from beyond the grave. There was no mistake.

Jason swallowed and clutched the coin tighter.

"It'll see to it."

* * * * *

Tarren stared into the surface of his guabo juice and didn't speak much. The Wilted Rose was raucous and spirited as usual, but all he could think of was the list that he put into Kierli's hands days ago. Then then the news of Patriarch Ragy's murder and nearly Captain Barnabas. She was already going to work on her plan.

And in the meantime, Tarren had taken to studying Dark Magic in the confines of his room. He needed to understand it —after all, how could he fight against something properly without knowing its intricacies? He told himself over and over he wouldn't allow himself to be consumed by it like Kierli was. Besides, he was stronger than her. He was Foreordained. A chosen spirit. Perhaps he could use it for his own purposes and nothing more. No one would need to know, and he could still serve as Advisor.

Niri scooted around the tavern serving drinks and teasing the patrons. Wherever she went, she left sparkles and smiles in her wake. And it didn't hurt that her pockets jingled from all the tips she collected. As she returned to the bar, she plopped down next to Tarren and wiped her forehead.

"Woo!" She sighed. "Busy night, huh? I haven't seen it like this since I started!"

"Yeah," Tarren said disconnectedly. "Strange."

"With all this money I can buy my own flat before long! Nothing fancy. Just a nice room that I can decorate myself. Not that the tavern isn't homey enough."

"Mmhm. Sounds nice."

Niri leaned over. "Are you alright?"

"Huh? Oh, yes, thank you… just thinking about Advisor things. Kierli and such."

"The sooner you catch her, the better," Niri grumbled. "Spreading lies about you and Jason keeping money stored up. What a bunch of tripe. And people actually believe it! Then there are the deaths of the Chief Patriarchs… do people not see how suspicious it all is? What's the matter with them?"

Tarren hummed and nodded.

"Hey!" a drunk patron called from one of the tables. "It's the Advisor! Why you hidin' all that money, Advisor? Got enough to share? Enough for a drink?" He held his empty tankard in the air and his friends laughed.

Niri jumped off her seat and put her fists on her hips. "*Oh, come off it!* There's no money at the castle—King Jason gave it to all of you years ago! Kierli's been lying to the lot of you!"

At the mention of her name, several people around the bar piped out, "Kierli for Queen! Kierli for Queen!"

Niri sighed loudly and dropped back in her seat. "I'm sorry."

"It's okay. Thank you, mother."

He reached out and put his arm around her shoulders, and as he did, she gasped horribly. It was so bad that he actually pulled his arm back. Niri was tense—her hands up and her back stiffened. Tarren frowned. "Mother? Mother, are you alright?"

"Yes, I'm fine," she said as she put her hand on her heart. "My... for some reason that got my heart up something awful. Made me think of the prison." She gulped. "I'm going to get back to work. Love you, sweetie. Stay as long as you'd like."

She kissed him on the cheek, took a couple more tankards and delivered them to their proper patrons. At his seat, Tarren frowned and drummed his fingers on the bar. He hadn't seen her that jumpy since he was young. If her madness was returning...

No, it was just a fluke thing. She was going to be just fine.

29

THE FOREST

That afternoon, Kierli spent time on the western side of Port Gala healing the sick and giving out money she had made from rusty iron bars. The poor people of the Western District welcomed her and took the money happily, all while chanting her praises and voicing their distaste for Jason. Soldiers tried to take her, but she kept them magically frozen in place, unable to move. With all the money people collected, they took boats to the Eastern District and started buying piles of fine goods, much to the chagrin of the city's upper class.

Kierli took on the appearance of Evelyn for the rest of the day and enjoyed the finer things around town. She bought some fine clothing. Went dancing. Got a massage. Then she watched lantern light dance on the reflection of the cool water as the sun dipped down. She drank in the smell of sea salt and made a note to visit here more often when this whole ordeal was over.

Last of all, she transported to the Western Forest.

Treetown still hadn't fully recovered from the Ash War. Three years ago, it was a quaint and delightful town bustling with hunters and lumber workers. But now, things were just a fraction of what used to be. So many of the villagers perished during the war and fewer people wanted to move back to the woods than expected.

Still, they managed to build a modest Cathedral in the center of town. It wasn't an extravagant building like the stone halls of Nezmyth City—just a lovely wooden cabin large enough for their needs. There wasn't even a Dragon statue or podium at the front, just ten pews and a prayer platform. It didn't matter. The locals blessed it and hallowed it as a place of worship, and it suited them just fine.

When the rumors reached the village about King Jason hoarding riches, Chief Kalyk dispelled them quickly. She had been to the castle multiple times during the Ash War and never saw any sign of gold there, and she knew Jason to be of the character to never withhold money from people who needed it. Unlike other communities across the kingdom, the people of Treetown trusted her and went about their lives without question.

When the decree arrived commanding every Foreordained person to be guarded day and night, Chief Kalyk frowned and coordinated rotations of the town guards to keep an eye on Patriarch Pila. Within a day, another decree was released saying guards had to watch the Foreordained people day and night, so that made things uncomfortable. But orders were orders.

Patriarch Pila was one of the younger Patriarchs in Nezmyth —an unmarried man in his mid-thirties that had just arisen to his calling before the Ash War. Before then, he was a lumber worker like most people in town. He was a subdued man that had a hard time being watched constantly. He slept in a little shed close to the Cathedral that was just large enough for a bed, a water basin, and a waste bucket. For that, only a few guards were necessary. One for the door, one for the window, and one inside.

Tonight, Chief Kalyk was in his room. She leaned against the wall while Chief Pila sat cross-legged on the bed. Her forest green eyes sparkled even in the dim lantern light, and she had shaved the hair on one side of her head. The rest of her wavy brown locks cascaded down to her shoulder blades. Her arms were folded, too, accentuating her muscles that had grown noticeably in recent years.

"You're not worried?" she asked.

"I don't fear for myself," Patriarch Pila replied, "but I do worry for my colleagues. If Kierli really is targeting us…"

"Well, we have the best soldiers in the village on guard," Kalyk said. "And if I hear anything, you know I'll come running, too."

Patriarch Pila smiled. "You always have. Thank you, Kalyk."

She opened the door and left. The guards snapped into position as she walked away. Her home wasn't far—another building that used to be extravagant before the Ash War, but had been rebuilt into something modest. She didn't mind. Extravagance never appealed to her anyway. As she walked, her weapons clinked on her back: a bow, quiver, and an unusually large ax.

A rustle sounded in the trees.

She stopped. Anyone else would have ignored it, but when you're one of the best hunters in the forest, you know which sounds are natural and which aren't.

Like she had done hundreds of times before, she slipped her bow off her back, nocked an arrow, and sent it flying into the trees. The sound was surprisingly high up—like a bird perched in a high branch. When the arrow disappeared into the foliage, she heard a cry. Not from an animal. A human leapt from the trees and landed like a cat in the clearing, ripping the arrow from their shoulder and throwing it to the ground.

Kierli. Chief Kalyk could spot her features even in the dark. The vagabond knew she had been spotted. The element of stealth was gone. To conceal her identity, her golden hair flashed into a crimson red and her face changed just a little bit. But it was too late. Kalyk knew what she saw.

"*Leave,*" the Chief commanded as she nocked another arrow.

Kierli didn't reply. She charged, raising a sword with pitch black steel. The Chief let her arrow fly. Kierli knocked away with a clang. With Kierli rapidly advancing, the Chief dropped her bow, focused magic through her arms, grabbed the ax, and swung it around. Kierli's dark blade connected with the head, making the metal sing.

As they locked their weapons in place, the Chief shouted to the guards. "Take the Patriarch to the Cathedral! *Now!*"

Kierli pulled back and attempted a swipe at the Chief's head, but the Chief ducked and kicked her away. Kierli backpedaled and clutched her wounded shoulder. She pushed magic into her arm to close up the wound. "You spotted me in the trees? That's incredible."

"Save it," the Chief said, clutching her ax with both hands. "You killed one of my friends. You won't get another."

"I had nothing against Ferribolt. It just needed to be done."

"Funny. That's almost how I feel about killing you."

The Chief lifted the ax and brought it down on the ground, creating a fissure that cracked and snaked toward Kierli. She bent her knees and launched herself into the air before the fissure came to her and sent out a deafening burst of earth. Kierli flew toward the Chief and brought her blade down, intending a vertical strike. But the Chief blocked it with a spin of her ax, sending the blade hurling through the air. Mysteriously, Kierli swiped her hand and the dark sword reappeared in her fist.

The Chief frowned. Kierli glanced at the head of the ax she carried. There were two names inscribed at the head, almost near the blade.

"You're incredibly strong to carry that ax," Kierli said. "*Adria* and *Patu*... hm. Friends of yours?" Her eyes flashed. "Or something more?"

"I've never been interested in love," the Chief narrowed her eyes. "Patu wielded this ax before she died in the Ash War. Not that you care."

"I do. My brother died in the war."

"So why do you feel the same as *they* did?"

She cocked the ax backward and gave a mighty swipe. With it, the veins in her arms glowed blue and a wave of magic soared through the air like a blade. Kierli ducked out of the way, but that's when the Chief brought her ax to the ground. Three simultaneous fissures cracked through the earth and snaked toward Kierli. This time, she was off balance. The shifting ground knocked her to her feet and a geyser of earth erupted where she lay, sending her dozens of feet into the air. She landed hard several yards away, dislocating her shoulder.

Kierli moaned and tried to shake the blurriness from her eyes. As she pushed herself up, she gripped her arm and forced it back into its socket, grunting. Meanwhile, the Chief bounded toward her like a gazelle, ax raised.

The Chief leapt into the air, ready to bring the ax down and chop Kierli in half. But Kierli regained herself. She held out her hand and constructed a translucent purple shield. The ax bounced off it and sent the Chief reeling backward. She tumbled across the dirt, dropping the ax and scraping her body. But she didn't wait—she slid to her feet and swung her bow around, nocking three arrows at once.

Kierli growled, swinging Starshadow into her hand. "You're a persistent one. I could use someone like you."

The Chief ignored her and released. Kierli swiped away two of them and dodged the third. Then she spun around and threw out her hand, making a claw with her fingers. Instantly, the Chief was lifted off her feet, the veins in her neck bulging. She dropped her bow and clutched her neck, but she couldn't peel away the invisible fingers around them.

Her windpipe constricted. Her feet flailed above the ground. Her heart pounded and she gurgled. Dozens of feet away, Kierli's eyes flashed. Just a bit more, and she'd be gone.

That's when an arrow lodged into Kierli's opposite shoulder. Chief Kalyk fell to the ground and massaged her neck, sputtering.

One hundred yards away, Patriarch Pila stood in the doorway of the Cathedral, nocking another arrow and glaring with eyes white hot. He launched another. Kierli was just able to dodge the arrow as it whizzed by her ear.

Kierli cursed silently. *This whole thing should have been much cleaner.*

"Surrender, Kierli!" Patriarch Pila called. "Take a look around! There are half a dozen archers trained on you, and people of the woods rarely miss their mark."

Kierli's head turned. Sure enough, there were seven other archers perched on rooftops—soldiers and townspeople alike. There was no way she could deflect a barrage of arrows from that many directions. She glowered at the sight. If only she had killed Kalyk sooner.

But Patriarch Pila was still standing just inside the Cathedral within arm's length. That was workable.

"Nezmyth will enter a new era," Kierli said. "I am a denizen sent by the one who rules above the Sacred Dragon. All those who oppose it will fall."

Chief Kalyk watched the scene, bewildered. "What are you waiting for? *Shoot her!*"

Everything happened fast. Arrows sailed true for Kierli. But she disappeared in her puff of purple smoke and reappeared at the Cathedral door. Two dark daggers materialized in her hands and plunged into the chests of the guards beside her. They toppled, then Kierli grabbed Patriarch Pila's collar. His eyes were wild as she yanked him out of the Cathedral, summoned Starshadow, and plunged it through his chest.

"*No!*" Chief Kalyk cried.

Kierli extracted Starshadow and Patriarch Pila slumped to the ground. Then she felt it again—the pain. It coursed from her limbs and made her blood like lava. And where she felt the pain, the purple cracks crept up. Her head swam as the searing hot strands finally dwindled. The cracks were now halfway up her forearms.

During the scene, more Treetown citizens launched arrows at her. There were five arrows inside her now, but the magic pumping through her blocked out the pain. She felt nothing but razor sharp euphoria. As her eyes spread around the scene, she noticed eight guards and villagers trained on her. As far as she knew, no one else in town even knew she was here.

Leave no evidence, she thought. *Make this look divine.*

In a series of flashes and smoke, Kierli disappeared and reappeared beside every archer. There were sickly gasps and dropping bodies, but no blood. The defenders of Treetown fell as hearts and throats were slashed. No evidence was left except torn clothing.

Chief Kalyk watched in horror as her people were slaughtered one by one. Then Kierli appeared right in front of her. Acting quickly, Chief Kalyk lifted her ax, but Kierli was too quick. She grabbed the Chief by the throat and slashed her belly.

The Chief gasped, blood dribbling from her lips, and Kierli dropped her to the ground. With that, the woods fell silent. Looking around, Kierli soaked in her handiwork. Twelve dead, including the village Chief and Patriarch. Only two soldiers by the Cathedral showed any stab wounds. From the look of things, everyone else just suddenly fell dead.

Good enough.

Kierli let out a deep breath and the arrows inside her dissolved. In their wake, the punctures they made were stitched up by invisible fingers. Her body tingled and felt like floating. She lifted her hand by Chief Kalyk's body and suddenly words appeared next to her lifeless eyes, curving in the dirt with glowing green letters. *The true god has spoken. Kierli for Queen.*

The shuffling of footsteps approached. More people were coming out to see the commotion. Excellent. The evidence had already been planted. The last thing to do was leave.

Kierli disappeared. Within the hour, a hawk arrived at Nezmyth Castle, alerting the King that Chief Kalyk and Patriarch Pila were dead.

* * * * *

A single candle flickered in Yorn's barrack. Fire was a symbolic reminder of the Sacred Dragon's power—the power to destroy, but also to give light and warmth. If there was anyone who needed the Dragon's light and warmth now, it was him. He bowed on one knee as his body faced the candle.

"Sacred Dragon," he prayed. "This is a dangerous time for not just me, but your entire kingdom. King Jason has entrusted me with a mighty responsibility... to be his *Inheritor.* I am honored, but overwhelmed." He paused. "Holy Dragon, I once loved Kierli, but she's become something I don't recognize. I'm following the King's instruction to serve by her side as a spy. Please, send your protection. Have my ancestors watch over me."

A cloud-like calm passed through him and the candle's flame swayed. He took in a deep breath through his nose, then let it out. He licked his fingers, pinched the candle into smoke, then took off his boots to get ready for bed.

But he got a visitor.

She appeared in her familiar smoke. Her breaths were hard and she pushed her fingers through sweaty hair. Blindly, she stumbled backward and dropped into a chair, closing her eyes and leaning her head against the wall. Yorn noticed her skin was mostly cracked and purple between her fingertips and elbows.

He got to his feet, but kept to a whisper. Silently, he hoped no one else in the barrack heard the intrusion. "Kierli, what happened? Where have you been?"

"Treetown," Kierli panted. "Doing what is necessary."

"Are you hurt?"

"No. I healed myself. Look."

Yorn could see through the tears in her garbs, but her skin was mended, leaving nothing but fresh scars. There were many of them reflecting puncture wounds on her arms and legs. What was most noticeable was the matching scar on her face.

During her fight with Barnabas, he thought.

"So you killed the Patriarch in Treetown?" Yorn breathed. "Just like Master Ferribolt and Patriarch Ragy?"

"Yes," Kierli said, wiping her hands on her armor. "And the village chief there. She put up a fight. She was worse than Barnabas."

Yorn shivered, but tried to appear composed. "Anyone else?"

"Almost a dozen villagers. They were witnesses. But they're all gone. Made it look clean."

Yorn flexed his hands as his insides shriveled with horror. *Twelve people. And she speaks of it so casually.* "So what you said about a new era coming to Nezmyth... are you getting rid of all the Patriarchs? Removing the pillars of the Old Ways, then putting yourself up when they're gone?"

Kierli didn't respond right away, but sat pensively wondering how much she should tell him. But it was Yorn. He was safe. "Yes. That's the plan."

Yorn swallowed. He sat down on the bed and held his hands together to keep them from shaking. "But I don't understand... how are you expecting the kingdom to just follow you after you've killed all of its leaders? The Patriarchs are loved by all, and over half the kingdom still favors King Jason."

"They'll never prove it's me," Kierli said. "I'm making things look like a divine act because, in a way, it is. A god higher than the Sacred Dragon has chosen *me*, Yorn. Besides, I made an alibi. I just spent the afternoon healing poor people in Port Gala, so when reports come that I was in Treetown tonight, they'll say, 'That can't be! It's more than a day's journey from Port Gala to Treetown!' My tracks are covered.

"Besides, every time I kill one of these Patriarchs, my power grows. I can feel it. And when every Foreordained servant is gone, I will have a power stronger than anything this world has ever seen." She leaned forward. "The era I've been talking about is coming, Yorn. This was meant to be. I am a denizen for glorious change, and Nezmyth will know freedom like never before. I don't love that this is how it's done, but nevertheless, it *must* be done."

Yorn prayed to keep himself from trembling. There it was. Her plan. Readily explained it to him. He had to tell King Jason. But until then, he still had a role to play. He swallowed again and forced a smile. "Then Nezmyth will be ours?"

Kierli smirked. "Yes."

She got up from her chair and strolled over to Yorn's bed, gently sitting next to him. She reached over and set her hand on his, holding it tightly. Moonlight seeped through the window and rebounded off her eyes. It made them shine like daggers. Only weeks ago, the sight would have made Yorn weak. And she probably thought it still did. But now, it just made his stomach hurt.

"I'm glad you're with me through all of this, Yorn," she breathed. "This has been a very lonely time for me. There isn't anyone else I'd rather share this with."

Yorn smiled, but her words were laced with insincerity. *She's buttering me up. Now will come the request.*

"Here is what I need from you," she said. "Come with me on my next excursion in two days. Meet me at our usual spot and I'll transport both of us to the next city. You're a strong warrior, and I may need you to help. And don't worry about being identified—I'll transform your face so no one recognizes you."

Yorn nodded slowly. "Of course. Where are we going?"

"You'll see," She squeezed his hand. "It's time for me to go. Goodnight."

She disappeared. Yorn put his boots back on.

30
THE UNREST

Soon after Jason retired to bed, a soldier burst into his room to tell him they received a hawk from Treetown. Chief Kalyk and Patriarch Pila were dead. Next to Chief Kalyk's body was the message: *The true god has spoken. Kierli for Queen.* Jason ground his teeth as he snatched the letter out of the soldier's hand and read it himself. He threw it aside, thanked the soldiers, and they dismissed themselves.

Not long after, Yorn was at the castle doors. Kierli had visited him again. Soldiers came in to fetch the King, who was still sleeplessly laying in bed. They both sat next to each other on the edge of the throne dais as Yorn explained everything Kierli told him. Her mission. Her meticulous work to make every murder look like a godly act.

"Yorn," Jason said. "You just confirmed an impression I received days ago. I had a feeling I should command every Foreordained person in Nezmyth to be guarded. Tarren disagreed on the matter, but I did it anyway." Jason deflated. "Killing every Foreordained person... Dear Dragon..."

"I can't do it," Yorn muttered. "I can't go with her to the next Patriarch's murder. I won't contribute to that."

"Do you know where she's going?"

"She wouldn't say."

Jason was quiet, thinking. "We can't do anything that arouses suspicion." He thought some more. "What if I beckoned you here that evening to help with something, and you weren't able to get away? Then you could report to her with some 'information' I gave you. That could work."

Yorn nodded tightly. "Yes, sir. That might."

"Go home. I'll send for you two days hence."

"Thank you, Your Majesty."

Yorn exited into the night and Jason was left alone, walking back to his room, thinking about recent events. Master Ferribolt, Master Ragy, Patriarch Pila… who was next? He could really use someone to talk to at a time like this. Maybe if he used the coin again, he could get a nugget of Master Ferribolt's wisdom from beyond.

Up staircases and through hallways he went. When he arrived in his quarters, he scooped Master Ferribolt's coin off his dresser and plopped down on the bed. He held it over his head, analyzing it, looking deep into the orange gem in its center. He polished it with his thumb. The oils in his skin made its surface a little glossier.

"Master Ferribolt?" he asked.

No response.

"Master Ferribolt?" he said a little louder.

Still nothing.

Jason sighed and set the coin beside him. He fell backward, hands on his chest, staring up at the ceiling. As the gears in his mind turned, he debated on whether or not to bother Tarren. He knew he should, but he had been so distant and irritable lately. And to disturb him in the middle of the night?

None of that should matter, Jason thought. *He's the Advisor. He needs to be told.*

Jason pushed himself out of bed and left his room, heading for Tarren's quarters. When he arrived at Tarren's door, he gave three gentle knocks.

"Hey Tarren, are you awake?"

"Sorry, one minute!"

There was a frantic rustling on the other side. Jason waited patiently, bending his eyebrows a little bit as he listened to the muffled commotion. Then Tarren's bare feet trudged up to the door and pulled it open just a crack. He cleared his throat. "Jason, it's late."

"I know, I'm sorry. But this is important. Can I come in?"

Tarren nodded and stole a glance inside. "Uh, sure. Come on."

Jason followed him inside and instantly felt something foreign. The air in here felt stiff and hollow, making goosebumps sprout on his arms and neck. It was also uncharacteristically cluttered. Usually, Tarren kept it much tidier and organized. But now there were books, sheets, and clothes strewn everywhere. Some of the musical instruments Tarren brought from his old shop were gathering dust in a corner.

"Sorry for the mess," Tarren scratched the back of his head. "Haven't really had the time to clean up in here."

"I don't mind."

Tarren and Jason sat across from each other—Tarren on his bed and Jason in his desk chair. Out of the corner of his eye, he glanced at some of the notes Tarren had on his desk. On the top, there were books of history and magic. But there were also bits of parchment shoved under them. It wasn't really his business, so he didn't ask about them.

"Sounds like my recent impression was right," Jason said. "Yorn came and visited just now. He said he talked to Kierli and discovered that her plan is to kill every Foreordained person in Nezmyth. That she's some kind of denizen for glorious change. I know you recommended against guarding every Foreordained person in Nezmyth, but it looks like it was the right move."

Tarren frowned. "So you're here to say 'I told you so?'"

"It's not like that at all," Jason said. "I'm just worried about you. You've been acting a bit different ever since your mother was healed. I thought you'd be happier when that finally happened, but if anything, you've been more distant."

Tarren folded his arms. "Well, I also thought when I healed her we wouldn't be hunting for a fugitive. Makes it hard to savor the moment."

"That's true…" The silence hung. Then Jason said, "How long do you think it'll be before she comes for us?"

Tarren's eyes went blank and glassy. His response was nearly inaudible. "I don't know."

"Well," Jason said. "The Sacred Dragon will show us the way. I don't know what it is, but I feel a calmness about all of this. It's hard to explain." He paused. "Is there anything else on your mind? Anything else bothering you?"

Tarren scoffed and rolled his eyes. "As if this isn't enough? Come on, Jason, don't be stupid. She's killed one of our friends and she'll kill more when she gets the chance. Why wouldn't I be upset and distant?"

Jason's face became dark. "Master Ferribolt isn't the only one. Yorn told me Kierli went to Treetown. Kalyk is dead, along with Patriarch Pila and a dozen villagers. Happened only a few hours ago."

Something in Tarren brimmed and ran over. His jaw clenched. His eyes misted up. His large frame shot from the bed and his hands balled into fists.

"*I hate her! I hate her!*" he cried. "How do we stop someone like her? She's turned everything upside down and she makes it look so *easy!* Why haven't we been better prepared for something like her? She's evil! That awful *wench!*"

He kicked over a stack of books, sending pages and notes flying. Then he sank onto the bed and covered his face, shielding his tears. The King moved next to him, putting his hand on his shoulder as he sniffed. A lump formed in Jason's throat. "I know. She's awful. But this isn't over yet. There's still more we can do. We'll figure this out together, okay? Just like we always have."

Jason's words should have been comforting, but to Tarren, they were suffocating bolts of guilt. Working against her? He didn't know about the list. He didn't know Kierli blackmailed him to sell out every Foreordained person in Nezmyth. The Old Ways teetered on the brink of collapse and it was all his fault. Tarren almost confessed everything—it was on the tip of his tongue. But then he thought of a healthy woman happily serving patrons down at the Wilted Rose. And a gorgeous warrior kissing him under the shadow of moonlight. Those thoughts stopped him.

"Well," Jason said, "if you're ever having an especially hard day and need to talk, I'm just down the hallway. Try to get some rest, Tarren."

He patted his shoulder and left the room. Tarren stayed in his bed for a while longer, listening for Jason's diminishing footsteps. Once he was comfortably distant, Tarren soundlessly reached under his bed. Hidden in the shadows were several glass jars filled with roaches. He retrieved a jar, unstopped it, then poured the roaches into one hand before he snapped his hand closed and crushed them all. Their dismembered legs twitched oozing green guts seeped between his fingers. But he wiped his hand with a rag and went back to studying Dark Magic at his desk.

✳ ✳ ✳ ✳ ✳

Barnabas grunted loudly as he swung his sword around the backyard. In the not-so-far distance, Kyleth Pond shimmered in the rising sun. Early risers strolled around its edges, occasionally glancing in the distance to see Captain Barnabas engaged in his morning exercises. They had scarcely seen him train this hard.

The remnants of Barnabas's breakfast were sitting on the chair under the oak tree, right next to the mound of earth. He meditated for an hour as he let the food settle inside him. In his heart, he tried to let his emotions align. Allowed himself to feel the anger that coursed inside him, then dismissed it.

Glossy sweat coated his body as he spun and stabbed and jumped. As he moved about, pushing his body to the limit, he kept seeing the faces of Nartikis, Master Ferribolt, and Patriarch Ragy. And with each flash, a surge of anger.

No, he thought. *Anger isn't my friend anymore. Sacred Dragon, give me peace and precision to avenge my friends. I cannot fail again.*

He stabbed his sword into the ground and threw out his hands. Plumes of fire shot from his palms in both directions. Then he clapped his hands together and a shell of electricity grew around him, encasing him in a sparking blue half-dome. Barnabas kept his hands pressed together, holding the shell for several seconds, then gasped and sat down, panting. The shell hissed and disappeared. His hands cooled down and he waved them in the air to dispel the smoke.

In the far distance, someone whooped in excitement. Barnabas looked up to see a single person clapping for him. He blushed a little bit then took his meditation inside.

Within the hour, he was in his armor and heading for the door. On his way out, he passed Artemis's perch. The fresh memory of Kierli's pointing finger and the flashing green light came blaring into view. Killing the horse was one thing, but Artemis was with Barnabas during his whole tenure of Chief Captain. The bird joined him during the Ash War and never left his side.

But now he wouldn't have that company. No more talons clutching his shoulder plate as he patrolled. No eyes in the sky as he rode through the city. No loose feathers to pick off the floor. Just a house that was emptier than before.

Barnabas caressed one of the branches, dipped his head, and locked the door behind him.

Through Eastern City and toward Center Court he rode. He kept a steady pace as he wove through the townspeople, receiving the dirty looks of Kierli supporters as he went. As he got closer to the Court, a frown spread across his lips.

A stampede of people was fleeing toward him, coming from Center Court. They clutched their children, gathered their goods, and warned other people to stay away.

I don't like the looks of this, Barnabas thought as he put his hand on his sword.

When the fleeing townspeople noticed Captain Barnabas, a group of them immediately made a beeline for him.

"Captain!" one of them said. "Captain! There's a fight at Center Court! The biggest one yet! There aren't enough guards!"

Barnabas's reply was a swift nod and a snap of the reins. The horse whinnied and galloped down the street. The knots of people quickly spread apart, making a narrow path for Barnabas to gallop through.

The horse barreled around a corner, and that's when Barnabas saw it—a crowd of nearly one hundred people in an open brawl. Most were fighting with their fists, but six had separated into duels and were flashing weapons at each other. There was a swarm of soldiers moving in on the struggle, shoving townspeople to the ground and binding them up with rope before they dove back in and tried to get some control.

Barnabas rode up to the edge of the crowd, staying atop his horse. He pushed magic through his mouth, put his fingers to his lips, and blew. A violently shrill whistle shrieked from his lips and rattled the windows all around the Court. And in the melee, everyone slapped their hands to their ears. They all turned to find the source, completely forgetting about the fight.

"Nobody move!" Barnabas roared, puffing out his chest and drawing his sword.

Instead, the Kierli supporters scattered. Soldiers and townspeople dove in and tried to wrestle them into submission, but most of them managed to squirm away and escape into alleyways. All in all, about a dozen people ended up in bonds.

Among them was the leader. Barnabas spotted him—he had seen him leading protests before. One of the more well-spoken slummies who ornamented himself with fine clothing as soon as he got a fistful of Kierli money. Barnabas threw out his hand and locked him in a Paralyzing Curse before he could get away. By the time he rode his horse up to the man, a soldier had already tied his hands behind his back.

Barnabas hopped off his horse and stalked up to the leader, grinding his teeth in his skull. The man looked up at Barnabas with a mix of stoicism and fear. Barnabas grabbed his collar and easily hoisted him to his feet.

"The true god has spoken!" The protester said. "Kierli for Queen! The true god—"

"*Shut up!*"

Barnabas gave him a swift punch to the jaw. The man staggered and blinked hard, spitting blood and trying to get his bearings.

"Make sure all the Kierli supporters hear this!" Barnabas called.

There was a shuffle as all the soldiers moved the tied-up Kierli supporters to the front of the crowd. They all seemed to be cut out of the same cloth—haggard, dirty-faced people garbed in fine clothing, jewelry, and fancy weapons. None of them lifted their eyes to see Barnabas, but kept their lips pursed and looked away.

Barnabas gripped the leader by the hair and led him to the middle of Center Court. During this entire display, everyone in the Court stopped and watched, not uttering a word. Finally, he took his head and forced his face toward the ground.

"Do you remember what used to be here?" Barnabas barked. "Answer me!"

"Your statue," the leader murmured.

Barnabas flipped him around and grabbed his collar, his eyes fiery. "That's right! The statue of one who usurped a throne. The statue of one who manipulated and murdered to gain power. You think I don't know what treachery looks like? Kierli is a shadow of what I once was, and you people worship her like a god! *Wake up!* She's playing you all for fools!"

Finding a shred of courage, the leader said, "You called her to Chief Captain, so who's the real fool here?"

Another surge of anger sprouted through Barnabas, and this time, he didn't control it. His hand balled into a fist again, knuckles white. His face burned red. He pulled back and launched a brutal punch. The leader fell to the cobblestone, half-dazed, moaning quietly from the blow.

Center Court fell even more deathly silent. Flustered, Barnabas growled like a gorilla and stood over the body. He was alive—not even unconscious. But this wasn't a good look as Chief Captain.

Anger isn't my friend anymore, he admonished himself. *Anger isn't my friend.*

Gathering himself, he muttered, "Take them away."

* * * * *

Down in the slums, not long after the event in Center Court, Kierli was healing those down at the Crossing. A line of people formed, be they blind, lame, deaf, or otherwise sick. With gloves to conceal the purple cracks, Kierli put her hands on each of them. The revived people ran away rejoicing with their friends and family. All the while, Kierli smiled. Each one was a link in the chain, and the chain was growing stronger.

"I know you healed my leg ages ago, but the pains have been coming back!" One villager said. "Can you please fix it up again? My friend, too, his cough is returning."

"Not to worry, friend, I'm happy to take care of it."

Kierli put her hands on the villager's leg and with a glow of purple light, the leg was made whole again. The villager put her full weight on it and instantly brightened up, thanking Kierli and hopping away.

The guards assigned to patrol the Crossing for the day were restrained by Kierli's magic. They just looked on helplessly, watching her mingle with the townspeople.

"I go to the tavern erryday!" a villager told her. "They said, 'she's killin' folks,' they say. But I know it's not you. Yer for the people. Yer helpin' folk that need it the most. Not like that Jason who sits in his throne all day sippin' wine and doin' nuthin'."

"I'm glad you understand, my dear man."

"I was at the fight hours ago!" Another said. "Soldiers almost got me, but I got away! I never stopped yellin' 'Kierli for Queen! Kierli for Queen!' I never thought I'd say it, but I think the Old Ways need to be just that—old and done. I feel like the Patriarchs dyin' away is a sign fer sure. It's time for Kierli to rule!"

"I'm so touched to hear you say that. Perhaps you're right—it's a sign to move on." She smiled. "If the time comes and the people of Nezmyth want me to lead, I'll do my very best."

"My my, what's this?"

Kierli's robes had slipped up her forearm, revealing the purple cracks just above her gloves. One of the villagers stared at it and lifted her sleeves to get a closer look, but Kierli pulled back. The villager's face got soft.

"Cap'n Kierli," the villager said. "You can heal others but not yourself?"

Kierli forced a smile. "It's not painful. I think as I heal others, it takes a toll on myself. But not to worry. I prefer this far more."

Tears welled up in the villager's eyes and she threw their arms around Kierli. "Bless you, Cap'n Kierli! Bless you and your heart!"

The line dissipated and the soldiers were magically unbound. Everyone at the Crossing glared at them as if daring them to close in. But they didn't. They knew what she was capable of. And she hadn't done anything wrong while she was here—aside from binding them up.

"Farewell, my friends," Kierli said to the people. "Take courage in your hearts. I must go to other villages that need my help. I'll return to you when time permits."

The villagers gave her a hero's farewell and she disappeared in a puff of smoke. When the soldiers continued patrolling, the townspeople stared daggers at them. It started slowly, but then the noise built. It wasn't a discordant noise of shouting and booing; no, the voices were unified.

"Kierli for Queen! Kierli for Queen!"

31
THE PORT

At dusk, Evelyn waited outside of Sue's for Yorn, but he never arrived. Her foot tapped on the cobblestone as she looked up and down the street. After several minutes, she left her tankard of booshum berry juice and walked away. When she crept into an alleyway, she vanished.

She reappeared as Kierli in Yorn's barrack. The bed was made and parchment stacks were neatly arranged on his desk... but no Yorn. There was a note, though, hastily written on his pillow. It was only a couple of lines long.

For anyone needing me, I've been called to the castle for some urgent business. No telling how long it will take.

Kierli scowled. He chose to visit the King instead of coming along like he promised? Maybe that would be alright. After all, he could be a useful tool if he's in the King's pocket. There would definitely be ways to leverage this later.

With a sigh, she disappeared again.

Up at the castle, Yorn sat at the dining room table with Advisor Tarren and King Jason. The three of them silently ate a meal of mutton, yams, apples, and asparagus. Jason left the asparagus on his plate untouched. Yorn gratefully dug into his meal, which was only slightly better than what he got as a soldier.

"Your Highness," he muttered. "Have you ever thought about reinstating some kind of tax on the people? Even just a small one? You're the only King that I know of that's never taxed the people."

"After the Harvest? No," Jason said. "I've tithed the wealthier citizens to provide for our needs, the needs of the army, and to donate to the poor. And we've always had sufficient. Except that someone keeps giving me *this*." He jabbed at the asparagus.

Yorn shook his head. "I can't believe people think someone like you would be holding riches from them."

"People believe what they want. Especially when they hear it from someone like Kierli."

In his seat, Tarren stabbed his mutton a little harder. After putting it in his mouth and chewing for a moment, he pushed his seat back. "I'm sorry gentlemen, but I'm already full. Your Highness, may I be excused?"

Jason ogled at his friend. "Tarren, are you sure you're well?"

Tarren tried not to snap back. "Yes."

"Alright then. You're excused."

Tarren nodded, bowed, and left the room. Yorn and Jason soaked up the quiet for a little longer before Jason said, "Yorn, you're in your early forties, right? And you're an accomplished man of rank and integrity. What's stopped you from getting married and having a family?"

Yorn chewed and swallowed. "I don't fall in love easily, Your Highness. I've always loved women who are strong, dedicated, and independent. So naturally, I gravitated to Kierli. At least until recently."

"There have to be loads of women in Nezmyth City that would be happy to be with you," Jason said. "Between you and me, I worry about Tarren sometimes. He longs for companionship, but he wants someone from Lower City who understands how to work hard. Not long ago, he was spending time with a girl from Lower City with dark hair and blue eyes that he adored. He said her name was Jesslin."

Yorn's eyes grew wide. "You're sure her name wasn't Evelyn?"

"See, that's what I thought, too! But he assured me it was Jesslin."

Yorn went back to eating, but slowly. After a long moment, he broke the silence with, "If you're not going to eat your asparagus, I'll take it."

Jason scooted his plate toward Yorn. "I'm going to check on Tarren. Make yourself at home, Yorn. Leave whenever you feel comfortable. Your 'important information' for Kierli is that I felt prompted by the Sacred Dragon to guard every Foreordained person in the kingdom. I don't think she'll find that too useful."

"Understood. Thank you, Your Highness."

Jason made his way through the corridors and staircases until he reached Tarren's room. He gave three gentle knocks on the door. This time, he didn't hear the familiar scuffle on the other side of the door. Tarren gently made his way to the door, unlatched it, and pulled it open. But he didn't invite Jason in.

"Yes?" he asked.

"Tarren, I haven't heard you talk about Jesslin lately," Jason said. "What happened to her?"

Tarren looked at the ground. "I lost track of her after my trip to Lunli Village. Haven't seen her since."

"That's too bad," Jason said. "And… you sure it's Jesslin, right? Not Evelyn?"

"Yes, Jason."

"Okay. Well… goodnight then."

Tarren didn't say goodnight, he just nodded and closed the door. Jason walked away with his hands in his pockets.

* * * * *

Nezmythians visited Port Runoff when they weren't wealthy enough to visit Port Gala. As the port on the southern end of the kingdom, it was a town of modest means with plenty of things to do, but not the worldwide destination that Port Gala was. The thick smell of fish down by the shore wasn't ideal either, but that couldn't be helped. Fish was Port Runoff's primary trade.

Most of the buildings in town were neat and tidy and saw an upswing in quality after King Jason withdrew the Harvest Tax. Buildings were patched up and more shops opened. People started to visit from across the kingdom to find a spot where they could see an ocean sunrise. And some argued the Eastern Mountains next to town made the sunrises even more exquisite.

Port Runoff had one Cathedral, which was down by the shore a brief walk from the market. It was one of the smaller stone cathedrals in Nezmyth that didn't have any stained glass windows, just clear panes of glass. When the sun cracked over the mountains, the orange light streamed through and gave the interior a warm glow. Many of the pews were worn and bitten from age, the lacquer rubbed away and reapplied over decades. And the Dragon statue at the front was actually made of wood. No one thought to replace it for the last hundred years.

With every sunrise at the Port Runoff Cathedral, Patriarch Cicily was already there, praying. A man in his fifties, his limbs and bones were tired from his service in the Nezmythian Army. He had achieved the rank of Captain in Port Runoff before his Foreordination came time to be fulfilled. After ten years of military service, the community loved and respected him even more.

He pushed his hands together as he knelt on the prayer platform. His thick eyebrows were turning gray and he had shaved all the hair from his head when he started going bald.

His back was straight and his shoulders square—perfect posture, even at his age. By the double doors, two soldiers stood guard, watching every move.

Night was coming on. The evening's golden glow was turning blue. Patriarch Cicily scooped up a walking stick. On wobbly knees, he ascended to his feet and let out a heaving sigh.

"Feels like it'll rain soon," he half-smiled.

The stick clacked against the stone floor as he made his way between the pews. The soldiers watched him in worry as he went.

"Sir," one of them said. "We're ready to escort you home."

"Thank you, my dear girl," Patriarch Cicily replied. "You all do such a wonderful job. Reminds me of my days back on the force."

They opened the Cathedral doors and surrounded the Patriarch as they stepped into the coastal air. The Patriarch lived only a quarter mile up the street from the Cathedral, and the soldiers were kind enough to keep his slow pace as they took him that direction. Their eyes scanned the rooftops as they led him along.

People passed by and wished the Patriarch a good evening as they went down to the wharf taverns. Patriarch Cicily smiled and thanked them. He took in a deep breath, drinking in the cool air and letting it fall from his lips. There was faint shouting from the fishing boats coming in, singing and drinking coming from the taverns, music playing along the wharf.

Home. What a lovely sight.

Houses sandwiching the street threw flickering light from their windows. It lit their way as their feet shuffled up the way. They stayed alert for some invisible threat, but nothing descended on them during their entire walk.

Finally, they reached the Patriarch's home, a one-room cabin with a stone chimney and curtained windows. Patriarch Cicily stood with his hands on his cane as he waited.

"We just need to sweep the building first, sir," one soldier said.

"Oh, I'm well aware."

Two soldiers cautiously opened the door and disappeared inside. After a minute of looking around, they came back out. "Everything looks good."

Patriarch Cicily thanked them and crossed the threshold with another soldier—the one to guard him for the next few hours. They closed the door behind them. The soldier planted his feet near the door as Patriarch Cicily went to work putting a pot of water in the fireplace. He struck stones to cast sparks on the logs. Some tried twigs at the bottom ignited and the fire started to grow.

There was a soft thud behind him. Patriarch Cicily didn't turn and look. He just listened to the presence move with careful footsteps then squat in a nearby chair. As he watched the fire sputter and grow in the fireplace, he took a deep sigh.

"You're very stealthy to have made it past them. Not many places to hide in here."

Kierli sat with her legs crossed, bouncing her foot. She smiled. "I've still got my set of tricks. I was hoping to transport in here, but it looks like every Patriarch's home is enchanted in a way that keeps me from using my magic."

"Rightfully so," Patriarch Cicily stoked the fire. "*Tepnoh Edomah* is a magic of death and destruction. Your magic cannot thrive where we dwell."

Kierli kept smiling. "If you'd like, I can wait until your tea is done."

"I'll leave that to you," Patriarch Cicily said. "I'm in no position to resist—I've done enough fighting for a lifetime. You know how difficult the life of a soldier can be. And I had to serve during the reign of King Barnabas." He sighed. "Those were long, difficult days, carrying out those orders. Many of them still haunt me, but I've felt the Sacred Dragon's forgiveness, and I know my hands are clean." He looked over his shoulder. "You can't say the same, can you? With the murder of Master Ferribolt, your damnation is sealed. The best thing I can wish for you is a quick, painless death when the Guardian of the Night disposes of you."

Kierli clenched her teeth, but hid them behind a grin. Then she threw a dagger. It found its mark and Patriarch Cicily collapsed by the fire.

Kierli's body tightened and convulsed as the purple cracks spread up to her elbows. She had to bite her lip to keep herself from crying. Then she helped herself to the tea Patriarch Cicily was preparing. The soldiers outside had no idea they were guarding a tomb until several hours later.

Just like in Port Gala, Kierli transformed into Evelyn and enjoyed some of the revelry down at the tavern. She danced at a tavern. A handsome man took her home and entertained her body. Halfway into the night, she left his home with another destination in mind—a home on the other side of town.

She moved through the shadows all across town until she arrived at a brick mansion at the foot of a mountain. Two guards stood outside the front door. As she walked by, she pushed the magic through her body to get an awareness of the people inside. Most of them were asleep except for some patrolling soldiers in the hallways.

She was able to detect the smallest pulse of a heartbeat on the west side of the house, just inside a window. Quietly, she kept walking until she was a fair distance away, then ducked behind another building. She forced more magic through her body, became invisible, floated up to the window, unlatched it, and slipped inside. The soldiers guarding the house never could have seen her.

It was a child's bedroom. Her parents were clearly of generous means, but the room wasn't decorated with lavish gifts. The bow and quiver leaning against the bed were of fine quality, but the bed, dresser, and water basin all had signs of lengthy wear. Clearly, this was a family that used things until they couldn't be used anymore.

The child slept soundly in the bed, nothing but a lump under the covers. By the door, a soldier stood sentinel. Kierli pointed at the soldier and his eyes rolled into the back of his head. While still invisible, Kierli caught him to break his fall and used more magic to muffle the sound.

Meanwhile, the child slept.

Krys, she thought. *So you're the next Foreordained King. After all, why wouldn't you be a King? A Queen hasn't been Foreordained in nearly a century.* She shook her head.

As if triggered by that thought, the child stirred and shifted, then sat up.

Kierli's jaw fell.

She couldn't have been older than thirteen, with deep blue eyes and golden blonde hair. And those eyes were filled with terror. She sat up in bed, petrified, trying to gulp in a parched throat.

The dagger was by Kierli's side—the same dagger that ended Patriarch Cicily just hours ago. But why were those eyes piercing her in such a way? She had killed loads of people. Why was she suddenly frozen, staring at this little girl? Why couldn't she move?

The girl swallowed and a tear rolled down her cheek. Her voice was still and hollow, barely more than a breath.

"You're here to kill me, aren't you?" she croaked. "You've been killing Patriarchs… and you know I'm Foreordained to be Queen."

Kierli couldn't speak. She couldn't move. Something like a fire overtook her. A fire of vanquishing admonition and justice —a warmth that was more vengeful than comforting. Her hand was still on her dagger. Why couldn't she move forward? Why couldn't she just lunge and strike?

"Will you…" the girls' eyes were still full of tears. "Will you let me write a note to my parents?"

Kierli bore her teeth together. She didn't say yes, but she didn't say no. Still, the girl reached with shaking hands into her nightstand and took out a writing stick and some parchment. With trembling fingers, she wrote two lines, then signed her name with a little heart on the end. Still shaking, she set the writing stick and the parchment on the nightstand.

"My name is Krys," she said. "I just thought you should know."

I already knew.

Still, Kierli couldn't move. Something restrained her. Krys blinked at her, waiting. She looked to the door, to the window, and realizing no one was going to come, she decided to act. In Kierli's hesitation, Krys slowly moved her hand toward her bow and quiver. Maybe, she thought, the Sacred Dragon was imbuing her with strength to fight against her assailant? She took a single arrow and pulled her bow onto her lap.

Finally, Kierli was able to do something. She found the strength to shakily push out one word: "Don't."

Krys raised her bow and nocked the arrow. She had to clench her jaw to keep her teeth from chattering. Three more teardrops rolled down her cheek.

"*Don't,*" Kierli said again.

Krys pulled back on the bowstring. And that's when Kierli found it in herself to move. She leapt forward, snatched the arrow from Krys's grasp, turned it about, and drove it in her chest.

Krys gasped and gurgled as the arrowhead stabbed her. Kierli held eye contact with her as her fist pushed against her breast. Krys's hands traveled up her arms to her neck and hair. Tears welled up. The girl mouthed the words "mother, father" as if either of them could running to save her. But no. Blood stained the bed sheets. Krys's eyes turned glassy, her hands fell by her side, and she exhaled her last breath.

The next thing that ripped through Kierli was the mightiest pain she felt yet. It dropped her to the ground, curled her up, and even kept her from breathing. The purple cracks stretched from her elbows to her shoulders. And with it all, an enormous swell of power inside her.

To mirror it, a void.

The parents heard the thump of Kierli's fall. But she disappeared before they arrived.

32
THE MANIA

Gus from the Wilted Rose sent for Tarren the next morning. He said it was something about his mother. Naturally, Tarren pushed away his notes and jars and left immediately. When he arrived, Niri was already at work, serving breakfast to the tavern—plates of corn and potatoes and various meats. There were dark circles under her eyes, though, and her usual pep was gone.

She waved and blew a kiss to Tarren as he walked through the door, then he pulled up a seat at the bar. The barkeep was there, wiping out tankards and looking across the room. He rubbed his eyes and leaned in close to Tarren.

"Mister Advisor."

"Morning, Gus. What's wrong?"

He cleared his throat. "Is your mother well?"

Tarren's eyebrows bent. "She should be. Why?"

"I woke up in the middle of the night hearing screaming down the hall," he said. "I ran upstairs to see what was the matter. Threw open the door and she was laying in bed hollering like someone was whipping her. I shook her awake and calmed her down, but it took a good while."

Tarren's face grew dark. "She did those kind of things years ago."

"Well, I hope she gets better," the barkeep said. "I can't have her here if she's screaming murder and scaring the customers. Could you talk to her?"

"I will."

Tarren waited until Niri was done running orders, then she dragged her feet over and sat next to him. She balled her hands and wiped her eyes, trying not to yawn. "Good morning, Tarren! I'm sorry, I didn't sleep well last night."

"That's what Gus told me. Nightmares?"

"Dreaming of the prison," Niri said. "It's the first time it's happened since I came home. But I'll be fine. It was just one time." She rubbed Tarren's back. "How are you? You don't look so well either. A little pale. You eating enough?"

"I'm fine, mother," Tarren reassured. "Just... try to keep yourself calm the best you can. Try meditating before you go to bed or something. Gus says you can't keep staying here if acting up becomes a regular thing."

Niri sighed. "I don't blame him. I suppose I could go stay with Gulaf again if I need."

"Are you okay with that?"

"No," Niri murmured. "But if that's what it comes to..."

Tarren deflated and forced a smile. Then he put his arm around Niri's shoulders and leaned in to kiss her on the head. As he did, she flinched—a split second of rigidity that softened quickly as it arrived. Tarren faltered, gave her the kiss, then squeezed her hand before he left. As he stormed out of the tavern, he flexed his hands.

Kierli was failing to keep her end of the deal.

The carriage door slammed shut and it started to crawl along the Southern Market Street. Tarren sat with his arms folded, fuming. Silently, he wondered if he could summon Kierli in any way. Maybe with some of that magic? He might have some fuel left from last night. He didn't know quite how, but he tried to focus on communicating with her, putting his feelings of anger and confusion behind it.

Amazingly, it worked. Within moments, she appeared in a puff of smoke sitting across from him. What was more shocking was that she was completely naked—every inch of her tight, strong body completely exposed.

Tarren scowled and his heart thumped loudly. "Have you no decency?"

"I thought you'd enjoy it," Kierli sounded surprised. "You've probably never seen a woman's body before. What troubles you?"

"My mother," Tarren folded his arms and intentionally looked out the window. "She's deteriorating again. Having night terrors and flinching whenever anyone gets near her."

"Oh?"

"*Yes*," Tarren said severely. "You want me to continue to work with you? Heal her. Restore her back to health. That was the deal, wasn't it?"

Kierli smirked, amused by Tarren's audacity. But she said, "Fine." She held up her hand, it glowed purple, then she snapped her fingers. "It's done. She won't have any more trouble."

That's when Tarren noticed the cracks running from her fingertips to her shoulders, like sleeves of purple spiderwebs.

"Looks painful," he muttered.

"It is at first, but it's worth it." Her voice died down to a purr again. "Is there anything else I can do for you?"

She was teasing him. Inviting him. Tarren stared at that body, letting his mind run free, picturing himself tangled up with her in ways he had always craved. No one would possibly know. They would be done by the time he reached the castle, then she would just disappear. His body trembled and he swallowed, but he shook his head.

"No."

"Too bad. I'm sure I'll see you again soon."

She smiled and vanished.

* * * * *

Two soldiers swung and twisted as they lunged at Yorn, brandishing their wooden weapons. Yorn clutched practice swords in each hand, arching and blocking as he moved about the area with surety and exactness.

They were surrounded by dozens of other soldiers in the Upper City garrison, hugging the edges of the battle area with leather armor and practice weapons. It made the entire room smell remarkably of sweat and leather. The soldiers around the edge cheered for their comrades, eagerly hoping to defeat their Captain just once. But those cheers were just fuel for Yorn. They made him smile. .

Yorn ducked, spun, and jabbed his sword into one of the soldier's bellies. The soldier swore loudly and laid himself on the ground as those around him booed. The one soldier remaining gulped as she dodged and parried Yorn's blows, but it didn't last long. The soldier swung high, Yorn ducked, reached up, grabbed her and flung her over his shoulder. She landed hard on the ground, face up, and Yorn poked his sword into her chest. Then the two soldiers got up and bowed to their leader. Everyone else clapped reluctantly.

Yorn smiled as he put his hands on his hips. His face was red and each breath came quickly. "If anyone else wants to try, you're more than welcome. The offer still stands—drinks on me if you can win with two or less."

"Awe, come off it Captain!" one said. "We've done this every day for a week! If Mara and Flik can't take you, no one can."

The rest of the garrison grumbled in agreement. Yorn just kept smiling.

"Looks like practice is over for today then!" Yorn said. "Everyone suit up and get to your posts. I'll be in my barrack if anyone needs me. Dismissed!"

The soldiers dispersed to their bunks and trunks. As they went to work strapping on their armor and leaving in pairs for patrols, Yorn retreated to his private barrack. He had scarcely closed the door and sat at his desk when he heard a voice behind him.

"Missed you last night."

He knew she'd be coming. Her voice was like flecks of ice in his ears. He didn't turn around as he began writing letters. "Yes, I'm sorry. King Jason called me to the castle to discuss some important matters. Ended up staying there for most of the evening."

"That's well enough," Kierli said, laying on Yorn's bed with her hands behind her head. "But he better not do the same thing tonight. Last night turned out fine, but I'll definitely need you tonight."

"Where are we going?"

"Pinegrove."

Yorn turned in his seat. "That village is still rebuilding from the Ash War. Why would you need my help there?"

"Because I heard the King's little magic teacher is from there," Kierli mentioned Alis with potent venom. "If there are other magicians like her there, I'll need your help."

"There's no one like Alis. She's a prodigy."

Kierli sat up, her face intense. "Are you coming or aren't you? If you plan on leading as part of this new era, I need better commitment from you! You do realize I'm changing everything, don't you? If you're not with me, you're against me!" Her body sagged and put her hand to her head. "I'm sorry, Yorn. I've just felt so tense these past weeks. Constantly running and hiding… why don't you come over here and lay with me for a moment?"

Yorn nearly shuddered. Nothing sounded less appealing than laying down with her right now. But he had to keep the act up—she still thought he was in love with her. So he put on a smile and stood from his chair, moving to the bed and sliding next to her. Kierli rested her head on his arm and caressed his chest.

She sneered. "You're trembling. Has it been a while since you've been with a woman?"

Yorn cleared his throat quietly, fearing the soldiers outside would hear him. "It… yes. It's been a while."

Please interrupt us, please interrupt us…

As Kierli stroked his chest, he took her hand in his. It was so strong. He ran his thumb along the cracks in her skin and frowned at them. "It's getting worse isn't it?"

"Better," Kierli said. "My power is growing. I bet this will cover my entire body by the time my strength reaches its fullness. But I don't mind. I think it makes me look more fearsome." She sat up and leaned her back against the wall, looking down on him with those sparkling blue eyes. "Meet me at the usual spot at sundown, alright? I'll take us to Pinegrove."

Yorn forced a smile. "Alright then."

She disappeared, and Yorn breathed a heavy sigh of relief. That's when a knock came to the door.

"Captain Yorn!" the muffled voice came from the other side. "Mika owes me five Bars from a bet we had on your fight earlier. Could you come make him pay up?"

* * * * *

Jason entered his bedroom and picked up the watering can by the door. Behind him, Alis leaned against the door frame with her hands clasped behind her back, admiring all the green.

"So these are all the plants the castle gardener recommended?"

"Yes," Jason replied. "They all thrive indoors as long as you keep them watered. They don't need much sunlight. You can come in if you'd like."

Alis shook her head. "I have unpleasant memories from the last time I entered a man's room. I'm more comfortable standing here."

"You know I'm harmless."

"From tales I've heard of you on the battlefield, I know that's not true," Alis smirked. "But I know you wouldn't do anything to hurt me. Regardless, I'll stay here."

"Alright then," Jason nodded. "But yes, these are all the plants the groundskeeper gave me—all twenty-five of them. Some of them need to be watered every day, but mostly every few days. My favorite one is the one by the door there; he said it only grows in some remote places at the base of the Eastern Mountains, but they thrive surprisingly well in—"

"Have you found that it's strengthened you magically like you thought it would?"

Jason blushed when he realized he was boring her. "Actually, yes. I feel like I've learned something from these things. They thrive on the necessities. They don't ask for anything more. I can't help but think that has spiritual implications." He paused. "Alis... if you don't mind me asking, what happened that made you nervous about men's rooms? You don't have to discuss it if you don't want to."

"No, it's alright," Alis said. She took a deep breath. "When I was fifteen I fancied a soldier in Pinegrove. We spent a little bit of time together, and I enjoyed it very much. One day we enjoyed some drinks together at the tavern, but I started feeling fuzzy and loose after I drank mine. It wasn't even mead, so I shouldn't have felt that way—I know he did something to it. My memories are hazy from the rest of that day, but I remember him taking me back to his barrack and taking advantage of me. My body was too weak to resist."

Jason's heart dropped and his body tightened with fury. For a brief second, he imagined it. Alis, this pure and sweet soul, violated in such a way.

"Tell me who did it," Jason said fiercely. "I'll make sure they're dealt with."

Alis shook her head. "It doesn't matter now. He died in the Ash War."

Jason rubbed his face and pressed his lips together. Not knowing what else to say, he said, "I'm so sorry."

"I am too," Alis said. "It took me a long time to heal. It was difficult trusting anyone for a long while. But I'm okay now. I even found it in myself to forgive him. I've felt like a new person ever since."

"How can you forgive someone who did something so evil?"

"I realized his action was turning me into a different person. Isolated. Alone. I didn't want that. It took help from others, but eventually I put it behind me. And now his power over me is gone. He's nothing but fragments of a memory." Her voice died down. "But some people never recover from that kind of pain. It eats them inside."

The sadness and anger swelled through Jason. But among those feelings, he felt a glow of admiration for Alis. A woman had never stood so tall and mighty.

"You're inspiring," he said. "I hope you realize the impact you have on others."

Alis smiled. "Thank you, Your Majesty."

"You can call me Jason."

Suddenly, the marching of soldier's footsteps came to the edge of the door. Two soldiers turned the corner. It wasn't just them. Yorn was there in his full armor, looking very distressed. When he saw Alis, he almost seemed relieved.

"Your Highness," Yorn said. "She plans to attack Pinegrove tonight. She's insisting that I go with her this time."

Alis's eyes grew wide, then she closed them and took an even breath with her hand on her heart. When she opened them, they were sharp and intense. "I'll be waiting."

33
THE GROVE

The crickets didn't chirp around Pinegrove that night. Something had entered the forest and all the wildlife felt it. Foxes stayed in their holes. Bears returned to their caves. It felt just like the Ash, and they hadn't forgotten.

Like Treetown, Pinegrove was a budding village in the wake of the Ash War. Thankfully, the lumber industry was in dire need after so much destruction, so there was no shortage of work to do. The returning settlers built houses, planted gardens, and hunted nearby game. Near the edge of town, a modest wooden Cathedral served their needs.

Tonight, Patriarch Calum was praying inside it. At twenty-nine years old, he was the youngest Patriarch in Nezmyth—the best looking, too. Women throughout the forest whispered about him as he grew older. His smile got brighter, his jaw got more pronounced, but his eyes always stayed a shocking green. He had no trouble finding a wife when he reached the proper age.

He stayed on his knees at the front of the Cathedral, pondering on the state of Nezmyth and the impending danger. He should have felt alone at a time like this, but there was another presence in the room—a sweet, petite girl with black hair and dimples sitting on the last pew. She kept her hands on her knees, meditating for over an hour.

Patriarch Calum let out a soft sigh and lifted to his feet. He looked over his shoulder. "What sad circumstances for a return home. I'm sorry, Alis."

"It's fine," Alis said, not opening her eyes. "How are Charla and the boys?"

"They're well, thank you."

"Do they know what's coming?"

The Patriarch's eyes sparkled a little less. "Yes, they know."

They let the silence settle around them. Outside, every window and door to the Cathedral was guarded. They weren't convinced it would be enough, but it would have to do.

"I know your spirit is special, Alis," Patriarch Calum said. "You've always been in touch with heavenly things. More than most people. So if you don't mind my asking... have you felt the same things I have?"

"About what?"

"About the end," Patriarch Calum said. "We all know this is the Final Era. The prophecies for centuries have said that Wevlia would last five thousand years. Well, it's been over five thousand years. So surely the time is coming, is it not? As I've watched this kingdom grow in commotion, I've thought about that. Perhaps this is the rumbling before the crash."

Alis opened her eyes and gazed blankly at the pews ahead. Something about Patriarch Calum's words echoed in the emptiness inside, like a truth she had been trying to ignore. The realization of its existence grew a great sadness in her, and with it, a resignation. Her shoulders rose and fell. "Yes. I think I've felt it too."

"What would you say is left for us to do?"

Her dark eyes became sharp. "Fight anyway."

Patriarch Calum smirked. "Always a person of passion. The Sacred Dragon has blessed you with much."

Alis smiled.

Another hour passed. The stars and moons were bright as they cast fractured light through the trees. On the edge of the forest, Kierli and Yorn suddenly appeared in a curtain of smoke, hiding in the bushes. Yorn's face was different—his blonde hair and beard were gone. Instead, his hair and beard were crimson and the structure of his face had been altered.

"There," Kierli whispered. "That should last about an hour. We'll take care of business long before that wears off. Then we can return to Nezmyth City."

Yorn didn't say anything. He just nodded.

"There it is," Kierli said, motioning toward the Cathedral. It wasn't in the center of town, but halfway to its edge. There were about eight soldiers guarding the perimeter. This made Yorn sweat, but Kierli was unphased.

"What's the plan of attack?" Yorn croaked.

She tensed. "Attack."

With that, she leapt from the bushes and stalked into the open. She flicked her hand and Starshadow appeared, soaking in the darkness around it. Centering himself, Yorn drew his blade and followed behind her. Then Kierli's stalking turned into sprinting. Yorn picked up his feet to follow pace. Together, they dashed for the Cathedral.

Kierli pulled back her hand and launched something like a jeroki, but as soon as it left her palm it bloomed into eight snake-like forms that soared through the air, twisting and writhing until they hit each soldier. But... they didn't hit each soldier. As soon as each beam was supposed to strike, they rebounded off invisible shields and immediately the guards went on the defensive.

Kierli frowned, still running for the Cathedral. "If it's her, so help—"

She didn't get to finish. The Cathedral doors burst open and Alis shot out like a dart, hurtling through the air. Fire blasted behind her, propelling her and scorching the soil behind her.

Kierli scarcely had time to lift her sword and block the impact. Alis's arms glowed white from her fingertips to her elbows. When she threw a punch at Kierli, her fist rebounded off her sword like steel.

Kierli toppled backward but quickly righted herself. In this window of time, Alis threw her hand toward Yorn, clamped him in a Paralyzing Curse, and threw him away from the scene. His stiff body landed carefully in the bushes outside of town. He would be useless now—nothing but a statue removed from sight. Kierli was left to herself.

When she noticed this, she snarled. "Stupid *bitch!*"

Alis planted her feet and cocked her fists. Then she snapped her fingers and the Cathedral was surrounded by a pillar of fire that lit up the entire town. Inside, the soldiers and Patriarch Calum could barely feel the heat, but everyone in Pinegrove noticed the orange light bursting through the clearing. Townspeople put their faces to their windows and stepped out their doors to behold it.

She's trying to bring witnesses, Kierli thought angrily.

"You should have turned yourself over last time," Alis said.

"No," Kierli glared. "Because now, I know I'm going to kill you!"

"Try, then!"

Kierli shot purple beams from her hands. Alis beat both of them out of the air, then thrust her palms into the earth. Her hands dug into the ground like the soil was water, then the area between her and Kierli rippled and cracked with brilliant light. The entire ground resembled the surface of broken glass, and with thunderous cracks, the earth broke and shifted like the sea during a storm.

Kierli fought to maintain her balance on unsteady ground. Meanwhile, Alis gracefully dashed over every dip and trough, headed for Kierli. As she got closer, Alis flicked her wrists and two white swords flashed into her hands. Kierli saw it. Just before Alis could close in on her, she leapt into the air.

Alis took a swipe but missed. She looked up. Kierli was hovering several feet above her, her purple cracks glowing as she hung suspended in the air.

Kierli narrowed her eyes and smiled wickedly as she pulled back her arms and thrust them down. With that motion, the oceanic surface of the earth demolished into a crater ten meters wide with Alis at the center. Alis crossed her forearms and pushed magic through them to keep the bones from shattering. The force on top of her was incredible—like a meteor smashing on top of her. Sweat beaded and dropped from her eyebrows.

Through the force, Alis took a deep breath and blew. From her mouth, a narrow thread of fire stretched up and up until it reached Kierli, then erupted into a red ball just inches from her body. The force of the crater ceased and Kierli was blown out of the air, tumbling toward the ground.

She landed haphazardly, breaking both her legs and her forearm. She bore her teeth through the pain and forced magic into her limbs, healing all of them. Then she scrambled to her feet and flicked Starshadow into her hand once more.

Alis leapt out from the base of the crater. At the crest of her jump, she threw her arms forward, casting a barrage of fireballs. Kierli danced on the ground as she swung Starshadow back and forth, dissipating all the blasts as the converged on her. By the time Alis landed, she pushed her hands together and yellow bonds sprouted around Kierli's ankles and wrists— just like last time.

Starshadow disappeared and Kierli fought against the bonds. Her face twisted and scowled as she locked eyes on Alis, who was panting and sweating several feet away.

"I've never wanted to kill anyone before," Alis said. "But I would rather kill one woman than see the Old Ways fall. Goodbye, Kierli."

She flicked her wrist and a white sword appeared in her hand again. She propelled toward Kierli. But Kierli was flexing her hands.

With one swift move, Kierli spread out like a star and broke her bonds. Alis dug her feet into the earth and slid to a halt, but Kierli was faster. She pushed her hands together and encased Alis in a black orb. As soon as Alis was stuck inside, smoke began to billow and spread until it was completely filled. Alis could only hold her breath for so long until she sucked in the smoke.

When she did, visions and memories flashed across her eyes. The destruction of Pinegrove. The Ash invasion. The screams of the people she knew and loved. The fire. The death. And another memory, vivid and awful. She was fifteen again. The soldier boy. The barrack.

Alis screamed.

Kierli flashed herself invisible before the townspeople could arrive at the battle and see her face. Unseen, she arrived at the pillar of fire and splayed her hands out, feeling every particle of flame that ascended to the sky. She flexed her palms. Great drops of sweat slid down the scars on her face. Her teeth clamped together and her entire body shook, but finally, dark energy overcame the embers. The flames quenched with a giant hiss of steam. The stars and moons were bright over Pinegrove again.

The soldiers jerked all around, searching for Kierli, but saw no one. Alis was trapped in a black orb several yards away, and the pillar of fire had somehow vanished into smoke. All the soldiers gripped their weapons tighter, awaiting the worst.

All the while, Kierli analyzed the situation.

He's not coming out, she thought. *And my magic is powerless in there. As soon as I walk in that door, I'll reappear. Need to improvise.*

An idea struck her. Yes, it could work. And it would look even more magnificent to the people of this town. It could be perfect.

She lifted her hands to the air, feeling her surroundings. On the edge of town, a single tree dislodged from its roots, cracking and snapping as the wooden fibers separated. The tree traveled through the air until it hovered over the Cathedral. The people of Treetown watched with awe, holding their breath.

With her fingers, Kierli felt through the tree's rings, splitting the fibers carefully. Overhead, the tree separated into one hundred javelins, their tips like spears pointed to the ground. Then Kierli dropped her hands, and the javelins sprayed into the Cathedral, breaking through the roof and piercing every square foot of the building.

The villagers cried with horror. Inside, Patriarch Calum didn't make a sound. Kierli knew she was successful when the pain rocked through her again. Her body buckled but stayed invisible. She felt the cracks stretch to her neck and breasts. And when the pain subsided, a new breath of power. She soaked it in, stretching and letting it have it live inside her.

The final touch. She held out her finger, and at the mouth of the Cathedral, wrote the same words in glowing green letters: *The true god has spoken. Kierli for Queen.*

She looked over her shoulder. Alis was still trapped in that orb. She could see that girl's fists and feet pounding against the edges every few seconds, the rest of her body shrouded by the smoke inside. Kierli smirked and said, "Good riddance."

Fearful whimpers peppered the village as Kierli marched to Yorn's petrified body. He was just coming to himself when Kierli arrived. He scarcely had time to behold the remains of the Pinegrove Cathedral before Kierli grabbed his arm and they vanished.

And it was in that moment, using her last reserve of magic, that Alis managed to punch her way through the orb. Smoke seeped onto the ground. The orb shattered and evaporated around her. Alis toppled onto the ground into the fetal position, still coughing up smoke as nightmarish memories stabbed through her mind.

As the townspeople crept out of their homes to see the awful wreckage of the Cathedral, they held each other and sobbed. When some of them saw the words outside the doors, they argued on whether or not it was another sign. But that's when one of the town healers noticed Alis's body curled up in the clearing. They hurried over to her, practiced some healing magic on her, then hurried her to the infirmary.

* * * * *

Tarren leaned his head against the wall, his arms folded. The room he had borrowed at the Wilted Rose was right next to his mother's room. She didn't know he was there, and he planned to keep it that way. It was just for one night to check on her—make sure she didn't experience any other night terrors. If she did, he was confident he could use his new magic to quell it.

A single lantern glowed on the nightstand. The furnishings were incredibly basic: a bed with a rope web instead of a mattress, a nightstand with a drawer that didn't pull out all the way, an empty chest, and a wobbly chair by the door. At least there weren't any mice. Looks like Gus kept the place reasonably clean.

From the next room, Tarren heard the creaking of the bed and a gentle groan. His ears perked up. It only lasted a second and it didn't return. The longer he sat, the easier it felt to simply nod off and sleep. But he kept himself awake. He could go sleep at the castle after sunrise. His carriage was waiting for him just up the street.

Suddenly, a flash of smoke appeared on the bed. Tarren's chest tightened. Sure enough, it was her. Kierli lay over the blanket and pillow, one hand on her hip and the other hand propping up her head. Thankfully, she was clothed this time, but not with much. Her legs were exposed along with her purple-cracked arms. She studied Tarren up and down.

"How is she?" She asked lowly.

"Fine," Tarren looked away from her. After a pause, he said, "Who did you manage to kill tonight?"

Kierli didn't answer the question, but replied with another. "What do you think of Captain Yorn?"

Tarren wasn't expecting this. Briefly, he thought of the day just recently that Jason appointed him as Inheritor. Kierli probably had no clue about this. If she did... he didn't think about it. Tarren tried to keep a straight face when he said, "I don't know him well. Why?"

"He's in love with me. Does that make you jealous?"

"No. I'm sure lots of people are in love with you."

Kierli's eyes flashed and she shifted her legs. "I don't know if I can trust him, though. They were surprisingly ready for me at Pinegrove tonight. And he was the only person I told about it."

Tarren was silent. Kierli narrowed her eyes.

"There's something you're not telling me, isn't there?" she said.

Tarren didn't look at her. *She'll kill him if I say.*

Kierli held up her hand. It glowed purple. She put her fingers together as if to snap them.

"You're not strong enough to heal her yet," she said. "But I'm strong enough to take it all away. Now tell me whatever it is you know."

Tarren clenched his teeth and finally let his stinging eyes fall on her. "I hate you. I hate you so much."

"How could you hate me?" She said almost teasingly. "I've given you everything you want. Your mother is healthy and my body is yours whenever you want it. These are great treasures that I'd prefer not to take away from you, but you must work with me. *Tell me about Yorn.*"

Tarren swallowed and tried to even his breathing. Niri was sleeping soundly in the next room. It had to stay that way.

"Yorn has betrayed you," he said. "He's a spy for King Jason. And he's the new Inheritor. Jason appointed him days ago."

Kierli numbly lowered her hand. For the first time, there was hurt in her eyes. She stood from the bed and paced the floor, her arms stiff and her eyes fixed on the steps in front of her. Yorn was the Inheritor. Working with King Jason. Why didn't he tell her? Because he was a traitor, just like Tarren said. He was never on her side. It was all a lie.

"Why didn't you tell me?" her tone was hot.

Tarren didn't answer.

Kierli continued pacing the floor. Her face grew harder and darker as she muttered to herself. Several feet away, Tarren watched with apprehension, waiting for his punishment. He thought she would erupt—scream and scowl and curse him. But that didn't happen. Instead, she wiped the frown from her face and pulled her lips into a smile.

"Thank you for telling me the truth, Tarren," she said.

Tarren blinked. "That's it? No punishment?"

Kierli's eyes sparkled as she shook her head. Instead, she made her way back to the bed and laid down. Tarren didn't resist analyzing her whole body—he knew she wouldn't mind. Her tight muscles. Her smooth skin. Even something about the purple cracks seemed… tantalizing.

"You know why I really asked you for that list, right?" she said.

Tarren said nothing.

"It's because I wanted you to be a part of this," she smiled. "I wanted you to be on my side. I like you. I have ever since I saw you at the castle that morning."

Tarren's cheeks burned. The verbal confirmation of her affection filled a hole deep down. She had said and done terrible things, but in this thing, Tarren could tell she was being… sincere. His heart started beating quicker. And he couldn't stop gazing at that body.

"Come here." She stretched out her hand, inviting him to lay down.

His hands grew clammy and he tried not to shiver. Tarren imagined himself running his hands across her hips and legs, his face close to hers. Breathing in her scent. Kissing those soft lips again. Cautiously, he laid down next to her and she nuzzled into his side, resting her head on his shoulder.

"You know things will never be the same," she said. "The Old Ways are coming to an end. You won't have to feel guilty about any of this because I'll be Queen, and I'll make sure you have everything you want. You'll be safe with your mother. I'll never leave you. It'll be time of total freedom."

How could words be so comforting and so hollow? Each syllable was a crushing weight to his soul. How could he betray Jason, Master Ferribolt, the memory of Nadiel? But still, there was an iron-clad truth. With that list, he had sold himself away —became a fragmented shadow of what he once was. The only path that remained was lined with Dark Magic and steely blue eyes.

She turned her head and looked into his eyes. Then she leaned in and kissed him. Tarren didn't resist.

He didn't resist for the rest of the night.

34
THE RECOMPENSE

Jason knew Tarren was staying the night at the Wilted Rose to look after his mother, so he didn't worry about training with him the next morning. He went through his physical exercises alone after he got dressed and watered the plants. Jason was pleased with the progress he had made physically since they started training again. He could run a lap around the castle without wheezing. His belly had trimmed down a bit since eating more vegetables. And generally he felt more calm ever since training with Alis.

Alis.

Yorn came to the castle in the dead of the night to brief Jason on Pinegrove. The news was devastating. The Cathedral was destroyed and Patriarch Calum was murdered. Alis put up an incredible fight against Kierli, but as far as they knew, Alis was dead. Kierli trapped her in a sphere of dark energy that choked her out.

Between his physical exercise and morning meditation, Jason quickly scribbled a letter and sent it on a hawk to Pinegrove. It was difficult to meditate peacefully until he knew for sure if Alis was safe or not. He didn't receive a reply for hours. By that time, he was sitting on his throne and Tarren still hadn't returned.

The return letter came in the hands of a soldier sprinting toward the throne dais. Jason sat up straight, broke the seal, and unraveled the parchment.

Your Highness,

You heard correct. The Cathedral is destroyed and Patriarch Calum is dead. His body is currently being prepared for burial at sunset. The village is mourning.

Alis is alive, but her health is dwindling. She's currently staying at the infirmary, but the healers say she was cursed with something they've never seen before. We're unsure how long she'll live.

Perhaps we need to consider that the Sacred Dragon has abandoned us and Kierli really is called by some higher god. The signs are there. Consider your position and do what is right, Your Highness.

-Chief Magladom

Jason tore the parchment and rained the pieces at his feet. Alis. It was hard to imagine someone so perfect and pure destroyed by someone so evil. He tried to swallow with a tight throat, his mind stewing in a vat of sadness. Then he had an idea. He transported during his practice with her the other day. Could he make it all the way to Pinegrove?

He ordered his guards to cut off his visits for the afternoon. The castle gates were locked. In his throne, Jason meditated for the next hour—remaining completely still, praying, breathing deeply, focusing every scrap of energy. He thought of the smell of pine needles, the soil of the forest beneath his boots. And threw it all, he tried to dismiss the anger and fear. Alis was alive. That was something to be grateful for.

At last, the time felt appropriate. His grip tightened on his knees. He pushed his magic through his whole body and focused on Pinegrove. The power ebbed through him inch by inch. And finally, like the snapping of a rope, he felt himself pulled through space.

For a few seconds, everything went white. He couldn't breathe or move, but then he was freed. The smell of pine trees fell upon him like a wave and he fell onto his rear. He was right in the center of Pinegrove, next to a well with a bucket dangling at the top. Out of the corner of his eye, he could see the wreckage of the Pinegrove Cathedral—skewered by a barrage of javelins.

The people passing by stopped and stared, exclaiming that the King had arrived. Jason struggled to his feet, but nearly fell over. His entire body was dizzy and tingling from expending so much magic. Clutching his head, he gazed around with blurry eyes. There was one woman at the well that stared at him with her mouth hanging open.

Jason called to her. "You! Ma'am! Where's the infirmary?"

She pointed. "Three cabins down, Your Majesty! On your left!"

Jason thanked her and ran as fast as his tired legs would go. When he arrived at the building, he threw the door open. Sure enough, the cabin was lined with a dozen beds, six on each side. Two people in healer robes busied themselves with spells and bandages. Only four beds were occupied.

One of them was Alis.

"Your Highness!" one of the healers said.

"I'm here for Alis," he said. "Is she well enough for visitors?"

"Well yes, but—"

"Good, thank you."

With the same pace, Jason hurried over to her bedside and pulled up a chair. But he wasn't the only one there. An older man with Alis's dark eyes and hair sat on the opposite side of the bed. He stood up and bowed when Jason came and sat down.

"Your Highness," he said, "it's an honor to be here with you."

Jason blinked. "You… must be Alis's father."

The man gave a sad smile and nodded. "My name is Fyal."

"The honor is mine, Fyal," he said. "I must apologize. I didn't mean to intrude on your time with her."

Alis was facing the other way with her eyes closed. But as she heard the commotion, her eyes fluttered open, and she turned her head. When those dark eyes focused on Jason, the corners of her mouth pulled into a smile.

"It's no trouble," her voice was a little raspy. "He's had twenty-four years with me. The least he could do is give us a few minutes." Her eyes narrowed quizzically. "How did you get here so quickly? It takes nearly a whole day to ride to Pinegrove."

"I transported," Jason smirked. "It's exhausting."

She lifted her head. "All the way here? That's impressive. Your magic will be out for hours if you don't get an elixir."

Without warning, she coughed horribly and her fist covered her mouth. Fyal handed her a clean handkerchief. She pressed it against her lips and hacked grossly, trying to push something out. When she removed the cloth, it was stained with some sort of black mucus. Jason scrunched his eyebrows and held her shoulder.

"The healers have tried everything," Alis breathed. "Whatever Kierli did to me last night was serious. I don't know how much longer I'll last. Maybe a few days."

Fyal's jaw shook and Jason's throat got tight.

"Or maybe you'll be just fine," Jason said. "Maybe you'll be out of here before you know it."

Alis smiled knowingly. "Come now, Your Highness. You and I are no strangers to death. Let it have its place. Besides, now that I'm so close, I can say that it doesn't feel that scary. It's like crossing a bridge or taking off a glove. I'll be okay. I'll see you again."

Jason swallowed hard, trying to flush out the lump in his throat. "I'm so sorry that things turned out like this. You've become a true friend to me. And I'll always be grateful."

Alis smiled again, her eyes half open. "Thank you, Jason. I've had many students through the years, but if I'm honest… I think you were my favorite."

* * * * *

Yorn was alone in the practice hall, sweating and panting. He spun and danced his way around a padded pylon, swinging a wooden blade with precision and gusto. But his mind was on other things: Pinegrove, Kierli, Inheritor.

The sweat made his chest and face glisten. After moving for a long while, he propped up his sword like a walking stick and leaned on it. He stayed like that and caught his breath before he turned and walked to the edge of the practice hall, searching for the canteen. It should have been next to his armor, but it wasn't there. He frowned.

"Looking for this?"

Yorn reflexively lifted his weapon, but stopped himself. He recognized the voice. Kierli held the canteen by his ear, sloshing it playfully. Yorn took it, gave her a half-smile, thanked her, and drank from it.

"You're still very dexterous for an older man." she said.

Yorn smirked. "I'm not that old. I've barely crossed into my forties."

Kierli's eyes twinkled. She watched him as he continued to drink. Then her eyes scanned their surroundings. The practice ring. The pylons. The weapons. The surrounding bunks and trunks of soldiers away on duty.

"A shame you couldn't help more during Pinegrove," Kierli said. "That Alis girl was clever."

Yorn stopped drinking. "Yes. She was quick. But you handled it well enough."

"It's true that she has been the King's magic instructor?"

"I've only heard rumors."

Kierli hummed, then clasped her hands behind her back. She strolled around the building as if it were a museum, looking around at all the shoddy fixtures that hadn't been replaced in decades. Meanwhile, Yorn watched her.

"How long did we work together at this garrison?" She said amiably. "Something like two years?"

"Just about, yes."

"Two years of working side by side, keeping the city safe. We did a very good job. I'd like to think we grew as friends. Maybe even more."

Yorn could feel it. She was leading up to something. His palms started to sweat.

That's when the amiable pretense fell. She turned her whole body on him. Those blue eyes became piercing, and her tone dropped to something dark and oily.

"So why would you betray me?"

Yorn's blood went cold. His heart thumped hard, but he tried to center himself. "What do you mean?"

"Don't feign ignorance," she said. "I spent the night with the Advisor and he told me everything. Told me that you're the new Inheritor. That you've been telling the King everything I've revealed to you. I know everything now."

Yorn stood frozen, his mouth shut.

"I'm going to kill you, Yorn. I told you I would." She started advancing. "But I want to hear it from your lips first… why would you lie to me and betray me? After everything we've been through?"

Yorn's jaw tightened and his lips pursed. This was it. There was no escaping this. He could try to fight back, but that would be pointless. She could tear the skin from his bones before he had the chance to raise his blade. It was over. He was a dead man.

So what reason was there to lie? He gave a silent prayer and straightened his shoulders.

"Because you're not who I thought you were," Yorn said. "For years I saw you as a shining pinnacle of discipline, loyalty, and grace. But I was a fool. You're a monster. You're a user. You're greedy, dishonest, and murderous. And you need to be put back in the Vault of the Damned where you belong—just like that boy that killed your brother."

Kierli didn't expect the words to cut so much. Her body trembled. Through her teeth, she hissed, "Is that all?"

"No," Yorn shook his head. "You played me. You knew I was in love with you and you leveraged that to your advantage. If you're going to kill me, at least have the decency of telling me what I really am to you: nothing. Don't perform to me, pretending you deserve pity or an apology. Because I see you now with perfect eyes, and loving you was my biggest regret."

Every word was a sledgehammer. Finally, Kierli couldn't take it. Starshadow appeared in her hand. She pulled back. Yorn closed his eyes. He didn't see the blade rip through his stomach, dying the blade a shimmering crimson. He struggled to stay on his feet as Kierli pushed him backward. She didn't stop until his body was pinned against a padded pylon.

And still, Yorn found it in himself to speak. Coughing up blood, he looked upon her with fading, iron-gray eyes.

"How... does it feel... to be used... like you... used me?"

"*Shut up!*" Kierli's eyes stung. She pushed the crossguard harder against his stomach. Yorn coughed up more blood.

"Your fight... will be... in vain."

Kierli pushed harder and gnashed her teeth together.

Yorn forced a smile. "Long... live... the King."

Finally, Yorn's body went limp. Starshadow disappeared. Kierli stumbled back and Yorn's body fell to the floor. Dead.

Something between a moan and a cry slipped through her lips. A battle of thoughts and emotions raged inside. Why did these tears form? He was nothing to her. Nothing. But... she was something to him. Or at least she used to be. No more adoring looks. No more juice on the Northern Market Street. One less tool to use—a tool that fought back. For once, a tool that fought back.

She didn't bother trying to make the scene look like an accident. She just vanished.

* * * * *

"Greatness cannot be achieved without sacrifice. Without making enemies. They would not understand."

Kierli sat cross-legged in the very bottom of the pool. The water filled her lungs minutes ago, but she breathed it freely. Every corner of her body pulsed with energy. As the voice spoke all around her, she let the power tingle and spin inside her. It made the cracks in her skin glow.

"You have done well," the voice said. *"The time is coming for you to reach your full potential. You are cunning and wise. For your reward, everything shall be yours. No one shall stand against you."*

Kierli tried to block out Yorn's words. But they barraged her brain like a volley of arrows. The voice knew this.

"Do not concern yourself with the words of the traitorous Yorn. He was naught but a stooge to King Jason. His betrayal will be remembered as folly for centuries."

"I want to finish it sooner," Kierli said, her hair swaying in the water. "Will you give me that power?"

The voice seemed to smile. *"Yes, my child. That power shall be granted."*

The water surged and pulsed more. It seeped in the cracks in her arms, shoulders, and breasts. With it, the euphoria—the pleasure.

It wouldn't be much longer now.

35

THE TRAITOR

Jason made it back to the castle shortly after visiting Alis. One of Pinegrove's magicians had a magic elixir to spare, so Jason drank it and used the energy to transport back to the castle. He was gone for less than an hour. When he arrived, Tarren still wasn't home.

As dusk fell, a soldier came to the castle to report Yorn's death. He was found stabbed in the Upper City garrison's practice hall, but there was no sign of struggle and no murder weapon was found. Jason already knew who was responsible. He thanked the soldier and dismissed her, then buried his face in his hands. Alone, he sat in the throne for several minutes mourning the death of his new friend and Inheritor.

Tarren didn't come back to the castle until that evening. By that time, Jason was still in his throne but ready to retire to bed. When the double doors swung open and he entered, Jason sat upright. There was a slowness in Tarren's pace that wasn't familiar. What's more, dark circles were under his eyes and his skin looked more pale than usual.

"Tarren!" He said. "Where have you been? I thought you'd be back this morning."

"Sorry," Tarren said. "Slept in a bit at the tavern then spent the rest of the day with her."

"Well, that's good. But I have more bad news. Patriarch Calum was killed last night in Pinegrove, Alis might not survive the next few days, and Yorn was found stabbed this afternoon in the Upper City garrison's practice hall. His body is already being prepared by his garrison, and I've allowed the garrison to appoint a new Captain until Barnabas can select someone new."

By now, Tarren was at the throne dais. He put his hands behind his back, let out a sigh, and shook his head. That was it.

Jason frowned. "What do you think we should do?"

"I don't know."

His tone was distant—almost dismissive. Upon detecting it, Jason prickled.

"Tarren, *what* is going on?" Jason pleaded. "I've felt it from you ever since Niri came back to town. And it's just gotten worse and worse. You know you can talk to me about anything, right?"

Putting on his best disguise, Tarren let a smile spread across his face and he put his hand on Jason's shoulder

"Thanks for being so concerned for me, my dear friend," he said. "But I'm well enough, I promise you. It's just been a long day." He paused. "I'm hungry. I'm going into the dining hall to see what the chef can prepare. You're welcome to join me."

Jason tried not to twist his face. *My dear friend?* "Uh—no thanks. I'm going to bed."

Tarren gave another smile with all the sincerity of old honey on stale bread. He was off—more so today than the days prior. As Tarren walked off, an itching in the crevices of Jason's mind grew stronger. Something was going on. He got up from the throne and retreated to his bedroom.

He closed the door behind him and went for the dresser. There, he scooped up Master Ferribolt's coin. The little orange gem glinted in the soft light, and as it did, Jason concentrated on the spirit of his late mentor.

"Master Ferribolt?" he said. "If you're listening, I could use some advice. Tarren has been distant and isolated lately. I've tried reaching out to him, but I have the feeling that he's hiding something. There's something going on that he doesn't want to talk about. What can I do? With so many of my other friends dying… I don't know who else I can talk to right now."

There was a long, profound silence, and in it, Jason sat on the edge of his bed and listened. He focused harder, imagining Master Ferribolt nearby. Nothing came for a while.

Then inspiration struck, clear as day. Jason could almost hear it in Master Ferribolt's voice:

Have Tarren sit in the throne, put a Paralyzing Curse on him, clamp his head between your thumb and middle finger, then supplicate the Dragon to see his mind.

Jason blinked. That was highly intrusive. But the feelings inside felt locked and sure—there was even a clear picture of it in his head.

Yes. That's what I must do.

Jason squeezed the coin resolutely. Then he slapped it back on the dresser and left the room.

His body shook anxiously as he descended to the great hall. The thought of using that spell on his friend… it was a major betrayal of trust. Had he just imagined it? What if it led to nothing? What if he was just imagining this revelation because he was so desperate for advice? This act could destroy their relationship.

But Jason couldn't shake the feeling that there was something festering inside Tarren.

Jason passed by the throne dais and opened the door to the dining hall. There, Tarren sat by himself next to the head of the table, hunched over his plate and scooping potatoes into his mouth. Jason dragged out his chair and sat next to him. Tarren never lifted his head to acknowledge his arrival.

After a moment, Jason mumbled, "I'm sorry if I've been pestering you."

"It's fine."

Tarren still didn't look up. Jason's chest was tight. He kept rehearsing the act in his head—getting Tarren into the throne, Paralyzing him, accessing his mind. He tried to breathe normally and look collected. Hopefully, Tarren wouldn't notice.

The chef brought Jason some food and he picked at it, but hardly ate. Both of them sat in taut silence for several minutes. Tarren didn't pursue conversation, and Jason was afraid if he opened his mouth, it would sound shaky and suspicious, so he tried to eat as much as he could. Finally, Tarren pushed away his empty plate and stood from the table, still not making eye contact.

"You worry too much, my friend," he said. "You've been through a lot lately—we all have."

Jason attempted a smile. His palms got clammier. Now was the time. They both stood from the table and Tarren said he was going to bed. Jason said he'd do the same, and together, they started walking through the great hall.

As they walked by the throne dais, Jason said, "Tarren, I'd like your opinion on something."

"What?"

"I think the cushion in the throne is getting a little flat. Should I get it restuffed sometime soon? Maybe I'm just being dramatic."

"Hm. Let me see."

Tarren trudged up to the platform, plopped down, and set his hands on the armrests. His lower lip stiffened, "No, I don't think it's—"

Jason acted fast. He threw his magic hand forward and locked Tarren into the Paralyzing Curse. Tarren was so unsuspecting that he didn't do anything to defend it. He just sat frozen in the seat, wide-eyed, his muscles completely constricted. A pang of guilt rang through Jason's heart, but nonetheless, he stepped onto the throne dais.

"I'm sorry Tarren, but I need to know…"

With his right hand, he put his thumb and middle finger on Tarren's temples, covering his face with his palm. Then he uttered a silent prayer. In that moment, images formed in front of him. He could see everything from Tarren's point of view in recent weeks. He watched his meetings with Evelyn, Evelyn's journey with him to Lunli Village, Evelyn healing Niri.

Then he saw the horrible truth: Evelyn revealing herself as Kierli, Kierli making demands of Tarren, Tarren writing the list of every Foreordained servant in Nezmyth, Tarren's practice of Dark Magic inside these hallowed walls, Tarren lying about Evelyn's identity, and Kierli seducing Tarren just last night.

Jason pulled his hand off Tarren's face and let out a startled cry. His mind raced. Kierli had healed Niri and Tarren had started practicing the forbidden magic. That's what was making him so off. His crushing guilt of being blackmailed must be excruciating. And the Dark Magic just compounded everything…

Jason backpedaled, his eyes stinging and his teeth clamped. Every fiber of his body shook. Tarren's mobility was gradually returning like a statue that gained life. The first thing was his face pressing into a scowl. His cheeks burned red and his purple eyes scorched. As this went on, every soldier standing around the edge of the great hall stared with mouths agape, waiting.

When he was finally able to utter words, Tarren said, "What did you see?"

"Everything," Jason croaked.

Silence. No one in the great hall breathed. Tarren's face burned redder and Jason's head swam.

"Jason," Tarren spoke softly, "she was too clever. She held my mother against me. You don't understand what it's like. I couldn't—"

"That doesn't matter!" Jason shouted, his eyes blurry. "Tarren, don't you realize what you've done? Other Foreordained servants *just like you* now lie in graves because of you!"

"What was I supposed to do?" Tarren stood from the throne. "I was forced into this, and this is my fate now! I have no other option! My soul is lost!"

Jason pursed his lips and shook his head. "You're wrong. You always had the choice. You could have turned her away and lived up to your sacred duty. You could have stood *with me* and worked against her, like we were Foreordained to do. But you allowed her to exploit your heart's desires. You had the choice, Tarren. You always did."

Tarren's jaw clamped. "It's too late now."

More silence. Then Jason's words were clear and threatening. "Tarren, son of Gulaf the stone mason, you are no longer the Advisor of Nezmyth. You're removed with dishonor for abandoning the Kingdom and betraying the Sacred Dragon." He paused. "Nadiel would be ashamed of you."

At the mention of his old master, a fire of humiliation and retribution swelled inside Tarren. With eyes white hot, he said, "You know you can't stop her, right? Nezmyth *will* enter a new era whether you like it or not. Your calling as King won't matter. My calling as Advisor won't matter. If we fight against her, we'll die like everyone else has. There's nothing we can do."

Jason blinked the tears out of his eyes. Is this what it had come to? He was supposed to stand with him through everything, just like he always had—like they were Foreordained to do. After he had stood with him through so much… the Ash War, Saryan's death… why fall apart now? Why betray his sacred calling now? What more could he have done?

But one thought was clear. As King, it was upon him to exact justice on those that threatened the prosperity of the kingdom. And this man, Tarren, Advisor of Nezmyth, had enabled Kierli in slaughtering those that stood as pillars in the last kingdom of the Old Ways. He knew what to do, and it pained him to do it, but nonetheless, he knew it was his duty. Banishing wouldn't be enough. Tarren's crimes were too great.

Jason reached down and drew Nightbane from its sheath.

Tarren's eyes turned to slits. "You really plan on fighting me?"

"You understand the gravity of your crimes. And you understand the consequences."

Tarren untied his cape, letting the royal blue cloth fall to the dusty floor. He kicked it behind him and whipped the daggers from his side. "I always beat you, Jason."

"Things change."

Tarren dashed off the throne dais and took three swipes. Jason dodged and ducked each one, but barely. Tarren was still at the top of his form—he always was.

All the soldiers around the room converged with weapons in hands. Tarren kicked Jason to the floor and sent out a flurry of spells. Within moments, every single soldier was constricted in a Paralyzing Curse, squirming on the ground.

Among them, Tarren attempted a Paralyzing Curse on Jason, but Jason caught the spell and attempted to Overcurse him. Tarren recoiled from Jason's power—it grew far more than he anticipated. Inwardly, he cursed himself for setting up lessons with Alis. Tarren managed to release the curse just before Jason Overcursed him, but that left him blurry-eyed and dizzy.

Jason leapt to his feet and sputtered some Ancient Nezmythian. His entire body took strength, surging with power that would make him faster and stronger—even the veins in his arms glowed. Then he dug in his heels and lunged.

Tarren recovered just enough to see Jason coming, and he dodged every one of Jason's strikes. Tarren dodged and took another swipe at him, but Jason wasn't able to fully evade. The blade's edge caught his cheek and he let out a yelp. He spun and kicked Tarren in the gut, but it only made him stagger.

Jason followed through by pulling back his magic hand and launching a jeroki in Tarren's gut. The force sent him flying backward.

Pushing Dark Magic through him, Tarren righted himself and slid to a stop before he slammed into a wall. Then he rushed forward. He was on Jason in the blink of an eye. He tried to ram his dagger into Jason's chest, but Jason twisted and tried to dodge. The dagger plunged into his shoulder instead. He gasped awfully as blood oozed onto his chest.

Jason leapt backward and cast a barrier around himself like a blue eggshell. Inside it, he pressed his hand against his wound and cast healing magic. It stitched up the skin and reconnected the muscles, but left an uncomfortable tingling sensation. Meanwhile, the cut on his face dribbled blood down his cheek and Tarren moved in a circle around the shell, stalking the barrier like a hungry wolf.

Jason closed his eyes and took a deep breath.

Find the peace. Acceptance.

The barrier started to fade. At any moment, Tarren would be upon him. And he was right—Tarren was outclassing him. He could very well die tonight.

There was only one other option—his Knightly power. But was this the right time? Would the Dragon even lend it to him now? Before, he thought this battle was too small—this wasn't against Nartikis or Barnabas or Kierli. But maybe… maybe in a way, this was more significant. This man had been Foreordained to lead the Dragon's people, and he had forsaken it, helping to demolish the Old Ways, tampering in Dark Magic. That's a damning betrayal.

So Jason uttered the silent prayer.

The barrier disappeared and Tarren lunged, but was thrown back. Jason's body caught fire. The markings appeared on his arms and legs. Orange hair, orange eyes, and the Blade of Nezmyth in his hand. The power was granted.

Tarren struggled to stay on his feet, and for the first time, fear crossed his eyes. He knew he had to match that power somehow. But did he have enough in him? He focused his energy and pushed the Dark Magic into every corner of his body. The veins glowed purple on his arms and face, and the whites of his eyes turned black. When he exhaled, his voice was layered with a raspy growl. And his body glowed with euphoria.

With it, he attacked.

To all the frozen soldiers watching, it was a barrage of flashes and sparks too quick to follow. But they could hear the sounds of clashing steel. Jason and Tarren swung and stabbed and danced around each other. But Tarren was panting—each stroke came with great effort. Meanwhile, King Jason fought with a power that no one had seen since the Ash War.

Finally, Tarren faltered. The Blade of Nezmyth swung and a dagger went flying. With a snap of his fingers, Jason evaporated the other one. Tarren was defenseless. He couldn't conjure daggers in his hands because all his Dark Magic was focused on his body. So Jason swept out his leg, forced Tarren down, and pinned him to the ground. Last of all, he held the Blade of Nezmyth at his throat.

The Dark Magic in Tarren evaporated, leaving him with a headache and sick stomach. But when the Knightly power left Jason, he felt invigorated and mended, still pressing Nightbane against Tarren's jugular.

Tarren was too tired to fight back, so he just lay there, defeated, his face sweaty and his jaw tight. He closed his eyes tightly, awaiting the final blow. Trickles of tears formed in the edges of his sockets. Silently, resolutely, he waited for the end he deserved.

Jason's lips shook. Tarren deserved it. This was the highest kind of betrayal. But at the same time... there had been so much death already. So much.

Were more of his loved ones dead than alive right now? In the space of how many weeks? And here was Tarren, his closest and oldest friend. The friend he collected bugs with as children. The friend that struggled with him during the Harvest Tax. The one that pushed him to train and work and be better than he was. Excluding his parents and wife, he hadn't loved anyone more than Tarren.

And Jason still felt that. For that reason, he leaned in.

"Leave this place," he said. "Never return. You're hereby banished from the Kingdom of Nezmyth with disgrace and dishonor. Go."

Jason stepped off, but kept Nightbane at the ready. Tarren stumbled to his feet, gave Jason a pitiful look, and turned away. As he did, he yanked the Foreordination Ring off his finger and dropped it to the floor. He kept his face hidden as he limped the length of the red carpet. Jason used magic to open and close the double doors and Tarren left the castle for the last time. The great hall fell silent. Meanwhile, all the soldiers regained their strength and groaned to their feet.

And in the middle of the hall, Jason bent down to pick up Tarren's Foreordination Ring. It was still warm. He clutched it tighter as if holding on to the memory of what his friend used to be. Then he dropped Nightbane to the ground, fell to his knees, and wept.

36
THE EDGE

Barnabas came to the castle the next morning to find Jason distant and quiet—almost exactly like he was when Saryan died. The King told him everything. Barnabas listened with a tight chest and felt a sharp pain in his stomach as Jason recounted his fight with Tarren. Through it all, Jason's countenance was hollow and ghostlike.

"How are you still able to trust the Dragon through all this?" Barnabas breathed.

Jason shrugged. "Sometimes I wonder the same thing. Maybe it's because soon the Dragon is all I'll have left."

Barnabas's face got iron-cold. "Not if I can help it."

The King wanted to smile, but couldn't.

Barnabas got back on his horse and started for home. The news was already spreading throughout the kingdom—the Advisor had joined Kierli and was on the run. If he was found, he was to be put to death immediately. When the announcement was read at Center Court early that morning, it gave a wave of confidence to Kierli supporters. To them, it reaffirmed that Kierli was called by some higher power to demolish the Old Ways. By the time Barnabas went through the middle of town, there was another full-on riot in the plaza.

This time, things turned lethal. Three townspeople were killed in open duels. Dozens were injured. Soldiers from all around the Market Streets had to converge on Center Court to stop the violence. And even then, it never really ceased. Throughout the day, there were fistfights and vandalism across the city aimed at Kierli supporters and Jason loyalists alike. Barnabas knew that it was probably the same throughout the kingdom.

He spent the next few hours trying to smooth things over and give instructions to soldiers, then he was able to get back to normal duties. There were two things he needed to do today— help with the funeral of Yorn and get his report from Captain Russ in Lower City.

Yorn's funeral that afternoon was a somber one. Besides Barnabas, there were only four people in attendance. There were his parents, who had moved from Port Gala to Upper City to follow their son's career. There was Captain Mara, a strong, brown-haired woman who temporarily replaced Yorn as Captain of Upper City garrison. And there was Sue, a woman who owned a restaurant on the Northern Market Street. King Jason wanted to attend, but Barnabas talked him out of it. It was too dangerous.

Barnabas gave a few words about Yorn's dedication and unconquerable integrity, and the casket was lowered into the soldier's section in the Nezmyth City Cemetery. That was that.

After the funeral, Barnabas traveled to Lower City with a small detail of guards to get that report from Captain Russ. The Captain was a raw nerve. He spoke frantically of slummies becoming impossible to control. They were sending people to the prison almost daily for fighting soldiers. They were convinced that the deaths of Foreordained peoples were divine providence and that Kierli was meant to be Queen. Every time he heard a cry of "Kierli for Queen," Barnabas's jaw tightened.

At length, the day was concluding and Barnabas returned to his home. As he changed out of his armor and into street clothes, he couldn't help but think of the day's events. The unrest. The battles. It all cast a dark blanket over the city that was already thick to begin with. And as he thought of Tarren, he also thought of Niri, who he heard was working at the Wilted Rose. She must be suffering right now.

He debated for a while, pacing the floor. Reconciliation felt appropriate. But would she even want to see him? Especially at a time like now? He paced the floor for several more minutes until his conscience got the best of him. He refastened his armor, locked the door behind him, and mounted his horse.

The horse's hooves clopped softly on the cobblestone as it made its way down the Southern Market Street. He didn't have to travel far west before he arrived at the tavern. He tied his horse to a post outside the building before he approached the door, smoothed his hair, stood up straight, and entered.

Noise filled his ears of people talking, tankards clanking, and the gentle harping of a bard in the far corner. The bitter scents of various alcohols wafted into his nose. Thankfully, Barnabas found a small table in another corner and sat relatively unnoticed. However, some patrons still noticed the disgraced King and avid Jason loyalist. It put him on the receiving end of some vengeful stares.

It wasn't long before a lovely woman approached him—someone whose appearance clearly reflected a heavy burden. Her chocolaty brown eyes were red and puffy but she still forced the corners of her mouth into a smile. What gave her away was her hair, golden and a little greasy, just like her son's.

"Hello," she said. "What can I get you?"

Barnabas swallowed. "My dear woman, I hope you'll forgive me… but you're Niri, aren't you?"

She nodded.

"Do you know who I am?"

She nodded again.

Barnabas deflated. "Then you know that I'm in desperate need of your forgiveness."

"Why?" Niri said, her head tilting. "And I hope you'll forgive *me*, but we're very busy tonight. If you're going to have something, say so."

Surprised at her directness, Barnabas cleared his throat. "I'll, uh… have some wine."

In less than a minute, Niri returned with Barnabas's cup of wine. But she didn't leave. She sank into the seat across from him, folding her arms on the table's edge. "Alright then. What do I need to forgive you for?"

Barnabas scoffed. "I'm surprised you need to ask. You wouldn't have gone to Lunli Village if it weren't for me. That led Tarren to pay any price for your wellness, even if it meant turning to Kierli… it's my fault."

Niri scratched at the table's grain and sighed. "Captain, I forgave you as soon as I came to the city. Tarren told me all that you had done during the Ash War. Nezmyth would have fallen without you. The man I needed to forgive is long gone— replaced by someone new."

Touched, Barnabas half-smiled and shook his head. "Why is it that I'm always on the forgiving end of people much better than me? After all I've done?"

"People change," Niri shrugged. "Sometimes they're awful and they turn good. And sometimes they're good… and fall away." Her voice trailed and her eyes became vacant.

"Words cannot express my sadness," Barnabas said. "Perhaps the Sacred Dragon will find mercy for him."

Niri was quiet, her thoughts distant. Her eyes glistened and her lips shook, but she collected herself and cleared her throat. "Is there anything else you'd like to order, Captain?"

Barnabas almost said no, then an idea struck him. "Actually, yes. Load a basket full of bread, fruit, and vegetables. But no asparagus."

Niri left and returned with the requested basket. By that time, Barnabas had only taken a few sips from his wine. When she returned, she handed him the basket and he thanked her.

"I wish there were more I could do," he said. "If you ever need anything, please contact me. Let me be of service to you."

Barnabas was surprised when she put her arms around his neck and held him. He tensed up a little, perplexed. As she hugged him, people all around the tavern gave looks—mostly bad ones. He tried to ignore them.

"Thank you," Niri said shakily.

When she let go, Barnabas bowed and left the tavern.

By the time Barnabas reached the castle, the sky had turned a blackish blue. When he entered, Jason wasn't on his throne. He checked the dining hall and the sparring courtyard before a soldier told him that the King was in his quarters. Up the stairs and through the hallways Barnabas went, keeping his basket of food in tow. When he reached the double doors, the soldiers guarding it nodded with sad eyes. But they let him in without question. He didn't even knock.

Barnabas could hear his sniffling on the other side even before he even opened the door. Across the room, Jason was laying in bed, above the covers with the crook of his elbow covering his eyes. Barnabas quietly made his way over and pulled up a chair by the bed. Then he waited.

Jason lay there and sobbed for a good while before he sat up and wiped his eyes. He moved with the energy of a man weighed down with decades of grief. Barnabas knew the feeling all too well. When he saw the basket that Barnabas was carrying, he said, "You didn't have to do that."

Barnabas set it on the edge of the bed. "I felt you could use another visit. I made sure they didn't put asparagus in it."

Jason almost laughed, but the hurt was too strong. Tears forced their ways out of his eyes and his shoulders shook.

"What happened to Nezmyth, Barnabas?" he said. "Haven't we served faithfully? Why is everything falling apart? After all the years we defended it?"

Barnabas kept his hands on his knees and his head down. "I wish I had words of comfort to give you, Your Highness. I'm sorry."

He glanced at the food basket and said, "Thank you for the basket. It was thoughtful."

Barnabas's smile was brief. "You know she'll come for you eventually."

"Yes."

"My recommended course of action is to keep you in the castle until she can be neutralized. If you'd permit, I'd like to move my residency here. That way I can guard you day and night. She'll have to kill me before she kills you."

Jason cleared his throat and tried to sit up straight—to appear Kinglike. He put his hands on the edge of the bed, stiffened his jaw, and nodded. "Granted. Move whatever you need. Tarren's old room is available."

* * * * *

"If they find you, they'll kill you."

"Same goes for you. I suppose we're a proper pair, aren't we?"

Kierli had abandoned the cellar and moved her place of residence to the slums of Lower City. Here, she was relatively protected by the locals. From the outside, her hideout was a worn-out tent with holes and patches. But when you crossed the threshold, it became a comfortable cabin with a fireplace, a desk, two chairs, and a large bed. Tarren was currently laying in the bed half-dressed while Kierli paced the floor.

"You're not worried at all about being discovered?" Kierli asked.

Tarren shook his head. "Even if they did discover me, what would they do? I'm stronger than any soldier I know."

Kierli smirked. "Very true." The smirk faded. "The time is getting very close. I can feel it. The throne will be mine soon. I went to the cavern yesterday to pray, and my strength was expanded once again."

"When are you thinking?"

"Tonight."

Tarren sat up. "So soon?"

"Yes. I see no reason to wait. Jason will be the last to fall, but tonight, I kill every last Foreordained in Nezmyth."

Jason will be the last to fall. His friend Jason. The one he betrayed. The one that cried after he saw the vision of everything Kierli had done to him.

His face must have given him away, because Kierli frowned. "Does this trouble you?"

Yes, deeply. "No."

"Don't lie to me."

"It doesn't."

Kierli stared, probing. Then she smiled. "Alright then. Go get me some supplies. I'll need a big meal and plenty of time to meditate for tonight."

Tarren's eyes flashed and his tone died to a purr. She took her hand and pulled her toward the bed. "Maybe we should spend a little quality time together before—"

Kierli yanked her hand from Tarren's grasp. Then she slowly stooped down and slid her fingertips down his neck. Tarren smiled, his skin sprouting into goosebumps. But it stopped being sensual very quickly. She wrapped her long fingers around his throat and squeezed. Tarren gasped for breath. Kierli's face was stoic and pale.

"I'm on the verge of the greatest achievement of my life and all you can think of is your filthy impulses," she said. "Leave. Don't return until you've got food. Money is on the table."

She released her grip and Tarren coughed, massaging his neck and trying to suppress the bubbling anger in his chest. Kierli meandered to the middle of the floor, sitting cross-legged and closing her eyes. Tarren pushed Dark Magic into his face to change his appearance, then he grabbed the money sack and stormed out the door.

He could have gone to the Crossing to buy bread and vegetables, but that wouldn't be as good as the products offered on the Southern Market Street. So Tarren walked northward. He tensed every time he passed a pair of soldiers, but they strode by him, completely unaware. As he made his way to the Southern Market Street, he passed by Tomm and Kara's house.

He slowed his pace. Anger and sadness mixed inside him. Jason's perfect parents—so loving and good. Always treating him like a second son. His cheeks burned and he turned his face toward the road.

This is my life now. I can't go back.

He did all the necessary shopping in a matter of minutes, filling a sack full of bread, apples, guabos, and carrots. There was still plenty of money left over, too. He thought of the Wilted Rose, wondering if his mother was working right now. It wasn't too far.

He stopped in the middle of the street, thinking about it. The thought of seeing his mother's face brought him feelings of both excitement and dread. Would she understand he did all of this for her? Or would she be angry? Perhaps not... she's always been a woman of kindness and understanding. But...

He needed to know. Within minutes, he was there.

The Wilted Rose was just as busy as it usually was. With Tarren's face altered, he walked through the tables and the chatter and pulled up a stool at the bar. Gus meandered his way over to him and tapped two fingers on the table.

"What'll it be, stranger?"

Tarren coughed and tried to alter his voice. "Uh, the house mead."

Gus nodded, poured a tankard, and set it in front of him. He furrowed his eyebrows. "You seem familiar. Have we met?"

Tarren shook his head. "Um, I was actually hoping to speak to that waitress there."

"Niri?" Gus said. "You're welcome to chat if you can catch her. She's been working herself to death ever since news of her son got out. He used to come in here, you know."

"You don't say?" Tarren took a sip. The mead burned his throat and he nearly coughed it up.

Gus frowned and nodded. "Used to be a good man. I'd even call him a friend of mine. You think you know a person." He sighed. "Well, let me know if you need anything else."

Tarren gulped a mouthful, forcing it to stay down. *Dragon, why do people drink this stuff?* After a moment, Niri came up to the bar to rest and sat not far from him. Her back was hunched and her eyes baggy. Quietly, she drank from a tankard of water and stared blankly at the wall ahead of her. Tarren almost didn't speak. His heart pounded and his palms felt moist. But he took his drink, moved a few stools over, and sat next to her.

He cleared his throat. "I, uh… I'm sorry about your son."

Niri's gaze was glassy, but she didn't look at him. "So am I."

"Maybe… maybe he had a good reason for it," Tarren said. "Maybe it was his way of trying to protect you. Kierli is rising to power, and he probably didn't want to see you hurt."

"What do you know about my son?" Niri glared.

Tarren shrugged and turned pink. "Just thinking out loud."

Niri shook her head. "If that's what he was thinking, he was foolish. He was Foreordained to serve as Advisor. That responsibility came above all else—even my well-being. His duty was to be a servant and a safeguard to the people of this kingdom. And what did he do?" She paused. "That Kierli is awful. *Awful.* But I'd rather go back to Lunli Village than live in a kingdom ruled by her. She's the one killing the Patriarchs and you can't convince me otherwise." She shook her head. "No. I love my son and I always will. But he's betrayed me along with everyone else in this kingdom. I hope I never see his face again."

I hope I never see his face again.

The words were a tidal wave crashing down on Tarren and drowning him in shame. His throat tightened and he couldn't bring himself to speak. After an awkward pause, Niri stood from the bar and delivered more drinks without another thought. In her wake, he reeled from her scorn, replaying it in his head over and over.

I hope I never see his face again.

Like a fractured specter of a man, he scooped up the satchel and moved to the door.

The march back to the slums was a hazy one. Niri's words now had permanent residence between his ears. The wound it made on his heart wouldn't scab over—it just kept bleeding.

When he made it back to the tent, he dropped the satchel and slumped onto the bed. Kierli was still meditating in the middle of the floor. She popped one of her eyes open.

Tarren stared at the space ahead of him, motionless, empty. Niri was well again. She's healthy. But now she's alone. And she wanted him out of her life completely.

And it was all her fault. The woman right there. The one meditating on the floor.

Tarren's gaze gravitated to her. He couldn't help but stare. The woman who surgically picked apart his deepest desires and exploited them. The woman who convinced him that he was too far gone to be with those he loved. The woman that stole his life and gave him reduced him to a rotten shell of what he once was.

Kierli stared back at him. "What?"

The thought crept through his mind. A horrible thought. An awful thought. But maybe it was the only way—the best way could atone. It was worth a try, but he had to be fast.

"You'll kill me anyway," Tarren murmured. "I know you won't *actually* keep me around. It doesn't benefit you... because you have to kill every Foreordained person to reach full power... right?"

Kierli frowned. That's when Tarren acted.

Pushing Dark Magic through him, Tarren's hand became lightning-fast and shot for his dagger. With just as much speed, he pushed the dagger to his own throat, trying to slash it. Seal her failure through suicide. Keep her from reaching her full potential. It should have been over and done in a second's fraction.

But even then, Kierli was too strong. The blade stopped right as it reached Tarren's throat, frozen by an invisible hand, drawing nothing but a soft cut on Tarren's jugular. He sat frozen in place, unable to move no matter how much more magic he pushed. Meanwhile, her eyes were fixed on him, blazing and furious.

"I was worried you'd have second thoughts," she muttered.

She stood up. Starshadow appeared in her hand. She came to the bed, stroked his face, gazed deeply into those purple eyes. Then she sighed and said, "It's a shame."

She slashed an X across his torso. It didn't draw blood. But inside his body, Tarren's organs were lacerated. She restored his mobility and Tarren gasped a sick, gurgling breath. Blood seeped out his lips and he struggled for air. Within seconds, he was splayed on the bed, his eyes wide open, lifeless. And that's when the pain rocked through Kierli again. The purple cracks stretched halfway down her stomach and up her neck. And when it was done, she heaved a deep breath and went back to meditating.

37
THE WARNING

It was swift and horrific.

Within the space of one hour, Kierli transported to every village and city in Nezmyth. Her methods of murder varied from house to house. Sometimes she barred the doors and lit the house on fire. Sometimes she dropped something massive through the roof. But usually, she would kill all the soldiers standing guard and stealthily slaughter whoever was inside.

And each time she killed, the pain and the power surged through her. By the end of the night, her entire body was coated with the purple cracks. That was, everywhere except her face.

Every single Foreordained servant in Nezmyth was dead… except King Jason.

* * * * *

Jason stood on the edge of Lake Lihya. He let the water gently lap on his bare feet while he pushed his toes into the sand, soaking in the bright sunlight and the clean air. The cabin wasn't far away—a beautiful building on the lakefront that he and Saryan would visit when they could spare the time.

She was standing next to him, her silver eyes scanning the conifers that crowded the lake's opposite side. Jason couldn't help but think of how beautiful she looked with the sunlight hitting her face like that. It felt like one of those moments that make you fall in love with someone again. Your breath becomes short and you ache to slip into their soul.

At that moment, she turned and looked at him. Then those perfect lips pulled into a smile. "The end is almost here. You've been feeling it, haven't you?"

Jason nodded. "Yes, I have."

"Are you ready?"

He had to think about it. "I don't know. I did everything I could, but every day I wonder if my best was enough."

Saryan smiled and took his hand. How he missed the feeling of those fingers intertwined with his. She squeezed gently. "I think you'll be pleasantly surprised."

Jason smiled in return, then gazed over the water again. So soft, so quiet. Birds chirped in the far distance and the gentle waves whispered in their ears. He only got to enjoy it for another moment before Saryan spoke again.

"She's coming," she said. "Do what you must. Remember, I won't be far."

Jason nodded. "I love you."

Her eyes sparkled and her lips pulled into a smile once more.

When Jason blinked, he was back in his bed, staring up at the ceiling. But he didn't feel tired at all. He threw off the covers, shoved boots onto his feet, and sprinted out the door in his night clothes.

As the doors banged open, the two soldiers standing guard jolted to alert. Both of them stared as the King flew away. One of them started to speak but Jason cut them off.

"Bar every door leading into this castle immediately!" Jason ordered. "On the double! *Move!*"

The soldiers sprinted down the hallway, headed for the great hall. Jason darted for Barnabas's room—the room where Tarren used to stay. He didn't knock. He grabbed the handle and threw it open. He expected to see Barnabas still asleep, but instead, he was sitting on the edge of his bed, lacing up his boots.

Barnabas looked up, then stood at attention. "You felt it, too?"

"Yes," Jason said. "She's coming."

Barnabas finished up his boots, grabbed his sword, then the two of them dashed down to the great hall. To their satisfaction, a host of guards were already at work barring the main doors. It was almost complete. As they stood there, three soldiers came running into the room to report that all other exits had been barred shut. No one was entering or exiting the castle.

"Kierli is coming," Jason told the soldiers. "We can feel it. Let the soldiers on the other side know that this is the time to fulfill their duty. However you can relay the message, do it."

"Yes, sir!"

The soldiers went to work, but it was useless. Before they could even run away, a loud *boom* slammed against the double doors, shaking the dust from its rungs. Muffled shouting was heard on the other side. An unsettling lack of weapons clanging. It was mostly cries of "For Nezmyth" and "Long live the King," followed by horrifying cries of agony, then silence. It didn't last more than ten seconds.

The castle grounds have nearly seventy soldiers, Jason thought, mortified. *Did she kill all of them?*

After a long, sickening pause, three gentle knocks came to the castle doors. Then her voice, right in his ear—almost as if she were standing next to him.

"It's a beautiful night, Your Highness."

Everyone else heard it. Barnabas ripped out his sword. Every soldier squared up. But she wasn't anywhere to be seen. Using his own magic, Jason could feel her presence just outside the castle doors. If he was right, she was leaning against the wood casually.

"Did you really kill all of my soldiers?" Jason asked through gritted teeth.

"Goodness, no," Kierli said casually. "Just the ones that resisted. Nearly half of them ran away. Can you blame them?"

"The Sacred Dragon warned Barnabas and I that you were coming," Jason said. "That should serve as a warning to you."

"And you should know you're the only Foreordained person left alive. *That* should serve as a warning to *you*."

Ice flushed through Jason's system. Every last one of them… dead? Across the entire kingdom? Including Tarren? That meant that the kind of power Kierli was now possessed with was… frightening.

"What did you do to Tarren?" Jason breathed.

"Doesn't matter," Kierli said. "As for the others, you'll probably get the hawks soon. They'll come from all over, giving you the terrible news. Once I've killed you, Nezmyth will be ready for its rebirth. I'll sort the affairs properly, don't worry."

Jason's legs felt weak. Pursing his lips, he said, "So you're not going to just kill me here and now?"

"It's tempting," Kierli said, "but no. I'll be merciful. I'll give you one day to come out of your hiding place and face me like a true leader. But after the sun sets tomorrow, I'll kill a family of Jason loyalists for every hour you stay shut up in there. I'll bring them to these grounds and slaughter them so they'll know exactly who let them down in their time of need."

Jason's whole body trembled.

"Farewell, Jason, Foreordained King," she said. "Until tomorrow."

The voice disappeared and Jason couldn't feel her presence anymore. A deathly hush fell on the great hall. Even the flickering torches seemed still. Jason noticed that every set of eyes were on him, faces painted with fear, bewilderment, and hurt. Barnabas's sword was still tight in his hand. Behind his eyes, he pictured every Foreordained person that was slain under his protection.

Jason felt brittle. Small. What more was there to do? But the faces of dozens of soldiers were upon him, and he had to say something.

"Well, brothers and sisters," he said. "I know I'm not strong enough to fight against her and win. But it looks as though I have no choice once night falls tomorrow. I don't want any other innocent people to get hurt because of me." He paused. "I know you took oaths, but I'm releasing you from them. If at this time you wish to leave, you are free to do so."

There wasn't an immediate response. But one soldier nearer to Jason shrugged her shoulders and said, "Your Highness… what greater honor is there than to die defending the last true King of Wevlia?"

Many of the soldiers buzzed in agreement. But among the crowd, there were dissenters. They shuffled toward the King, dishonor and fear in their eyes. They dropped their helms and weapons at his feet. The rattles and clangs echoed off the walls. None of them looked him in the eye before they turned and left. As they retreated, the remaining soldiers glared at them or spat curses under their breath. Finally, Jason was left with the loyal ones, which was most of them.

There was something about these ones that remained—the ones that chose to stay and fight. Had their eyes always been this bright? Or did they glow more just now? Whatever it was, it didn't matter. Jason's heart swelled. He swallowed to keep a lump from forming in his throat.

"I've, um…" he said, "felt very alone lately. Thank you for showing me I'm not." He paused. "If it's true and I am the last Foreordained person in Nezmyth… that means I'm entitled to a certain level of authority. If you would like, and if the Sacred

Dragon is willing, I'd like to pronounce a blessing upon all of you."

In unison, all the soldiers set down their weapons and knelt before the King. Jason raised his gaze upward. The sacred duty of every Patriarch and government leader was on him now—all of that power and responsibility. Silently, he prayed and asked if what he was about to do was acceptable. He felt no admonishing or dissuasion, so he continued.

Jason looked upon his followers and put his fingers to a triangle, just like Master Ferribolt used to do. Then he breathed deep.

"Sacred Dragon," he said, "give these soldiers power. Expand their abilities and make them mighty in battle and spirit. And when it comes time to them to enter their eternal rest, give them warrior's welcomes at the Gates of Paradise. From now until the edge of eternity, these shall be known as the Knights of the Final King."

Jason lowered his hands, and everyone shuffled to their feet. Under their helmets, eyes glistened and lips were tight. Jason didn't know what to do with this feeling—no one had looked at him like that before. As if he were their father, leading them into the unknown. Through it all, his insides glowed.

These are the ones that stayed.

"Thank you," Jason said. "Tomorrow, we fight for Nezmyth once more. Likely for the last time."

* * * * *

By the time the sun was rising over the Eastern Mountains, Kierli wouldn't see it. She was back in the Chasm, meditating in the bottom of the pool. Her golden hair waved all about her head as the water filled her lungs and filled her with pleasure. The purple cracks glowed brighter, turning her into a purple and black monolith. With every passing minute, she felt her strength enlarge.

"Tonight," she said. "I will be the Queen of Nezmyth. No… the world."

"*Yes,*" the voice around her said. "*You have grown mightier than ever. At last, you take that which you deserve. But there is one final piece.*"

"What is it?"

"*This.*"

The water began to swirl and twist in front of Kierli's face. It thickened and curled until the water formed itself into a ball, shiny and black. Perfectly round. Kierli stared at it, mesmerized, until finally it stopped twirling before her. Then the ball drifted until it rested in her palms. As soon as she touched it, she could feel it stirring like a lion awakening from a slumber.

"*When the King is slain,*" the voice said, "*Destroy the Oracle Stone and replace it with this. Your power has grown far beyond what it once was, but the door of your truest desire is still closed. This is the key. Then, you shall be truly unstoppable, and Wevlia will be yours.*"

Kierli held the stone in both of her hands, feeling the tingles it put up and down her forearms. She nodded, then the stone shrunk and disappeared in a fit of purple sparkles.

"It shall be done," she said.

* * * * *

Kierli was right. As the day crawled by, the hawks trickled in. Port Gala, Widow's Rest, Lunli Village… every Foreordained person in Nezmyth had been murdered last night, young and old. So it was just as Kierli said. Jason was the last one.

A hawk from Pinegrove came, too. The letter was to alert him that Alis died last night in her sleep. Whatever toxin Kierli filled her with during their battle caused Alis's mind to grow foggy and her muscles to grow weak. The healers did the best they could, but in the middle of the night, she lost the strength to breathe. They had plans to bury her in the local graveyard within the next two days.

Through it all, Jason felt numb. But he still wrote responses to every city, letting them know of the current state. He was the last remaining piece of the Old Ways, and he would soon fall as well. Kierli would likely kill him by tonight, then her supporters would try to appoint her as Queen. Be prepared.

He also wrote one more hawk, this one going locally. He kept it short:

Mother, father,

Kierli has killed every Foreordained person in the kingdom except me. She plans to finish that tonight.

Please don't come anywhere near the castle. Do what you must to stay safe. The end is coming, but something tells me there's nothing you need to fear.

I love you both. Thank you for everything. I'll see you soon, I'm sure.

-Your Jason

Jason tearfully rolled up the parchment and stamped it with his seal before handing it to a soldier. Everything stayed within the great hall today. Jason, Barnabas, all the soldiers… the only exceptions were for meal breaks. They had enough food in the castle to last everyone through the day, but they couldn't be picky. Jason even found himself eating some strands of asparagus.

His hand was sore after writing so many letters. He kept his station at a small table near the end of the hall. Meanwhile, soldiers all throughout the room practiced their drills and meditated, somberly preparing for the end. Barnabas was among them. After an hour or so of practice, and after Jason's twelfth letter, Barnabas approached and sat across from him at the table.

He didn't say anything at first, but finally, his gaze finally lifted from the table to Jason's eyes. "How are you feeling?"

Jason rolled up the letter and sealed it with another stamp. A soldier standing right over his shoulder took it and marched away. Jason sighed. "I don't think I have sufficient words to explain everything I'm feeling. But... I think I'm ready."

"To die?"

Jason nodded. Barnabas was silent.

"My only worry is our people." Jason's eyes glossed over as a myriad of thoughts bombarded him. "What will become of them after we're gone and Kierli takes power? She won't be benevolent. She won't be good like she thinks she is. Just look at the destruction she creates." Jason rubbed his face. "I never thought Nezmyth's greatest threat would rise from inside. I should have been more prepared." Barnabas opened his mouth to speak, but Jason cut him off. "And don't give me that 'It's all my fault' rubbish. We've been over this. I'm tired of being pestered with your guilt and I don't intend to be oppressed with it in my final hours. Do you understand?"

Barnabas closed his mouth.

Jason's shoulders sagged. "I just wish I could have done more. But what? What more could I have done for my kingdom? Did I not always pray for guidance? Did I not act as a steward for the Sacred Dragon? Then why did it come to this?" Jason took off his Foreordination Ring and rolled it in his fingers. "How can I stand in the presence of past Kings when I let everything fall apart?"

Barnabas leaned in with a serious face. With absolute certainty, he said, "You were a fine King if there ever was one."

"I'm not so sure."

Jason wiped his eyes with the back of his hand. Barnabas leaned forward more.

"Your Highness," he said, "there is a lot I don't know. I don't know if I'll be in Paradise or Darkness when death takes me tonight. I don't know if I'll ever see my son again. But this I do know: you saved me. You reached down and pulled me from the abyss when I was broken. You helped me atone for my crimes when the kingdom cursed you for it. Everything I am now is because of you. No matter where my soul goes, I'll live forever with pride knowing I served Jason, the last true King of Wevlia."

Jason tried to smile. "I never thought you'd be the last person to stand by me."

Barnabas smiled for him. "It will be an honor."

At that moment, a soldier came bustling up. He gave a little bow and said, "Your Highness, some of us were talking, and we'd like something to signify our loyalty to you. A symbol or marking of some sort. Is there anything you would like?"

Jason blinked. What an odd request. He racked his brains for anything they could possibly use, but had a hard time coming up with anything. All the while, his eyes absently locked on his hands, tired from writing letters all day.

That's when it struck him. His right hand. The one he hid for eighteen years. On his palm, the marking that signified his divine power. The triangle under his index finger with one side longer than the others.

Now, it would mark them, too.

38

LONG LIVE THE KING

As daylight turned to sunset, everyone in the great hall grew tense. Their weapons were sharp, muscles loose, minds alert. In the throne, Jason sat with his hands on the armrests, his face pulled in a frown, his eyes closed. He meditated for hours, keeping his fingers on Nightbane's pommel as it leaned against the seat. Before him, Barnabas sat cross-legged, also meditating with his sword across his legs.

Blackness filled the sky. Light stopped shining through the windows. The chandeliers magically ignited as they did every night. The world itself seemed to grow still, then distant thunder rumbled. Cracks and shatters ran across the sky, then the patter of rain grew on the widows. They started small, then swelled until each droplet slapped the glass in a fierce downpour. This late in fall, they knew the rain would be freezing cold.

All the soldiers gathered to the front of the hall, forming ranks inside the doors. Jason opened his eyes and wrapped his hand around Nightbane. With intensity, he thrust the sword into its sheath as he stood. In front of him, Barnabas arose with the same bravado, but tore his sword from its sheath and marched to the head of the soldiers.

The soldiers parted as their Captain strode between them. His armor clinked with each step. When he reached the front of the ranks, he snapped around to face them. His eyes were electric again—focused as he read the faces of every remaining soldier. Through them all, he saw King Jason, garbed in his royal armor. They held a gaze for only a moment.

"Ladies and gentlemen," he said, "I wish I had more comforting words to give you. Of a truth, we advance into an almost certain death. But I know the Sacred Dragon has Its eyes upon this struggle tonight. Show It that you were one of the few that chose to defend Nezmyth in its final moments. Fight with fire. Fight like the heavens are watching. And I hope to gaze upon your faces as Paradise welcomes you in a blaze of glory. May the Dragon be with you, Knights of the Final King."

The soldiers stood a little straighter and held their weapons close. Their armor was polished and strapped on tight. But on every breastplate, there was a red hand print, freshly painted. And inside each hand print, a triangle below the index finger. The mark the King wanted.

Barnabas's eyes met with Jason's again. It was time.

Taking an uneven breath, Jason said, "Unbar the doors."

The soldiers at the front followed the order. That's when the voice came.

"People of Nezmyth, it is I, Kierli."

Everyone prickled and stiffened at the sound of it. Jason gripped his weapon tighter and Barnabas ground his teeth together.

"The true god has spoken has led us to this glorious day," she said. "Within moments, the shackles of the Old Ways will be no more and a new age of freedom will dawn. There will be no need for fear. I will lead you into a new era—an era of power, prosperity, and security. All shall be equal and free under me, and none shall suffer."

"*Liar! Long live King Jason!*" One soldier shouted. The rest of them cheered.

The doors were unbarred and pulled open. Darkness spilled into the great hall along with the humid embrace of rainfall. Outside, wind abused the trees and bushes. The grounds were already littered with stiff, cold bodies—those that Kierli had slain last night.

And there she was, standing in front of the Knightly fountain. Even from hundreds of yards away, everyone could see the purple strands of light cracking across her neck and arms. Her dark blade jutted from her hand and her hair whipped around her face like a yellow flag. She stood still, a specter against the storm.

Lightning flashed and thunder roared. The clouds above were a great billowing mess of gray, shielding the stars and moons. And just inside the castle doors, Barnabas stood at the lead of nearly seventy soldiers. His first order was clear.

"*Fire!*" he shouted.

Archers launched a volley of arrows. Kierli lazily lifted her hand. Before they could reach her, half the arrows reduced to dust. The other half halted in midair, turned around, and soared back at the assailants.

Some soldiers didn't react quick enough. They took arrows to their arms and stomachs, falling to the ground. Most of them were able to cast barriers in time, including Barnabas. The arrows aimed for him clattered to the ground. He cracked his knuckles and brandished his sword.

"*Volley two!*" Barnabas commanded.

This time it wasn't just arrows, but a barrage of jerokis and other projectiles. Again, Kierli lifted her hand and stopped everything coming her way. This time, when she launched them back, the soldiers were quicker to react. Those that weren't killed in the first wave yanked the arrows from their bodies and speedily cast healing magic.

Kierli started to move forward, her boots trudging across the wet stone and kicking bodies out of the way. Her chin was down and her eyes glowed with something otherworldly.

Barnabas hated to do it, but he knew there wasn't much more they could do. She's just too strong, and he knew she would be. He brought up his sword and bent his knees.

"With me, brothers and sisters!" He called. *"For tradition! For truth! And for Nezmyth!"*

"For Nezmyth!" they echoed.

Like a great wave, they charged into the rain. In the stampede, the soldiers bellowed guttural cries of loyalty to Nezmyth and the King. Per Barnabas's orders, Jason stayed behind. So he saw it all.

It was magnificent. His blessing from earlier was answered, because each soldier radiated a glory and shine he had never seen before. Each of them became a glowing beacon against the stormy landscape, running and jumping and casting magic surpassing their capacities. They truly had become something more. The Dragon had blessed them.

But it wasn't enough.

Kierli raised her hand and shot lightning from her fingers. Enormous green bolts ripped through the bodies of multiple soldiers, dropping more than a dozen in a single blow. As more soldiers descended upon her, it was a massacre. She vanished and reappeared at their weak points, stabbing and slashing them into oblivion. With every second, someone new fell, their blood mixing with the fallen rain. More flashes of lightning. More slashing. More death.

At last, the final soldier was brought low. The entire castle grounds were littered with them—only Barnabas was left. Jason stood in the castle doors, shivering with sadness and horror. He felt a brimming hate for what was to come—an anger for the inevitable. But he still held on to a spark of hope that she could be stopped.

Barnabas's chest rose and fell with each heaving breath. Half his face was spattered with blood and he held his blade with both hands. Rain soaked his entire body, dripping down his chin. He glared at his oppressor with squinting eyes.

"I should have never appointed you," he spat.

Kierli smiled and shook her head. "It wouldn't have mattered."

Barnabas cast up a silent prayer, then released one hand and shot a plume of fire at Kierli. She blocked it with a purple barrier and pushed forward, raising her weapon against him. Barnabas dove and rolled out of the way as the weapon came down and chipped the stone below him. He raised his blade to the sky. In that moment, a deafening crash of lighting shot down from the clouds, igniting it.

Jason watched with a dangling jaw as Barnabas reeled in the lightning's power, spun, and slashed it at Kierli. The blast actually connected and threw her back. She slammed against the fountain, her entire body sparking. Barnabas staggered from the force. But Kierli recovered in an instant. With a shake of her head, the sparks dissipated and rose to her feet as if lifted by invisible hands.

Barnabas spat some blood from his lips and said, "Long live the King."

The hope in Jason's heart flared up. Barnabas was winning. Perhaps the deaths of those soldiers wouldn't be in vain.

But then Kierli smiled.

It was so sudden. Too sudden. She dashed on him in a fraction of a second, and suddenly, her dark blade was stained with blood, spiking out of Barnabas's back. The blade's handle was pushed all the way to his stomach. Barnabas gave a wet gasp as his eyes snapped open.

"No!" Jason couldn't help but scream.

Barnabas coughed. The strength left his legs. Blood trickled from his lips. He still had the strength to turn and look at Kierli, and as he did, they locked eyes. Behind those steely blues, there was nothing but a shadow. No shimmer. No light. Regardless, her lips stayed in a smile.

With one hand, she held Barnabas's shoulder. And with the other hand, she slowly extracted Starshadow from his body. When the tip was free, she spun around. Barnabas's body collapsed as his head left his shoulders and landed with a sickening thud on the wet stone.

Inside the castle, Jason felt sick. His eyes filled with tears and his chin shook. Two droplets slipped down his cheeks. Anger and a thirst for vengeance boiled inside him.

So this is what it is to be totally alone?

But with that thought, a feeling. Like a hand on his shoulder. He turned and looked, but there was no one there. That's when he remembered Saryan's words, and the rage inside him cooled to an even calm.

No. I'm not. I never was.

He held Nightbane tighter and swished it as pushed his feet forward. As he crossed the threshold and stepped into the rain, lightning flashed again. Kierli's gaze turned to him. She could sense her absolute power edging nearer. Whether it was that or the Dark Magic, she was still hungry—hungry for one more kill.

Please, Sacred Dragon. If it is Your will, give me the power to avenge my friends.

His body ignited. The marks appeared on his limbs, his hair turned orange, and the Blade of Nezmyth flashed into his hand. And with the Knightly power upon him, he could sense Kierli's spirit even stronger than before. Around her body was a thick veil of darkness—a gaping void of astounding magnitude. Never had Jason seen anything like it before.

He walked by the bodies of his Knights. The handprints on their breastplates were washing off in the rain. His heart rang in agony for them.

Forgive me, brave Knights. I wish it wasn't so. He looked up. *I fight for you now.*

He crouched his legs and launched himself, hurtling through the air. As he flew, the raindrops were like needles on his face. They made his eyes like slits as he careened toward Kierli. She was ready. She squared up, holding Starshadow high, ready for the strike.

When they collided, the air was filled with a deafening *clang*. More of them sounded, an impossibly fast barrage of clashing. They stayed on the ground, dancing around each other's bodies as they swung and stabbed, ducked and dodged. Finally, Kierli launched herself into the air, soaring into the rain. Jason planted his feet and jumped, pursuing her.

As Jason's body soared against the storm, Kierli looked down on him. From her hands, she launched black balls of magic that were almost impossible to see. But Jason could feel them. He evaded them as he flew, but when they got close enough, the black balls exploded into green ribbons. He dodged them the best he could, but some of them still managed to graze his arms and neck. They stung like jellyfish and made his vision blurry. He shook his head, trying to overcome the poison.

Jason vanished the Blade of Nezmyth and charged up a blast of his own—the force of it nearly shot him back. From his hands, seven beams of fire scattered and converged on Kierli. She anticipated them. She threw her hands out and encased herself in a dark purple sphere, blocking them out. The fire swallowed her, making her sweat and shake inside her cocoon, but she still remained unharmed.

Jason frowned, pondering how to break that barrier. That's when he remembered his battle with Nartikis. He lifted his hand to the dark clouds and petitioned the weather. The answer was swift. As if reading his thoughts, three bolts of lightning tore from the clouds and converged on Kierli. It was blinding. Thunder ripped through their ears. And in its wake, Kierli's cocoon shattered. Her smoking, half-conscious body plummeted from the sky.

She was soaring toward Jason. In the air, he readied himself with the Blade of Nezmyth. He cocked back, ready to strike. But as she flew by, she regained herself. She expertly twisted in the air and evaded the swing. The Blade of Nezmyth got within an inch of her nose.

She kept flying downward, hurtling towards the ground. Jason growled and flew after her.

She was heading right for Center Court. Thankfully, there wasn't anyone on the plaza—Jason could feel it. With that in mind, he focused his energy on the cobblestones in the courtyard. Down on the ground, the stones began to jitter and rumble free of their mortar. As the plaster around them severed and cracked, the stones flew into the sky like thousands of stony jerokis. Each one headed right for Kierli.

Kierli narrowed her eyes. She maneuvered her way around the speeding cobblestones in a way that was unnatural. It was almost like her body was able to bend and reshape. Jason was having trouble sensing it, but part of him thought some of the stones even went *through* her.

Whatever it was, he forced the stones that missed her to reverse course and rain down on her. He could feel each one of them cascading through the air. If they were coming at her from every direction, she wouldn't be able to dodge.

Thus it was. As Kierli perfectly swerved and dodged every stone, all of them converged on a giant sphere around her—thousands of them. They hovered for a second, then imploded. She didn't tense or prickle. Instead, she turned and looked at the King, those blue eyes searing. As she disappeared into a hail of rocks, an eruption sounded.

Blam!

Kierli was suddenly blasting toward Jason at top speed. She soared through the stony onslaught, bursting out of it and sending rock through the air. What's worse, there were six of her, all flying toward Jason with glowing eyes and raised blades.

Jason tried to use his Knightly sense to feel out which one was properly Kierli—the other five had to be projections. But no. Each of them was *one sixth* of Kierli. He bore his teeth. He threw a barrage of jeroki beams at them as they pelted toward him, but just like the cobblestones, they evaded all the attacks. They were almost upon him. Then three disappeared in puffs of smoke. Jason closed his eyes. He had to trust his senses now —he had to feel them out.

They encircled him, charging while swinging their swords at breakneck speeds. With his eyes tightly shut, Jason could feel each attack coming. But even in his Knightly state, repelling each blow was becoming impossible. He felt sweat coating his face. Breaths came sharply.

In his mind, he pleaded, *Knights past, please, help me.*

No response.

Jason fought off more swipes, the clang of steel ringing through the air. He was moving slower. Getting tired.

No. I can't. I can't stop.

He shot energy through his body that made his entire skin hard as metal. Two of the Kierli copies shot toward him from opposing directions. He didn't bother to block the blows, and their blades connected with him. What's worse was his metal skin wasn't enough to block the blows completely. Blood seeped onto his arms and torso.

Need to regroup. Create some space.

Jason turned and soared toward the castle, face-first. As he flew, he flipped around and faced backward. The Kierli copies were in pursuit. He released another barrage of jerokis, beams, and fireballs, lighting the air with reds and yellows. But they all dodged and swerved effortlessly, just like before. Then, all at once, the Kierli copies converged into one. She was back. And she blasted toward Jason so speedily that he couldn't react.

She tackled him in the air and didn't let him go until they both hurtled into the Knight statue, sending a geyser of broken rock and dust into the air. Jason's entire body felt broken. The Knightly power mended his bones, but slowly. Meanwhile, his vision was blurry and his mind foggy. With that, Kierli held nothing back.

She disappeared Starshadow and launched a flurry of blows on Jason with her bare fists. His face, torso—everywhere. The force and frequency of each blow made Jason's insides rupture. He simply couldn't keep up and block all of them, even with his Knightly power. She really had become something insurmountable.

Finally, he got some relief when she grabbed his face and threw him out of the rubble. He tumbled across the slippery stone of the courtyard. When he finally stopped, he propped himself up and vomited blood. His body shook as he tried to get on his hands and knees, but everything was smeared and hazy and his body felt like sludge. But despite his struggle, the Blade of Nezmyth appeared in his hand.

Through the pouring rain, Jason saw Kierli stalking toward him, almost looking bored. He breathed heavily. Blood dribbled down his chin. He clutched the Blade tighter.

As she got closer, Jason bent down as if to launch himself at her again. But she threw out her arm and stopped him. He felt himself suspended in midair, his arms and legs outstretched like a star. Then Kierli rotated him until he was upside down, his head dangling just above the ground. She got close and inspected his body—dozens of broken bones, punctures, half covered in blood.

"I thought you'd be much more of a challenge," she mused. "I'd heard stories of your power. Seems they were exaggerated."

Starshadow appeared in her hand.

She started with the shoulders. Starshadow ripped through each one, tearing his bones and muscles as blood oozed out. He gritted his teeth and gasped. Then Kierli stabbed each thigh. Slit each wrist. More pain. Jason couldn't help it—tears started dripping from his eyes.

What more could I have done?

King Thomas nor anyone else sounded in his head. But Kierli kept working.

She stood back and watched Jason bleeding in the rain, admiring him like a painting. The blood stained his royal armor in slashes and mixed with the water as it fell to the ground. All the while, he gasped for breath and moaned pitifully. She gave a little laugh before she cocked back Starshadow and rammed it through his chest.

Jason felt the blade pass all the way through him. And that's when things finally started to fade. His Knightly power flickered away. His entire body slackened. The light inside him diminished. As his eyes darkened, memories started to burst forth.

Learning to play the flyra as a child. Blasting a hole in Tarren's wall. Crying after receiving his Blessing of Fate. His first meeting with Barnabas. The kingdom cheering at his Ordination Ceremony. Kissing Saryan when they became Melded. Losing Garrit in Unbuntye. Cradling Nartikis outside the western wall. The tears after Saryan's first pregnancy. Burying Saryan and Prince Garrit. The words from Barnabas's final speech:

Fight like the heavens are watching.

I did.

Kierli dropped him. Jason's punctured armor creaked horribly. And as raindrops pattered his face, he let out his final breath.

Before he faded completely, he heard a voice. Floating. Soft.

"Well done, Your Highness. It's time to come home."

39
THE AWAKENING

It's warm here.

That was Barnabas's first thought. He couldn't remember how he had gotten into this dark corridor, only that the tunnel behind him didn't seem to have a beginning. The last thing he remembered was Kierli at the castle. Was it a dream? It felt like so long ago… but no, it was only moments ago. Wasn't it?

It didn't take long before he saw a light in the distance. He moved toward it, shuffling his feet. That's when he noticed the clothes he was wearing—the same street clothes he wore at the castle, with the same tears and punctures from the fight with Kierli. Strangely, his body was completely healed. No scars, nothing. His eyebrows furrowed as he looked upon himself.

Then he stopped. A feeling of dread washed over him.

I'm dead. I'm in the Third Life. Which means judgment is coming.

He pinched himself to make sure this was real. Yes. He could feel the sharpness of his finger nails. He stole a glance behind him. Could he just go back? But what kind of escape could he find? He was *dead*. What was ahead of him was inevitable, so what was the point of running?

He had to clamp his jaw to keep his teeth from chattering. Inside his chest, his heart thumped horribly. At least, he thought it did. Did he still have a heart if he was dead? What was this body then?

Another glance behind him. It was endless black, and who knew how far it went. Ahead of him, a growing light. This corridor got warmer the more he approached it. And something about this place felt... familiar.

There was no use resisting. He knew he would end up here eventually. It was time. He faced the light, puffed out his chest, and picked up his feet.

At length, he arrived at the opening in the tunnel. What he found made his jaw drop—a cavernous dome carved out of beautiful white stone, marbled with designs that no human hands could do. As Barnabas looked closer, he realized the designs contained faces. At the top, the faces were of dragons, noble and majestic. Halfway down, there was a great empty space. Then as it got closer to the bottom, the faces were human. He did a double take as he recognized three of the faces at the bottom level. One was Thomas's. Then his. Then Jason's. There weren't any more after that.

But that wasn't the most astonishing thing in the room. On the opposite end of the dome, there were two doors. And between them, a massive, green-scaled dragon. It had to have been the length of fifteen carriages end-to-end, with a long curving tail and claws large enough to crush his entire body. Its eyes were yellow with slits like a cat's. As Barnabas came into the room, the creature perked up. Not threateningly, but curiously.

Then, it smiled.

"Greetings, Captain Barnabas," the dragon said. Its voice was deep and strong enough to make Barnabas's insides tremble.

Barnabas's throat was dry. "Are... are you the Sacred Dragon?"

The dragon laughed in its throat. "Nay, my human friend. I am Ugviir, the Last Dragon King. It was I that ruled Nezmyth before Wevlia fell to the Dark Era."

Barnabas nodded, still gazing around the massive dome. His tone was distant and detached. "What is this place?"

"The Hall of Judgment," Ugviir said. "Constructed for souls such as thine."

Barnabas's eyes fell. "The damned?"

"The conflicted."

Silence. Barnabas just kept his head down in thought. With that, Ugviir continued.

"Thou art a man of complexity, Captain," Ugviir started strolling around the perimeter of the room. His tail dragged along the ground like a snake and he kept his wings tucked in. "Thou art the bearer of a great many sins. Thou didst cast my beloved Nezmyth into disrepair, abandoned thy son, and caused the death of great many…"

Barnabas shriveled.

"However," Ugviir continued. "Thou hast also atoned for many of those sins. Thou didst become reacquainted with The Sacred One during thy tenure in the Vault of the Damned. Thou didst lead Nezmyth to victory during the Ash War. And thou didst kindle a love for the young Nartikis with what little mortality he had left. In every way, thou hast sought to repair what thou didst break. And what was last…" the dragon paused. "Thou wast the last friend that stood beside the Final King before his murder. When all else had left."

Jason is dead, too? Barnabas thought. *So the Old Ways are lost?* His heart sank and despair took him. Ugviir could see the sadness growing on his face. He arched his long neck down, looking into Barnabas's eyes. "Why the sadness, human friend?"

"I couldn't protect anyone," Barnabas said. "No matter how much I tried."

"Has it not occurred to thee that a plan was prepared?"

Barnabas looked up. "What plan?"

Ugviir smiled and pulled his great head back. "Mortality is but a drop in the ocean of eternity. Thy growth did not end in Nezmyth. His Majesty, King Jason, has fulfilled his role. As thou hast. And it is time to move on. The Sacred One knows all."

Jason fulfilled his role admirably. Of course he did. He was valiant and good and true. But what about Barnabas? Once again, Ugviir could see the concern riddled across his face. "Thou art troubled still. Come closer, human friend, and I shall open thine eyes."

Barnabas swallowed and dragged his feet to Ugviir. As he got closer, he could see the dragon's features in greater detail. The ridges in his greens scales were thin and long like the pine needles of the Western Woods. Those brilliant yellow eyes had spots of red, brown, and amber in them. And those teeth... they had to be the size of his forearms, but perfectly white and clean. It was a wonder any creature like this could ever go extinct.

When Barnabas got close enough, Ugviir spread his wings like a great canopy, then took his claw and reached forward. With the claw's point, he delicately touched the middle of Barnabas's forehead.

His mind opened.

* * * * *

Jason groaned and kept his eyes closed. How long had he been asleep? It must have been ages. He couldn't remember his bed ever feeling this warm—at least he thought it was his bed. It didn't feel like the mattress back at the castle, but it didn't feel foreign either. He pulled the covers over his shoulders and nestled himself deeper.

Then he remembered the fight. Kierli. The pouring rain. Her cracked body. Her dark blade ripping him over and over.

Under the covers, he put his hands on his shoulders and legs. No punctures. And someone had slipped off his armor. What was stranger was that the clothes he wore weren't his street clothes. Whatever these were, they were far too comfortable to be his. Even as King, he never owned anything this fine.

He groaned again, then started to hear voices—whispers of people closeby. He tightened his eyelids then forced them to open. In that moment, he felt a weight ease down next to him on the bed. Shapes were starting to form around him. He blinked harder.

The weight next to him was a person, beautiful and clean. They leaned in closer and Jason could make out their face. Golden blonde hair. A smile with even teeth. Freckles around their nose.

Jason's eyes grew wide.

When they saw the surprise and wonder on his face, they held back a laugh. Tears welled up anyway, and they couldn't push down their smiles.

"Hey, big guy," Saryan said with bright eyes. "It's been a while."

She put her hand on his face and kissed his forehead. As soon as Jason felt that warm touch, it was like everything inside him caught fire. Is this a dream? Another vision? It couldn't be. He actually *felt* her lips on his forehead. With a shaking hand, he reached up and touched her face. It was real—warm and smooth. Not a spirit, but a real body.

It was her.

He couldn't help himself. He pulled her on top of him, pushed his face against her neck, and wept. Both of their bodies pressed together, trembling, laughing, crying. Saryan didn't fight it, but held him like a child, stroking his hair and kissing his head.

"It's you," Jason said, his voice shaking. "It's you. It's finally you."

"It was less than two months!" Saryan teased him through her own tears. "Pull yourself together! Didn't I tell you I was never really far? Besides, we're all here now."

"All...?"

Jason hadn't looked around because his face was buried in Saryan's shoulder. But she got up and stepped aside, and that's when Jason saw where he was.

Oh my, Jason said. *This is the same room I Awakened to when Barnabas killed me years ago. King Thomas was standing right there when he told me I was a Knight of the Holy Order...*

King Thomas wasn't there, but Kara and Tomm were.

Jason found the strength to sit up on the edge of the bed. Together, Kara and Tomm came up to him and wrapped their arms around him. The three of them embraced tightly, smiling. Kara kissed her son on the cheek and whispered in his ear.

"We are so *proud* of you," Kara said.

When they let go, Jason looked up at them, his face pressed with confusion. "You two... should be alive, shouldn't you? Did Kierli do something to you? What happened?"

Kara and Tomm traded glances and shrugged. Tomm answered. "We heard Kierli's voice, but not long after, a spirit appeared to us. Told us to be at peace, and the time to leave had come to leave. We didn't know what that meant, but we didn't feel scared. Somehow we felt... ready." Tomm and Kara shared another beaming glance. "And here we are."

"It was that way for a lot of people," Kara said. "Although we haven't talked to many. Just some of the people that are here."

"Here?" Jason said. "What do you mean 'here?'"

"Oh, you'll see," Kara said brightly. "But right now, there are two people we want you to meet." She turned to Saryan. "Do you think he's ready?"

Saryan nodded vigorously. Kara and Tomm shuffled for a door on the far side of the room. Jason looked on, still waking up, his face pressed with perplexity.

He looked down at his hands. They were clean and soft—his mark still blazed under his forefinger. He couldn't find any scars or callouses all along his skin, not even the slit wrists Kierli gave him. It was like his body was renewed, cured from all ailments or past signs of struggle. Every breath he breathed felt clean and pure.

Is this my body now?

While he was thinking, Saryan bent down and looked him squarely in the eye. "Jason, the Sacred Dragon has blessed us very much. These are Garrit and Lea."

The door opened just a crack, but Tomm and Kara crowded it and made it hard to see. Kara took a parcel carefully into her arms. Tomm leaned down and spoke soothing words to a small figure. They turned around and Jason saw who they were bringing into the room. His eyes grew and his heart jumped into his throat.

Tomm walked with tiny steps as a little girl kept pace with him. She had sandy brown hair just like Jason's and bright silver eyes like Saryan's. The little girl didn't tear her eyes off Jason as Tomm led her to him. As for Kara, she carried something tightly wrapped in a blanket—something the size of a large loaf of bread.

Tomm heaved the girl onto Jason's lap. Words escaped him. She had to have been a year or two old. That little face was so clean. So new. But something about this child was like looking in a mirror. He could see traces of himself in her. But there was something more. She was Saryan and she was Jason, but also... *more.*

She was his.

In this moment, the words from his Blessing of Fate returned to him. The promise that he would be a father. His eyes locked onto those little silver orbs. As his throat filled with a lump, he managed to croak out one word.

"...Hello."

Lea stood from his lap and put her tiny hands on his face, examining him. Jason let her. Meanwhile, everyone held their breath. Then something like a smile crept across her face. Yes. This was her father. And with that, she leaned forward and put her little arms around his neck.

Something inside Jason glowed and swelled. She was so small! And where was this love coming from? How could he care so much for someone he just met? He wanted to protect this small human. Care for her. Teach her. Show her everything. The thought was exhilarating and terrifying, but above everything else, the love. The love was unlike anything else. He held her close—held her for the first time.

When she unwrapped her arms from around him, Tomm took her back and Saryan put the parcel in Jason's arms. It was a baby boy—wrapped up in a blanket, sleeping soundly. He had a small shock of blonde hair growing from his scalp. Jason felt the same swell of love for this child as he did with Lea. A lump stayed in his throat as he smiled wide, holding the child against his chest.

"He's got my eyes, too," Saryan teased as she stroked his tuft of hair. "Looks like my blood is stronger than yours."

Jason laughed quietly. The tears dripped down his cheeks. "This… this is amazing." He looked at Saryan. She returned his gaze. She leaned in and gave him a gentle kiss.

"Alright, come on," Tomm said as he lifted Lea into his arms. "The welcome feast is probably ready by now. Don't want to keep everyone else waiting. Jason, are you ready? Can you walk?"

Welcome feast? Everyone else? "Uh… yes, I feel fine. I think I'm ready."

Kara opened the door and walked out. From the other side, there was an immediate rustling of people shushing each other in anticipation. Everyone filled out, allowing Jason to bring up the rear. The floor beneath his feet was smooth and warm, and his body felt strong with each step. Saryan looked back at him and held out her hand. Jason took it. Then they crossed the door. His eyes grew again when they walked out.

They must have been in an elaborate cabin the size of a mansion. The room they were in connected to a great hall with a long dining table, complete with fine dinnerware and covered with fresh vegetables, roasts, and baked goods. The roof was held up by a grid of supporting beams. Tall windows streamed in brilliant light. A fireplace roared on one side of the room. It was finer than any mansion Jason had visited in Upper City. Everything was exquisite, cozy, and lovely.

But the best part was the people.

As soon as he crossed the door, Jason was blown away by rousing cheers and applause. And nearly every face was familiar. Master Ferribolt and Rosie. King Thomas. Nadiel. Alis. Yorn. Garrit and Melody. Kalyk. Chief Patu and Adria. Even Patriarch Willows and Kristof. Every face was smiling, cheering. Healthy. Alive. Beaming.

This pushed Jason over the edge again. His joy ascended in his chest until it made his eyes leak. Saryan put her arm around his shoulders and walked him to the dining table. There, everyone surrounded him, showering him with hugs, welcomes, and congratulations.

It took a while for Jason to calm himself down—the emotions were so strong. But Master Ferribolt was the first person he threw his arms around. The Chief Patriarch's body was stronger than he remembered—less rotund. And he had a head full head of hair! But Jason could never mistake those stony gray eyes and rosy cheeks.

With their embrace, Jason uttered a simple, "Thank you."

"You did well, and I am proud," Master Ferribolt smiled. "Rosie, this is Jason."

Rosie was a lovely woman with a soft face and short, curly hair. She said hello and gave Jason a firm handshake. Jason got the impression that she was the quiet one in the relationship.

"The Final King!"

King Thomas was already on Jason. He scooped him up in a bear hug and swung him around before finally dropping him to his feet. Everyone laughed as they watched. Jason had never felt King Thomas before, only seen him and talked to him. He couldn't help but laugh as Thomas held him like an older brother. Then he set him on the ground and held his face between his hands.

"You did it," he said with absolute glee. "You did it, Jason! You're a legend, Jason. An absolute *legend*."

Jason's face scrunched. "How? With my death, Nezmyth is gone. Wevlia and the Old Ways fell."

"There's more," King Thomas shook his head. "You'll understand—"

"*Outta my way!*"

It was the second time Jason was lifted off his feet, but this one was much more forceful. Chief Patu was all around him, crushing his body against hers while his feet dangled above the ground. It would have snapped him in half if he wasn't already dead.

"Great teh see yeh, Yer Majesty!" She bellowed. "'Ow I've waited fer this day!"

Jason coughed as she set him back down. He went one by one through his loved ones. He talked with Kristof about life down in the south. He loved it until he was taken up by a spirit much like his parents were. Patriarch Willows was slain just the day before Jason, so he hadn't been here long. Garrit introduced Jason to Melody—a graceful spitting image of an older Saryan. Jason apologized for not being able to save him in Unbuntye, to which Garrit shook his head and smiled.

"I was reunited with my wife sooner than expected," he said. "I have no room for bitterness."

Alis threw her arms around Jason's neck like a little sister. Then Yorn came up and hugged them both. For some reason, Jason felt a strong gravity toward these two. They were in the thick of Kierli's conquest. They fought against her. Worked with him to defend the kingdom. They were loyal, good, and true.

Jason put his hands on both their shoulders. "I am so grateful to you both. I hope the Dragon rewards you beautifully."

Lastly was Nadiel. Those red eyes were just as bright and piercing as ever. But he somehow seemed younger. His hair was jet black and his face was devoid of wrinkles. The magician waited patiently with his hands behind his back as everyone else got to speak to Jason. Finally, they parted so they could see him.

They didn't hug immediately, but looked each other over. Nadiel smiled.

"Welcome home, Your Highness," he said. "It's been a little while."

Jason smiled back. "It has been. You saved Nezmyth, you know. Your sacrifice is what ended the Ash War."

"We all played a part," Nadiel said. "You. Me. Tarren."

At the mention of Tarren, everyone became still. No one spoke a word. And for the first time in several minutes, Jason felt sad.

But that brought someone else to mind.

"What about Barnabas?" Jason asked. "Where is he?"

Everyone exchanged looks. Saryan had been putting baby Garrit in a crib off to the side. She looked up and said, "We haven't seen him yet. He could still be in his In-Between."

"His what?"

"In-Between," Nadiel said. "It's the state you're in right now —the state before you go to Paradise or Darkness. It turns out the afterlife is slightly more complicated than we thought. Everyone has an In-Between specific to them. Then once you arrive at Paradise, you can visit the In-Betweens of your loved ones as they enter the Third Life."

"I was told that Barnabas's In-Between is restricted," Master Ferribolt said. "I pressed the messenger for more detail, but they wouldn't give me any. That was all."

Jason said, "So will he join us eventually? Do we know?"

People shook their heads or shrugged.

"I hope he does," Jason muttered. "He was the last friend I had left."

Another hush settled. Then Master Ferribolt said, "Perhaps he will. As for now, let's feast. We're here, and we want to celebrate you."

So they did. They gathered around the table and dove into the feast. It was absolutely delicious—better than anything Jason tasted back in Nezmyth. He asked out loud how they could enjoy this feast when vegetables and animals were all living things, too. Adria explained that they could still enjoy all the things they loved back in mortality, but in the Third Life, no living things are harmed. No one quite understood it yet, but they enjoyed it all the same.

As they ate, everyone swapped stories about life back on Nezmyth. They made it a point to go around the table and share their favorite memory of Jason. Of course, Kara and Tomm shared embarrassing stories from his childhood, like the time Jason took off all his clothes at the market or threw up in the hat of a girl he fancied. Everyone howled with laughter and Jason shrunk in his seat.

But there were also touching stories. Saryan tearfully recounted the day of their Melding Ceremony and Jason had a hard time keeping his eyes dry, too. Chief Patu proudly reflected on fighting with Jason in the Ash War. Nadiel recounted a quiet time that Jason gave him a gift on a difficult day. Jason didn't even know he was struggling at the time. The thought touched his heart.

While everyone feasted and laughed and sang, Saryan reached out and held Jason's hand under the table. Jason squeezed it firmly.

This moment… could it possibly be better? The woes of Nezmyth felt like a distant dream now—almost like they never happened. His loved ones were here, all safely gathered. Safe from the Ash, safe from tyranny, safe from Kierli. It was all over. But his smile faded as he realized everyone *wasn't* here.

Tarren. Barnabas.

They took their time, but everyone finished the feast. As soon as they stood from their chairs, the messes disappeared from the dishes. Nothing to clean up—it was just *gone.* Jason blinked in surprise, thinking about how this was going to take some getting used to. Everyone came up to him and gave him another hug before they got ready to leave. It was another round of welcomes and congratulations and I-love-yous.

Master Ferribolt was one of the last ones. He gave Jason a firm embrace and said, "We'll be waiting for you in Paradise. From what I understand, the Sacred One wants to meet with you before you join us there."

Jason's jaw fell. "The Sacred Dragon wants to *see me?*"

"Why are you surprised?" Master Ferribolt almost laughed. "The Sacred Dragon sees everyone when they pass! Besides, you're the Final King. I'm sure It has something special in store for you. I can't wait to hear of it." He winked, squeezed Jason's shoulder, and said, "Welcome home. Your real home." Then he took Rosie's hand and they walked out the front door.

The only people that were left were Jason's family and Nadiel. Jason gave a sly look to his former Advisor. "Why are you lingering, Nadiel?"

"If you wouldn't mind," he said sheepishly. "I was wondering if I could accompany you to the gates of the Sacred Mountain. I have matters with you I'd like to discuss."

Jason smirked. "Just like the good old days, huh?"

Nadiel smiled. Jason shared looks with Saryan and the rest of his family. They all agreed that would be just fine.

"So where do we go?" Jason said. "Where do we find the gates?"

"They're outside," Saryan said. "Come on."

At that moment, Lea came scampering up to Jason and held her arms out. He picked her up and held her so her little head could rest on his shoulder. She relaxed as soon as she was in his arms.

Jason followed everyone as they filed out the front door. Outside of whatever building they were in, there was a lush, grassy field that seemed to stretch forever. Through the middle of it, a long road eventually led to a magnificent set of golden gates. Most of their friends had left through those gates, but they made it out in time to see Master Ferribolt and Rosie pass through.

But there was another path branching off the road, heading to the right. That path ended in a set of massive stone doors that didn't seem to open to anything at all. It was just a set of enormous stone doors stretching up from the grass.

With those doors in mind, they all started forward.

Jason looked behind him. The door to the house they just left looked like they didn't lead to anything either—just a door in the middle of a road. Jason turned all around and took everything in.

"So every time I go through one of these doors," he thought out loud, "it's like I enter somewhere completely different?"

"That's right. We haven't learned how or why it works, either."

Jason was quiet for a moment, then he turned to Nadiel. "So what did you want to talk to me about?"

"Just a couple of things," Nadiel said. "First, I have been given a chance much like yours. The Sacred Dragon has helped me find love. I've been seeing a charming woman I met soon after arriving here years ago. I look forward to you meeting her. It will take some time, but we're currently working out the Melding details. It's a bit more complicated to perform after you've passed."

"Nadiel, that's wonderful!" Jason's eyes brightened. "Why didn't you bring her to the feast?"

"It felt a little sudden, I didn't want to overwhelm you. Secondly… I wanted to discuss our friend, Tarren."

Immediately, Jason's heart dropped. Lea was falling asleep in his arms, but she stirred a little. He let out a heavy sigh. "He should be with us."

"Jason, Paradise is a wonderful place," Nadiel said. "I wish I had the proper words to describe it. For centuries, it's been described as a perfect place without suffering. But I've found that's not quite true. There is one suffering that remains, and that's remembering those who should have joined you there."

Jason's bottom lip shook. The stage of his mind played the memories of Tarren and him growing up together, serving the Kingdom together, working through hard times together. But it was all gone now. All thanks to Kierli.

"However, I've heard whisperings," Nadiel said. "Nothing confirmed, but many things alluded to. Perhaps this isn't the end for Tarren or Barnabas." He scratched his chin. "Eternity is a very long time. It holds to reason that those of us who made mistakes in our Second Life would have chances to recompense in the Third Life. I've had the opportunity to commune with the Sacred One a number of times, and I'm frequently surprised at Its passion for *mercy*. Perhaps there isn't reason to despair quite yet." He smiled. "Just a thought."

Jason's eyes shimmered as he forced a smile. "It's a nice thought."

The party had turned right and made for the giant stone doors. When they got closer, Jason discovered that they were heavily ornamented with carvings. He could make out Ancient Nezmythian characters, several dragons, and landscapes around Wevlia. They were magnificent, and the stone was creamy, smooth, and white.

"This is where we leave you," Nadiel said.

"We'll wait for you outside," Kara said, holding Prince Garrit close.

Jason swallowed, suddenly feeling nervous. "So… this will take me to the Sacred Mountain where the Sacred Dragon dwells?"

Everyone nodded. Saryan came up and took Lea from Jason's arms. Lea whimpered slightly. Saryan bounced up and down with their child in her arms, then smiled at her husband.

"It'll be great," she said. "We'll be here when you're ready. Good luck."

Jason swallowed again, turned, and knocked.

There was a great unlatching, then the doors fanned open. They didn't creak or groan, but swung smoothly, hardly with a sound. Taking a deep breath, Jason walked in, then the gates started to close behind him.

40
THE GODS

When the doors boomed shut, Jason was at the beginning of a five-hundred foot corridor with tall, vaulted ceilings—almost like a stretched out Cathedral. The walls were lined with artwork that seemed to reflect the entire span of Wevlia. The sculptures and paintings at the beginning were simple and rudimentary, but became more refined near the end of the hall. There were no torches or windows, but everything was comfortably lit. Crystal chandeliers formed a long line down the ceiling, and on the ceiling itself, a mural of Wevlia's history.

As Jason meandered down the hall, he couldn't keep his eyes off the mural. He saw the Formation, the founding of each kingdom, the hunting and extinction of dragons, the era of darkness, the time of illumination where Foreordination was born, and the eventual fall of each kingdom. He had gotten so preoccupied with the art that he scarcely realized he had reached the end of the corridor.

A tiny spark of fear jumped inside him. The old storybooks said no mortal person could lay eyes on the Sacred Dragon and live—Its might and majesty were too overwhelming.

But he wasn't mortal anymore.

Before him was another set of double doors even more fine than the ones behind him. Gold and silver were mixed with the creamy white stone in designs that were intricate and fine. The Sacred Dragon had to be on the other side, waiting for him. Well… it would be rude to keep It waiting.

Trembling a little, Jason reached out and knocked three times. His knuckles rapping would surely be drowned in the thickness of the doors, but nonetheless, they swung open.

The doors parted to reveal an expansive, cavernous room. Again, comfortably bright. Everything was cream stone illuminated by a brilliant light that felt warm and all-encompassing.

And in the middle of the room, curled up soundly, It was waiting.

Its scales were perfectly clean and white, and when the light hit them just right, they reflected a rainbow of colors like a magnificent scaly prism. From snout to tail, the Dragon had to be one hundred and fifty feet long. Its claws and legs were strong and thick, Its tail like a great snake, and Its head was larger than Jason's wingspan.

It was large, majestic, and mighty, but all fear fled out of Jason's heart as soon as he saw It.

And It noticed him.

It perked up like a delighted house cat. It blinked its brilliant eyes—completely black if not for the oceanic blue slits in the middle. And when It spread Its wings, they were great sheets of leathery pink.

It was smiling.

"Jason, my son," Its voice was like the rushing of rivers and the moving of mountains. "Come forward! You have made this Ancient Dragon very happy."

Jason couldn't help it—his feet seemed to do the work for him. He broke into a run, his steps echoing on the white stone until he careened into the Sacred Dragon's great face, feeling its smooth scales against his arms. The Sacred Dragon laughed softly in Its chest, nuzzling Its face against Jason's whole body. Everything inside Jason glowed as he embraced It, as if reunited with someone he deeply loved at the edge of the world.

"Oh, my dear Jason," the Dragon said. "You saw so much hardship, and you bore it so well. You were the last stone that remained, and you stood steadfast. I hope the welcome to your In-Between was a warm one."

"It was!" Jason said as he finally let go. "My whole family is here!" He paused. "Wow… this is really you…"

Suddenly, propriety leapt into his mind. He dropped to his knees and bowed, nearly putting his face to the ground, arms outstretched on the stone. The Sacred Dragon smirked at him, amused but flattered.

"You've given me so much," Jason groveled. "You've given me a chance to be a father even after death took me. For that, I can never give you the end of my thanks. But I must ask one more thing of you."

The Sacred Dragon tilted Its head, curious. Jason's face was still inches from the ground, his body splayed out in worship.

"I would like to advocate for the redemption of my friend, Barnabas," Jason said. "He did many awful things during his life, but he did everything he could to reconcile with his crimes. What's more, is he was the last person to stand by me at the end of it all. Please, Sacred Dragon, have mercy on him. He—"

"There is no need to remind me of his deeds, my dear Jason," the Sacred Dragon nearly laughed. "For now, the fate of Barnabas is in his own hands. As for your fatherhood, I made a promise, did I not? In your Blessing of Fate? And you fulfilled the requirements for that promise. If I did not keep my word, I would cease to be holy. Besides," the Dragon smiled, "nurturing another life is one of existence's purest joys. To care for another far beyond yourself—to love purely—is a sweetness that nothing else can touch. You may rise now. I have a final task for you."

Jason got to his feet and cleared his throat. "A final task?"

"Yes. One I'm eager for you to complete. It involves the recent events in Nezmyth."

Jason's tone darkened. "Kierli. The Old Ways." He dipped his head. "I failed. I'm sorry."

"Quite the contrary. I'm happy to inform you that we sealed our victory over the Guardian of the Night."

...what?

The gears in Jason's mind turned with great effort, but no matter how hard he tried, he couldn't put the pieces together. Victory? Over the Guardian of the Night? But Kierli killed *every* Foreordained person in the kingdom, including him. The Old Ways were *gone*. Destroyed.

Jason furrowed his eyebrows. "Dear Dragon... I don't understand."

"I will tell you," the Dragon said. "But first, do you remember the objective of the Guardian of the Night from the old tales? From the Legend of the Formation?"

"It wanted Wevlia for itself."

"But why?"

"From what I understand, it was jealous of your creation and wanted to control it."

"That is partly correct, but there is more," the Dragon said. "The Guardian of the Night is a miser for power, glory, and the control you mentioned. You saw what *Tepnoh Edomah* does to someone. They aspire for more power and glory until it becomes all-consuming. They also become so attached to Dark Magic that it becomes a constant source of need. You see? Power, glory, and control.

"The Guardian of the Night wanted to usurp Wevlia as its supreme ruler, as I am. But it wanted Wevlia for its own glory and power, not for the happiness of its children." The Sacred One suddenly became serious. "Jason, your happiness and the happiness of all my creations are the entirety of my thoughts and desires. You'll see it more in Paradise. But under the

Guardian of the Night, people would live forever as slaves, oppressed and dominated."

Jason felt somewhat illuminated, but there were still pieces missing. "I'm sorry, Sacred One. I'm still confused."

"Consider your experiences so far in your In-Between. Then ponder it. Tell me what conclusion you arrive at."

Jason tucked his chin down and mulled it over. The Guardian of the Night wants absolute control—tyranny, supremacy. It had effectively taken down Foreordination and the Old Ways in every other kingdom except Nezmyth. Once the Old Ways were done away with, everything should be able to fall into its hands. The gate would be wide open for it to come in and exact control over all living things.

All living things. Most of his friends died during Kierli's conquest. Not all, though—his parents and Kristof were taken to the Third Life by heavenly guides. They were simply instructed that it was time to go. All of them would be untouched by the Guardian of the Night because they left the world before the Guardian could come into power.

That's when the thought struck him.

Jason scratched his beard. "My parents and Kristof said they were taken up by spirits before Kierli could kill me and destroy the Old Ways—before the Guardian of the Night could take control." He looked into the Dragon's eyes. "Did you do that for more people? To protect them?"

The Sacred Dragon smiled wide. "No. I did it with every living thing."

Jason's jaw fell. *"Everything?"*

"Yes, everything," the Dragon said. "Not just the people— all of Wevlia is now devoid of life. Not even a sunflower or beetle crawls along the soil. They've been taken safely up to Paradise or Darkness—wherever they belong. What the Guardian has inherited now is a world of desolation." The Dragon leaned in. "And you're going to be the one to let it know. The Final King. The last piece of the Old Ways."

Jason's eyes grew and his mouth went dry. *"Me...?* Sacred Dragon, why not you?"

"I want it to come from the last piece of its so-called victory. The irony will be delicious." It looked at Jason out of the corner of Its eye. "Being almighty does not rob me of my sense of humor."

Jason chortled, then his smile faded. "So how will it be done? You'll send me back?"

"Yes, as a spirit. Much like how King Thomas visited you on Grace Mountain. I will put you at the castle grounds just moments after your death. When the Guardian of the Night appears, you shall be the first thing it sees. It may try to frighten you, but I assure you, you have *nothing* to fear. It cannot hurt you.

"Additionally, there are other punishments I am bestowing upon the Guardian, and they may look familiar to you, but they will be made known to you in the proper moment. Then you can tell it of its fate in whatever way you choose. You are my vessel for one last time, Jason, then you may rest in Paradise forever. Are you ready?"

Jason nodded. "I am."

"It is well. Close your eyes."

* * * * *

Lightning flashed as Jason's punctured body collapsed to the wet stone of the castle courtyard. His lifeless brown eyes faced up, kissed by the falling rain. He was no more.

And with it, the most intense bolts of power shot through Kierli's body. The cracks in her skin stretched across her face, covering her cheeks and touching the edges of her eyes. As she lay on the ground, curled up, painful surges rocking her, she laughed through her agonized shrieks. She actually laughed.

When the convulsing ceased and she found the strength, she pushed herself to her knees. Letting the rain swallow her, she held her hands to the sky, cackling like a lunatic.

"*Yes!*" she cried. "Do you hear me, true god? I've done it! I have destroyed the Old Ways! Nezmyth is *mine!*"

"*Well done, my child,*" the voice was in her head now. "*Do not forget the final task.*"

"Yes," Kierli said hungrily. "The Oracle Stone."

Jason watched the whole thing, but they couldn't see him. He was a spirit, hovering over her shoulder, invisible as she stalked through the castle grounds. She kicked over the bodies of the soldiers as she moved toward the doors. Their watered-down blood soaked and swirled and pooled between the stones. Jason kept quiet and simply watched.

"*The room is on the bottom floor,*" the voice said. "*I will guide you.*"

"Yes, master."

Kierli entered the castle. The great hall was gravely silent, like a candle that had lost its flame. The red carpet was pushed and wrinkled. As Kierli passed the throne, she eyed it eagerly, knowing it would be hers within minutes. But as Jason looked around, he knew there was a brightness that this castle would never see again. It made his heart shrivel.

With the direction of the voice, Kierli made her way to the Oracle Stone room. Through the correct door, down a hallway, through a few sets of stairs. When she arrived at the double doors with the Ancient Nezmythian on them, she pressed her hands against them. The veins in her arms lit up and a purple blast erupted from her palm. The doors scattered and flew as if struck by a cannonball.

Inside the room was the Oracle Stone, sitting on its usual pedestal, the smoke inside swirling soundly. That changed as soon as Kierli approached it. The smoke turned pitch black and churned like an awful storm. Kierli noticed, but didn't care.

"*Take it,*" the voice said. "*Destroy it.*"

Kierli advanced on the pedestal and took the Oracle Stone in both hands. She pressed it between her palms and her face twisted into a scowl. The purple streaks in his arms glowed brighter. The Oracle Stone vibrated violently in her hands—resisting, fighting. She clenched her jaw and shrieked as the Oracle Stone finally burst into a mess of shattered glass, slicing her hands and arms. But the cuts stitched themselves together as if they never happened. She smiled as she looked at the broken pieces scattered around her feet.

"*Very good,*" the voice purred. "*Lastly…*"

In a puff of smoke, the black orb appeared in Kierli's grasp. She reached forward and gingerly set it down on the pedestal.

There. It was done.

And unbeknownst of them, the world outside changed.

"*Excellent,*" the voice slithered.

That was when something lurched inside Kierli—like a stomach ache that grew too fast. At first it made her grimace, then it lurched so horribly that it dropped her to her hands and knees. It bubbled violently like something was struggling to break out. It burned in her veins. Even the back of her eyes felt like they were searing cold and electric. She screamed. Something was taking over her—her body was moving on its own, abandoning her commands. She gritted her teeth and tried to push it out, but it was too much.

"What is happening to me?!" She cried.

Involuntarily, her head jerked and cackled with a voice that wasn't hers. Then her head snapped back into place.

"*Foolish girl!*" the voice said with her own lips. "*It is I, the Guardian of the Night! The Sultan of Darkness! The Prince of the Void! With you, I have sealed my victory over the Dragon! Wevlia is finally mine! Did you honestly believe I would let you rule? A pathetic little girl desperate for adoration? You were exactly what I needed. But now, your usefulness has run its course.*"

"No—no!" Kierli screamed. "Get out of my body! *Get out!*"

"Oh, I'm afraid this body is very much mine now," the Guardian said.

"No!!" Kierli shrieked.

"Farewell, Queen Kierli," the Guardian said. *"The pit awaits you."*

Kierli let out one more soul-ripping scream, then her head snapped back, she gasped, and was no more. The Guardian exhaled a long, perverted breath, and as it did, long curling horns stretched out of its forehead. It lifted her hands to her face, examining them, admiring the long purple cracks, running her hands all over her body, caressing her face. It blinked hard, and when it opened her eyes, the eyes were completely black.

"This is what it feels like," the Guardian said. "Flesh and blood. Magnificent."

The Guardian turned and gasped. Its black, doll-like eyes filled with fear. King Jason stood in the remains of the doorway, arms folded, girded with full royal armor. The fiercest scowl was slashed across his face.

The Guardian bore its teeth and summoned Starshadow, then hurled it at Jason. The blade should have stabbed him in the chest, but instead, the blade phased through him and clanged against the opposite wall. The Guardian scowled nervously, then regained itself. It roared so loudly that the building shook, agitating the stones and mortar. *"Get out of my castle!"*

"Your castle?" Jason said. "According to my understanding, you didn't do a single thing to build this world, let alone this building. All the stones that comprise this great building are the works of the Sacred Dragon's claws. And now you want to claim it for yourself? That's a tad presumptuous."

"Silence!" The Guardian spat. "The Old Ways are dead! Now it is just *me. I* am Wevlia's ruler!"

Jason hummed. Silently, he wondered if the Guardian could feel pain in that body. There was only one way to find out. In his spiritual state, he summoned the Blade of Nezmyth. It appeared into his hand and he moved so quickly that the

Guardian couldn't retaliate. Jason slashed the Guardian across its chest, then flashed right back to his spot in the doorway. The Guardian cried out and staggered backward, but its body mended immediately.

The Guardian slapped its hands where the wound was, then cackled delightedly. "*Pain!* So awful! So wonderful! No matter. With this body and my power, I cannot die."

"Seems like you hatched the perfect plan," Jason said.

"Yes. Now *leave!*"

"I don't think I will. There are some important things to show you."

"I said *begone!*"

The Guardian flashed Starshadow back into its hand and attempted more swipes at Jason, but every time, the sword just phased through him. Jason sighed irritably, summoned the Blade of Nezmyth, then dealt several devastating slashes on the Guardian, finishing with a decapitation. As its head landed with a gross thud, the Guardian's body healed up, picked up the head, and stuck it back on its shoulders. The head rejoined the body with wet, muscly cracks, then the Guardian shook its head like a dog.

"Don't try that again, it's pointless," Jason said. "Now come along."

"*You do not command me—*"

Too late. The Guardian and Jason both transported to Center Court. The rain had stopped. Not a soul was around. In the distance, the castle loomed like a dark, diseased fortress on the top of Upper City hill—just like it did seven years ago. The Guardian of the Night looked around, its eyes furrowed at the ghostly silence surrounding them.

"I… don't feel anything," it said.

"Oh?" Jason replied. "Let's try somewhere else. Maybe you'll have better luck."

In a flash, they were suddenly in Mumbi, the capital of Mumbano. Being at the edge of the desert, the city was an enormous cluster of square houses constructed out of clay and sand. They were standing in the middle of the Mumbi market, which was populated by tightly-packed carts and canopies. But just like Nezmyth City, there wasn't a single soul around.

The Guardian could feel this. "Where is everyone?"

"Let's do another, shall we?"

In a snap, they were on the tropical shores of Kyne. There should have been palm trees, but there was just sand. Even the water wasn't as blue as it once was. No forests in the distance, just endless dirt. Huts and cabins on the beach were uninhabited. Empty.

"Cease this charade!" The Guardian spat. "Tell me where the people are!"

Suddenly, they were back at Center Court. The Guardian was still reeling, calculating. In its moment of confusion, Jason stalked up to it and touched his index finger to its forehead. The Guardian tried to resist, but didn't have the power. Its eyes snapped wide open and it saw the entire land of Wevlia—every particle of sand and dust. When Jason removed his finger, the Guardian couldn't stop staring into oblivion.

"No," the Guardian breathed.

"That's right, Guardian," Jason said. He threw out his arms. "All hail the emperor of desolation! Let's all bow to the monarch of the endless nothing! You succeeded in your goal. Wevlia is yours. But what good is that now that the Sacred Dragon has taken up every living thing to its eternal rest? Everything is *gone*. There is not an insect or a blade of grass for you to bend to your will. You worked for thousands of years. You achieved your goal. But now the only living thing left is *you*."

"No," the Guardian stammered. "No no *no no NO!*"

The Sacred Dragon's reveal suddenly flashed across Jason's mind. What shocked Jason most was that it was familiar. Terribly familiar.

Sacred One...! he thought with wonder.

"But that is not all," he said. "Now, you will live forever facing the hot vengeance of the mightiest ones you slaughtered. For thousands of years you ravished this world with your suffering, lies, and deceit. But those who seek retribution against your crimes will be appeased. After three thousand years of slumber."

Jason snapped his fingers. And with it, the entire Upper City hill erupted in a geyser of rubble and soil. Nezmyth Castle was no more—reduced to bits of stone, glass, and mortar hurtling through the sky. In his heart, Jason mourned for the destruction of his home. But it was short lived. A distant groan from inside the hill was growing. A chorus of rumbles and roars. Shapes took up to the sky—long, white, and mighty. It filled Jason with wonder. It racked the Guardian with horror.

Dragons.

The bones of the Dragon Kings soared out of Upper City hill—dozens and dozens of them—those that were slaughtered by dragon hunters and their *Tepnoh Edomah* thousands of years ago. Their screeches filled the air. The torn fabric from their wings carried them to the sky.

Jason heard rumors that Upper City hill used to be the mountain where the Dragon Kings dwelt before the Dark Era. The story went that their remains were housed and put on display there by the dragon hunters before the mountain collapsed at the end of the Dark Era. But it was all just stories. Apparently not. Dragon Mountain was the foundation on which the castle was built.

The Guardian's body shook with dismay and terror. Jason started pacing circles around it.

"Pain really is awful and wonderful, isn't it?" He said. "Well, I'm sure you'll get more than your fill. I've never been ripped apart by a dragon before, but you will. Forever."

The sky was now filling with them, flying despite their decomposed limbs and wings. The thought struck Jason that there had to be more in every kingdom across the world. And they'd all be focused on one person: the Guardian of the Night.

Dear Dragon, he thought with awe. *What a fate...*

Suddenly, there was a turn. Every dragon in the sky became instantly aware of the Guardian. They spun in the sky and dove for Center Court, belting out roars that made the air itself tremble.

"It appears as though the tormentor has become the hunted," Jason muttered. "Farewell, Guardian of the Night. May you relish forever in your victory."

With wide, panicked eyes, the Guardian of the Night flicked its wrists into long, curving black swords. It bent its knees and launched off the ground, hurtling toward the dragons that were quickly closing in. It collided with the dragons in a mighty clash, swinging and twirling through the air as it slashed its blades—but its magical weapons only bounced off the dragons' skeletons. It shot lightning and ice from its hands, but they had no effect.

The dragons swiped their claws and snapped their jaws at the Guardian. The Guardian was only successful in evading the attacks for a while, then it was overwhelmed. The dragons ripped off limbs. Shattered bones. Jason could hear the shrill cries from the ground as the Guardian's body tore and regenerated. The last thing he saw was the small outline of the Guardian turning tail and streaking across the sky, only to be pursued by hundreds of flying skeletons.

All of them disappeared over the horizon. Jason looked around at the remains of Center Court. A ghost of a city. Never to be filled with song or dance again. But it was better this way.

"Sacred One," he said, "it is finished."

41

THE GATES

Ugviir pulled his claw away from Barnabas's forehead. That's when Barnabas realized his cheeks were wet with tears. Blushing a little, he wiped them up. He had just witnessed every moment of his life as if living them over again. Last of all was his final stand for Nezmyth and King Jason. And now he was here.

"Thou seest clearly now," Ugviir's voice rumbled.

"I do."

"Thou hast lived a life of great pain," Ugviir said. "But it is thy pain that has refined thee. For a time thou wast lost, but thou hast also been restored."

"But how can that atone for everything I've done?" Barnabas whispered.

"The place where thy crimes still lives the strongest is in thine own heart," Ugviir said. "Thou hast recompensed for a great deal of that thou hast destroyed. The past tortures thee because thou dost will it so. Many have forgiven thee, but thou hast failed to forgive thyself."

Barnabas was silent as Ugviir let him soak up that last statement. Finally, the great dragon lifted his head. The ground rumbled as he stepped aside, freeing a path between Barnabas and the two doors. "Now, thou must choose. On the left, Darkness. On the right, Paradise."

Barnabas's throat went dry. "It's my choice?"

Ugviir nodded. "Such as it is with all of the conflicted. Thou art free to choose. It is according to my understanding, however, that thou hast many friends in Paradise."

"What about Nartikis?" Barnabas muttered. "Where is he?"

Ugviir shook his head. "For now, the boy is in Darkness."

Barnabas's heart sank. Of course he'd be there. What could he have possibly done to redeem himself after the Ash War? After all, he was stuck down in that Vault for years before he died. Barnabas's throat got tight, then he noticed a detail in Ugviir's statement.

"You said 'for now.' You mean he has the chance to get out?"

Something like a smile crept across Ugviir's face. "Eternity is a long road, my human friend. There shall be many chances to grow and reconcile as the eons ebb and flow. That is all I shall say of that."

Barnabas nodded silently. That gave him some kind of hope, but it still wasn't what he wanted. "I wish I could see him right now."

"My apologies. But nonetheless, a choice lies before thee. Thou must choose."

"Where do you think I should go?"

"I must not say."

Barnabas's eyes shifted between the two doors and tried to feel what was in his heart. Where did he belong? After so much wrong, but after trying so hard to do right. But it was his choice. He had many friends waiting for him in Paradise. But he also had a son in Darkness.

He stole a glance to Ugviir. "Thank you, King Ugviir, for helping me see."

Ugviir smiled and bowed.

Then Barnabas stepped forward.

* * * *

Jason opened his eyes and he was back in the Sacred Mountain, face to face with the Sacred Dragon. A grin had spread across Its great scaly face, and it nodded with approval.

"It is well," It said.

Jason took a deep, cleansing breath, as if the weight of the world was finally off his shoulders. "That's it then. Wevlia has fallen, but there's no one for the Guardian of the Night to rule." He paused. "I just wish it didn't have to be this way."

"As do I," the Dragon said. "I would have loved to see Wevlia grow and flourish for thousands of more years. But all has ended as I have foreseen, and I thank you for being ready to assist in its final stages. Now," the Sacred Dragon bent down, putting its eyes level to Jason's, "it is time to build something new."

"Really? You're going to build a new world?"

"Not I, my dear Jason. You."

Jason's face must have betrayed him, because the Dragon gave a small rumbling laugh.

"*Me?*" Jason stammered. "I don't know anything about building worlds! Do I even have that kind of power?"

"All in due time," the Dragon smiled. "You are not expected to understand the intricacies of eternity right away. You will have eons to expand your capacities and learn. And what's more, I shall be right beside you, as your god and your mentor."

Jason's smile touched his ears. The Sacred Dragon bent Its head down and Jason wrapped his arms around it. The Dragon's scales were so warm against his face. Jason exhaled a comfortable sigh.

"Thank you. For everything."

"It was my joy and my pleasure," the Dragon said. "Go now, King Jason. Be with your family. Come visit me when you wish."

Jason bid the Sacred Dragon farewell and jaunted out of the Mountain. So much to tell the others! The Guardian of the Night, Wevlia, their victory…

When he exited the massive double doors, it was like he never left. Everyone was still waiting for him, filled with anticipation. Saryan was cradling baby Garrit while Lea clung to her leg. Once Jason emerged from the mountain, Lea stumbled over to him with arms outstretched again. Jason hoisted her into his arms, then leaned in and kissed his wife. Those silver orbs sparkled.

"Well?" Saryan said.

Jason scoffed and a smile spread across his cheeks. "So much happened."

"Can't wait to hear more about it," Saryan said. "But I want to show you our home in Paradise. It's beautiful. It's right next to our parents, too. We're all close."

They all started back up the path toward the gates. The air was cool and gentle around them. Lea started falling asleep in Jason's arms again. Kara and Tomm held hands as they walked behind Jason and the others.

"I wish I could have seen your first moments with the Sacred One," Nadiel mused. "It's everything we could have imagined and more, isn't It? I try to visit It often. It teaches me so much."

Jason thought about what the Dragon said about building a world. "Yes. I'm sure that'll be necessary as time goes by."

The gates of Paradise were getting close now. They were wide and tall, barred with gold, shimmering in the light. As they approached, Saryan reached out and took Jason's hand. Those silver eyes shone as they locked on him.

"Your adventure is finally over, Jason," she said.

Jason smirked. "You know… I'm starting to think the adventure is never really over."

The gates opened.

THE END
OF THE KING JASON SAGA

ABOUT THE AUTHOR

Aaron N. Hall is the author of The Wevlian Chronicles, the Hammerfist Series, and multiple collections of stories and poems. When he's not writing (which isn't often), he's doing nonprofit work, exercising, reading a book, or sipping a cup of tea. He lives in Utah.

For updates on future books, visit **aaronnhall.com**